CARRY ME HOME

OTHER BOOKS BY ROSALIND JAMES

THE ESCAPE TO NEW ZEALAND SERIES

Prequel: Just for You

Book 1: Just This Once

Book 2: Just Good Friends

Book 3: Just for Now

Book 4: Just for Fun

Book 5: Just My Luck

Book 6: Just Not Mine

Book 7: Just Once More

Book 8: Just in Time

THE KINCAIDS SERIES

Book 1: Welcome to Paradise

Book 2: Nothing Personal

Book 3: Asking for Trouble

CARRY ME HOME

Paradise, Idaho: Book One

Rosalind James

This is a work of fiction. Names, characters, organizations, places, events, and incidents are either products of the author's imagination or are used fictitiously.

Published by Montlake Romance, Seattle

www.apub.com

ISBN-13: 9781477830734

ISBN-10: 1477830731

Cover design by Eileen Carey

Printed in the United States of America

This one's for my dad, the best teacher I ever knew. I miss you.

PROLOGUE

Amy Corrigan's body was screaming.

The tension gripped her forearms even as her hands clenched the steering wheel, and she was driving anything but smoothly. Not that she'd have minded being pulled over. She was praying to be pulled over. The muscles of her thighs were so tight that she could barely move her foot on the accelerator, and the car lurched forward as she jerked her head to the side to check the rearview mirror again.

He was still there. Hanging back. But still there.

She didn't know why she was so sure it was a man. It could have been Bill's old girlfriend Stacy following her, trying to scare her off. Not like Stacy would get Bill back that way—Bill had been clear enough about that. That hadn't stopped her from trying, though.

But somehow, Amy knew it wasn't Stacy. Stacy didn't have a car, and this wasn't the first time Amy had noticed lights behind her, or felt that prickling at the back of her skull. But the prickling had never been as bad as this, because the feeling had started long before she'd gotten into her car.

She'd felt the hair rising on her neck and arms as she'd dug into the bulgur wheat bin in the bulk-food aisle of the Co-op, filled her plastic bag, and twisted the tie around its neck. There she'd been, surrounded by people, lights shining overhead, still smiling from the teeny bit of harmless flirtation she'd engaged in with the cute guy in the produce aisle. Just living her everyday life in one moment, and the next as frozen as a doe grazing in a meadow, raising her head with the sudden certainty that the hunter was there, that he had her in his sights.

She'd finished her shopping, telling herself she was being imaginative, that she was nervous and jumpy. Premenstrual, maybe, or worried about the test tomorrow, because Dr. Santangelo had warned the class that she was a tough grader.

Geology had sounded easy. That was why she had signed up for it. It was just rocks, right? Who'd known there would be so much memorizing? She wished she had a great big rock in the car with her right now, though, one big enough to be a weapon. But she didn't have a rock, so she was going to have to think of something else.

She turned onto Pine, and the headlights followed, and the tingling at the back of her neck was so strong that she would have raised her hand to rub at the skin there if both hands hadn't been hanging on to the wheel so tightly.

Onto Adams, and the lights made the turn behind her. She wasn't going home, because she wasn't stupid. She was driving at random, and he was following, and she was more than scared, because this wasn't the first time, and Paradise was a very small place with very little traffic. She could tell it was a pickup back there, but that was all she could tell, and that ruled out just about nobody in North Idaho.

She couldn't call Bill, because he'd gone to his parents' place in Coeur d'Alene for the weekend, and that would be no help at all. He'd invited her to go with him, but midterms started tomorrow. Her dad had told her in no uncertain terms, when the grades had come out at the end of her freshman year, that if she wanted her parents to keep paying the bills, playtime was over. So she'd stayed on campus to study. Right now, that was feeling like the worst decision she'd made in her admittedly checkered college career.

She might not be a model student, but, she reminded herself fiercely, she was a smart girl—no, a smart *woman*. Too smart to ignore a sixth sense that was doing everything but screaming and clanging alarm bells in her ear. She swung onto Spruce again, then back into the Co-op parking lot, grabbed her purse from the seat beside her, leaped from the car, and ran for the door, not stopping for her coat despite the bite in the late-October air. *Snow by morning*, her farmer's-daughter brain told her irrelevantly.

Once she was inside the store again, she peered out into the street, but the lights, whomever they belonged to, were gone.

Or else the person—*he*—had driven into the parking lot himself, or stopped on the street, even, while she'd been running for the door. She couldn't tell. She didn't know. She couldn't remember whether she'd heard a car stopping or not, and she nearly wailed with fear and frustration. Why hadn't she listened for it? But it wouldn't have mattered anyway. For all she knew, he was in his truck now, somewhere in the dark, across the street, maybe, waiting for her to leave so he could follow her home, where there were no lights and no crowds, where it was dark and she would be alone.

Or waiting for his opportunity to ram her, her overactive imagination suggested. To pin her in her much smaller car, pull her out and into his truck. There were a hundred ways this evening could end up, and most of them were bad.

She pulled out her phone and dialed Monica, her best friend. She couldn't stay in the Co-op all night. It was closing in half an hour, and then she was going to have to walk out those doors again. Into the dark, where he would be waiting. She couldn't call the cops, not for a pair of headlights and a bad feeling in her stomach. But she wasn't leaving here alone.

◆ ◆ ◆

The man watched the girl—Amy, he told himself, rolling the syllables on his tongue like wine—running into the store like the hounds of hell were on her heels.

Which they were. He'd relished the sight of Amy darting those quick glances into her rearview mirror, taking the turns without signaling, like that would have mattered to him, like he couldn't follow one scared girl through the nearly deserted streets of downtown Paradise at nine o'clock on a cold Sunday night. She hadn't had a hope of outrunning him, not a chance of escaping, not if he'd really wanted to catch her, and the knowledge was sweet.

She'd pulled into the parking lot again, but that just made the game more fun. What kind of challenge was there in shooting a deer from the cab of your truck? None at all. No bone-deep satisfaction in that, not the kind you felt when you'd hidden, when you'd waited and watched, when you finally saw that doe thinking she was safe, and when you knew she wasn't, because you were there, and you were stronger. Because you were the predator, and she was the prey.

Just like Amy was his prey now. She'd been jumpy before, and after tonight, she'd be terrified. But not as terrified as she'd be when he caught her.

What was it they said? Getting there was half the fun? Yeah. But being there, doing it . . . that was the other half.

IN THE DITCH

The meeting had been on Zoe Santangelo's schedule. The ice wasn't.

When she hit it, she didn't even realize what it was. One moment she was approaching the turn, admiring the black-and-white beauty of the snow-covered curves and hollows around her and wondering if she had time to get a coffee before her two o'clock Geology 101 class, because sitting in front of the room monitoring that midterm was going to get boring. The next instant, she was turning the wheel to sweep around the bend in the road, and . . . not sweeping.

She was still trying to turn the wheel, but the car wasn't responding. Not at all. Instead, the whole thing was going sideways, her back end swinging wide to the right. She saw the semi heading toward her through the light mist of blowing snow, and her mouth opened wide in a soundless scream as she tried frantically to turn the wheel the other way, away from the eighteen enormous wheels, the heavy, crushing load that loomed over her like an ocean liner.

The driver's horn blasted through the frigid air, through the fragile layer of glass that was all that separated her from the tonnage bearing down on her. She'd have prayed, but she didn't have time to pray. She just slid.

A fraction of a second later, the semi was blowing past, the sound of the horn trailing behind it, and the back end of the car was hitting the frozen ditch at the side of the road, tipping remorselessly over the bank despite the foot she'd jammed onto the brake, and all the momentum her Elantra hatchback possessed stopped in a single heartbeat.

Her rear bumper landed against the far bank with a dull crunch, and her back slammed into the seat with the impact, the shoulder belt tightening, grabbing her even as her head bounced a little off the hard fabric headrest.

And then it all ended and everything was still, only the heater's fan breaking the silence.

She stayed there, dazed, for a moment, heart thudding, body starting to shake with freshly released adrenaline.

"All right," she said aloud, and heard the tremble in her voice. "All right. All right."

There. That sounded better. All right, she was in the ditch. She'd slid on ice she hadn't seen and, stupidly, hadn't anticipated.

"Watch for black ice," somebody had said as she'd left her very first meeting as a groundwater consultant, but she'd barely registered it, because she'd been thinking about the check. The nice, big, fat check that would help so much, and everything it represented as the next step on her career path. And now she was in the ditch.

Call Triple A. She had AAA, because when you moved to a new job in a new city—well, a new town—three very large Western states away from home, in your twelve-year-old car with more miles on it than God, you had AAA. Thank goodness.

Her fingers were still shaking, but she got her shoulder belt unfastened; reached uncomfortably uphill and scrabbled around to find her purse, which had slid under the passenger seat; found her phone; and got the number dialed.

Just call. Call, wait for the tow truck, cross your fingers you haven't done damage, and hope it doesn't take too long.

Damage. She couldn't afford damage, not until she had that check. And she couldn't afford to be late to class on the day she gave her first exam, to make that kind of impression. But both things were looking like real possibilities.

She was on hold. Of course she was on hold. *Damn.*

She was concentrating so hard, trying so fiercely to hold herself together, that she jumped a full two inches when a face appeared at the window next to her.

A face. A man. She was alone on a lonely highway, in the snow, incapacitated in the ditch, and there was a man at her car, trying to get in. She could feel him jiggling the handle, and he was talking to her.

"Are you all right?" He said it loud, so she could hear him even through her closed window.

She nodded, trying to look as in-charge as a short woman in a red hatchback upended in a frozen Idaho ditch could look. She held up the phone and shouted, "Triple A. I'm good."

He looked a little amused, a little exasperated. "Roll down your window," he shouted, and made rolling-down motions with his hand.

He was probably just trying to help. She realized that her car was still running, pushed the switch to lower the window a cautious two inches, and focused on him, since the phone was still playing elevator music.

He wasn't all that comforting a sight. In his thirties, probably. Scruffy, dressed in a blue sweatshirt printed with "Paradise Pumas" that had seen better days, and a black baseball cap with "CAT" in big white letters. Not the animal, the equipment company—she knew that much. The square jaw, the bright-blue eyes that matched the sweatshirt, and the shoulders that blocked the whole driver's-side window were all fairly overwhelming. On the other hand, he wasn't exactly trying to ingratiate himself, which a predator would surely do. Instead, he had a frown on his face.

"Turn the car off," he told her.

She blinked at him.

"Dangerous," he said. "Your tailpipe's blocked. Turn the car off."

"Oh." She switched the phone to her left hand, because she was still on hold, and turned the key. "Thanks."

"Need some help?" he asked.

"No, thanks," she said, trying to sound brisk. "I'm on the phone with Triple A. I'm okay."

"Uh-huh." He scratched his cheek with the knuckles of one big hand. "They tell you how long it was going to be?"

"Uh—no. Still on hold."

"Triple A dispatches out of Union City. Day like today, it's going to take an hour or two to get around to you. You won't be the only one going into the ditch in the first snow of the season." He glanced toward the front of her car. "There'll be a few more Californians out there, betcha anything."

He'd seen her license plate, she realized, and she wanted to tell him that she wasn't from California. That is, she was, but she lived in Idaho now. But it didn't matter, and she'd had it drilled into her head that if you had car trouble, you locked your doors and waited for the police, or for the tow. You didn't trust random men who approached incapacitated women on lonely highways.

The phone came to life in her hand. She grasped it more tightly in gratitude and gave her information to the voice at the other end. "How long will it be?" she asked hopefully.

"At least an hour," the voice said.

"What? I can't wait an hour. I have a class."

"Sorry," she heard. "I'm getting an hour."

The man hadn't gone anywhere. He was still looking in at her—crouched down on the bank to do it, she realized, with her car at its awkward angle—amusement lurking in his blue eyes, and a telltale quirk at one corner of his mouth.

"All right," she said reluctantly into the phone. "Could you ask them to hurry?" She hung up and looked at the man. "Okay," she sighed. "You were right."

He scratched his cheek again. "So what do you think? Still want to be all proper and Californian and wait for your tow? Hope you've got a coat."

He cast a sweeping glance at her suit, and she realized that her black skirt had hiked up well above her knees. She thought about tugging it down, forced her hands to stay right where they were, and stared back into those devilish eyes instead, offering him her own best above-it-all expression.

"Or, if you like," he said, "seeing as we're in Idaho and all, I could just tow you out right now."

Don't get out of the car, she reminded herself. *You don't know this guy.*

"Uh . . ." she began, then heard, to her relief, the blip of a siren, saw the reassuringly official SUV with "Sheriff" emblazoned on the side pulling to a stop on the shoulder, behind what she belatedly realized was the guy's black pickup truck. Of course he had a black pickup truck, just like every bad guy in every action movie she'd ever seen. With a big, ugly brown dog in it, looking just like every bad guy's dog.

The guy outside her window looked around, straightened, and turned to give her a view of the back of a pair of tan canvas work pants with "Carhartt" stamped onto a leather badge on the back pocket. The very nicely shaped back pocket, because that was some rear view. Well, she could hardly miss it, not right outside her window.

She buzzed her window down the rest of the way, the cold instantly rushing into the car, and watched the—officer?—walking up in his reassuring dark-gray Smokey Bear hat and uniform. Thank goodness, help at last. Help she could trust for sure, because his big, broad frame inspired nothing but relief. *Wait for the police.* And here they were.

"Hey, Cal," she heard him say as he approached. "What's going on?"

"Happened to be passing by, saw this lady hit that ice and slide right into the ditch," the guy—Cal—answered.

"Ma'am?" The officer bent to look into the car, and she saw his "Deputy Sheriff" badge. "You all right?"

"I'm fine," Zoe said, still upended in her little car and trying not to shiver in the frigid air, wishing she'd thought to tug her skirt down while Cal's back had been turned. "I'm just waiting for Triple A."

"What, Cal didn't offer to give you a tow? Losing your touch, man," Smokey said over his shoulder to Cal.

"I offered," Cal said in what Zoe was beginning to recognize as his amused drawl. He crouched down again beside the other man, and Zoe fought back a sudden, horrifying urge to giggle at the ridiculous picture they all made.

"The lady's from California," Cal went on. "She thinks I've got designs on her virtue. Wants to wait for her tow."

The deputy laughed. "Take an hour, maybe more," he told Zoe. "I'd take Cal, if I were you." He winked at her, to Zoe's outrage. "Gotta go. Bound to be more than one unprepared Californian spinning out today, weather like this. See you, Cal."

And he left her, just like that.

A PRETTY NICE ARMFUL

"So . . . am I taking off here, or what?" Cal asked again, wondering why he was pushing it. Not like he was dying to crawl under a car in the snow. Not like he didn't have things to do.

Well, yeah. But driving to town for replacement scraper blades for the soil saver wasn't exactly urgent, not with the cold keeping him from plowing anyway. And besides, she was cute. Great legs, and he admired the spunk that had kept her from tugging her skirt down. He could tell she'd wanted to do it, but she'd refused to show weakness. Good for her. Not easy to be on top of the situation when you were sitting ass-over-teakettle in the ditch, but she'd managed to act that way.

She cocked her head, the cloud of shoulder-length dark-brown hair a little disheveled, or maybe that was her normal style. He liked it. She stared at him out of round, thick-lashed brown eyes, chewed on a plump pink lower lip, and distracted him. "How do you know him?"

"Huh?" She was doing the lip thing again.

"The cop. How do you know him?"

"Oh." He smiled. "My cousin." He put out a hand to shake hers, careful not to breach the sanctity of the car's interior. "Cal Jackson."

She didn't react to his name one little bit, just reached her own hand out, with the nails he'd noticed weren't painted, and shook his. She had a firm grip, and he liked that, too. "Zoe Santangelo."

Pretty name, and it suited her. "Well, Zoe Santangelo," he said, and tried another smile, "what do you think? Want a tow?"

She smiled back, finally, and it lit up her eyes, accentuated the high cheekbones he'd already noticed in her round face, and she looked better than ever that way. "You think you're trustworthy?"

Ah. Sass. He loved sass. He especially loved it in a woman who should be crying, or begging, right about now. He wouldn't mind hearing her beg, come to think of it, but he could live without crying.

"Hey," he told her, "you just heard a cop vouch for me."

"A cop who was your *cousin*."

"Yeah. Well." He grinned. "I've got lots of cousins. Want a county commissioner? Got one of those, too. Or do you just want a tow?"

"Yes," she said, and damned if she didn't have two dimples, one at either corner of that luscious mouth. "Yes, please. I want a tow. What do I do?"

"Nothing yet. I got it. Hang on." He was back at his rig in a few quick strides, hopping up in the cab and pulling forward, turning on the flashers so, he hoped, he'd be seen through the light snow that was still falling, and maneuvering so he was nose-to-nose with her car. He'd tow her from the front, where he had the weight for leverage, because it was going to be a slippery son of a bitch in the snow, with her wedged into the ditch like that.

He yanked his cap off, tossed it onto the seat and pulled on his wool watch cap instead, grabbed the coat he was glad he'd thrown in, and went around to get a tow strap from the box in the bed, then tugged on a pair of heavy leather work gloves.

When he turned around, she was struggling out of the car despite his words. She was wearing heels, low ones, but not shoes you got out of a snowy ditch with. Her feet started to slide out from under her just as she got vertical, and he raced for her, saw her flailing for the top of the open door, and starting to go down all the same.

She didn't fall, because he was there, grabbing her under the arms, pulling her upright. And then, all right, maybe he held on to her a moment too long, because she felt good there.

She wasn't tall, that was for sure. She barely topped his shoulder. But she was a pretty nice armful all the same. Not skinny, which was good, because he liked girls with curves, and she had some very nice ones, although the severely cut black jacket and skirt and the blue blouse beneath weren't exactly showing them off.

"Whoa there, darlin'," he said, setting her carefully back against the door. "You might want to stay in the car, like I said."

She wrapped both arms around herself. Tightly, which pushed her breasts up to the neckline of that boring blouse in some very interesting ways. *Don't look down*, he told himself.

"I thought," she said, through teeth that had begun to chatter, "that you might need my help. To . . ." She gestured to the tow strap. "Fasten it on. And please don't call me darlin'."

He couldn't help smiling, even though he probably shouldn't. "I'll try to keep it in mind. And nope, I got this. Anyway, were you planning on crawling under the car in your good suit, Miss Zoe? Before your class? You a student?"

"No. I'm the professor. It's Dr. Zoe, actually. I mean, Dr. Santangelo."

"Whoa, a doctor and everything? Well, then, Professor, I think you'd better just let me do this. That way you won't be dragging in there all wet and muddy."

She narrowed her eyes at him. "Are you making fun of me?"

"Now, why would I do that?"

"You—" she said, then stopped herself and laughed. "I'm some grateful victim, aren't I? I'm being rude, when here you are stopping and helping me and everything, and about to crawl under my car. Either I have no manners, or you're pushing my buttons. I'm not sure which."

"Oh," he said, "I'm probably pushing your buttons. It's been mentioned. I'm button-pushing, and helpful, and all that good stuff. And if you'll get back in the car, I'll be the guy who got you out of the ditch, too." He dropped his tow strap across the hood of the little hatchback—hell of a car for an Idaho winter—and got a hand under her elbow to help her back into the car, and enjoyed it.

The rest of it wasn't nearly as much fun, but he'd been under a fair number of vehicles in his thirty-two years on the planet, and once he was back in his rig, it was as satisfying as always to feel the big Cummins diesel growl out its full-throated roar as he eased down on the accelerator, kept it steady and smooth, backed it up, and saw the little hatchback clearing the ditch and coming to rest on the snow-covered asphalt shoulder again.

He maneuvered both vehicles off the roadway and then, keeping the flashers on, jumped down and unhooked the strap from both ends, and ended up looking in her window again at a considerably more vertical Ms.—*Dr.*—Zoe Santangelo. Whose skirt, unfortunately, was all the way down over her thighs again, but then, you couldn't have everything.

"Do you think my car is badly damaged?" she asked, serious now, unable to keep the edge of anxiety out of her voice, and he guessed that somebody driving what he'd estimate was about $2,000 worth of metal probably couldn't afford much of a repair bill. Professoring must not pay that well.

"Nah," he said. "Not too bad. Got a pretty good dent in the back bumper, and you'll want to take it in. You may have a couple hundred bucks' worth there, but I don't think you've done much more than that."

"That's not good," she said, "but I guess I'll just be glad it's not worse. And thanks. Really, thanks." She put out a hand, and he reached to shake it again, then realized that it held a twenty.

"No," he said, putting a gloved hand firmly around her own and closing her fingers over the bill. "This is what we call being a neighbor. It's what we do. And I don't need your money."

"Oh." She looked confused. She made to stuff the bill into a pocket that didn't exist, and he got the feeling she usually wore pants. Which was a real shame. "Sorry. I thought . . ."

"Yeah. Never mind. I'll wait for you to get on the road, follow you into Paradise, if that's where you're going, make sure I'm not wrong about that damage."

"Oh," she said again. "No, that's all right. I'm fine."

Did she think he would be following her? As in, *following* her?

"Staying a careful distance away." He measured the words out, scratched the idea of asking for her phone number right off his list. "Turning off at the Deere dealership on the highway. I won't even wave good-bye."

"I didn't . . . sorry. It's just . . . being careful, you know."

"Yeah. Well. You might be able to ease up on that. I think you'll find that we have a distinct lack of serial-killer types in Paradise. We kinda pride ourselves on that."

THE ROCK LABELED "A"

Amy fought down panic for the second time in less than twenty-four hours. *Think. Go. Write something.*

She couldn't think, though. She couldn't concentrate. The clock on the wall was ticking remorselessly, clearly audible in the nearly silent room. That damning tock each time a minute clicked over, the sound competing with nothing but the scratch of pens on the flimsy pages of blue books, the shuffle of feet, the occasional sniff from somebody's autumn cold. And the periodic, maddening disturbance of another student getting up, grabbing his stuff, and walking to the front of the room to set the blue book on Dr. Santangelo's desk and leave the room.

She hadn't done too badly with the multiple-choice part. But after that, everything had gone downhill.

Give the names of the rocks labeled A, B, and C, and explain the environments that led to their creation.

She'd managed that one. Barely. She thought. But when she'd been staring at a sketch of a rock marked with all sorts of lines and zigzag marks, with arrows pointing to randomly placed spots labeled A, B, C, D, and E, and asked to identify what was going on . . . she'd gone into overload, and she'd blanked. And from there, it had just gotten worse. How did she know which layer was older? They were all mixed up!

The worst part was, she *knew* she knew. But it was all lost in the fog of anxiety. She was stumbling around blind, the tears choking her throat. She was going to flunk the test. She was going to fail the class, and it was too late to withdraw and change to something else she could pass, and her dad was going to tell her that was it. Her chance at college was going to be gone, and she was going to be working at the dime store in Wilson's Ferry all year, not just during the summer, until she got married just because there was nothing else to do. She was going to be stuck, and it wasn't even her *fault.*

"Five minutes," Dr. Santangelo called out, and there were only four students still working. There were three questions she hadn't even started, and she raced through, putting down answers at random. *Folding. Faulting. Sedimentation. Pressure.*

"Time's up," Dr. Santangelo said. "Pens and pencils down."

Amy couldn't look at her as she shoved her pen back into her backpack, slid the Scantron form into the blue book with shaking hands. She forced herself to walk to the front of the room, set the book on the desk. She was the last to finish. The last one, and the worst one. She had flunked the test.

"All right?" Dr. Santangelo asked her.

Amy nodded, gulped, and opened her mouth to tell her. "I was . . ." She had to stop, get hold of herself, or she was going to cry in front of Dr. Santangelo, who was always so cool and smart and in control. She probably thought Amy was an idiot. An idiot who hadn't even tried. But she *had.*

"Remember," her professor said with a gentleness Amy would never have expected, "you'll get another chance. On the essay part of the midterms, once we've gone over the answers in class, you can redo the ones you missed, turn them in again, and get half credit. This isn't about flunking you. It's about teaching you."

Amy bobbed her head in a jerky nod. The tears were escaping despite herself, and she just wanted to leave before she lost it entirely. "I know. I will."

"You came to the study session last week," Dr. Santangelo said. "I thought you had a pretty good handle on it. What happened? Did you panic?"

It sounded so stupid. "Yeah. Because . . ." She ran her knuckles under her eyes, tried to get herself back under control. "I was ready. I just had to do some more studying, you know. Last-minute. Just to make sure. But then . . ." She swallowed. "This guy was following me. Last night, and I . . . I got so scared, I had to sleep at my friend's, on her floor in her dorm, but I couldn't sleep, and I didn't have my notes with me, and I was scared to go home to get them, and . . ." She trailed off, because she was crying again. "I know that sounds like an excuse, but it's true, I swear. And I *studied.* I know you won't believe me, but I did."

"Sit down," Dr. Santangelo said, and she was frowning. But not at Amy, at least Amy didn't think so. "Tell me what happened."

She was frowning some more by the time Amy finished her story. "Did you call the police?"

"No," Amy admitted. "I don't have any proof. I mean, yeah, somebody was definitely following me, but it could have been some kid playing a game. I mean, I realize that. It could even have been just a coincidence. That's what they're going to say, I know."

"I think you should report it all the same," Dr. Santangelo said. "Take it seriously. Sometimes our bodies know things that our minds try to reason away. And it could be that other women have been experiencing the same thing. If none of them report it, nobody will even know there's a problem."

"Maybe," Amy said, unconvinced. "I'd feel stupid. I mean . . ." She laughed a little, although it was pretty watery. "I already feel stupid."

Dr. Santangelo stood up. "You aren't stupid, and I doubt you're that easily scared. Go home, and don't worry about this. You may not get an A, or even a B," she said with a smile, "but if you're willing to work, you'll pass the class. Keep trying, keep working. And Amy?"

"Yeah?"

"Take care."

◆ ◆ ◆

Later that day Amy was grateful that somebody had believed her. Because when she told Bill over coffee in the student union, he wasn't as easy to convince.

"I'm sure you saw *something*," he hastened to say after she'd tried to explain, had seen his skepticism, and had gotten increasingly heated in response. "But don't you think you're being a little . . . hysterical? I mean, what happened?"

"Nothing," she admitted, her hands twisting in her lap, tugging on her napkin. "That's because I went back to the Co-op, though, don't you think? I mean, because I got away, it was all right. But he was *behind* me. He *was*."

"Did anybody follow you to Monica's?"

"I don't think so. But . . ."

"Then they weren't really following you, were they? Not for more than a little while. Maybe the person was just going to the Co-op, too. It could be as simple as that. You were nervous about the test, and your fears got away from you."

He stayed with her that night all the same. Which probably wasn't any big sacrifice, because he took full advantage of the opportunity to hold her, but then, that was fine with her. She wished she could stay with him all week, because she'd have felt safer away from home, but he was in a frat, so it wasn't possible. And her roommate was usually around during the week, of course.

As the days went by and nothing else happened—nothing but the vague sense of eyes on her—she started to doubt what she'd seen herself, what she still felt. Maybe she really *had* overreacted, had gotten an idea in her head from watching too many slasher movies, had spooked herself. She'd probably made a whole big deal out of something that wasn't anything at all. Nothing like this had ever happened to anyone she knew, or even anyone she knew of, because it only really happened in those movies, or in the big city. It didn't happen in Idaho. It sure didn't happen in Paradise.

LADIES' NIGHT

Zoe made an unsuccessful attempt to tug the yellow lace dress a little farther down her legs. "You sure this outfit works?" she asked her friend.

"I'm damn-straight positive it does. And quit messing up my dress. Here." Rochelle took Zoe by the shoulders, spun her toward her, and attacked her with the eyeliner.

"I'm going to look like a raccoon," Zoe complained.

"Will you stop? You're going to look like a girl who just might want to get laid in this decade, instead of somebody who's spent her Friday nights for the past two years working on her dissertation."

"Five years," Zoe muttered, careful not to move her face too much. "Counting the coursework. And I *was* getting laid. Sometimes. I had a boyfriend." Until she hadn't, because she wasn't that good with men. She didn't flatter them enough, or concentrate on them enough, or something. Whatever.

"Oh, yeah, honey, and I can tell he was a pistol. Under the covers, right? After you both got ready for bed? Every Wednesday and Saturday night?"

"As opposed to what? On the kitchen table?"

The eyeliner wand stilled in midapplication. "Oh, man," Rochelle sighed. "It's been way too long."

"Are you overdoing me?" Zoe asked, feeling the applicator moving beyond her upper eyelid. "Wings are stupid. At least on me."

"Wings are hot, but I'm not doing them on you. Just smudging you up a bunch," Rochelle said, flipping the applicator in her hand and putting the soft end to work. "You've got these fantastic big eyes, and it'll be dark in the bar. You want a guy to keep his own eyes up there on yours, right? Give him a reason to look. I've got little squinty eyes, so no hope for it."

"You do not have squinty eyes," Zoe said. "You have really pretty blue eyes, and you're tall and blonde, too. All the good things."

"Doing your lips. Open up a little."

Zoe obeyed, feeling like a Barbie being dressed by a particularly obsessive seven-year-old, and Rochelle went on. "Yeah, I do. Squinty as hell. Of course, no guy in this town has looked past my neck since the seventh grade, so it's pretty much a hopeless case, but I'm still giving it a shot. That's why the hair."

She finished Zoe's mouth off with a coating of gloss, and Zoe spoke at last. "So the hair isn't real, but . . . ?"

"The hair's fake, the boobs are real. Go with the one that counts. Every single woman around here knows I started life as a muddy ol' brunette, and no man gives a damn that the blonde's from a bottle, because they know I grew the parts they care about most all by myself." She bent from the waist, scrunched her fingers into the long blonde tresses, then stood up and shook it into disheveled order. "Just out of bed," she said, looking in the mirror. "Perfect. Do it."

"Because I want to be messy?"

"Oh, yeah. You want to look like you just tumbled out of bed after some extra-good lovin' from a man who knows how." She put a hand on the back of Zoe's head and gave it a little push. "Over you go."

Zoe bent over, scrunched, stood up, shook, and looked at her reflection in front of the full-length mirror in Rochelle's North Main apartment. "Just out of bed in full makeup," she said dubiously.

"Big soft eyes because he did you so good, a mouth that's all pink and swollen because it's been worked out so hard, hair he's had his hand twisted up in while you've been lying underneath him," Rochelle said. "You're three for three, and he is *gone*."

"Thanks. Now I'm all turned on," Zoe grumbled. She adjusted the delicate brown leather belt defining her waist in the yellow dress, posed a bit in the tooled leather boots that were actually her own. Put her hand on a cocked hip, stood on one toe, and looked over her shoulder at the smoky-eyed temptress who gazed back at her.

It was true; she felt like a different person. A whole lot less like Dr. Zoe Santangelo, assistant professor of geology at the University of the Palouse, and a whole lot more like the babe she'd never been.

She shouldn't have bought the boots, but looking at them with the lace dress, she couldn't help being glad she had. She'd been moving to Idaho. She'd needed cowboy boots, right? And if they were purple and would never come within yards of an actual cow, well, they had just been too pretty to pass up, and for once, she'd succumbed.

It wasn't that she was never tempted. It was just that she almost always resisted.

"That would be great," she told Rochelle. "Looking good, I mean, if I were actually in the market. Except I'm not. Turned on or not, I am not picking up a guy in a bar."

"Ego feed," Rochelle said. "Entertainment. You look, you dance, you drink. And then you walk on home with your girlfriend, safe and sound, feeling a little bit prettier, a little bit sexier, and knowing that more than a few of those boys are watching you walk out, imagining what you and I are getting up to, and wishing like hell they could join the party."

Zoe stared at her in astonishment. "They are not."

"Oh, yeah," Rochelle assured her. "They are. They love to think about that."

"I've heard that," Zoe admitted. "But why would they? What's the appeal? If they wouldn't even be . . . involved in it?"

Rochelle shrugged. "Guys' minds. Who can understand them? You ever want to do it with a girl?"

"No. Never. Despite what some of the guys I turned down in grad school had to say. Seems they just couldn't understand why I couldn't get enthusiastic about their skinny bearded selves. Or why I was better than them in class. Somehow, it made it a lot easier to understand if I was a lesbian. Who knew that attraction to women translated to IQ points?"

"Me neither," Rochelle said. "Never wanted to, I mean. And it sure doesn't do anything for me to think about two guys gettin' it on. Passing that image right on by. But for some reason, the idea of two girls features big in guys' fantasy lives. I guarantee you, they'll be thinking about it tonight. Makes me laugh. I might just give you a hug while we're out there, fan those flames a little. If I kiss you on the cheek, do me a favor and don't wipe it off."

"As long as you don't get too excited," Zoe said, "I'll go for it. But you've got me wondering now. Is this really about taking me out on the town? Or is it more about your nonlamented ex-husband?"

"You mean showing Lake the Snake that I'm better off? Well, I'm not saying that doesn't figure into it, too."

Their eyes met in the mirror, and they both smiled. "Well," Zoe said, "that's a worthwhile goal. I'm more than happy to contribute to that effort."

◆ ◆ ◆

She'd met Rochelle when she'd come to the university for an interview and a guest lecture, hoping that this would be it, the tenure-track position that would start her on her way. Never mind that it wasn't exactly the Ivy League. All she needed was a start, and she could make it to those ivy-covered halls. She knew she could. She had to.

An administrative assistant in the dean's office, Rochelle had been in charge of the details of her visit, and she had made Zoe laugh more than once in the nervous weeks leading up to the interview trip. Since then, she'd helped her find her apartment, given her a tour of the town, and made her laugh some more, and an unlikely friendship had been born.

They'd gone out for lunch in the student union in those early days before school had started, when Zoe had known barely a soul other than her all-male colleagues, who seemed to regard her either as unwelcome competition, the product of preferential hiring, or a potential conquest. And Zoe had learned that Rochelle needed a friend herself.

"Yep. Separated three big months," Rochelle had said, eyeing the lasagna with a sigh and passing it by in favor of a salad. "Divorce sucks. On the other hand, not having to cook is a plus, especially the crap Lake liked. He thought it was scarily gourmet if I put red peppers in the Ragu spaghetti sauce, spent all dinnertime picking them out. Mr. Culture. Besides, the problem with marrying a good ol' boy is that he stays just that."

"What? Good? How's that bad?"

"No. A boy. A bunch of buddies and a keg of beer and a baggie full of weed is a good time in high school. That's where I met him, thought he was wild and crazy. Women just love a bad boy. And 'Lake'? I thought that was some sexy name. I found out later that his mom had read a romance novel where the hero's name was Lachlan while she was pregnant. Turns out that was about as close as he ever did get to romance. Eventually he hit thirty, and that same old good time? That was still pretty much it. Well, that and the waitress on the breakfast shift down at the Kozy Korner."

"So the divorce was . . . his idea?" Zoe asked delicately.

"Oh, no, honey," Rochelle said. "That was me all the way, the day I came home with the flu and found out what happened after her shift was over. I moved to town, left him in that farmhand's house with the wind blowing through the cracks, that splintery wood floor, hardly any heat and always about twenty below in the winter. I got my own apartment, first place of my own I ever lived in. Not that it isn't crappy," she admitted. "One tiny window in the bedroom at the back, looking out on a 'courtyard' that's really just a paved yard and a couple lousy trees, one more window in the living room that I have to keep the curtains pulled on if I don't want to give a show to everybody walking down Main Street. Way too small, way too dark, and furnished right out of the Goodwill store and every garage sale in town, that's my place. But hey, it's mine. My paycheck goes for *me* now, not for beer and cigarettes and more of that weed. You'd be surprised how good that feels."

"No," Zoe said, "I don't think I would. It's important to know that you don't have to depend on somebody else, that you can make it on your own. To be independent."

"Yeah," Rochelle said, stabbing unenthusiastically at her salad and heaving a sigh. "That's what I tell myself. It's just too bad that I still like 'em big and tough. My sister keeps telling me to find some nice engineering professor. She married the guy who runs Owl Drug, you know the one?"

"I think so," Zoe said. "The pharmacist? That him?"

"Comb-over and all," Rochelle said. "I swear, he about had that comb-over in high school. And have you had the lucky chance to cast your eyes over the engineering professors yet?"

"Not so much. Other than a new faculty orientation."

"And did you see anybody there worth my while?"

"Uh . . . not that I noticed. But maybe some of the other departments would be better. I was mostly talking to the ones in engineering and physical sciences. Math, too."

"Oh. Math," Rochelle said glumly. "Yippee-ki-yay."

Zoe laughed. "Yeah. I'd give it a pretty definitive no."

"Same difference in engineering. Besides, who wants to be a perk of the job? Not me. Don't want anybody who thinks he's slumming because I didn't go to college, that's for sure. Anyway, men are all lying bastards, and I'm not divorced yet. So I'm not looking."

Except that they were going out to the Cowboy Bar, because, Rochelle had insisted, Zoe needed to "live a little."

"You've been here two months," she'd said during their Thursday lunch date the day before, "and what have you done for fun?"

"Uh . . . two-for-one margarita night with you at Senor Fred's? I don't have time for fun, and I don't have clothes to go out dancing in anyway. I guess you don't wear jeans."

"Not your jeans, anyway," Rochelle said. "Honestly, where do you shop? Geeks R Us?"

"I don't like fashion," Zoe said. "It confuses me."

"And see, you didn't even have to tell me that. Look at it as doing me a favor. Showing Lake that I don't miss his lazy, lying ass, that I'm out on the town and looking good on the Divorce Diet, eating all those green vegetables he hated, clear eyes and shiny hair and not a care in the world. Besides, I've been looking at flat engineer butts in khaki Dockers all week long. Give me a pair of faded Wranglers and a long, slow, sexy smile, a fiddle and a guitar playing soft and sweet, a cold beer and a hot man. That's all it takes. Back home again, and it's off to fantasyland. Got Bob in my bedside table all ready to satisfy me, and between him and my imagination?" She sighed. "That's a hot-damn guaranteed Friday night good time. A whole lot more likely to get me there than Lake ever was."

"Well," Zoe said, "if it's for as good a cause as that, I guess I'm taking the plunge and going to a bar."

◆ ◆ ◆

As they got closer, though, she started to lose her nerve.

"You're sure we won't see anyone I know?" Zoe hustled across the street, tugging the inadequate silver-studded jean jacket more closely around her against the chill.

"No, and who cares anyway?" Rochelle demanded, her long legs keeping up with ease. "You planning to strip naked? You're allowed to go to a bar. It's in the Constitution."

"It is not in the Constitution."

"Well, it ought to be. And quit fidgeting," she ordered Zoe, who was trying to tug the dress down again. It stopped only a few inches above her knee, but that was a good couple inches higher than she wore her skirts—on the rare occasions when she wore skirts. "You look hot," Rochelle said. "Think of it as research. Research is the deal, right? Exploring the local geography. Isn't that the job?"

"The geology. Which is rocks. This isn't rocks."

"But it rocks," Rochelle said helpfully. "You'll see. It rocks solid."

"And anyway," Zoe said, "the Cowboy Bar isn't really the geography the tenure committee will have in mind."

"The tenure committee is never going to know. You aren't doing anything wrong, for God's sake. When they start the wet T-shirt contest, I promise to hold you back. Just in case the dean's hanging out near the cigarette machine, hoping to hook up." She sighed when Zoe stared at her. "Joke. Lighten up, will you? It's not a Den of Sin. It's a friggin' bar. Dance, drink, flirt with cute guys, go home with me. Exactly like we said."

"I should have said," Zoe told her, "one more thing. I'm not good at dancing. I mean, I can stand there and sort of move awkwardly."

"Ah," Rochelle said. "Guy dancing."

Zoe laughed. "Yeah. That's about it. I don't know how to do this, I'm pretty sure."

"I'd say that's the least of your worries," Rochelle said. "Because I suspect we'll find out that somebody's just dying to teach you. I told you. You look hot. Trust me. I'm very good."

They were outside the bar now. A couple of guys in jeans, jackets, and boots cast an appreciative eye over the two of them on their own way in. The wooden door with its heavy cast-iron handle swung heavily open, and a swirl of music, all guitars and fiddles and drums, came out on a gust of warm air.

"All right," Rochelle ordered. "Shoulders back. Stick 'em out, swing your hips, and we walk on in like now we're here and the party can start. Own it, baby. It's your room, and they're just visiting."

BAD GUY OR GOOD GUY

"Oh, holy hell."

Cal turned his head at the exclamation. He'd been leaning backward against the bar beside Deke Hawley, one booted foot on the rail, casting an eye over the dance floor and wishing he'd see somebody new out there, somebody who wasn't a college girl. Wishing he was attracted to nineteen-year-old girls with fake IDs like any red-blooded thirty-two-year-old man ought to be, and didn't just want to put his jacket on them and tell them to go on home before they got themselves into trouble.

Another Friday night at the Cowboy Bar, in other words, and he'd been wondering why he'd come.

Because he hadn't wanted to face another night talking to his dog, that was why. Junior was a great listener, but lately his eyes had been looking much too weary and patient. Same old story, same old song. He was even boring the dog.

The Cowboy Bar wasn't much better, not until Deke busted out with his exclamation, and Cal was setting his beer down on the bar and straightening up, along with just about every other guy in the place.

"Heard Rochelle Farnsworth was fixin' to get single," Deke said. "Looks to me like she's done it, and like she's lonely, too. Might have to do something about that. I've had a thing for that woman since junior high. Damn, she's looking good."

"Rochelle Marks again, now," Cal said absently. "Not a moment too soon."

Deke shot a look across at him. "Why? You interested? Man, I can never catch a break. How am I supposed to compete with you?"

"No," Cal said. "I've seen her a few times lately, that's all."

"Then I'm going for it. Who's that with her?" Deke asked idly, still with an eye on Rochelle, who was gliding hip-first over to a table, working that slimmer figure of hers for all it was worth, her mane of blonde hair falling down her back.

And yeah, she looked good. But Cal's attention was all for the woman with her. He'd always gone for the tall, long-legged ones, back when he'd been going for them at all. Before he'd found the girl he'd thought he'd keep, the one everyone had wanted. The girl he'd won, like he'd won every other prize. Then.

Dr. Zoe wasn't blonde, and she wasn't tall. And those legs weren't long, but they looked better than ever. There was something about a girl in a pretty dress and cowboy boots that did something to his . . . heart.

She was walking like she meant business herself, pulling out a chair and shoving that mess of dark hair back from her face with the other hand, laughing at something Rochelle was saying, and despite the way their last meeting had ended, Cal's own boots were carrying him right on over there. He was headed right smack-dab over to their table, beating out every other guy in the place, and throwing out a look along the way that told them to back off. He let Deke come along, though. Deke wasn't after his girl.

"Well, ladies," he said, dropping into a chair and setting down his beer, "what a pleasant surprise. Here I was thinking this night was looking pretty boring. How you doin', Rochelle?"

"Oh, not too bad. Hey, Deke. This is Zoe, guys. Cal Jackson, Deke Hawley," she said, nodding around the table. "I'm just showing her the local sights. She's from California. Gotta keep her from getting into too much trouble, you know. Let her know that not every man wearing a hat is actually a real live cowboy."

"Yeah," Cal said, sliding his eyes on over to Zoe. She was sitting up straighter now, forgetting to look sexy and just looking prim and proper instead, and damn if that wasn't even sexier. "I've met Dr. Zoe. And you're right, she's not too . . . well acquainted with Idaho, I'd say. Here's a little tip to help you out tonight," he told her. "Don't believe him when he tells you he's a cowboy. Not until you see him ride."

Deke snorted, but he ignored that.

"Oh. Wow. Is that innuendo?" She opened those big brown eyes wide at him. She was made up tonight, and he liked it. "Nobody told me there would be innuendo."

He laughed. *Damn.*

"So I shouldn't believe you're a cowboy, that what you're saying?" she went on, those round eyes nothing but innocent. "Even though you've got the boots and the pickup truck and everything? Because I haven't seen you . . ."

"Oh, I can ride," he assured her. "I can ride real good. But I'm not a cowboy. I'm a farmer."

Rochelle snorted. "You could say that."

He kicked her under the table, and she jumped.

"You owe me a beer for that, bud," she told him.

"For what?" Zoe asked.

"Never mind," Cal said. "Rochelle's just reminding Deke and me of our manners, that's all. Here you two ladies are, looking just that fine, and nobody's bought you a drink yet. What can I get you?" he asked Rochelle, finishing off his own beer with one final swallow.

"Oh, the good stuff," she said. "Corona with a lime."

"Want a glass?"

"Nah, haven't got that fancy yet," she said. "Bottle's good."

"How about you, princess?" Cal asked Zoe. "Let me guess. White wine. No. White wine *spritzer*."

There were some sparks flying in those dark eyes now, and he had to smile a little, even as he wondered why he was taking chances with the only woman to capture his fancy for months. Because it was so much fun to tease her, that was why.

Sure enough, she rose right up to it like a trout rising to a fly. "You think I'm too good for beer? I'm a geologist."

"Um . . ." He put a hand to the back of his head, gave it a scratch. "Is that like star signs or something? Astrology?"

She sighed. "I know you know. It's rocks. I study rocks. Actually, I study water in rocks. I'm a hydrogeologist."

"I'll take your word for it, Professor. So . . . wine? Beer? Let me guess. Tequila straight up, bring the bottle, leave the worm." He gave her a wink, and she laughed.

Oh, yeah. He'd made her laugh.

"Beer," she said. "But I'll buy it. First one's on me," she told Rochelle. "Do you want another?" she asked Deke.

"Well, sure," he said. "And next round's on *me*."

"It's not actually a crime to let the guy buy," Cal told her. "Just like you can let him give you a tow. At least, I'd think so."

He saw the light dawning in Rochelle's eyes. "Ah," she said. "Hot mystery man to the rescue."

This time, he was pretty sure it was Zoe giving her the kick, because Rochelle was jumping again, and he was smiling again.

"I'm not going to argue with you," Zoe said, all business now, standing up and grabbing her little purse from the table. "Because I did appreciate my tow. And actually, that's *why* I'm buying my own beer," she said with what was clearly a flash of inspiration. "All right, you wouldn't let me pay you for your trouble. But surely I could buy you a beer. What do you want?"

"You're going to buy Cal a drink," Rochelle said slowly. "This happen to you a lot, Cal? You like a take-charge lady? That where I've gone wrong all these years? Here I thought men liked to do the chasing."

"Nope," Cal said, standing up himself. "She's not." He decided not to answer the rest of it. No way to come out ahead on that one. "I'm buying my own beer. And I'm going to keep her company, too. My mama always told me, you never let the lady walk up to the bar alone."

Zoe just looked at him, those dimples trying their best to come out, then turned on her cute little boot heel and sashayed off, and he followed right after her.

"Your mother told you that?" she said when she was leaning against the bar, worn dark and smooth by generations of elbows, waiting for Conrad, the overworked bartender, to make his way down to them. "She gave you etiquette advice for drinking in bars with women?"

"Nah," he said, the slow grin spreading, because damn, but she made him smile. "I made it up."

"Hmm. Well, *that's* reassuring."

He laughed. "Hey. We work with what we've got."

Conrad made it over to them at last. "Hey, Cal," he said. "Another cold one?"

"Yeah," he said. "And the lady'll have . . ." He raised an eyebrow at Zoe.

"Three Coronas with lime," she said. "Please."

"Glasses?" Conrad cast an experienced eye over the pretty yellow lace, the silver-studded jacket.

"Bottles," Zoe said firmly, and Cal smiled again.

Conrad brought them over, threaded between the fingers of one beefy hand, set them on the bar, and started popping tops and shoving in the lime wedges. Cal had pulled his wallet from his jeans, but he was too late. She was holding her credit card out, and she hadn't been kidding, because she was buying his beer.

"Please," she told Cal. "It makes me feel better about the tow."

"Lady's paying," Cal said in resignation at Conrad's raised eyebrow.

The bartender turned to the register, was back in a moment, his heavy face apologetic. "Sorry," he said. "Not taking the card. Got another one you'd like to try?"

Cal shot a look at her, saw the dusky red creeping up her throat, into her cheeks. Before she could answer, he had the wallet out again, was pulling out a twenty and a five, dropping them on the bar.

"Keep the change," he told Conrad.

"Thanks," Zoe said after a minute. "It was . . . the repair bill, I guess. I thought there was still enough on it. And we only get paid once a month." Her mouth snapped shut. "But thanks."

"No problem. And see, here I am again, getting my way. Kinda makes you think it was meant to be, doesn't it?"

She laughed at that, and that was better, and they headed back to the table, where Deke had his elbows on the varnished wood, smiling into Rochelle's animated face and looking like he was set to stay awhile.

"Honest," Cal said, sitting down with her again. "I'm an all-right guy, even though I stop to help women on lonely highways and buy them drinks and all."

She looked a little startled at that. So she *had* been worried about him. Another reason he didn't live in California anymore. He'd hate to be that suspicious. "Ask Rochelle," he said, "if you're worried about it."

"Ask Rochelle what?" Rochelle asked, because if you said a woman's name, no matter how loud the music was or what else she was doing, she'd hear it.

"Am I a bad guy?" Cal demanded. "A deviant?"

"Not that I know of," Rochelle said cordially.

He groaned, laid his head against the table and banged it a couple of times, sat up again, and told Rochelle, "You have known me since the seventh grade."

"The sixth," she corrected him. "He doesn't remember," she told Deke tragically. "I'm doomed to go to my grave hopelessly devoted to Cal Jackson, with my love unreturned."

"Never mind," Deke said. "Give it to me. I'll return it."

"And?" Cal demanded, ignoring Deke.

"And what?" Rochelle asked.

He sighed. "Tell Zoe. Bad guy? Or good guy?"

"All right." She set down her beer. "Other than a lack of taste, as witnessed by his never once asking me out, yes. Good guy. Told the guys to knock it off when they snapped my bra strap. That was their big game. God, that was obnoxious."

"Did you?" Zoe asked. "That's good."

"He said," Rochelle pronounced, "'You guys are assholes. Leave her alone.' And they did, of course."

"You have such power over all you survey?" Zoe asked.

"Oh, honey, he was king of the *school*," Rochelle said.

"Aw, I'm blushing and everything," Cal said. "So we sitting around here drinking? Or is anybody planning on dancing tonight? Deke and I hustled on over here to claim the two prettiest girls in the bar. Going to put us out of our misery, take us for a spin?"

"Well, I am," Rochelle said. "If somebody asks me."

Deke got right up, put a hand out. "I'm asking."

She smiled. "See ya, guys."

"What do you say?" Cal asked Zoe, watching Rochelle sway out there, put her hand in Deke's, and start right in enjoying herself. "Seeing as I've got my Good Guy badge and all, think you could risk dancing with me?"

"I don't know how," she admitted. "Whatever it is they're doing."

"Ah," he said with satisfaction. "Nobody's ever taught a pretty thing like you how to dance country? This is your lucky night, then." Teach her? Hell, yeah, he'd teach her. "Because here we are. We've got the band, and you've got the man."

TEXAS TWO-STEP

Zoe looked at him, raised her eyebrows with a cool she wasn't feeling one bit, and shrugged out of Rochelle's jean jacket, reminding herself to move slowly, to pretend that she'd expected this, that she wasn't surprised he wanted to dance with her. Even though she was. Surprised, that is. All right, shocked. She guessed the clothes worked. Too bad the woman in them had less than a single clue.

Call it practice, she told herself. *Flirting practice.* And boy, did she need practice.

His complete confidence should be bothering her, just like it should be bothering her that his eyes had dropped to her breasts for a split second while she'd arched her back to shrug the jacket off, then flown hurriedly back to her face again. It hadn't been for long, but she'd seen it.

Unfortunately, her body didn't seem to be getting the proper messages, because the only thing that glance did was send a few more sexy tingles down her spine. She turned, draped the jacket over the back of her chair, put her little shoulder bag across her body, looked at him and tossed her hair back, and he watched that, too. She would never doubt Rochelle again.

"All right, cowboy," she said. "Teach me something new."

He went still, and the fire burned just a little bit hotter. She was better at this than she'd ever realized. Or maybe it was him.

Flirting had never been fun. It had only been awkward. But it felt fun tonight.

He was up, helping to pull out her chair, taking her hand in his and leading her to a spot not too far from the stage. The music was loud up here, the dancers' energy infectious. His hand was warm and solid around hers, big and hard and a little bit rough, and she liked that, too.

The song, a quick, swinging number that had turned the crowded floor into a twirling mass of bodies and had her wondering if she'd ever keep up, ended with a crash of drums as she stood there with him, hovering at the edge of the smooth hardwood dance floor.

"Hang on a second," he told her. She stood and waited as he jumped up onto the low stage, and the lead singer turned to him. The man listened as Cal talked, nodded once, and Cal was jumping down again, coming back to her with his easy, loping grace, and some of her newfound confidence left her.

Shoulders broad as Texas, slim hips, boots and faded Levi's and a black T-shirt stretching over a chest that kept right up with those shoulders. Square jaw, firm mouth, nose that wasn't quite smooth or straight—broken, maybe. And those thick-lashed eyes, as blue as a midsummer sky in late afternoon. Not quite handsome, but tough? Oh, yeah. Every woman's dark, dangerous barroom fantasy.

Could she really dance with somebody like that on the bare courage of one lonely beer? She wasn't some hot babe, no matter whose borrowed clothes she wore or how much makeup she put on. She was a geologist, a geologist who didn't know how to dance. She was going to make a fool of herself, and he'd realize his mistake. He'd be too polite to humiliate her, but she'd be humiliated all the same. She'd spend the rest of the night sitting at the table with a smile pasted on her face, watching Rochelle dance and trying to look like she didn't care, wishing they could go home so she could quit pretending. Exactly like the ninth-grade dance.

◆ ◆ ◆

The ninth-grade dance. Her first school dance, and her last. She hadn't even started out sitting at a table for that one. She'd had nobody to sit with, so she'd stood against the scuffed wall of the gym in the dress her mother had said was "so cute," that made her look "so slim and pretty," her hair painstakingly curled, her blue-framed glasses sitting squarely on her round face and flashing in the lights, but thankfully disguising her shining eyes. Standing there with that lump rising in her throat until swallowing had been hard, and not crying had been torture.

Her one real friend and her one almost-friend had finally showed up, and she'd sat with them for the rest of the interminable evening. Except for the times when she'd sat there alone, because neither of them had been quite as relentlessly unpopular, quite as decked out with hardware, quite as chubby or as geeky as she was.

She'd actually danced twice, and she remembered both of them, and her gratitude at finally being released from the Table of Shame. Rainer from Math Club, who hadn't seemed much more at ease than she was, and her friend's brother, because Sylvia had told him to, although he hadn't exactly disguised his relief at returning her to her table.

She wondered now why she hadn't just danced with her girlfriends. Why had it seemed to matter so much that she be chosen by a boy? Why had she been willing to give them that kind of power over her? Over even her innermost thoughts, her most tender feelings? But she had.

Her dad had been waiting outside for her with the car afterward, thank goodness, so she hadn't had to stand there alone, and she could slide in next to him and escape. He hadn't said much—he never did, not about things like this, because he didn't think they mattered, and look how right he had been.

Her mom, though, had said plenty. She'd been waiting up to hear all about it, and Zoe had disappointed her. Of course she had, because she always did, and what was the point in even trying?

"So how did it go, honey?" her mother asked eagerly. "Did you dance with all the cute boys?"

"No," she muttered. "It was totally lame."

"Oh, sweetie," her mother said. "Did you smile and look like you were enjoying yourself, like I told you? Boys like a cheerful girl. If you look all mopey, they'll move on to somebody else."

"Maybe they don't think braces and glasses are a hot look," Zoe said. Not to mention girls whose extra pounds were in all the wrong places.

"Of course they are," her mother said. "Maybe not exactly," she amended as Zoe looked at her incredulously, "but remember what I always say. A smile is the best makeup. You ask them about themselves, act interested, and the boys will come to you, just like they're the bees and you're the flower."

"Except I'm not a flower. And they have to be in the general vicinity first," Zoe said. "Which they're not. You don't get how it is. You don't have a clue." A smile is the best makeup? *Please.* "Besides," she said, her voice rising along with her frustration, "that's what *you* want. I don't want the same things you do. How hard is that to understand?"

"Well," her father said, "if you don't want it, why did you go? No point in getting emotional about it. It matters, or it doesn't. If it doesn't, what do you care? Save your energy for the important things."

"But it's . . ." she tried to explain, and wondered why he couldn't understand. Why nobody could understand. "I don't *care*. Just . . . *forget* it, okay?"

She'd fled to her room, slammed the door, wrenched the dress over her head, stuffed it savagely into the wicker laundry hamper with its flowered liner, and gotten ready for bed. She'd pulled on her rose-printed pajamas, taken her glasses off and set them on the bedside table next to the canopied bed, switched off the lamp with its frilly shade and, finally, in the forgiving shelter of the dark, had allowed herself to cry.

She'd never done anything wrong. She'd never hurt anybody, not like the Mean Girls who looked and smirked and made comments not quite under their voices, because they wanted you to hear. She was nice. She was smart and funny. She was a good friend.

And none of it mattered, because all boys cared about was whether you were pretty, whether you had the right body—a Southern California body, tall and thin and tanned—and the right clothes to put on it. Whether you knew how to flirt and how to look cool and sound cool. She didn't have any of that, and she was sick of trying to play a game when she didn't even understand the rules.

That was the year she'd ripped the stupid girly canopy off her bed. She'd gotten rid of all the flowered stuff, refused to let her mother go shopping with her anymore, and changed her wardrobe to jeans and T-shirts, to her mother's constant distress.

She wasn't one of those girls, and she never would be, and if she was going to disappoint her mother, it was going to be by choice, because she wasn't trying anymore to be something she wasn't. She was a geek, and she was chubby, and she had glasses and braces, and she was smarter than almost all the boys. They didn't like her, and that was all right, because she didn't like them, either. Most of them were jerks, or idiots, so who cared?

She'd made friends, guys as well as girls, guys who laughed at her jokes, but she'd never gone to another school dance. Not even when she'd lost the braces, when the glasses had been replaced by contacts. She'd finally had a boyfriend, but he hadn't been cool, and he sure hadn't been hot.

◆ ◆ ◆

But right now, one seriously hot farmer had his hand around hers again, was looking at her with something in his eyes, something in his smile . . .

What white teeth you have, she thought. *And the big bad wolf said, "The better to eat you with, my dear."* She couldn't help the delicious shiver that went down her spine at the thought.

He pulled her out onto the floor, set his right hand on her shoulder blade, the fingertips just kissing bare skin, and that shiver was coming from more than her thoughts. He wasn't trying to do anything else, but she was as aware of those fingers as if he'd been touching her someplace else. Someplace really good. He was looking down at her, those blue eyes holding hers, and the band was playing again. The drums and the bass starting it, a steady, slow beat, the lead guitar kicking in, and the singer crooning low and deep, an incongruously smooth sound coming from his scrawny body.

"Okay. Two-step. First thing you do," he told her as the music filled her, swept her up in its insistent throb, "is put your hand on me. Right up here," he said, patting his right shoulder. "And then you hang on for the ride."

She set her hand tentatively where he indicated, felt the ridge of muscle rising under his black T-shirt, and very nearly took it right off him again.

He felt the hesitation, smiled a little. "Feels kinda close, huh? Not the way you dance with some guy you just met, back in California?"

"Sort of." Well, not "sort of" at all, but he didn't need to know that.

"You've got a secret weapon here, darlin'," he said. "Called your thumb." He took his hand off her back, put it over hers, maneuvered her thumb so it was resting on his collarbone. "You give this arm a little muscle," he told her. "Give me some tension, push back a little. Not a bad thing at all. Where we go is up to me, but how close we dance? That's entirely up to you."

"I like that part," she said. "And you know that thing I said about darlin'?"

"I'm going to keep forgetting," he said, "because I can't seem to help myself. So maybe you could pretend it's all right, this one time. Pretend you're a pretty girl in a bar, dancing with a man who thinks you're the sweetest thing he's seen in months, and that he's mighty lucky to be the one holding you. Just for tonight."

Her eyes widened, and he smiled, a little crookedly. "Just pretend," he said. "I'll never tell."

She had to smile then. She didn't know if it was true, or if he was just pretending, too . . . but she couldn't help smiling.

"And damn," he groaned, "there go those dimples again. You're distracting me. Here we go. Backwards, off your toes. Quick-quick slow-slow. Step-together, slow, slow. Just like that."

He coached and teased, and surely the band was playing chorus after chorus of that song, and she was dancing backward after all, starting to feel just a little bit like somebody else, like a woman who would be dancing in a cowboy bar with Cal Jackson, and having him look at her like that.

"That's real good," he told her. "All you need to do now is relax into it and let me drive. I've got you, and I'm not going to let you fall or mess up."

"Maybe it's that I'm used to being in charge," she said, trying to maintain her equilibrium. It wasn't easy, not with his broad chest so close to hers, not looking at the muscular brown column of his neck, the faint shading of beard from where he'd shaved that morning. Dark, because his hair was dark, the hair she hadn't seen under that hat on Monday. Dark, thick, and cut close to his head.

His skin was dark, too. Tanned and warm and firm, and covering all that muscle, everything she could feel under her hand, everything she was trying not to look at. He was so big, so sure. He made her feel feminine, and small, and . . . pretty. And just for tonight, maybe that was all right. Just for tonight.

"You can be in charge all you want," he promised. "But not right now. There's only a couple of places where a man gets to be in charge, but we're pretty jealous about those couple of sweet, sweet places."

Another rush of heat at that, and she swallowed, and knew he saw it.

"Come on, sweetheart," he said, his lips curving into a slow smile. "Just relax and go with it. Let me do the driving. I'll get you there, I promise."

"I hope all this innuendo is entertaining you," she managed, trying not to count her steps, to ease into the steady beat, "because it's not doing a thing for me."

There were crinkles of amusement around his eyes. "You just keep right on trying. I like that no-quit in you. Hope you don't mind if I keep trying, too. Can't seem to help myself."

Somehow, they were on a different song now. The second? The third? She didn't know. Still not too fast for her, and she was keeping up. She was dancing.

And then he was coaching her through a twirl, and the feeling of being spun around, her boots sliding together like they belonged to somebody else, of being caught again with his hand warm and strong against her back . . . it felt good. She surrendered to it at last, moved with him, exactly where he wanted her to go.

"That's right," he told her, moving across the floor like he'd been born doing this. "That's real good. Just feel the music and let me take you along with me. Just like that. Just that easy. Just that sweet."

MY NEXT BROKEN HEART

Cal couldn't actually dance with her all night, unfortunately. The band finally played a good fast one after a raised eyebrow from Wayne, the guitarist, and an answering nod from Cal. Cal twirled her and turned her forward and back again, felt her going right along with him, letting go, letting him move her every way he wanted to. And then, much too soon, she was laughing, stepping back, saying, "Wow. Give me a second. I think I need a beer," and not even raising any objection when he took off to get it for her.

"Though I know you'd rather have bought it yourself," he said when he brought it back. "Being the independent kind of woman you are."

There was that curve of pink mouth as she smiled right back at him. Her lipstick was all-the-way chewed off by now, and not only didn't she care, he could swear that she was totally unaware of it. And her mouth looked great.

Rochelle and Deke showed up, too, then, Rochelle laughing as she took her seat. "What do you think, Cal? Think you owe me?"

"Yeah. I do." He slid out of the chair. "Now, don't drop anything in my beer while I'm gone, Professor," he told Zoe. "I know you want my body, but control yourself. I'll do most things if I'm asked nicely." He winked at her. "Give me ten minutes and I'm right back here, ready to show you a few more things."

He hadn't been planning on having to bribe a whole band to play things his way while he was out tonight. Like it or not, he was taking a trip to the ATM. But it was going to be a quick one.

Less than fifteen minutes, and he was back there. And she wasn't at the table. Nobody was.

His eyes roamed the dark, crowded dance floor, looked for that yellow dress, that dark head. And saw her. He leaned back in his chair and watched them circle the floor. Watched Greg Moore, that sleazy bastard he had the misfortune of calling his cousin, giving Zoe a double spin and catching her again, his hand landing a little too far from her shoulder blade, pretty damn close to where it had no business being, sliding casually around again, none too quickly, to its proper place.

She still had that thumb clamped, he saw. At least there was that.

He waited until the song ended, then vaulted onto the stage again and said a couple words into Wayne's ear. Wayne nodded, long hair swinging, set his guitar in its stand, and Cal was jumping down again.

"We'll take a short break, folks," Wayne announced. "Back in fifteen."

Cal got back to the table before the others did, pulled out Zoe's chair before Greg had a chance. He saw Greg about to sit his self-satisfied butt in the chair beside her, too, not getting the point at all.

"How's Kathy doing?" Cal asked him. "And how's that new baby?"

Zoe turned, looked up at Greg in surprise, and Greg glowered at Cal.

Cal kept his expression innocently inquisitive. "Heard the second one's tougher," he said. "She at home with them tonight? Well," he said with a laugh he didn't mean one bit, "of course she is. Not like a woman with a newborn's up for much dancing."

"Her mom's there," Greg got out between his teeth. "Thanks for your concern."

"Uh-huh." Cal raised the bottle to his lips, took a sip. Warm, but who cared.

Greg looked like he'd have loved to say something else, clearly thought better of it. "Nice to meet you, Zoe," he finally decided to say.

"Uh . . . yeah," she said. "Give my best to your wife. And the kids."

"Don't forget his mother-in-law," Cal said. "Aunt Doreen doesn't like to be forgotten."

Greg beat a scowling retreat with as much dignity as he could muster. Cal let a little smile of satisfaction curl his lips and watched Zoe drain her beer. That was her third, he was pretty sure, and she didn't look like a big drinker to him.

Rochelle came back at last, sitting down with Deke, who looked happier than a pig in shit.

"Falling down on the job, aren't you?" Cal asked Rochelle. "You didn't happen to mention Greg Moore's interesting—and increasing—family to Zoe? Speaking of bad guys and good guys," he told Zoe, "I'm not saying Greg's a criminal, but he's not exactly a saint, either. I wouldn't say your radar's too accurate so far."

"Oh, is that who you were with?" Rochelle asked, sounding a little distracted, or maybe just like a woman with a good buzz on. "No, really, he's not the best news, Zoe."

"Yeah. A little late, aren't you," Cal said. "Good thing I was on the job. And darlin'," he told Zoe, "just because he's not wearing a ring, that doesn't mean he's not married."

"Look for the little dent," Rochelle put in, fingering the spot where her wedding ring had been. "That means they pulled it off right outside the door. Or that band of white where their tan stops."

"Oh, *now* you're helpful," Cal said.

"Hey," Deke said, "maybe she was having a good time. Dancing's not a crime, even with a lower life form like Greg. She wasn't taking him out into the parking lot. Just dancing."

"Thought I'd filled up your dance card for the night, anyway," Cal told Zoe. "I'm gone five minutes, and it's all over? Did all our promises mean nothing to you after all? Have the flowers of spring all withered and died?"

"What?" She stared at him.

"What, don't geology ladies have any poetry in their souls?"

"Ah . . . no, I guess. You've got me there." She was struggling not to smile. "And anyway," she went on, doing her proper thing again, seeming to forget that she was in a yellow lace dress and purple cowboy boots, and that that dress had dipped a little lower, ridden a little higher, while he'd been gone. There was quite a bit of firm, warm bare thigh right there next to him, and some—not cleavage, but call it just the barest bit of a shadow, up above. Which he wasn't looking at. Much.

"Anyway," she said again, sitting up straight and putting her shoulders back, running a hand through that hair, and distracting him for a minute, "who died and made you the boss of my body?"

She got a muffled snort out of Rochelle and some frank goggling from Deke for that.

"Well, now," Cal said, "that's a real interesting question. Let's get you another beer, get you out on the floor for another lesson, and see if we can come up with an answer. I've got a step I'd like to teach you. Called the Sweetheart. And I think you'd look real good doing it."

◆ ◆ ◆

"You know that thing I told you about the thumb?" he asked her when he'd got her on his hip and sashayed across the floor with her, then had twirled her back into place, her feet moving perfectly with his now, her eyes sparkling to the driving music and the beer and, he sincerely hoped, him.

"I remembered it," she said.

"Yeah, I saw that. Good job. But I may have neglected to mention one little item."

"What's that?"

He danced her backward toward the band, lifted his hand briefly toward the stage, moved it down in a flat motion, then put his hand back and spun her as the song ended. He waited a minute, kept hold of her until the drums started in again, as steady and insistent as the beating of his heart, and the guitar commenced a slow, sweet wail.

He didn't start dancing quite yet, though. Instead, he ran his hand up her arm, right over the smooth skin, all the way to that thumb gripping his shoulder. He stroked his own thumb over it, felt the way it tightened on him, then loosened under his caress.

"The thumb's optional," he told her. He took his time sliding his hand back to her shoulder blade, enjoying every bit of the journey. He looked down into her eyes, and he could swear they darkened. No question, the pink lips had parted a little.

"The thumb . . ." she said, swallowing with an effort, because he could see her slim throat working. "The thumb stays. You want to dance close, I'll bet you could find a volunteer."

"Tempting," he said, even though it wasn't, not a bit. "But I guess I'll stick with you."

They danced like that, nice and slow, but not nice and close, until Wayne ended the song, shrugged behind Zoe's back, and switched it up. Up-tempo again, Wayne grinning at Cal, then launching into the next one, and Cal had to smile at Wayne's choice.

Because, yeah. Maybe so. Maybe he was.

Working on his next broken heart.

◆ ◆ ◆

And that looked like just what it was going to be, because there he was an hour later, walking a girl home from a dance like he was fifteen years old. Worse, walking her home with her girlfriend as a chaperone.

When Zoe and Rochelle had exchanged one of those complicated woman-looks and gotten up to leave, he'd gotten right up with them.

"I'll walk you to your car," he said.

"We walked," Rochelle said. "My place is only a couple blocks away. Plus, you know . . ." She waggled her final empty bottle. "A few too many."

"What about Zoe?" Cal asked. "This a sleepover?"

He saw the smile the girls exchanged, caught the startled look from Deke, met it with one of his own. *Damn.* Nah. Couldn't be. Or could it? Wouldn't that be something?

"Nope," Rochelle said. "I'm walking Zoe home first."

"Then I'm coming, too," Cal said. "Since you gave me my Good Guy badge and everything. Call it protection."

Deke had come along, of course. No shaking him.

Cal had taken one look at the girls when they'd stepped out into the high-forties chill of a late-October night in Paradise, and asked in astonishment, "You're walking home like that? You'll freeze."

"Nah," Rochelle said. "Zoe lives up by City Park, that's all. What's that, six blocks? We'll walk fast."

"Hell you will," Cal said. "Got my truck right here. Five minutes and you're there. Both of you, since I can tell the professor isn't about to climb up in my truck alone with me, Good Guy badge or no."

"No, thanks," Zoe said. "You've had as many beers as I have." At least she tried to say it, but her teeth were chattering so bad, Cal could barely hear it.

The buzz he was feeling wasn't coming from the beer, but he wasn't telling her that. "Right," he said. "Walking." He opened up his truck, grabbed his sweatshirt, and tossed it to Rochelle. "Put this on."

She didn't argue, and he was already shrugging out of his heavy wool jacket, draping it over Zoe's shoulders. "Here, princess. Can't do anything about those pretty bare legs of yours, but this'll help."

"You'll be cold, though," she said, but she was putting it on all the same. The ends of the sleeves dropped inches past her hands, and the tails of the jacket hung to midthigh, so far you could barely even see the dress. She could be naked under there. And wasn't that a nice little thought.

"Me? I'm pretty much immune by this point. Besides," he said with a grin at her, "I tend to run hot."

Rochelle snorted, and Zoe laughed, too, and kept on laughing. "I thought this was going to be good practice," she told him with a little snort of her own that told him that four beers were about three more than she was used to drinking. "Flirting with you. I kind of need practice, in case you can't tell. I can't decide if you're practicing, too, or if this is your normal mode."

"You think? And this isn't even my A game. I'm a little rusty, you could say." He set off down the broad sidewalk of a nearly deserted Main Street with her, leaving Rochelle to follow along with Deke. "But I was practice, huh? Who am I the warm-up act for? Got your eye on somebody up there on campus?" He sighed. "And here I picked the hay out of my hair and everything."

Another snort. "Nobody. Practice for nobody."

"Ah." He pretended he understood, even though he didn't. Could she be into girls after all?

No. Those had been signals she'd been sending. Confused signals, contradictory signals, but signals all the same. He was glad, though. She didn't belong with some professor. She needed loosening up, needed to let that woman inside her go. Or maybe that was just wishful thinking on his part.

"I like the paintings," she said, checking out the storefronts they were passing. The antique store, the mineral shop, the hardware store. All of them were decorated as they had been every Halloween for as long as he could remember, with ghosts and pumpkins, witches flying on brooms across big, round harvest moons like the one shining right now, all applied with poster paint by clearly young and inexperienced hands.

"It's so . . . small-town. It's nice," she continued, smiling at a crudely drawn Superman flying over a skyscraper on Owl Drug's front window. A skyscraper painted after watching some movie, because the tallest building in town was about three stories.

"Yep," he said. "Every year."

"Did you do this, then, when you were a kid?"

"Oh, yeah. My brother and me. That is, until the time I painted a mermaid. Got her a little too . . . bodacious. But hey, that could have been a costume, right? Maybe she was getting dressed. I got carried away by my artistic vision, you might say."

She laughed. "I'll bet."

"Yeah." He sighed. "Worst part was, it was on the window of Paradise Flowers and Gifts. About the worst possible place. Mrs. Hodgins didn't just make me wash it off and start over, she told my mom and dad. That was the end of my career in public art."

"The innocence of childhood lost," she said, huddled in his jacket, looking up at him, her eyes dancing with laughter.

"Yeah, well, farm kids. You never have all that much innocence to start with. But could be I had less than most."

"How old were you? Thirteen?"

He grinned. "Very nearly ten."

"And shaving."

"Nah. That one took all the way until the ninth grade. I was an early bloomer."

"Ha. I'll bet. I was a late one. Not sure it's happened yet."

He was the one laughing at that. "Oh, it's happened. Trust me."

She smiled, and they crossed Main, headed up the Maple Street hill toward the high school. She was shivering, he could see, even in his jacket. It wasn't that cold, but then, she was from California. When he'd lived in California, he'd kept wishing it would snow, or at least get chilly from time to time. Clearly, though, opinions differed.

"So," he said, "on that note, my irresistible manliness and all, want to . . ." He had to stop and rack his brain. "Go to breakfast with me, say, Sunday? I'd do better by you if I could, but unfortunately, as you've probably noticed by now, the Breakfast Spot is the best restaurant in town. No candlelight at Pizza Hut."

"Don't you have to go to church?" she asked, teasing again.

"Does the Catholic show that much? Not every Sunday. I'm saving that for later. Doing my sinning while I've got the chance."

"Is that how it works?"

"Well, for me, anyway. I feel a sin or two coming on right now, in fact. Could have something to do with dancing with you."

"Thanks," she said after a moment. "For the invitation, I mean. But I've got a lot to do on Sunday. Tests to grade, lessons to plan." She seemed to catch herself up short. He waited, but that was it.

So busy she couldn't have breakfast? "Uh-huh," he said. "You know, it'll be broad daylight. Other people all around."

"I know," she said. "I'm just . . . I can't."

"Well, how about this? You want another dance lesson, you can show up next Friday night with Rochelle, and I'll give it to you. No strings, no moves. Not unless you want them. I'll even shake your hand at the door, or whatever it is guys like that do."

"Guys like what?"

He smiled. "Scared guys."

"Maybe," she said. There was no doubt about it, that door was slamming shut, and damned if he could see why.

They'd turned onto Jackson, and she stopped in front of a sagging little house, its yard a bit overgrown and unkempt.

"This is me," she told him, shrugging off his jacket and handing it to him. "Thanks for walking me home. And for your jacket. And the lesson. I had a good time."

She already had her keys out, and she was taking off around the side of the house, down a couple concrete steps, then opening a door, the window beside it glowing bright a second later. The door slammed shut, and she was gone.

She lived in the basement. The old car, the maxed-out credit card, and the basement. Professoring really *didn't* pay that great.

Rochelle came up to join him. "That went well."

"Yeah." He rubbed the back of his head, sighed a little, and shrugged his jacket on again. "Pretty much shot down in flames."

"Gotta be a first," Deke said, as they all turned around for Rochelle's apartment.

"I've got an ex-wife, remember?" Cal said. "I know all about getting shot down."

Nobody had much of an answer for that one, and they walked in silence for a couple minutes.

"All right. Why?" Rochelle demanded at last.

"Why what?" he asked.

"Why couldn't I tell Zoe who you are? When has that ever not worked out for you? Couldn't have worked much worse, anyway."

"Call it a hunch. I figured I'd win her over with my looks and personality instead."

"Huh," she said. "Yeah. That worked."

"Rub it in, why don't you."

"But so you know," she said, "I did it for you tonight, but I won't do it for long. There's a Girl Code, too."

"That bra strap," he pointed out.

"Only gets you so far. You're a big boy, and you're going to have to do this one all by yourself. Never seen you lose yet. Of course," she had to add, "Zoe's a cut above. I actually *like* her. And she actually likes women. That might be new for you."

"Likes women how?" he asked, exchanging another of those glances with Deke.

"Ha," she said. "I knew it. Don't get your hopes up. I mean that she has friends, girlfriends. She knows how to *be* a friend. She's not a snob. In fact, she just might be too good for you."

"She just might," he said. "And I just might be good for her. Guess we'll see."

SWEET PLACES

It took Zoe almost all week, and a fair amount of self-discipline, too, to stop thinking about Cal.

She'd left him standing on the sidewalk, had barely thanked him, she'd realized later with chagrin, before she'd hustled herself into her apartment. She hadn't trusted herself to spend any longer out there.

So she'd escaped inside; had leaned back against the scratched, faded white paint of her front door; and had taken a moment to catch her breath, with her hand patting the lace covering her galloping heart, thinking about the way he'd smiled. She'd known exactly how much her body had responded to him, because it was still humming, still lit up from the electricity of his touch, the memory of his smile.

It had been a night out, and that was all. Exactly what Rochelle had said: dancing, drinking . . . and flirting, too, which was an added bonus, right? Coming home with a fantasy or two to help her through the lonely nights, and what was wrong with that? Even when she'd been with Mark, her latest and not-so-greatest boyfriend, she'd needed the fantasies. The sad truth was, it hadn't been any better with Mark than it was by herself, so what would even be the point of finding someone new, somebody she could have in the flesh? Once, because Cal wouldn't be interested in more than once. And even if he wanted something more—and there was no way he could, because men like him didn't go for women like her—she couldn't do a relationship. Not now.

But a fantasy was something else again, and the mere thought of Cal was doing more for her than the very real, very solid Mark ever had. Maybe because Mark hadn't had shoulders like that, or muscles like that. He hadn't looked at her like that. And he'd sure never affected her like that. Cal had touched nothing but her back and hand, but her body still remembered exactly what his own hand had felt like against her. Firm and sure, but gentle, too. He had never grabbed her. He'd just . . . steered her. Showed her. Taken her where he'd wanted her to go.

She made herself move at last, went and sat on the couch to pull off her boots. They said that the mind was the most important sex organ, and she guessed it was true. Before heading to her bedroom, she shrugged out of the jean jacket, unfastened the belt from around her waist, and left them on the coffee table to give back to Rochelle. She closed the door, pulled the lace dress over her head and dumped it into the hamper, then switched on her portable heater, her major indulgence, turned as usual to its highest setting.

She shivered at the pleasure of the heated air hitting her chilled body, let it warm her. And then paused, arrested by her reflection in the full-length mirror on the back of the door.

She looked . . . good. And she felt good, too. She ran her hands down her sides to her hips, over the delicate floral lace of the pale-blue bra and bikini panties she'd worn tonight. Some of her favorites, because if you were going out, if you were going to try to get pretty, it was important to *feel* pretty. And she did. She felt pretty, and curvy, and *good.* And she looked that way, too.

Standing in her underwear, in her bedroom. The one place she felt safe being soft, being feminine. The one place where she didn't have to fit in, to be as tough as any of the guys, where she allowed herself to remember that she was a woman who felt, and yearned, and needed. That it was all right to want . . . whatever she wanted. That her fantasies were her own, and that they were allowed to be everything she wanted. Anything she wanted.

If the mind *were* the most important sex organ, she was right there, because the woman looking back at her looked *sexy.* Cal hadn't even kissed her, and it didn't matter. Just the way he'd danced with her, just the way he'd held her, and her lips looked plumper, her eyes looked softer, her curves looked lusher. For once, she wasn't wondering if she should try to diet away five or six—or ten—more pounds. The way he'd looked at her . . . she'd seen how much he'd wanted to touch every inch of her, how much his hands had longed to trace every curve. Almost as much as she'd wanted him to do it.

You can be in charge all you want, but not right now. There's only a couple of places where a man gets to be in charge. But we're pretty jealous about those couple of sweet, sweet places.

◆ ◆ ◆

Fantasy was one thing, though, and reality was something else. And when she was grading midterms on Sunday, thinking about how she could have been having breakfast with Cal right now instead, flirting some more . . . This was the danger zone, and she'd been right to say no, exactly because she'd wanted to say yes so badly.

But just because a guy flirted, just because he danced and smiled and talked like that, just because he was funny and charming and so sexy, that didn't mean he was in love. It didn't even mean he was in *like.* It just meant that he hadn't seen anyone he'd wanted to go after more on that particular night. She couldn't handle a one-night stand, and if it were more than that . . . she could handle that even less.

And if her body still wanted him, so what? He probably couldn't hit an actual erogenous zone with a set of blueprints and a guide dog. Men who looked like that didn't have to. It was all about the fantasy, and he was one heck of a fantasy. She could leave it at that, and she was going to.

But it was so quiet here. All right, it was lonely. She needed to talk to somebody, because it was so much harder than she'd thought to be up here in Idaho all alone. She was with students so much of the day, but somehow it wasn't the same.

Well, she needed to make this call anyway. She only wished . . . she wished . . . well, it didn't matter what she wished. She needed to make it. She picked up her phone from the coffee table and dialed.

"Santangelo."

He always answered the same, even in the age of caller ID, when he could see it was her. That had always sounded so professional. But today she wished for something else.

"Hey, Dad." She tried to inject some energy into her voice. "How are you? Working?"

"When you love what you do, it isn't work."

She'd heard that one a *lot*. "What on?"

"I've got a grant proposal due Monday. Going to have to cut one of my RAs loose, because I'm going to spend the whole day fixing this. Well, my own fault. Should have known he didn't have what it took, but I gave him a chance."

"Oh, that's too bad. For both of you."

"Too bad for me, but a good lesson for him. I gave him a chance; he didn't make the most of it. That's life. You're working, too, I assume."

"Yep. Of course. The apple doesn't fall far from the tree," she tried to joke.

"Something special you wanted to talk about?" *Get to the point.*

"Um . . ." She closed her eyes, rubbed her hand over her forehead. "I went into the ditch with my car this week. Skidded on some ice. And I . . . I wondered," she finished in a rush, "if I could borrow three hundred dollars until the end of the month. Just for ten days or so, for the repair bill."

"Zoe." She could hear the sigh, and her stomach twisted. "You need to budget for emergencies."

"I know. Of course." She'd known this would happen. As soon as she asked him for money, she invited him to examine her finances. That was how it worked. "But moving was expensive, and first and last month's rent, student loans . . ."

"Maybe you should have rented a cheaper place. And as for the loans, we've talked about this. I paid half of everything, all the way through the PhD. That's more than fair. This is the struggle everybody goes through, because you don't value what comes too easily. Everybody was poor once, at least anybody worth knowing. I ate tomato soup and scrambled eggs and rice every day through graduate school."

She'd heard that before, too. "I'm not asking for anything different," she said. "I'm just asking for a loan for ten days. I know how to be poor. I'm being poor. And you only ate those things during graduate school," she couldn't resist pointing out. "Not once you were teaching. Times have changed. This job pays less than being a high school teacher in California."

"I thought you said you were doing some consulting."

"I am. Union City hired me to look at their groundwater table, the job I told you about. That's when I skidded on the ice, coming back from a meeting. And I'll get paid for that in another month or so, and it'll help a lot. But meanwhile . . ."

"All right," he said. "I'll put the money into your account today. You can put it back into mine on the first. But be more careful in the future. Driving *and* budgeting."

"Sure," she said with relief. "Thanks."

"And remember," he said, "that's exactly why you're working so hard. To move up and out of there, to get the job and do the research that will bring you the consulting contracts. There's your motivation. That's what life's all about, working toward that goal."

"I know. I know it is. And actually, it's really nice here." She looked out the sliding-glass door opposite her tiny living/dining room into the backyard. Nothing special, but the trees were pretty, lacy branches mostly bare against blue sky, and the sun was shining. She'd take a walk later to the university pool, go for a swim, give herself a reward for getting her work done. "It's peaceful," she went on. "It's like a real community, you know? Where they have Girl Scouts and 4-H and county fairs. There's a real downtown where people shop, and kids around after school playing in their yards, skateboarding at the park. And babies in the baby swings in their snowsuits. Everybody's not just holed up in their own houses. I even know my neighbors. So, really," she said, trying to cheer herself up, "it's all good."

"Hmm," her dad said. "I'm sure Mayberry R.F.D. *is* peaceful. Just remember, 'peaceful' doesn't usually translate into 'career progress.' There's a time in your life to stop and smell the roses, and there's a time to plug away. This is your time to plug away. The first ten years of your career set you up for the rest of it."

Another maxim. "But you know," she said slowly, "in ten years, I'll be thirty-nine."

"Yes, you will," he said. "And set up."

"But . . ."

"What?"

"Well, you know." She tried to laugh. "What if I decide I want the whole deal, after all? I guess my biological clock is ticking. Must be those babies in the snowsuits." Cheeks pink with cold, warm hats and mittens and boots, stomping on the frozen puddles in City Park because it was so much fun to crack the ice. Being lifted into swings by mothers . . . and dads. Dads who were there to do that, who wanted to do it. Babies shrieking with glee as they flew through the air on those baby swings. They made her smile. They made her feel . . . something. Something new.

"Have you met somebody?" her dad asked. "Is that what this is about? It's too soon for that. The first year of teaching is the critical one. You don't have time for relationships this year. It's the easiest thing in the world for a woman to fall off that track, and this is exactly how it happens. We've talked about this, about how few women make it, and this is why."

"I know," she said. "Never mind. I'm probably just lonely. Don't listen to me."

"I was reading an article the other day," her dad said, surprising her, because she'd figured they were done, "about some of the tech companies who are paying for their female employees to have their eggs frozen. And I thought, that's brilliant. You can put it off until you're established, but still know you've got healthy eggs, without the increased risk of having an imperfect child."

An imperfect child. "Sounds . . . practical," she managed.

"And if you want that, that's one thing I *would* be willing to pay for, because it would be an investment in your career. We can look into it when you're down here at Christmas, schedule it for next summer when you'll have the time. I understand it's quite a procedure, and you'd want to have it done at the best facility, of course."

"Whoa. I mean . . . thanks." *I think.* "The future Mr. Santangelo or whoever might not be willing to go along, though."

"Well, the beauty of this is," her dad said, "even if there isn't a Mr. Santangelo, you can still choose motherhood down the road. Use a sperm bank, get a med student donor so you know you've got the right genetic background, and delay it until you can afford to give your child the best, like I gave you."

"Well, I had a mom, too. This all sounds kind of Future World, doesn't it?"

"No," her father said, "it sounds like a solution that would set your mind at ease and help you keep that focus where it belongs But we'd both better get back to work. I'll put the three hundred in, just to cover you. Until the first of the month."

"I promise, it'll be back in your account on the first. Thanks."

It wasn't until she hung up that she realized he hadn't asked her if she'd been hurt when she'd gone off the road. But then, he'd have figured that she'd have told him if she had been. That was her dad. Focused on the practical details. Eyes on the prize.

Freezing her eggs. Wow. It was practical, she could see that. It just sounded so cold. So bleak. But maybe that was the answer. Maybe so.

She glanced over at the cowboy boots that had cost half of that $300. She'd known they were a bad idea. Why was it that everything that felt good was a bad idea?

She thought about calling her mom. Her mom would understand about the boots. But she'd also want to know how Zoe's dad was doing, and that was so depressing, and so exasperating, too. *Give it up, Mom,* she always wanted to say. *He doesn't love you anymore, and he never will again.* But it was too cruel.

Her dad was right. Relationships were confusing, and they got you off track. And men were fickle anyway. Her dad was the prime example of that one, too. She'd focus on work. She knew about work.

She'd call her mom tonight, tell her she'd gone out dancing, describe what she'd worn. Her mom would love that. Meanwhile, she needed to finish her grading, and then she could take a walk, have that swim. She could say hello to people along the way, and they'd say hello back. She could even look at babies in the park. But she had a stack of tests to grade before she could do that, and she was only halfway through, so she picked up the next one, opened it, and got started.

Amy's. Her handwriting had become increasingly wild as she'd gone along. It was obvious that, for whatever reason, she had indeed panicked. During the test, anyway.

Zoe sighed, read, marked, and hoped Amy would keep after it, would do those corrections. She reminded herself to encourage the girl if the opportunity arose, because she hated failing a student who was trying. It was the worst.

CANDY AND FLOWERS

Wednesday night, and Halloween, too. Amy walked the last few blocks toward home in the dusk, her coat buttoned against the increasingly chilly late-afternoon wind. There was going to be frost tonight, and all the kids would have to wear their jackets under their costumes, and they'd complain about it, just like she always had. It was pretty hard to feel like a beautiful princess with a puffy jacket stuffed under your Snow White dress.

She hoped she'd get some kids, but the apartment complex was student housing, so probably not. She'd bought some M&M's just in case, hoping she could restrain herself from eating them. When you were short anyway, five extra pounds were five pounds too many, and she'd gone to a Halloween party at Bill's frat house on Saturday night, had drunk too much, and beer was fattening, everybody knew that.

She didn't have to eat M&M's, she reminded herself sternly, because she was in control. Of her body, and her life. Even though she'd finally gotten her geology test back in class today, and it had had a big red "61" on it. She'd turned the book over fast, looked around and hoped nobody had seen, and swallowed against the sickness that rose at the grade distribution Dr. Santangelo had posted on the whiteboard, because her 61 was third from the bottom. She was going to do the corrections tonight, though, and then she was going to stay caught up. The next midterm, she wasn't getting a 61.

She climbed the final hill to the apartment complex, saw the splash of color outside the sliding door to her apartment, and her heart lifted a little. Bill had never sent flowers before, but then, he'd walked home with her on Saturday night after the party, had come in to say good night . . . and it had been really good.

They'd both been a little drunk, and her roommate had been at a party of her own, so they'd had the apartment to themselves. Bill had pulled the plunging top of her belly dancer costume right off her when they'd barely been inside the door, and they'd never even made it to the bedroom. They'd done it right there on the living room rug, and it had been the best sex she'd ever had.

"Damn, baby, you looked hot tonight," he'd gasped, grabbing her by the hips and grinding into layers of transparent skirts. He'd gotten everything off her except the jangling bells around her ankles, and when he'd been doing it hard and fast, those bells had rung like crazy, and so had hers.

Right in front of the window, in the dark, and that had been exciting, too. And now there were flowers outside that same window. Which told her it wasn't just sex. Flowers were romance.

She bent down on the concrete slab, picked up the plain glass vase full of chrysanthemums in bronze and gold. Fall colors. Halloween colors. She balanced the vase on a hip, opened the sliding-glass door and locked it behind her, set the vase on the coffee table, and plucked the white envelope out of its holder.

A Halloween card. Aw. That was sweet. *Prepare to be spooked*, the outside proclaimed. She opened it and laughed. Bigfoot, holding a sign. *Have a hairy scary Halloween.*

Trick or treat, pretty girl, was printed in block letters beneath. Not signed, because he hadn't had to sign it. She smiled and sighed.

She'd already gotten her treat. What had happened the other night, and flowers. Two pretty good treats.

She pulled her phone out of her pack, texted him.

`Just wanted to say I loved it. Thank you.`

She carried the phone with her while she took her things into her bedroom, and sure enough, it dinged within five minutes.

`Anytime`, he'd texted back. `See u tomorrow.`

She wouldn't eat any M&M's, she vowed. Not a single packet. Next time she got naked with him, there was going to be a pound less of her. Meanwhile, she'd heat up some soup and do those corrections. This was going to be her new leaf, because there was no way she was flunking out of school and going home, no matter how many panic attacks she had during a midterm. She was in charge of her life, and she was going to stay in charge of it.

HAPPY HALLOWEEN

He swung himself up, balanced for a second on top of the wooden fence, then dropped to a crouch on the other side, his navy-blue sweatshirt and dark blue jeans blending into the shadows.

He could have walked straight up the driveway and around the sidewalk. Not like there was anybody around, not at three in the morning. The witching hour, when sleep was deepest, defenses were lowest. His favorite time of night.

But you never knew. Somebody up late studying, some guy banging his girlfriend, then coming outside to smoke a cigarette? He'd gotten away with this so far not just because of his . . . advantages, but because he was smart, and he was careful, and he planned.

Fail to plan, he reminded himself, *or plan to fail.* He didn't plan to fail. Not tonight. Not ever.

Amy had been savvier, more aware than most of them, but that just made her more of a challenge. She'd picked up on him faster, although not as fast as she could have, because she hadn't caught him shadowing her on foot, had she, during his preliminary reconnaissance? But once she'd figured it out, she'd definitely taken more precautions, had slowed him down. He'd had to lie low longer than he'd expected, hadn't had more than those few nights of fun chasing her in the truck, the entertainment of watching how jumpy she'd been ever since.

He'd have to make tonight extra good to make up for it, that was all. There was no big, strong boyfriend to help her now. It was just going to be the two of them, him and his cute little Amy. His dream date.

She'd had a good time with Billy-boy on Saturday, and he'd enjoyed the view he'd gotten of it from his spot right here by the fence. He'd used his night-vision goggles to make sure he hadn't missed a thing, and he'd enjoyed the hell out of it. Bill had warmed her up pretty good for him, and now it was his turn.

They always got complacent eventually, and Amy was no exception. They always doubted what they'd seen, what they'd felt. Women were so easily swayed. Face it, they were stupid. They were weak, and the strong preyed on the weak. That was the law of the jungle.

He unzipped the pocket of the sweatshirt, felt for the thin, sticky latex of the surgical gloves, worked them onto his hands in the dark. His fingers found the reassuringly jagged edges of the zip ties, gave them a little pat. Two, and two extra, because he always brought extras. There was that planning again.

A gloved hand in the other pocket, and he pulled out the black ski mask, tugged it over his head, aligned the eye and mouth holes. Now he looked like a bona fide nightmare.

He smiled inside the woolen mask. *Happy Halloween, Amy.*

He didn't need anything else. He never did. Fear froze them for those first critical seconds, and by the time they woke up enough to know what was happening, it was already much too late. A few threats, a good hard slap or two if they needed it, a hand on their throat, and by the time he started, their minds had gotten ahead of them and they were just praying to survive. That was all it took.

His heart was beating harder, but it wasn't unpleasant, not at all. He was on edge, but it was a good edge, knowing he was at the top of his game, that he was in charge. He never felt better than he did right before. Not even afterward. He could get off anytime. But he couldn't get this. This was special. This was his.

Mask, gloves, zip ties, penlight. He was ready. He wondered again if he should change it up, start blindfolding them. Use a pillowcase, maybe. Shove it over her head, and he wouldn't have to worry one bit about her identifying him.

But if he did that, he couldn't see their eyes, and their eyes were his favorite part. Seeing the fear in them, the desperation. The pain. And then there was the bargaining, the reasoning. When they tried using their freshman Sexual Assault Awareness training on him—Christ, that made him laugh.

So no blindfold. Because it would take away half the fun, and the fun was the point. That and the danger. The danger . . . that was the extra spice in the stew.

But that was enough time savoring the pleasures to come. Time to make his move. He looked around once more, stayed low, and crept across the yard. Then he was standing on the concrete slab, lit by the dim illumination of the so-called security lights, the most dangerous part of his mission.

The sliding door was aluminum, but he knew that already, because he didn't take chances. He'd checked it out weeks ago, when he'd picked his Amy. He tried it, just to make sure. Locked.

Well, that would have been too easy. No fun at all. Anyway, locking one of these things was like taking your shoes off for the airport security scanners. Didn't keep anything safer at all, just made stupid people feel like it did.

He put one hand up to the corner of the aluminum frame, the other on the handle. A couple hard, sharp jerks in exactly the right place, and he felt the snap. He smiled. Piece of crap. Easy as pie. He slid it open, left it that way, ready for a quick exit, and stepped inside. Unzipped his sweatshirt pocket, touched the ridged edge of a zip tie. Party time.

"Honey," he breathed. "I'm home."

MONKEY PAWS

Amy sat up in bed, her heart knocking against her chest. What was that? Was that something?

She'd sat up in the dark with her heart beating exactly like this, over and over and over again, every night for more than a week. But this was the first night she'd been alone.

It's all right, her brain said. *Just the wind.* But her body was telling her something else. That it was the very furthest thing from all right. Every muscle had tensed. Everything in her was screaming *danger*.

Her eyes were fixed on the doorway. It was pitch-dark in here, the shades drawn, but she could sense something. Not quite hear it, just a feeling. And then she heard the hint of a rasp that she somehow knew was the doorknob turning, saw a sliver of a break in the shadows, a wedge of gray that grew slowly wider. The door was opening.

Her right hand, the one that had been resting on the switch, hit it hard, and her bedside light went on.

She saw him standing frozen, his hand still on the doorknob. And then she had leaped to her feet, on the side of the bed away from him, even as he rushed around the end of the bed, straight for her.

She didn't try to run, didn't scramble across the bed. She never even thought of it. Instead, she charged him, shouting at the top of her lungs, a wordless, primal scream of fear and anger and aggression, lifted the maple wood bat that had been beside her bed and swung it backhanded, because there wasn't enough room between her bed and the wall. And because she had seen him telegraph his move.

He'll go for your right. Go for his left.

She didn't swing for his head. Too small, too uncertain a target.

Center mass. It had worked when she'd been standing at home plate facing the pitcher, and it worked now. She swung, hard and fast, and that right hand that had been reaching for the bat missed, but she didn't.

Wham. Into his left arm, and he was spinning, gasping.

Wham. Into his back as he spun, and he was catapulted forward, and then he was scrambling, running away, and she was still screaming at the top of her lungs, no words forming, just screaming. And chasing him.

Out of the bedroom, through the dark living room, out the open sliding door, into the shock of the freezing night, her bare feet hitting concrete, then grass as he ran for the fence, hunched over, hugging his left arm.

Three steps, four, and her foot was sliding out from under her on the frost, and she was flailing, falling backward, the other foot going out from under her.

She hit the grass hard, the wooden handle flying out of her grasp, into the darkness. Her head banged against the frozen ground, and she saw stars, but her feet were scrabbling all the same.

She rolled, looked up, and he was there. The face she'd seen only for those couple of terrifying seconds before she'd struck. Nothing but black, the white edging visible in the moonlight outlining his eyes and mouth, a staring, screaming mask. His hands glistening weirdly, curled monkey paws reaching for her.

"Bitch," he hissed, still favoring his left side. "You *bitch*."

She scrabbled back like a crab on palms and feet, reached desperately behind her for the bat.

He didn't let her get there. He grabbed her left ankle in his right hand, was pulling her toward him, her short nightgown riding up over her hips, above her waist, nearly to her breasts, her bare skin burning against the frosted blades of grass, sharp as needles, and she was kicking desperately, screaming with every ounce of breath in her lungs.

"You're going to *pay*." It was a snarl, and he grabbed her right ankle as well, pulled harder, toward the bushes, and she was hauled up on her elbows, naked now from the shoulders down, still trying to kick, still screaming.

"*Hey!*" It was a shout from behind her. "*Heyheyhey!*"

She didn't stop kicking, didn't stop screaming. Her attacker froze, dropped her ankles, turned and took off. It was Tom, her neighbor, running after him, and the man in the ski mask was running, too, still hunched, leaping for the top of the fence only yards ahead of Tom and heaving himself awkwardly across it.

Tom was up and over seconds later, and Amy heard the pounding of feet, Tom still shouting, the sound fading into the cold night.

She was sobbing, pulling herself up, tugging her nightgown down with shaking hands, then standing, hunching over with her arms wrapped around herself, and the yard was full of people now. Lights coming on along the row of apartments, students pouring out, milling around, talking. Tom's girlfriend, Janice, was running across the grass, grabbing her.

"What happened?" she asked, panting. "Who was that? Was that Bill?"

Amy couldn't answer. She was crying too hard, shaking too violently.

Tom appeared at the top of the fence again, dropped down, came over to the two of them, stood over her, hands on hips, breathing hard, and Amy shrank into Janice's arms, sobbed and sobbed, and couldn't stop.

ANOTHER BORING COLLEGE FUNCTION

Five o'clock on Friday afternoon, and instead of getting a start on Tuesday's lecture for her Groundwater Hydrology class, Zoe was about to use a precious couple of hours to go to a cocktail party.

Which she had no interest in attending, and which would take time she couldn't afford. Teaching three classes, preparing lectures and labs for all of them was way too much work, especially on top of that consulting job, and was leaving her dangerously close to the edge of panic most of the time. The first year teaching a full course load, she knew, was a sink-or-swim proposition. And she had to swim.

"Just use the slides that go along with the textbook," her next-door office neighbor, Roy Blake, had advised before the semester had begun. "Somebody's got to teach Geology 101. Last few years, that lucky camper has been me, and I can't tell you how glad I am that they finally filled that position. With anybody. Although having it be you, of course, is a bonus."

"Oh, thanks," she said. "Because I brighten the place up. With my femininity and all."

"No," he said, "because you occasionally laugh at my jokes. But you want my advice? Don't spend too much energy on it, and don't let the students suck all your time. You have to keep your office hours, or somebody will tattle to Daddy, but other than that . . ." He mimed slamming a door. "Keep it closed."

"But that isn't . . ." *The point. The idea.*

"You think? Just wait. I've been slogging in these trenches for a long, long time. You want to move up and out, that's how you do it. Guard your time for the things that'll help you do it."

"Uh . . ." She wasn't sure how to respond. Had she been that transparent?

"You've got it written all over you," he said. "Ambition. I recognize it, vaguely. What, we thinking Colorado School of Mines here? Virginia Tech? Or the really big leagues? MIT? Stanford?"

"If . . . if I can," she managed.

"Well, you know as well as I do what's going to get you there. Consulting and research. Publish or perish, baby. You don't have to publish much to stay here, which is, of course, why I'm here. Got tenure now, and that means they'll be carrying my cold, stiff body out on a slab. But you sure do have to publish to leave here. I'm not telling you not to care about teaching. I'm just telling you not to care too much."

He was right. But she still couldn't keep her office door shut, not if there were students who needed to talk to her.

Like Amy. She frowned again, thinking about the girl. She hadn't showed up for class today. Zoe hoped she'd make it on Monday, and that she would turn in those test corrections, too.

She sighed. Sometimes, students were nothing but baffling. But she couldn't shortchange them, which meant that she couldn't lecture from the slides that came with the Intro to Geology textbook. So she was stuck working eighty hours a week to keep on top of everything, and *not* researching, and *not* publishing. Not yet.

It was only her first semester. It would get easier. She got up reluctantly and put on her suit jacket and coat for the cold, if short, hike to the student union and the stupid cocktail hour that the new faculty had been elected to attend.

She got there on time, of course, and was one of the first ones. Too conscientious once again. She found her name tag on the table at the front of the banquet room, stuck it onto the front of her black jacket, spotted Rochelle across the room talking to the caterers, and felt a little bit better.

"Hey," Rochelle said when Zoe approached. "I saw you were coming. Some Friday night fun, huh? Not quite the Cowboy Bar." She looked Zoe over critically. "In fact, not the Cowboy Bar at all. Did you actually look in your closet to find the most boring, least attractive outfit possible? It's hard to believe you'd have picked that by accident."

"What?" Zoe looked down at her pantsuit. "This is my interview suit."

"No, it's not," Rochelle said. "I saw your interview suit, remember? Same ugly black jacket, same totally sexless blue blouse, same black pumps your Aunt Constance wears to her Library Committee meeting. But at least a skirt."

"It's cold," Zoe said weakly. "And I have to look like everybody else."

Rochelle looked at her in astonishment. "I hate to break it to you, but you don't look like everybody else. Wear all the ugly pantsuits you want, it's never going to happen."

"If I wanted to hear about my unfeminine clothes," Zoe said, trying to summon a little spirit, "I could fly home and talk to my mother."

"Well, you know," Rochelle said, "even mothers are right occasionally."

Zoe snagged a glass of wine from a tray carried by a passing waiter, took a sip, and grimaced.

Rochelle laughed. "Yeah, I'd tell you what a bottle of that cost, but the truth is too painful." Her gaze shifted to a spot beyond Zoe. "Gotta go check on the front table. See ya. Don't have too much fun."

"Ha," Zoe said glumly as Rochelle took off. She looked around, feeling alone and conspicuous. She saw a few guys she'd met during her new faculty orientation, and contemplated going over to chat. She took another sip of wine to help get her there, then looked around for someplace to put her glass down, because really, even for courage . . . no.

"Yeah, it's pretty bad," she heard at her elbow. "Beer's always a safer bet at places like this."

She whirled. Cal? What? Why? How?

"Why are you . . . here?" She looked at the front of the white cotton button-down that stretched over his distractingly broad chest. No name tag, of course. "How'd you get in?"

She could see the amusement crinkling the corners of his eyes. "Whoa there, princess. Don't you worry about me. It'll take more than a couple professors to toss me out. I'm bigger than they are. Come on. I'll buy you a beer. You look like you could use one."

"It's an open bar," she pointed out. "Such as it is."

"And see," he said, "that means you don't even have to compromise your principles. Long as you can live with me asking for it, that is. That going to work for you, or do you have to place the order, too? They only have one kind, so you don't have to worry that I'm making your decisions."

"How do you know? Are you here for the . . ." *For the beer*, she almost said, then realized how insulting that would sound. "I mean," she stammered as he started to laugh, "it can't be for the entertainment value. I know *I* sure wouldn't be here if they hadn't made me come."

"Aw, see, I knew you were smart," he said. "The truth is, I'm hoping to get wasted enough to make Dumpster diving look like a good idea afterwards, because I'm hungry, too." He snagged a cracker with a piece of cheese on it from a passing tray. "And this isn't going to do the trick."

She was following him to the bar despite herself. She took the glass the bartender poured, sipped a little as Cal took his own glass with a nod of thanks, stuffing a five into the tip jar that had the young man smiling.

"Hey, Cal." The voice came from behind them. Another big, good-looking guy. Nobody Zoe had met, because she would've remembered him. This one did have a name tag. *Lucas Jackson.*

"Yeah, beer's the beverage of choice today, I'd say," the guy told Cal. "How about pouring me one of those?" he asked the bartender.

"Sure thing," the bartender said, and Lucas took his own beer, moved away from the bar with the two of them.

"Another cousin, I take it. The mystery solves itself," Zoe said. "Why you're here, I mean," she explained to Cal.

"Does it?" he asked. "Good to know, because I was wondering. And nope, this one's a real live brother. The only one I've got. And since I know you read real good, Professor, I don't even need to say his name. Luke, this is Dr. Zoe Santangelo. I *will* say her name, just because it's so pretty."

Zoe extended her hand, and she couldn't help it, she had to smile at that. "Do you teach here?" she asked Luke.

There was a definite family resemblance. Luke was a little more handsome, a little leaner in build, with a shock of dark hair that fell across his forehead, and brown eyes instead of blue. A little younger, too, or maybe he just spent less time outdoors, because his face didn't have the frown lines Cal's did on the forehead, or the laugh lines beside the firm mouth.

"Nope," Luke said. "Principal over at the high school, believe it or not."

Cal shook his head. "Still getting over that one," he told Zoe. "Let's just say the principal's office wasn't unfamiliar territory to him."

Luke laughed. "Man, you're always messing me up with pretty girls."

"Yeah, well," Cal said, "I saw this particular pretty girl first, so back off, Bozo. Although I have to say," he told Zoe, "I liked what you were wearing last time better. At least you could have worn the skirt and not the pants."

She gasped in outrage as Luke burst out laughing again.

"Never mind," Luke said, still grinning. "I'm not one bit worried about Cal cutting me out, I just decided. Yeah, man, insulting her appearance. That's going to work."

"Rochelle told you to say that, didn't she?" Zoe demanded of Cal, ignoring his brother.

"No, what, you hear that already today? Let me guess. That yellow dress was Rochelle's."

"Maybe."

"No maybe about it," he decided. "Rochelle's all the way. Go shopping in her closet a little more, will you? I loved you in that dress."

She did her best to ignore the glow that gave her. "And pleasing you would matter to me because . . . ?"

"Now, then, Professor," he said, that drawl back in full force, "I'm sure you can think up the answer to that one if you put that fine mind of yours to it."

"Uh-*huh*," Luke said, his eyes dancing. "I knew I needed to come to this thing. I hear the speeches are going to be lousy, but the entertainment's not too bad all the same."

"Welcome."

The sound boomed out almost directly behind her, and Zoe jumped, nearly spilling her beer, and turned to look. The trim middle-aged woman at the podium stepped back and laughed a little, and a young man leaped onto the elevated platform in a corner of the room, did some adjusting to the microphone.

"Off to a rousing start," Cal muttered.

"Now that I have your attention . . ." the woman said. She acknowledged the answering scatter of laughter with another smile. "I'd like to welcome all of you here today. As many of you know, I'm Dena Calvert, and I have the privilege of administering the university's development office. We're here today to acknowledge a very generous gift, and to announce a program we couldn't be more excited about. In fact, it's *so* momentous, it's too big to come from me. So here to do it instead is the president of the university, Dr. Franklin Oppenheimer."

"With a name like that," Cal said, "no other job he could possibly have."

"Shh," Zoe hissed. They were standing too close to the podium for her to get the giggles. It didn't matter that Dr. Oppenheimer didn't have a clue who she was. He'd find out soon enough if she started laughing at the sound of his *name.* But her unfortunate sense of humor wasn't cooperating, and she was having a hard time controlling her face.

"Thank you for that wonderful introduction, Dena," the gray-haired man at the microphone said graciously.

"What? That she got his name right?" Cal asked, and Zoe snorted again, slapped a hand over her mouth, and shot him a glare that he answered with a cock of his head.

Dr. Oppenheimer was still talking, but Zoe was too focused on not giggling to listen. *Generosity of one of our community's most notable citizens, blah blah. Although sadly not an alumnus . . .* She drifted off a little.

"Yeah, yeah, yeah," Cal muttered beside her, still not quietly enough. "Wrap it up, cowboy. Your eight seconds are up."

She had to pretend to cough into her napkin at that one, and she didn't even dare look at Cal.

"Although no longer making us proud on the playing field," Dr. Oppenheimer said, "today's honoree is still very much contributing to his hometown and its university. And it is my very great pleasure to announce tonight that he has donated the astonishingly generous sum of $800,000 to the university for the purposes of expanding its efforts in the physical sciences, engineering, and technology, and in particular to foster the inclusion of women and students of color in those fields. I couldn't be happier to ask you to join me today in being the first, although surely not the last, to thank Mr. Calvin Jackson for his generosity." He was smiling now, beckoning. "Cal?"

Cal handed a stunned Zoe his beer. "Don't drink it all, now, darlin'," he told her. "I'm going to need that later."

He strode to the platform in his cowboy boots and black jeans, jumped up onto it exactly the same way he'd jumped up onto the stage at the Cowboy Bar, and the room echoed with applause and even a few whistles. He shook hands with Dr. Oppenheimer, adjusted the microphone upward with a practiced hand, and waited for the crowd to quiet.

"Well, thanks for all that," he said when silence had fallen. "You know, when I was first talking to Dr. Oppenheimer about this idea, and he asked me what had led me to it, I said something noble about improving the quality of education for Idaho students, not losing our best and brightest to the other states, making the playing field a little more level, some sh—shinola like that."

He grinned at the ripple of laughter. "When, really," he confided, "the truth is, I was just hoping for a parade. So I hope that's in the cards," he told a chuckling Dr. Oppenheimer. "I'm kinda countin' on riding on the float."

His speech didn't go on much longer than that, or get much more serious. Another couple minutes, and he was saying, "Thanks, everyone. The wine and cheese and crackers are on the house. Go wild, because I'm not taking all that home."

He jumped down again as the room erupted in laughter and applause, came over, took the beer that Zoe had forgotten she was holding, and drained it.

"Do we get to leave now?" he asked. "Because I'd love to get out of here with you. If I talk real nice, I figure I might just get you to go dancing with me. Seeing as how I'm a donor and all."

SOME COGENT POINTS

Zoe was still groping for words when Luke spoke.

"Whoa, bro," he said. "I didn't realize how much it was for."

"Yeah," Cal said. "I figured, why not? I can use the tax write-off."

"Uh-huh," Luke said. "You mean you wanted to make the folks proud, do something worthwhile with some of the dough. Oh, the horror. You know, if you keep doing stuff like this, that decent streak of yours is going to show no matter how hard you try to hide it."

Cal shrugged, not looking nearly so comfortable. "Maybe I just wanted to piss some people off, you think of that?"

Luke laughed. "Hell, yeah. What's Jolie going to think about it when she hears?"

Cal's expression hardened. "She'd have something to say if we were still married. But we're not, so she doesn't."

"I hope it burns her," Luke said with satisfaction, clearly not seeing what Zoe saw. "Thinking about you giving away all that gorgeous money. Imagining, what? The vacation house you could have bought her down in Puerto Vallarta? But hey, too late now."

"Yeah," Cal said shortly. "But I was thinking about Steve."

"Our brother-in-law," Luke explained to Zoe. "He'll have something to say for sure."

"I swear," Cal said, clearly doing his best to shake off the moment. "He lives in terror as it is that I'll blow everything and not pay the ground rent. The rent for the land," he told Zoe. "How I buy out Luke and Theresa's share of the farm."

"Okay," she said, although she wasn't much wiser.

"He was telling me at Easter," Luke went on, "that it wasn't looking now like you'd have kids, and what did I think? Like it was such a sad story, like he was fooling me. With him counting the zeroes, adding it all up in that calculator he calls a brain."

There was that tension right back again in Cal's face, and Zoe wondered why Luke couldn't see it. She waited for Cal to answer, but he didn't, so she spoke up.

"Wait," she said. "Back up for me. I'm sure you both know exactly what you're talking about, but I'm completely confused. Who *are* you? You said you were a farmer. And you're talking about buying people out, and million-dollar donations . . . how?"

"Not a million," he said. "And I *am* a farmer. Want to see my farm? Amber waves of grain and everything."

"More like black contour lines of dirt right now," Luke said. "Not sure how impressed she'll be."

"Then . . ." Zoe said. "What exactly are you growing out there? Or don't I want to know?"

Luke laughed again. "Before he was a farmer," he said, "or before he took over the farm, let's say, he was a little bit of a football player. What, you didn't know?"

"No, I didn't know. How would I know?"

"Oh, nothing," Luke said. "Had his ugly face on TV every Sunday for quite a few years there, that's all."

"In a helmet," Cal pointed out.

"And your name in the paper. A fair number of commercials, too," Luke said.

"Mostly during football games," Cal said. "And somehow, I doubt the professor's a big fan."

"No," she said. "Not a fan."

Dr. Oppenheimer was approaching them now, though, even as the speeches continued, and Zoe fell silent as he touched Cal on the arm. Cal turned, and the president shook his hand again, chuckling.

"You caught me off guard there," Dr. Oppenheimer said. "Not much of a speech."

"Leave 'em wanting more," Cal agreed. "That's the idea. Do you know Zoe Santangelo? Dr. Santangelo was just giving me some ideas on how we could do more to encourage women to pursue the hard sciences. Making some really cogent points there."

Zoe gaped at him, then snapped her mouth shut. Cogent *points*?

"I haven't had the pleasure, I don't believe," Dr. Oppenheimer said smoothly, shaking Zoe's hand. "But I think I recognize the name. One of our newer faculty, is that right?"

"Uh . . . yes," she said, then got hold of herself. "Yes, I am. In the Geological Sciences Department, just hired this year as an assistant professor."

"That's right," Dr. Oppenheimer said. "The first female professor we've had there, I believe. I remember the appointment. Quite a coup for us, getting you."

Yeah, right. Such a coup that he hadn't had a clue who she was.

"And I was thinking," Cal said, "you were mentioning a committee, Frank, when we spoke earlier. Seems to me that a couple of younger women faculty members like Dr. Santangelo here, with boots on the ground, you could say, might have a lot to contribute. Ideas about how women can break down those invisible barriers, or how we can help remove them."

"An excellent idea." The president beamed. "We'll be setting up that working group right away, and we'll be looking for members who can give us the view from the trenches, as it were. I hope I can count on you to be one of them, Dr. Santangelo. Zoe, if I may. And please, call me Frank."

"Yes," Zoe stammered. "Of course. Frank." She didn't dare look at Cal. "I'd be happy to."

"I was thinking about the high school as well," Cal went on. "Get the students thinking about it ahead of time, get them aware of the opportunities out there, open up those AP Physics, AP Calculus classes to more of them. Ruin the curve for the guys, of course, just like I'll bet Dr. Santangelo did. Isn't that so, Professor?"

She couldn't help smiling. "Could be."

Dr. Oppenheimer looked at Luke. "Can we count on your participation on the committee as well? That's an excellent suggestion, too. A real partnership."

"Sure," Luke said. "How about mentoring? I'd love to have some of the engineering students over there tutoring, helping out."

"Nothing like teaching it to help you learn it yourself," Cal said. "Don't you think, Dr. Santangelo?"

"Yes," she said. "Yes, I do."

"Yet another good idea," Dr. Oppenheimer said, actually rubbing his hands together a little now. "I hope you're going to sit in as well, Cal. I'd love to have you steering this." *And pumping more money into it,* he didn't need to say.

"I'll come when I can," Cal said. "Until spring work starts, anyway. Share a few ideas I've got going in. But don't worry, I've got no plans to run the show. Give the money and go away. The ideal donor profile."

"No, no." The president laughed. "Not true at all. Look how much you've contributed right here."

"Uh-huh." Cal grinned. "Well, I'll try to keep the . . . contributions coming. Now, if you'll excuse me, the professor here had a few more insights she wanted to share with me."

"Of course." Another smile, another shake of hands all around, and Cal was shepherding Zoe across the room with a hand resting lightly on the small of her back, a hand she was aware of right through her jacket and blouse. Luke came along, too, although the little procession kept getting stopped along the way, because it seemed like Cal—and Luke, too—knew half the room.

"Phew," Cal said when they reached the foyer. He gestured at the cloakroom, looked at Zoe. "Got a ticket?"

"I do." Zoe pulled it from her pocket and handed it to him. "But wait a second," she realized. "Maybe I didn't *want* to leave."

"Oh." He looked genuinely taken aback, then grinned. "Yep. There I go again. Disregarding your agency, that what that's called, Luke?"

"I think that's the buzzword," his brother said. "And yeah, I think that's exactly what you just did. You want to go back inside, Zoe, talk to professors and have another fine beverage, you go right ahead. Just tell this arrogant SOB where he can shove his assumptions and head on back there."

"Well," she conceded, "as it happens, I'm ready to leave. But I'd rather have said so myself."

"Got it," Cal said. "See, Professor, I'm trainable." He held up the ticket. "So . . . coat?"

She was going to do it. She was going to walk out of this building with him. And with his brother, of course, who was an educator, just like her. She tried to tell herself that that was why she was doing it, and she knew she was lying.

She made her decision. "Yes, please."

ZOE'S LIST

The shock of cold that hit her as soon as they stepped outside the building brought her straight back to reality. No snow now, but it was *freezing*. Literally. She was never, ever going to get used to this.

"That pumpkin of yours somewhere in the lot, princess?" Cal asked.

"No," she said, willing herself not to shiver. "My *perfectly fine* car is at my apartment. I walked to work."

"Huh," he said. "I would've thought you'd have been driving, being so safety conscious and all, but hey. Happy to drive you home. Or wherever. Because I know how you love to hit that ditch."

He grinned, and she laughed. He *always* made her laugh, even when he was teasing her. It really wasn't fair.

She'd been surprised, too, actually, that she'd felt safe walking. But Paradise *did* feel safe, even after dark, when she was walking through the busy campus, up the wide sidewalks of Maple Street with its line of, yes, maples, past the comfortable, historic houses with their expansive yards. Not many fences, not many walls, just lawns and gardens and brightly lit windows, and even other people walking home.

"Uh . . ." Luke was looking a little bemused. "Guys. It's cold. You two planning on standing around in the parking lot bantering all night? If you are, I'm leaving. Or am I leaving anyway, because three's a crowd? That's what I can't figure out. Because if you're trying to make points here, bro, all I can say is, you need lessons. Now you're ragging on her driving?"

Zoe was laughing, because Cal had his mouth open and actually looked at a loss for once. "All right," she told him. "It's official. I like your brother."

"Leaving your fondness for my brother strictly out of it," Cal said, "because he and I are going to be having a little talk later, I'm hungry, and I know you're freezing your pretty little butt off. I propose that we get into my nice warm truck and go get a burger, and then plan out the rest of your night. I've got a couple ideas there, too."

"I bet," she said. "Did I mention that I like your brother?"

By now, she really *was* shivering. Her laptop and files were back in her office, but she could always come back for them tomorrow. One night off wasn't so bad. Maybe.

Cal sighed. "Come on," he told Luke. "Chaperone duty. I'm buying you a burger."

"Uh-*huh*," Luke said. "This is looking like a whole new development for you."

"What do you think, princess?" Cal asked. "Dinner at one of our fine establishments with two upstanding pillars of the community, or a ride back to that basement of yours for some Top Ramen that you eat standing up at the kitchen counter? Just guessing here."

Luke was shaking his head. "Maaaannn . . ."

"It wouldn't actually be Top Ramen." Zoe tried to say it loftily, as difficult as that was through chattering teeth as the wind wrapped her in its chilly fingers. "But otherwise, you're pretty close. Sure. Thanks. I'd like to have dinner."

Cal looked at Luke. "Never doubt the master's methods. Whatever works." He ignored her indignant gasp at that, led the way across the parking lot to his big black pickup, and opened the passenger side door for her. "You all right sliding your fine self over to sit by me," he asked, "or are you going to make Luke snuggle up to me while you hug the door for eight blocks?"

"Don't be ridiculous," she said, and tried to make it sound more definite than she felt.

But when she was sitting between the brothers, Cal's thigh much too close to hers, his broad shoulder actually touching her own, she wasn't so sure. Especially when he reached for the gearshift lever, and his arm very nearly brushed her breast. He didn't seem to notice, so she pretended she didn't, either, even when he was twisted around to look over his shoulder, his forearm resting on the back of the seat directly beside her face. His proximity, the smell of him, something about fresh air and soap and man . . . they shouldn't affect her like this, and she wasn't going to show him that they did, or who knew what could happen?

He must have felt her stiffen, because he reached to shift again, looked down at her, and smiled. "Just think of it as a little more dancing," he told her. "A little more . . ."

"What?" she asked. "Foreplay?"

She heard the words come out of her mouth, slapped a hand over it, and groaned. "Please tell me I didn't just say that."

Cal was laughing, and so was Luke. "Yep," Luke said with satisfaction. "Definitely a new development."

Cal drove the circle to the lot's exit, pulled into the street, and began to turn left, toward town.

The car was around the corner and on them in an instant, its headlights flashing through the dark. A university police cruiser, Zoe barely registered in the split-second of time she had to see it. No red-and-blue lights, no sirens. But traveling much too fast, barreling down the quiet street, swerving at the last second, sweeping past Cal's front bumper with inches to spare. Only because he'd already hit the brakes. Hard.

His arm shot out across her in the same moment, catching her even as her upper body hurtled forward. She let out a strangled *whoof* as her chest hit his arm and bounced off it, and she slammed against the seat again.

She sat there, too stunned to say anything. Too stunned to move.

"*Damn*," Luke exclaimed from her other side. "What the hell was that about?"

Cal didn't answer. "You okay?" he demanded of Zoe.

"Sh-sh-sure," she managed. "I'm fine. Fine."

"Thinking Idaho's not that safe a place to drive?" he asked. "Want to get on back to the freeways?"

"The thought had occurred." Her body was still trembling, her heart still beating too fast from the near miss, but she did her best not to show it.

"All right," Cal said. "We'll shake it off, then. So much for the university's finest keeping the streets safe. Onward. Burger Barn okay by you, Zoe? We're a little light on French cuisine in Paradise."

"Of course," she answered automatically. She felt a little steadier, her heart rate returning more or less to normal. "You've got quick reflexes. I would've hit him."

"Well, that was kind of the job for a while there," Cal said. "Keep your eyes peeled and react fast. Get hit, get over it, make them pay later on. Comes in handy from time to time, even now."

◆ ◆ ◆

"I should tell you," Zoe told Cal fifteen minutes later. "I know what you did back there. And thank you."

They were sitting in the cozy leatherette booth inside a warm, bright space, painted yellow and cheerfully decorated with antique farm implements hanging on the walls. At least Zoe assumed they were farm implements.

They were in the Burger Barn, in other words, with three more beers in front of them. Somehow, she was next to Cal again, with Luke facing them. Well, really, no *somehow* about it, because Cal had stood back to let her slide in first, and then had slid right in after her.

"What?" Cal asked. "Catching you? I told you. Instinct."

"No." Zoe traced the rim of her glass with a finger, then looked up at him again. "Making Dr. Oppenheimer put me on the committee. That's going to be a high-visibility spot. It's a real coup to get on it, especially for somebody as new as I am, who wouldn't normally have had a hope at it. I know you know that, and I know that's why you did it. I still don't know *why* you did it, but . . . thank you."

Cal exchanged a look with his brother. "You don't know why I did it?"

"Some joke of your own, probably," she said. "It all seems like it's a joke to you, but I don't believe it really is. People don't give away that kind of money, not for something serious like that, for a joke. And you had good ideas about it, too. You've thought a lot about it, and I can tell you care. I can't figure you out at all," she admitted. "Maybe the part about me was just to tease me. I can't tell."

"Maybe if you stick around," Cal said, "you'll start to get an idea why I want to tease you."

Her eyes flew to his face again. His smile started in the laugh lines around his eyes, extended down to that firm mouth. Slow, and sweet, and sure. She tore her gaze away at last and took a hasty sip of beer.

"Is it hot in here?" Luke asked of nobody in particular. "Or is it just not me?"

Their waitress bustled up with a tray, brown hair swinging in a ponytail that matched her brown uniform dress. "Double-bacon cheeseburger, cheeseburger, plain burger," she announced, setting the plates down. She added the big paper-lined red plastic basket of skinny-cut fries to the center of the table. "Going to have to start watching that cholesterol pretty soon, Cal," she added. "That's a heart attack on a plate."

"Aw, thanks for your concern, Terri," he said. "All my vital signs are real good so far. It's all that healthy living."

She gave a ladylike snort. "Yeah. Well, you watch yourself. You grow a gut, and life around here just got a whole lot less beautiful."

"Where's the love?" Luke complained. "It's all about the prodigal son, huh? Here I am, beautifully single, eating right, looking good, a full head of hair, and all my own teeth. Fully employed, too. What am I, chopped liver?"

"Nope," Terri said. "Grade A prime cut, just like your big brother. But with that boy of mine coming home with two detentions last month, I'm scared to flirt with you."

"You can always flirt with me," Luke said. "I'll give up a lot for this job, but that's one privilege I'm not about to lose."

She laughed. "You're both a menace. Your mama ought to keep you on a leash. You all good on beer?"

"Yeah," Cal said. "I'm holding the professor here back. She tends to get a little frisky after more than a couple."

"Hi," Zoe told the waitress ruefully. "Zoe Santangelo."

"Up at the university." Terri nodded. "I heard you and Rochelle were over at the Cowboy Bar last week with Cal. Welcome."

Zoe was gaping again, but Terri had bustled off with her tray to the song of a furious couple of *dings* from the bell on the counter leading back to the kitchen.

"I didn't realize I was news," she said.

"Maybe not you so much," Luke said. "But Cal's news. Welcome to Paradise."

Cal didn't seem to be listening. He had his eyes closed, was working on his first bite of double bacon cheeseburger. He opened them again with a sigh. "I swear, that's what I missed most, all those years in the wilderness. All that tiny food in California and Seattle. Seems like it's not gourmet unless you can put it in your mouth in two bites. I just decided on my number one criterion for dating a woman from now on. Must Eat Hamburgers. Not rabbit burgers, not salmon burgers, and definitely not portobello mushrooms pretending to be burgers. Just a great big, juicy, American, aneurysm-inducing slab of ground beef on a great big soft bun, with lettuce and tomatoes and even some onion, if both parties are prepared to brush their teeth afterwards. And for the record," he told Zoe, "you're doing real good, though you could put some cheese on there next time for full points."

"Full points?" she gasped. "Full *points*?"

"Maybe we'd better hear Zoe's dating criteria," Luke said, after working his way through a couple bites of his own. "I have a feeling this could get interesting."

Cal waved his burger at Zoe. "The floor's all yours, Professor."

"Okay." She set her own burger down, wiped her hands on her napkin. "Item One." She ticked it off on her index finger. "No jocks."

"Aw, shoot," Cal said, not looking all that crestfallen. "Fortunately, as we know, I'm a farmer. But why don't you like jocks? Got something against a man with a physique and a game plan?"

"Well, yes," she said. "I do. A bit."

Luke cleared his throat. "Moving on. Since Cal's a farmer and all, hasn't knocked himself out of the running."

"Item Two," Zoe said, shaking it off. "Good sense of humor. Three—kind. A kind person. Four—intelligent. Five—can talk."

"So no mutes, then," Cal said. "Or mimes. That's a good one. I'm putting that on my list, too."

"You know what I mean," she said. "Can have a conversation about . . . subjects."

"I've got subjects," Cal protested.

"You've got *a* subject, anyway. And all right, yes, you can talk. Boy, can you ever." She took another sip of beer, and then another, because it was tasty.

"And?" Cal prompted.

"And what?"

"That's the list?"

"Well, I don't really have a *list*. I mean, I'm not looking. But if I *were* looking, that would be my list."

"So good-looking doesn't matter," he said dubiously. "Or at least looking good to you."

"I was going to say," Luke said into his own beer. "Because, bro. Broken nose."

"No," Zoe said determinedly. "Looks are overrated. Good smile, though. That matters."

"Good in bed?" Cal suggested.

She choked a little on her beer. "That's supposed to go on my list? How am I supposed to know?"

"You don't think you can know?" Cal asked. "By how he touches you, how he looks at you? By how you feel when he does?"

"I think that can be deceptive," she said, trying to ignore the tingle as he, yes, looked at her. At her mouth, specifically, as she ate another fry, licked the salt off her finger. She realized what she was doing, flushed, and reached for her napkin. She ate alone too much.

"Deceptive, huh?" Cal said softly, still watching her. "How? I think it's a pretty damn good test. How I feel when she looks at me. How I feel when I touch her, and when she touches me. How much I want it. How much I can feel her wanting it."

Everything in her was trying to lean into him, to respond to that. But she needed to answer this. She needed him to know. "Guys can lie, though," she told him. "You know they can. They promise what they can't deliver. Or worse, they promise, and then they just . . . hurt. Because they want to win, and that's all. That's why no jocks, because it's just a game to them. It's all about winning, and when you need everything to end in a win for you, that means you need the other person to lose. I don't want to be the loser. I don't want to be the tool for somebody else to get another win."

The booth went quiet for a long moment. Luke's eyes went to Cal, then back to her. She barely noticed. She was still watching Cal, her eyes steady on him.

"Now, see," he said at last. "You've got me, because I don't have a comeback to that. Except to say that I don't want you to be that, either."

DOUBLE DATE—OR NOT

She was still looking at him, and he was still looking right back at her, trying to let her know he meant it, when Luke broke the silence, because Luke always did.

"Damn," his brother breathed. "Could we just eat some dinner here? The sexual tension—I'm all hot and bothered. And now I'm all sad, too. It's putting me right off this excellent hamburger."

Zoe shook her head and laughed, although Cal didn't think she'd been joking. Not one bit. "Yeah," she said. "Sorry. It's your guys' fault. Asking me for my list. Like I have a list. What's on *your* list?" she asked Luke, trying to shake it off. Again. She had some guts.

He pointed to himself as he chewed, his eyes widening. He swallowed, then answered, "Me? Well, yeah. Look good and show up. Take her clothes off, preferably. It's a pretty short list."

"And now, see," she said, "I don't even believe that." She looked at Cal again, and he could tell she was trying hard to keep it light. He tried to smile at her, let her know it was all right. He wished he knew who had made her feel like that. He'd like to pound him.

"That what's on your list, too?" she asked Cal. "Besides the hamburger thing, I mean. She just has to show up and take off her clothes?"

"No," he said, not smiling now. "She has to be all kinds of wonderful. I'm pretty picky these days. But I don't really have a list. That was a joke. I know what I want when I see it."

She dropped her eyes, picked up her burger again, and took a bite. Like she couldn't believe it. Like she *wouldn't* believe it, and he sighed and ate some more himself. Leave it to him to finally find somebody he wanted, and have her be a project. Good thing he liked a project.

"So, tell me," she said when she'd done some more eating, and Luke hadn't said anything for once, because he was sitting back and watching. More entertainment, Cal guessed. "Tell me why the donation. The truth, not the jokes."

"You mean you're not going to believe that I'm giving it because it's too hard for engineering students to get a date otherwise? If you have a tough time talking to girls, maybe at least if they're in your classes, you can form a study group or something. Could be I'm just charitable to my fellow man that way."

"Uh-huh," she said. "You mean you're not going to tell me. And I'm starting to get really suspicious here. You love to act like you're just some hick, or some jock, and that's so obviously not true."

"Isn't it? Maybe jocks and hicks aren't all exactly what you think, you ever consider that?"

Clearly, she hadn't, because she looked a little startled. "Exactly what was your own major? And where?" she demanded.

"Man, you're tough," he said. "Bet your students are scared to death of you."

She just looked at him, her eyes narrowed, and he sighed. "Mechanical engineering. And Stanford. Of course, Stanford. That's where I played football. Oh, wait. You don't know that."

"Mechanical . . . engineering," she said slowly. "At Stanford."

"It's actually kind of fascinating," he said. "It's like I can see all the cogs working, all the assumptions reshuffling, even as we speak. Yeah. I'm a jock, and a hick, and a farmer, and I have a degree in mechanical engineering from Stanford. Not the very best degree, I'll point out, so you can feel better. I wasn't any scholar-athlete or anything. But I managed to make it through without them kicking me out."

"While you were on a football scholarship," she said. "While you were playing. How?"

"Because I'm not as dumb as you think, maybe?"

She sighed. "I don't think you're dumb at all. I just know how much time athletes spend outside the classroom, how tough it is for them to keep up even in a . . . less rigorous major."

"Well, it *was* a less rigorous major for me," he pointed out reasonably. "If it had been English literature or something, if I'd had to write ten-page papers about Shakespearean sonnets, I might have had a rough time. But when you grow up looking at machines, poking around in there, taking things apart to figure out why they're not running, you tend to see how they're put together, too. And I'm good at math, even when I can't take my shoes off to count on my toes. It comes pretty easy. Just like you. What was *your* major?"

"Physics," she admitted.

He stopped with his glass halfway to his lips, pointed it at her. "There you go. I'm not a dope, you're not a dope, Luke's not a dope. Can we take that as a given, go on from there? In fact, could we go back to flirting again? I liked that a whole lot better."

"Is that what we were doing?" she asked, but at least she was smiling again.

"Oh, now, Professor. A smart woman like you? You've got to know that's what we were doing. And I'd like to segue right into talking about what we're doing after dinner, because unless I can buy you another beer, we're about done here, and that's pretty much a tragedy."

"After dinner?" she said. "After dinner, I'm going home. I'm doing some catch-up reading on my journals, since I decided to give myself a night off from preparing for my classes, even though I shouldn't. And then I'm going to bed. There you go. My plan for the night. Not sure how exciting it is to hear about, but you asked."

"And see," he said, "that's just a crying shame. Luckily, I've thought up an alternative plan." He ignored her sarcastic huff and continued. "You get yourself dressed up in something pretty again, and we go dancing. Of course, we'd have to get Rochelle to loan you another dress, because I don't trust you to go for the gold by yourself."

Luke was shaking his head again, Zoe was sitting up straighter and looking outraged, and Cal smiled at her, picked another french fry out of the basket, and waited for the explosion.

"If I can't get pretty enough for you," she said, "then it won't be any problem when I say no. You go on over there, though, find somebody who meets your standards. Knock yourself out."

"I didn't say you couldn't get pretty enough for me," he said. "I said I didn't trust you to do it without some help. You've got a gift like that, and that's how you're using it? You need to burn that suit, darlin'. It's a crime against nature."

"A gift like . . . what?" she asked, a dangerous glint in her eyes.

"Once you get the right dress on," he said, "a little shorter, a little tighter, and a whole lot prettier, like the one you had on last week, you won't have to ask me. You'll look in the mirror and see for yourself. You'll see exactly what I saw when I looked at you."

Her color was higher, and her breath seemed to be coming a little harder, too. Of course, he couldn't tell if she was turned on or mad, but either one was better than cool and indifferent, on the verge of turning him down flat, which was where she'd started out.

"What do you think?" he asked his brother. "What's Dr. Zoe's color?"

Luke looked at her, his head a little on one side, considering. "Mmm . . . red," he said.

She snorted. "What a surprise."

"Deep red," Luke said. "Wine red."

"Think Rochelle's got a red dress?" Cal asked him.

"Rochelle, huh?" Luke laughed. "Yeah, bet she does. Of course, it might not be Zoe's red."

"Who knew," Zoe asked the air, "that I was eating hamburgers in the Burger Barn with two experts on women's fashion?"

"Isn't that lucky," Cal agreed cordially. "Here's an idea. We give Rochelle a call right now. Take you on over there, get Luke to find you that red dress, although I'd settle for the yellow one again, and Luke and I take you girls dancing. Double date, nice and safe, featuring your very own non–scholar athlete."

"Good of you to volunteer me," Luke said.

"You got an objection?" Cal asked.

"Nah," Luke decided. "Other than on principle. Just felt duty bound to point that out."

Zoe was already shaking her head. "Thanks," she said. "But no."

Cal sighed. "It's the jock thing," he decided. "Still holding that against me?"

"I'm not holding anything against you." And she wasn't going to be, either, not tonight. Unfortunately. She pushed her mostly eaten burger away in its plastic basket, swallowed the last of her beer, and put the glass down. "Like I said, I appreciate your help getting me onto the committee. I appreciate you catching me in your truck. I appreciate the dinner. I do. And I'd really appreciate a ride home."

OFFICE HOURS

"Excuse me? Dr. Santangelo?"

Amy's professor lifted her head from where she'd been focusing on her laptop. She looked so serious that Amy almost lost her nerve, except that she couldn't afford to do that.

Dr. Santangelo eyed the blue book in Amy's hand. "If this is about your test corrections," she said, "I'm very sorry, but they were due on Friday."

"But . . ." Amy's hands were shaking, and her voice was, too, just like it had been all week. "I can explain. Please. I can't . . . I can't flunk. Not now. *Please.*"

Dr. Santangelo looked at her more closely. "I think you'd better sit down and tell me."

Amy wasn't going to cry. She wasn't. She sat down, and Dr. Santangelo got up and shut her office door, then came back to her desk and shoved the tissue box across. "What's going on?" she asked.

The concern in her voice made Amy choke up more. She wiped her eyes, shook her head violently, and put the blue book on the desk. *Get it together.* "I know I missed class," she said. "I know I missed the deadline. I had to go home for a few days."

"A family thing?"

"No. I was . . . I was . . . attacked." Amy's throat worked. "Wednesday night. In my apartment."

Dr. Santangelo's expression changed. "Oh, no. What happened?"

"It was . . . you remember I told you about that guy? Or whoever? Following me?"

"A couple weeks ago. Of course I remember."

"I think it was him. Not because anything else happened then," Amy hurried on. "I mean, I got scared, but then it seemed like it was nothing, like I was imagining it. And everybody *said* I was imagining it."

"But?"

"But . . ." The trembling had started again, and she couldn't help it. It kept coming back. "Wednesday night. Halloween. That night. I woke up, and he was in my bedroom. In a ski mask. And . . ." She shuddered. "And gloves. Doctor's gloves, because his hands were . . . shiny. Like . . . monkey paws."

"Oh, no," Dr. Santangelo said again. "I'm so sorry."

"But I hit him with a baseball bat," Amy said. The memory made her feel better. Still. Always. "I chased him out of my apartment. He tried to . . ." She swallowed hard. "Catch me again outside, to pull me into . . . the bushes, I think, and he almost did, but then my neighbors came out."

Dr. Santangelo let out a breath. "Good for you. Did they catch him?"

"No. He got away." He'd gotten away, and he was still out there, and she couldn't forget what he'd said, because he'd meant it.

"But you reported it," Dr. Santangelo said. "Of course you did."

"Well, *I* didn't. Somebody called the cops. They did a report and all that. And I went home for a couple days, for the weekend. I know I missed class. I know. But I had to. And then I came back, because I have to go to school. I *need* to go to school." She pushed the blue book across the desk. "So . . . please."

Dr. Santangelo finally put her hand on the book, slid it across her desk, and the relief nearly knocked Amy over. It seemed like she bounced from one emotion to the other, completely unable to find stable ground.

"Of course I'll make an exception, for this," her professor said. "And I'm glad you came back. Sounds like you did well all the way around. But are you getting some counseling?" She reached into her desk drawer, pulled out a card. For the counseling center, Amy saw at a glance. "That's what it's there for, and I do urge you to go."

"Yes," Amy said, not taking the card. "At least, yeah, they already gave me that. The police did. I guess they have to. But I'm not sure how much good counseling's going to do."

"Oh, you might be surprised. I know it doesn't sound like it would help much to talk it over, but I think you'll find it does. Please do try."

"Everybody says that," Amy burst out before she could stop herself, because she was so tired of hearing that, like that solved everything. "But if they're not going to even try to catch the guy, how is counseling going to make me feel better? And if I don't have a place to *live* . . . I get that it's good to talk about it. All right, fine. I'll talk about it. But what good is it going to do?"

"Whoa." Her professor held up a hand. "Let's take this one at a time. Why do you think the police aren't trying to catch him?"

"It doesn't seem like they are, that's all. I don't think they even believe—well, at least the cop I talked to. I don't think he even believes that the guy meant to rape me. I mean, I *know* that's what he was going to do. I *know* it," she insisted, getting agitated all over again, because she couldn't help it. Why wouldn't anyone *believe* her? "He didn't tell me so, I realize that. He didn't *have* to tell me so. What's he supposed to do, say, 'I'm here to rape you'? The cop said he could have just been a burglar. That he probably thought the apartment was empty, being Halloween and all. He wasn't a burglar. I know it. I was *there*."

"I hope you find that you're wrong," Dr. Santangelo said. "Not about the burglary," she went on hastily as Amy stiffened, "but that they're investigating. If you find they aren't, let me know. But for now—you don't have a place to live?"

"I don't want to stay there," Amy tried to explain for what felt like the tenth time. "He broke in through a sliding-glass door. They replaced the lock, like that's supposed to make it all right, after he *broke* the lock once already? And my roommate moved in with her boyfriend, because she's scared, even though she wasn't even there. My boyfriend said he could stay with me, at least for a while, but he's in a frat, and my dad doesn't want him to, and *I* don't want him to. I'm not ready to live with somebody, and we're not that serious. But I don't know what else to do. I can't stay there alone. I *can't*. I don't even want to be there. I went in this morning to get my stuff, and I was so scared. I wanted to run."

She was weeping again, tears trickling down her cheeks despite her efforts at self-control. She'd come back to school, and she'd been determined that she was going to stay here. But right now, it seemed impossible. "I'm going to have to sleep on my best friend's floor again," she got out, "but her roommate won't want me to, and I don't know what else to *do*."

"Okay." Dr. Santangelo held up her hands again. "Whoa. Okay. This one is solvable. Have you talked to the housing office about finding you alternative housing?"

Amy reached for another tissue, blew her nose, and nodded. "I called them on Friday. My dad tried to talk to them, but they said it had to be me."

"Because you're over eighteen. And what did they say?"

Amy shrugged in helpless defeat. "They said they didn't have space. That on-campus housing was full. That I could look for an apartment off-campus. But what can I find now, in the middle of the semester? Nothing. There won't be anything left now, and I need it *now.* They said they'd put me on the list, but I can't wait for the list. I called the counseling center to see if they could help, and they said I could ask about it at my appointment, but they couldn't promise. They told me to call housing, but I already *called* housing. And I don't know what else to *do,* because I can't go back there. I just can't." She was crying again, and she hated it.

"All right," Dr. Santangelo said hastily. "Come on, now. It's going to be all right, because we're taking a field trip. You and me. This one, at least, we can solve."

"Really? You'll help me? Because they said . . . that there was nothing."

"There's never nothing." Dr. Santangelo looked at her watch. "I've got office hours coming up. Right now, in fact. I need to open my door again. But if you can come back here at eleven thirty, I'll help you, and we'll get some answers. And some action."

POWER PLAY

"Sorry," Zoe told the middle-aged woman at the front desk in the housing office a few hours later. "I'm afraid I'm going to have to insist on seeing the director himself, because it's urgent. Richard Winston, is that right? Could you please call Mr. Winston and tell him we're here?"

The woman sighed, her heavy face a mask of resignation. "Look. Everybody's got an emergency. I told you. You need to request an appointment."

"I'm sorry," Zoe said again, "but it can't wait." That was one thing she was positive of. The way Amy had looked this morning, and then hearing her story—Zoe had known that however much she had on her plate, nothing was more important than this.

Now, she looked at Amy's white face, then back at the staffer, impatiently tapping a pen, and made her decision. "Come on," she told Amy, and set off around the edge of the cubicles and down the hallway, eyeing the nameplates beside office doors.

The woman had gotten out from behind her desk, was hustling after them. "You can't do that."

"Ah." Zoe stopped, rapped on an open door, then stepped inside with Amy following her, the staffer puffing up behind them.

The man behind the desk looked up in surprise. "Well, hello," he said, taking in the little procession.

"I'm sorry, Mr. Winston," the woman said. "I told her she needed an appointment, but she just came on back. I couldn't stop her. Do you want me to call security?"

"Oh, I don't think that will be necessary. I think I can handle it." He smiled at Zoe. He was pretty good-looking in a fit, sandy-haired way, and she smiled back. Maybe charm would work. She might as well start with that.

"Thank you," she said. "As I explained, I wouldn't have insisted, but it really is urgent."

He looked at his watch. "I'm afraid I do have a lunch meeting, but I can give you five minutes."

He didn't invite them to sit, but she took a visitor's chair and gestured to Amy to do the same, then put a hand across the desk to shake his.

Winston held up his hands in response, and she realized for the first time that his dress shirt concealed braces covering both wrists. "Sorry," he said. "Carpal tunnel. Take my advice, don't get this thing. It's a bear."

She pulled her hand back again. "Sorry to hear that," she told him. She smiled, didn't get much in return. It looked like her feminine wiles weren't going to help much after all, not that they usually did. Back to her default mode. Businesslike. "I'm Zoe Santangelo. Assistant professor of geological sciences, and a member of the president's task force on Recruitment of Underrepresented Students in Science and Engineering." She gave it a name it didn't even have yet, because that was how the game was played.

"Didn't realize we had such a thing," the man said. "Rich Winston here, by the way."

"It's being set up now," she said. "Frank just invited me to be part of it, to help work out the most effective use of Cal Jackson's recent donation. You may have heard about that. Exciting times." Which was a blatant power play, but whatever it took.

"Well," Winston said, favoring her with another smile, "that does put a little different light on things, doesn't it?" He opened a leather-bound notebook case and pulled an engraved pen from an onyx holder. "So how can I be of help in this effort?" he asked. "All hands on deck, that the idea? I'd be happy to set up a regular meeting to discuss it, although I'm not sure I see how housing fits into the picture."

"Ah. Well, it's an issue of female students feeling safe living on campus," Zoe said. "Which we think could be quite important for recruiting." She didn't specify who *we* was. "This is Amy Corrigan, by the way. One of those female students."

"Hi," Amy said.

Winston merely glanced at her, then looked back at Zoe. "And are women not? Feeling safe, that is? We're not exactly a hotbed of crime here in the Palouse."

"I don't know if it's a hotbed," she said, "but it looks to me like you've got a rapist on your hands. That's why we're here, because Amy needs your help."

"Excuse me? A rapist? Are you aware of an issue I'm not?"

"It sounds like I am. Amy was attacked last week, after a man broke into her apartment in the middle of the night. Luckily, she was able to chase him off and a police report was filed, but the police don't seem to have much to go on, and he's still out there. That's the issue."

"I didn't hear that we'd had a break-in," Winston said. "I'm sorry to hear it," he told Amy. "I'm glad it wasn't more . . . serious, I take it?"

"No," Amy said. "I chased him off, like Dr. Santangelo said." She sounded a little stronger, and Zoe guessed it helped her to say that.

"And . . ." Winston said. "I still don't see how this involves me."

"Well, I think there are two issues," Zoe said. "Both of them pretty urgent. First, it seems like a good idea to let female students know that you might have a problem, warn them to take precautions."

"And if the campus police tell me we've got a problem," he said, his voice not quite so cordial anymore, "I will certainly do that. Thank you for bringing it to my attention. And now," he said, rising from his chair with a smile that didn't reach his eyes, "I'm afraid that meeting's calling my name."

Zoe didn't budge. "The second thing you can do, the reason I'm having to press here, is that Amy needs new housing. Right away. I know that might take some extra effort, and that's why I insisted on seeing you personally. Because I'm sure that you're the one person who can do it."

"I'm sorry," he said, "but I'm afraid that's not possible. If you'd like to apply for a change of on-campus housing," he told Amy, "you're free to do so. There's a waiting list, though, I believe."

"Yes," Zoe said before Amy could answer. "There is. And there are times when exceptions need to be made. I'm sure you'll agree that this is one of those times."

"And you would be the one to decide that?"

"No." This wasn't going so well. Time to press harder. "I'm just the one pointing it out so you can help Amy find a safe living environment. She was the victim of a serious assault, and her roommate has already moved out, leaving her alone. Her attacker was stalking her previously, and now he's broken into her apartment by force and uttered some very serious threats. It's not possible for her to stay there. I'm sure you can see that."

He looked at her a minute more, then turned and punched a few keys on his computer. "Can you give me the address of your apartment, please?" he asked Amy.

"One-forty-one Hawthorne," she said, her voice coming out a little shaky again, and if even saying her address scared her, she really did need a new place. "Apartment 115."

He put in the address, did some scrolling. "I show that there was an incident there," he said. "Last Wednesday."

"Yes," Zoe said. "As I mentioned."

He raised his eyebrows again at that. "And that we fixed a lock." He lifted his hands from the keys, swiveled to face them again. "Looks to me like we corrected a security issue, and the problem is solved."

"But it was broken because he *broke* it," Amy said. "It wasn't broken before."

"Uh-huh." Winston didn't sound convinced, and Zoe's blood was beginning to boil. "We always advise that our female students take care. That they watch where they're walking, watch their drinking, keep their windows and doors locked. And nine times out of ten, they don't. They come from little towns where nobody locks a door, where they know everybody and everybody knows them. Then they get to college, go to parties, drink too much, and . . ." He shrugged. "We're a college campus with a transient population. Incidents happen, and that's more than regrettable, but there's only so much advising we can do. If you're worried, though," he told Amy, "you might consider installing some inexpensive alarms. Perhaps that would make you feel safer."

"No," she said. "I can't go back there." The words came out in jerks, and Zoe could tell she was fighting the tears again.

"This isn't just Amy's problem," Zoe said, keeping her voice level with an effort. "It's housing's problem, too. You've got an issue here, I'm sure you can see that. A lawsuit waiting to happen, if you don't mind my mentioning it." He minded, she could tell, and that was good. "Amy signed a contract to live in campus housing and abide by its rules. She's kept her part of the bargain. In fact, you could say she's done more than keep it. She kept herself safe under some pretty extreme pressure. Now it's up to the university to keep your—to keep *our* part of the bargain, by finding her someplace safe to live."

"It is?" He sat back and stared at her, and she stared right back at him. "What exactly do you propose that I do? I can't magically conjure up a new apartment for her. There's a waiting list."

"I'm guessing," Zoe said, "that those apartments she's in are pretty coveted. Apartments generally are, aren't they? Here's my idea. You take a couple big, strong guys living in a dorm, tell them it's their lucky day, put them in that nice, safe . . . furnished . . . ?" She glanced at Amy, got a nod. "Furnished apartment, with its fixed door and all. You put Amy and her roommate in a dorm, on a high floor, and the problem's solved. Today. Just like that."

"You seem to have a lot of answers," he said, his voice as cold as his eyes. "I don't know how things were at . . . wherever you came here from, but that's not the way it works around here. People tend to ask for their favors a little more nicely, and brand-new assistant professors generally don't ask for many favors at all."

"Ah." She pulled her phone out of her bag. "If that solution won't work, maybe we should get Dr. Oppenheimer on the phone. He might be able to help us figure out another one. In fact, I think he has a lunch meeting with Cal Jackson today. I know Cal pretty well, too. Maybe he could help. He's a pretty helpful guy." She'd made up the meeting. She hoped she hadn't made up the help. Except that she didn't actually know Cal's number. Damn.

Winston still had a faint smile on his face, but his eyes were anything but friendly. Zoe sat still and met his gaze, and the seconds ticked away, one after another.

"I'll see what I can do," he said at last, and Zoe tried not to let the relief show. "You'll have to give me a few days. Leave your phone number with the front desk," he told Amy, "and we'll let you know if we can find you a spot."

"I'm afraid that isn't going to work." Zoe sat back, settling into her chair as though she were planning to stay awhile. She'd bluffed once. She could do it again. "She needs a safe place now, tonight, even if that place is temporary. Even if it's a room you keep at the campus inn for visiting professors or those star athletes you're recruiting. It could even be the VIP suite at the faculty club, but she needs to sleep someplace safe tonight. I know that might take a while, but that's all right. We'll wait."

FAMILY TIES

"Stay," Cal told Junior, pulling his key from the ignition and grabbing his workout bag from the floor of the truck.

The dog wagged his tail twice, then, as Cal slammed the door, lay down across the seat.

Cal didn't bother to lock it. Sixty pounds of ugly brown mutt was a pretty good antitheft device. He took off across the high school's parking lot, populated by only a few cars at six thirty on a Friday morning. Luke's truck was here, he noticed, in the "Principal" spot near the door. His brother liked to get in early, get a jump on the day. Came from growing up on a farm.

He opened the front door with his key and entered the familiar lobby, uncharacteristically silent now. His athletic shoes didn't make a sound as he crossed to the gym, past his old locker. He wondered how old you got before you forgot your locker number.

One last door, and he was dropping his bag onto a bench in the boys' locker room, stripping down to a T-shirt and gym shorts, going on through to the weight room, and climbing on the rowing machine to warm up.

A dancer took class every day, the routine of studio and barre as familiar as family. A jockey rode horses. And a jock went to the gym. Except during the very busiest weeks of the year, when he didn't do anything but work, eat, and fall into bed, Cal always got in his hour or two. His mind settled as the sweat flowed, and the problems seemed to solve themselves. However he felt when he walked in, he always felt better walking out.

Not that he anticipated feeling bad today, because he was seeing Dr. Zoe again in a few hours. He'd need his wits about him, though, and a workout was good for that, too. He smiled at the thought, rowed a little harder.

He'd worked his way through his Friday program and was on the bike, doing a little aerobic conditioning to finish things off, when the door behind him opened. He turned his head, expecting Luke, coming in with some last-minute idea. Or some last-minute insult, more like.

Unfortunately, it wasn't Luke. It was his cousin Greg, heading over to the weight racks, and Cal's heart sank a little.

Why he was here, Cal couldn't imagine. Greg normally did his workout at the university rec center. He hoped his cousin wasn't going to start coming to the high school instead, because a little Greg went a long way.

"Hey," he said now, giving the other man a nod.

Greg didn't look much happier to see him, although he didn't look surprised. He stacked weight onto his bar, winced a little as he lifted it over his head, settled it on the meat of his upper back. Probably put too much weight on it to impress Cal, as if Cal would care.

"I didn't know you were still coming over here," Greg said, beginning a set of squats, because of course he had scorned his warm-up. Always looking for a shortcut, always thinking there was an easy way. "I figured you'd have built your own weight room by now."

Cal didn't stop pedaling. "Nope." And because Greg was his cousin, and that mattered, he added, "Kinda enjoy being back in the old stomping grounds, actually. Scene of our former triumphs."

His former tight end answered that one with nothing but a grunt, and Cal gave a mental shrug. Well, he'd tried.

Greg stood, hoisted the barbell overhead, his face twisting with the effort, and dropped it from a little too high up so it bounced on the mat. "I wouldn't know," he finally said. "I don't live in the past."

That one about had Cal choking. He grabbed his water bottle instead, took a sip. "Good for you."

"Heard you gave a bunch of money to the university last week," Greg said after a minute, hoisting the bar again. "Only a matter of time until they name the high school after you, I guess. Funny, I always thought football was a team sport."

"Yep," Cal said. "It is. I remember you blocking for me, back in the day. I remember that you're my cousin, too. Trust me, if I didn't remember, I'd have kicked your ass a long time ago."

Greg snorted, started another set. "You wish."

"You know," Cal said, "we're not actually in high school anymore. It's not about who's got a bigger dick, or more money."

"Easy for you to say." Greg leaned over for a set of dead lifts. "When you're handing it out like candy."

"Well, hey," Cal said with a sigh, "tell you what. When I pay to replace the urinals in the locker room, I'll have them name them after you, how's that?"

He could see the red rising up Greg's dark, thick neck, into his unshaven cheeks, black with beard. He shouldn't push him, he knew. But since nothing else was working, why the hell not?

"Knock yourself out." Greg dropped his bar again, wiped down his dark hair, still cut nearly Marine-short after all these years, like if he didn't keep reminding people, they'd forget he was ex-military. Like anybody cared. "But then," he continued, "I suppose if I had as many things I wanted people to forget as you do, I'd keep shelling it out like that, too. Otherwise, people might remember that even with all those millions of dollars, you still couldn't keep your wife in line."

Now Cal was the one whose color was rising, try as he might to control it. The taunt wasn't new, and neither was the satisfaction he could see on Greg's face, so why should he let it bother him all this time later?

"But hey," Greg said, "what can you do? I guess some guys know how to control a woman, and some guys don't."

Cal climbed off the bike, wiped it down with deliberate motions, then walked over to stand in front of Greg. His cousin had switched to the lat pulldown machine now, was sitting on the bench, his hands behind him as he worked the bar.

Cal shot a hand out, grabbed the metal handle in the middle while the weights were at the top of their extension, felt Greg straining to hang on. "If you're pushing Kathy around," he told his cousin quietly, "you watch yourself. I don't know what all's happening over at your house, but I've heard rumors. And if I hear anything more . . . I'm not going to ignore it."

Greg's face was purple with effort and temper by now. He finally let go of the handles, because he had no choice. Cal felt it happening and loosed his hold at the same time so the weights crashed down with an almighty *clang*, making Greg jump.

"Oh, so now you're out to get me?" his cousin asked, swinging his leg around to stand with the bench between the two of them. "Just because I don't kiss your ass like everybody else? What happens between me and my wife is none of your goddamned business."

"Oh, yeah," Cal assured him. "It's my business. I'll make it my business."

"What, you going to make a report?" Greg laughed, short, sharp, and contemptuous. "Ever hear of the thin blue line?"

"I won't be making any report." Cal stood for a minute, let it sink in, then turned on his heel, veered back to the bike for his water bottle and towel, tossed the towel over one shoulder, and headed for the locker room.

He could feel Greg's eyes on him, the red heat all but radiating off him, but didn't look back. Greg wouldn't be coming after him, he was almost certain of it. Greg was a bully, and a coward.

The tension remained all the same through his quick shower and change. He left the building and headed back across the lot to where his truck was parked, with Greg's own glossy black rig, shinier than Cal's, newer than Cal's, parked right next to it. And when he got around to the driver's side, he saw the fresh ding in his door, too.

Not that he cared about the ding. The day you cared about messing up the paintwork on your truck was the day you handed over your man card, as far as he was concerned.

He threw his bag inside, climbed up, and gave Junior, who had sat up to watch him, a pat. "Hey, boy," he told the mutt. "Next time Greg bashes my truck, how about doing me a favor and biting him? I won't rat you out to animal control, I promise. It'll be our secret."

Junior had stopped listening. He was on his feet, staring out of the passenger window, the hair on his back standing up in a ridge, a low, soft growl coming from his chest at the sight of Greg coming out of the building.

Cal turned the key, backed up, and drove past his cousin without speeding up, slowing down, or looking at him, because ignoring him, he knew from long experience, was the ultimate insult.

"Yep," Cal told the dog. "He's an asshole. Every family's got one."

MONEY AND WOMEN

A week after she'd turned Cal down—if he'd even been all that serious, which she doubted, because one thing was for sure, he loved to tease her—and here Zoe was sitting next to him again. His shoulder, in another white button-down shirt, touching hers again. His broad thigh, in black Levi's again, which she guessed was his version of dressing up, so close to hers in the folding chair that she could have laid her hand on it. If she'd wanted to, that is. There was just way too much of Cal, looking way too dangerous. Way too distracting.

Worse, they were on stage, and she was supposed to be listening to Luke, because he was introducing her. In another minute, she was going to be standing at the podium and addressing about five hundred high school students, so she'd better start concentrating. On something else.

Luke had called on Tuesday afternoon when she'd been in her office, trying to focus on writing up her findings for the Union City consulting job so she could get paid, and trying not to fume about Amy's problems. She had to stop getting so invested in her students' issues. She'd done it over and over again as a teaching assistant in grad school, and here she was doing it again, because she just couldn't help caring. But she'd gotten Amy housed safely, and that was all she could do.

"I wanted to get a jump on the whole scholarship deal," Luke had said on the other end of the phone, and she'd brought her attention back to the call with an effort. "Or whatever it turns out to be. On the increasing opportunities for Idaho students in science and engineering, we'll call it. How does that sound?"

"Well . . ." she began.

He sighed. "You're right. Boring. The minute I got my butt in this chair, I could feel the boring start. I'll think of something better. And that's why I need your help. I want to get them fired up about those hard classes they'd just as soon avoid while they're still planning their schedules for next semester. Would you be willing to come talk to them for a few minutes? I can yap at them until my face turns blue, but there's nothing like hearing it from a real live professor. Not to mention a real live woman."

"When would this be?"

"Well, that's the deal. Friday morning at eleven. Short notice, I know. But you don't have to prepare a whole speech or anything," he hurried on. "I'll have the teachers talking, too. Just get up there and say a few words, maybe answer a few questions. Show them it can be done."

Which mattered, so she'd said yes, of course. And somehow, she hadn't been surprised to find Cal sitting in Luke's office when she'd arrived, or to find out that he was speaking, too. But then, he was the one giving the gift. It only made sense.

"I'm not going after Cal, though," she told Luke when the three of them were sitting down, with Luke looking incongruously authoritative behind his desk in a button-down shirt just like Cal's, dress slacks—and cowboy boots, of course.

"Excuse me?" Luke said, exchanging a glance with Cal.

"I mean, I'm not following him talking. Speaking," she said, trying not to blush. "I'm not going right after him. He's too hard an act to follow. Literally."

Luke smiled. "Yeah, that's been pointed out. Never mind. I've got a couple teachers between him and you, talking about those fascinating AP classes. You'll be a big step up. You're the grand finale. And you're right," he added with a sigh, "if he hadn't so inconveniently been the one to give all the money, I'd never have invited him."

That startled a laugh out of Zoe, and caused Cal, leaning back in his chair with his long legs stretched out in front of him, to put his head back and groan.

"No respect," he told the ceiling. "Not one damn bit of brotherly love."

"Because no matter what he says about engineering," Luke said, "half the guys in the auditorium will be hearing, 'Come play in the NFL and get money and women!'"

"How about if I tell them they can get money and women by going into engineering?" Cal suggested. "Remind them of all those software millionaires?"

"I thought this talk was partly *for* girls," Zoe pointed out. "Women are at least half your audience."

"Hmm," Cal said. "Good tip, Professor. Quick rethink here. What do I have besides sex and money? That's a toughie. I normally keep it right there, and bang, I'm done. You're actually going to make me work for it."

"Oh," Luke said, "I think that goes without saying, doesn't it?"

"You know what they say," Zoe told Cal. "Things you work for are better."

"Oh," Cal said, with a silky promise in his voice that made Zoe shiver despite herself, "I'm kinda counting on that."

"Sex and money, huh?" Luke said after pausing a beat for an answer from Zoe that didn't come. "You need me to show Zoe your bank balance? You imagining that's going to do the trick?"

"Nope," Cal said. "Somehow, I have a feeling it's not. I'm doing my best here to figure out what will."

"Anybody ever tell you that you're inappropriate?" she asked him, even as the tingle started. She crossed her legs in the deep-blue sweater dress she'd worn today in the hope of his being there. She hadn't wanted to admit it, but it was true. He was still looking at her, his eyes not drifting south to her legs, because in spite of all his teasing, he was polite. He was, in his own bizarre way, a gentleman. She knew, though, that he'd watched her cross her legs, and that he'd liked it. "That you're . . ." she said, and stopped. She shouldn't get drawn into this again. Not here. Because then *she'd* be inappropriate.

"An arrogant SOB?" Luke finished. "Yeah. He's heard it."

Cal sighed. "And the pro athlete is, what? Zero for three? Four? I've lost track."

"I told you," Zoe said loftily, trying not to giggle, because Cal brought out the strangest reactions in her. "I like your brother better."

Cal shot a glare at Luke. "Don't even think about it."

Luke put up both hands. "Not saying a thing. Not doing a thing."

"Yeah," Cal said. "That'll be the day."

◆ ◆ ◆

Now she was on stage, and the students were applauding, although not too enthusiastically, as Luke finished his introduction. It was nothing like the ovation they'd given Cal, but no surprise there.

She got up, walked to the podium, and adjusted the microphone downward. *Way* downward.

She looked out at the sea of faces, reminding herself to focus on a few of them, one after the other, to make eye contact, to pause until she had their attention, until they were wondering what was coming next.

"You know," she said at last, "when I was in high school, the jocks pretty much ruled. That still true?"

Some scattered laughter at that, and she smiled. "Yeah. I thought so. I went back for my tenth high school reunion last year, and a few of those popular kids . . ." She paused, gave it a beat. "Hmm. Let's just say, and I'm being charitable here . . . a few of them hadn't aged too well. Oh, present company excepted, of course," she said, turning and smiling at Cal, garnering another laugh from the students. "But in my class? *Our* quarterback . . ." She shuddered a little. "He sells used cars, does those shouting commercials. True story. Boy, I'm glad I never had a crush on him, huh? What a blow *that* would have been."

She got another ripple of laughter at that. "So, yeah," she said with a sigh. "The popular kids and the jocks? They weren't necessarily all that, in the end. And you know what else was interesting? You know who really ruled the school at that reunion? Here's a hot tip for you. It was the geeks."

She clicked the mouse, and a hugely enlarged image of an eighteen-year-old boy in an ill-fitting tuxedo appeared on the screen behind her. Brown hair falling unfashionably over his forehead from a side part, glasses, skinny shoulders, uncertain grin, and all.

"Alan Johnson," she said. "Voted Biggest Brain, as I recall, back then. You could call that a compliment, but . . . not so much. He wasn't there, of course, at the reunion. Too busy. His startup just went through an IPO. The last I read, his stock options were worth something like two hundred thirty million dollars."

She clicked again, pulled up a shot of the same face. The haircut wasn't much more fashionable, but he'd lost the glasses and was standing with a blonde in a long gown. Had an arm around her, a smile on his face. He looked happier, that was for sure. And he was wearing another tuxedo, cut a whole lot better this time.

"His wife," Zoe informed the students. "Angela Lawson. VP of finance in his company before they started dating, in case you were thinking he married a supermodel. She was a geek, too, by the way. I know, because I've met her. Nice person, and super smart, too, both of which mattered to Alan."

Another click. A teenage girl this time. Asian, serious, straight hair parted in the middle. And glasses again.

"Karen Nguyen," Zoe said. "Valedictorian. I'm not sure she ever had a date in high school. She was always studying, or helping out at home, because she didn't have it too easy. Any students here like that?"

She looked around at a few cautiously raised hands and smiled. "Yeah. Me, too. I didn't have too many dates, either. Didn't go to my prom. Know what I did that night? I hung out with my friends, told myself prom was dumb, and tried not to feel like a loser."

She clicked again to an image of a doctor's office, all sleek, rounded reception desk, blond wood inlaid with strips of stainless steel, modern seating areas upholstered in pale, glove-soft leather, and glass-block dividers.

"Karen's a cosmetic dermatologist these days in Beverly Hills," she said. "Not doing too badly at it, as you can see. Helping her family out, and let me tell you—her skin is *gorgeous*."

She rode the laughter, clicked once more, and another picture came up. Not a yearbook shot this time, but a casual group, four young people sitting around a table. Three guys and one girl at the front of the shot.

"There you go," Zoe said. "Four star members of the Math Club, sitting in a corner of the cafeteria, huddled together for warmth to eat their lunch far, far away from the popular kids. What a bunch of losers, huh?"

She got some nervous laughter at that. She smiled back at her audience, then used her laser pointer to focus on each face in turn.

A chubby white kid with wildly curling brown hair. "Software engineer."

An Asian boy, tall and thin. "Physicist at Lawrence Berkeley Labs."

A short red-headed kid. "This one . . . well, he kind of went downhill. I'm afraid he turned out to be a corporate lawyer. Got tall, though, somehow. He's actually really good-looking now. All the girls were flirting at that reunion, not realizing who he was, which we all thought was pretty funny. It *is* funny how people change, isn't it?"

She turned back to the screen, and the red dot rested on that final plump face. The girl's mouth was open in a laugh, which was unfortunate. Her braces gleamed, light reflected off her glasses, her dark hair was pulled back in a ponytail, and her jeans and T-shirt weren't doing a thing for her pudgy figure.

"And, of course," Zoe said, "this one turned out to be a physicist, a hydrogeologist, and, in the end, a professor. Yours truly, Zoe Santangelo, PhD. Math and science geek. Me."

She stood tall, looked out at them, her gaze sweeping the room again. No laughter this time.

"So, if you think this is all there is," she said quietly, "whatever you're going through, here and now in high school? You're wrong. Cal thinks I'm a bit of jock basher, but that's not really true. If sports are your thing, that's wonderful. But what else are you working on? Even if it's all going well for you right now, even if high school's just great, you may want to ask yourself what you're doing to keep your life that good, what steps you're taking toward the future you want to have. Because one thing I can tell you for sure—it's not going to stay the same. Life doesn't work that way. Even Cal Jackson's life can change. He's just told you so."

She paused, turned back to the screen behind her, moved her pointer among the four figures around that table. Happy together, if nowhere else. "And if it isn't so good?" she asked. "If you're one of these guys? I've got a secret for you, and I want you to listen really hard right now, because this is the truth. It gets better. It gets so much better. You can get better-looking, like Randy—" Her pointer hovered over the red-haired figure again, then moved inexorably on. "Or like me."

That did get a laugh, a nervous one, maybe.

"Yeah," she said, looking out at them again, "you bet it's possible. It's totally possible. As far as looks go—you can get prettier, you can get thinner, or in the case of the guys, you can join a gym and get bigger. You can get contacts or Lasik surgery, and those glasses are gone, and your beautiful eyes are there for everybody to see. Your braces will come off, and your teeth will be straight. You can get a really good haircut. All of that, for what it's worth. You can get better-looking, and you can even get more popular, although I think you'll find that both of those things matter less as time goes on."

Another pause, and she pulled the microphone out of its stand, walked out from behind the podium, walked back and forth as she talked, never losing eye contact.

"But the main thing you can get," she told them, "is successful. Successful in your career. Successful at your life. If you like math, and you like science, even a little bit? Now's your chance to give them your very best try. Even if you're not sure you can do it, even if you're the first person in your family to go to college. Because if you do the things everybody's talked about here today, take those hard AP classes, do that hard work? You can use your brains and your drive and your ambition and your work ethic—and Cal's money," she added, getting another laugh for that one. "You can use all that. You can become the person that everybody talks about when you show up here for your own reunion. And you know what's even more important? You can use them to become the person you want to be, to create the life you want."

She stopped a minute, stood still, let it build.

"And if there's somebody out there today," she told them, "somebody like that girl up there on that screen, or one of those guys. If you're not pretty, or not handsome. If you're good at math and bad at sports, if you're overweight, or skinny, or gay, or poor, or unattractive in any of the hundred and one ways high school students can find to make each other feel unattractive. To that person, wherever you are, whoever you are, let me promise you this. It gets better. It's all out there for you. It's all possible. If you commit, if you work, if you earn yourself some of Cal's money, if you use it well. If you never stop trying. It gets better."

DARK SECRETS

Cal had insisted on taking her out to lunch. "You've got to eat anyway," he'd pointed out reasonably when they were back in Luke's office so she could collect her purse, so they could both get their coats. "You don't have class until, what?"

"Two," she said.

"There you go. Two. And what are you going to be doing otherwise?"

"Uh . . . eating lunch?"

"Uh-huh." He put two fingers to his forehead and closed his eyes. "I see . . . a peanut butter sandwich and an apple. Maybe carrot sticks, if you went wild. The vision gets a little fuzzy down there at the bottom of the paper bag."

"No," she said, trying not to smile. "A turkey sandwich. And celery sticks. And all right, you got me on the apple."

"And you're just dying to eat all that?"

She glanced at Luke, who was leaning back in his desk chair, his eyes going from one to the other of them as if he were watching a tennis match. He held up his hands. "Got to stay on school grounds. Kinda goes with the job. And yeah, I've got the sandwich in the bag, too. You don't see Cal here offering to pick me up a big fat meatloaf sandwich and deliver it, do you? Guess I don't count. Go someplace well lit with him and you could be all right. Keep some space between you, and remember what your mama taught you about what your knee is for."

"Nice," Cal complained as Zoe burst out laughing. "Next time, don't help me."

"Who's helping you?" he asked. "I think I was talking to Dr. Zoe here."

She went, of course. It was just lunch, after all. She had to eat lunch. She'd fixed her sandwich the night before, and it would be a little soggy. It didn't sound that good at all. That was why she agreed to it. Of course it was.

"Now, in sports terms," Cal said conversationally from his side of the table at the Garden Café, "we'd call what happened back there bringing in a ringer."

"Pardon?" she asked innocently, taking a sip from her iced tea through the straw and smiling at him.

"Or," he continued, "you could come right out and call it being sucker-punched. I've never been so upstaged in my life. You must be one hell of a teacher. You're obviously one hell of a motivator."

The glow spread through her, and she was smiling some more. "I can't pretend I keep my students that riveted, though. If you came to hear me lecture, I'm afraid you'd be sadly disappointed."

"I'll have to give that a try," he said. "Might even learn something useful about rocks. Or . . ."

"Hydrogeology," she reminded him. "Of course, you're an engineer yourself, so you might actually be able to stay awake. But it's true that some subjects are easier to make fascinating than others. To the lay audience, that is. Anytime you want an analysis of the water table under your farm, though, please do feel free to inquire about my services. My rates are still quite reasonable, being so new in the profession and all. I'll even do diagrams. Color-coded."

"But will you use the pointer?" he asked. "That's the real question."

"For a consideration," she said solemnly, "we can do slides and the pointer and everything. Of course, it may cost you extra."

"So worth it, though," he said. "Especially if you wear that." He cast an appreciative eye over her V-necked sweater dress, which she could have sworn, this morning, wasn't anything like too short or too tight. And certainly not anything like too sexy. "I'm doing my best to remember all those manners my mama taught me, but damn, Professor. I'm afraid that if I'm going to behave myself and get a shot at taking you dancing again, I might have to insist on the black suit next time, after all, because you're way too distracting this way. Although red would be even better, don't get me wrong. I'm still holding out for you in that red dress."

"Really," she managed to say. She was warming at his words, the look in his eyes, but then, what woman wouldn't be? "Another vote in favor of the black suit, then, because this clearly isn't professional enough."

"Oh, you're professional enough," he said. "It's just that you're so much else, too. You can't help it, and why should you have to hide it?"

That one actually took her breath away, and she couldn't answer.

"So was that really you back there, in the picture?" he asked after a moment, taking a bite of his ham sandwich. "Hard to believe."

"Oh, yeah," she assured him. "And that was possibly one of the more flattering shots. Let's say I didn't exactly keep a scrapbook of my teenage photos."

"And I'm going to throw out a wild-ass guess here," he said, "that some of those jocks gave you a hard time in high school."

"Some," she admitted. "Although mostly, I wasn't even on their radar. I was pretty much invisible."

"You're not invisible now," he said. "And they didn't know what they were missing. Not just how you look, but that person you are underneath. That's some woman underneath."

"Well, thank you." She did her best to keep her balance, but he made it so hard. First he teased, and then he was so . . . so sweet. "They seemed to stumble through their days despite the loss, though."

"So if not high school," he said, "when?"

She took another sip of tea, a forkful of salad. "When what?"

"Jocks. Or *a* jock. What happened? And when? Tell me who it was, and I'll go beat the . . . crap out of him for you. I promise."

"Violence doesn't solve everything."

"Well, no," he conceded. "But it solves some things. All I need is a name."

She had to smile at that. "It's a long story. And I'm fine." She turned her attention to her salad, which featured way too much iceberg lettuce and carrots, and way too little of anything else, and wasn't actually that much of an improvement over the sandwich in her drawer.

"I suppose it's just going back to high school," she said after a minute. "Even somebody else's high school. Still a little painful, I guess, even though it was a long time ago. And it's such a hard time for so many kids. It should be about the future, and instead, it's all about the present. It shouldn't be about looks and popularity, but it is. And sports, of course. It can be so hard on kids who don't have any of the three, and that can keep them from focusing on that future, and that's a shame." She caught herself with a laugh. "But I guess you know how I feel about it. Since you just heard me give a whole talk about it."

"You're right," he said. "That I know how you feel about it, and that it's a shame. That's why I gave the money, you know.

Because I got lucky. And because I know that not everybody gets that lucky."

She felt the hot color rise in her cheeks. "And now I'm ashamed," she said. "I'm lecturing you, when you're the one donating all that money and setting up the program to help those same exact kids. You're so casual about it, I keep forgetting. Or maybe you're just too hard to figure out."

"I should go back to teasing you, you think? That make you feel better?"

"Maybe," she said, losing the battle against the smile again. "Or maybe you could go on and let your guard down some more. But then, I know you don't like to show your soft side."

She got a smile from him for that, another of those Cal Jackson specials. Slow, sweet, and so sexy. "Could be," he said. "And could be I'm saving my soft side for a special occasion."

"Oh?" she asked, because she couldn't help it. "That's going to be your *soft* side? Oh, man, that's disappointing."

He laughed. "Damn, Professor. You're just too good. Let's go back to talking about you, because I'm losing. When did you get so pretty?"

"What?" she asked, off-balance yet again.

He gestured at her. Her face, and . . . the rest of her. "All that. When did it happen? Or do you not know it happened? I find that hard to believe."

She looked down at her plate, stabbed at an anemic tomato wedge, and contemplated it on her fork. "Freshman year of college. No glasses, and no braces, of course. And most kids gain weight that first year. I lost it. Guess I've always been contrary."

"And you got pretty."

"Prettier, anyway."

"Pretty."

"You know what's really terrible?" she asked him with a sigh.

He smiled again. "What? I can't imagine."

"That I can't ask you to show me your picture from back then so I could laugh at you, too. Because I already saw it, right there above the trophy case in the front hall of your high school. You know, from when you led the team to the state championship. Of course you did. You looked pretty good in that uniform, didn't you? But then, I think it's obvious that you were born good-looking."

"Nope," he said. "I was born . . . I don't know. Strong, maybe. *Luke* was born good-looking."

"Yeah," she said, eyeing him. "Your body's probably better than your face."

He choked on his ice water, had to spend a minute coughing into his napkin. "So if I put a bag over my head," he managed once he could talk again, "you might consider it?"

"Well, I guess all of you is fairly acceptable," she conceded, trying not to laugh and failing completely. "And you know it, so don't pretend."

"I thought good-looking wasn't on the list," he said. "Just a good smile. And by the way, you've got one hell of a smile yourself. That's going on my own list for sure. Those pretty dimples of yours . . . I've lost a little sleep over those."

The flush was rising again, for a completely different reason this time. "No fair remembering everything I say. Especially after a couple of beers."

"So, I should be a dumb jock and just stare vacantly out of my not-good-looking face, is that it? Smiling, of course."

"You're not a dumb jock, and there's no way anyone could miss it, all right?" she said with a sigh. "Except me, but as we've just discussed, I was prejudiced."

"I like that *was*."

"So," she said, working determinedly on her salad again, "not so many dark secrets of your own, huh? Football star from about . . . oh, junior high, I'm guessing. Money, stardom, good-looking . . . body," she added to another grin, "and the hometown hero, too? You really do have it all, don't you?"

"Don't have the football career anymore," he reminded her. "Only have half the money, too, since the divorce. Less than half since that little gift to the university. Don't have a wife, either. And as you pointed out," he said with a sigh of his own, "I don't even have a handsome face. Dang it."

She wanted to ask him about the wife, but how could she? She was beginning to wonder why any woman would have left Cal, but that's what had happened, according to Rochelle. "I suppose there are worse things than being the hometown hero," she said instead.

"Yeah. The good part is, you get to live in your hometown again. The bad part is, you have to live in your hometown again. Not everybody loves a hero."

She looked up from her salad. "Jealousy," she guessed.

"Yep. Everything's got a price. Most people around here take you for who you are, though. What I like about living here. *Why* I'm living here. It's not about what you do for folks around here, or about how much you've got. It's about who you are. If I set myself up all fancy, that wouldn't impress anybody. Just the opposite. They'd think I was a jerk."

"And you're not."

He shrugged. "Well, I don't know. What do you think?"

"That it's pretty obvious you're not a jerk, not underneath. And," she went on, because it had been nagging at her for days, "speaking of that gift of yours . . . I like this town, too, don't get me wrong. But you do know, don't you, that everything that goes on everywhere else goes on here, too?"

"Like what?" He looked startled, and no wonder. Why couldn't she just flirt? Why did she always have to make things serious? Because she *was* serious, and she couldn't help it.

"Thinking about recruiting women to the university . . ." she said. "We keep overlooking one thing. That they need to be safe there."

"And they're not?"

"Have you heard that statistic, that one in five women is sexually assaulted in college?"

"I have," he said, shifting gears right along with her, because Cal was anything but slow. "And I believe it. I went to college on a football scholarship."

"And were in a fraternity, I'll bet."

"Yes," he said, "I was in a fraternity. Although I don't think that's the only place parties happen, or rape happens, if we're putting it on the table here. But I wouldn't have said this university has any worse record than anyplace else. Probably better. And aren't there training sessions and things like that now? I'm sure I saw something about that recently. Kind of a big deal, isn't it?"

"You'd think," she said, "if things were really changing."

"So this is happening? You're hinting around, and I don't have a clue. Where is this coming from?"

"Remember when we were in your truck," she said, "and the police car went by so fast? And you said something about the university's finest keeping the streets safe?"

"I'm not likely to forget that, am I? Scared me to death, with you not in a shoulder belt."

She set aside the feeling that gave her. "Well, I don't think your campus police, or the university administration, either, is exactly with the program. However well the sexual assault prevention program is working, and I'm not sure it is, because I've done some research this week. Even when you've got straight-up attempted forcible rape, the classic case, breaking and entering, they don't seem nearly as concerned as they ought to be."

"All right." He set the remains of his sandwich down. "Let's have the story." He beckoned to her. "Come on. Let's have it."

SECURITY FORCES

It was Wednesday, and Amy was walking into the low wooden building that housed the campus police department. It was her second time here, and the first had been pretty bad. But this time, she was here with Dr. Santangelo.

Her professor had asked her after class on Monday how the investigation was going, and when she'd heard that it seemed to be going nowhere, she'd announced that they were paying the police a visit. Which had been such a relief, because her dad hadn't been able to get any answers on the phone, and Bill had refused to come.

"We already went to talk to them," he'd said when she'd asked him. "It's only been a week. You need to let them do their job."

"I need to make sure they're taking it seriously," she tried to explain.

"They said they were investigating, so let them investigate," he said. "You moved into the dorm. You're safe. It's all over. You can let it go now, and I think you should. You're letting it take over your life."

"I don't think I am," she said. "At least, no more than normal. That's what the counselor said, that it's normal to still . . . cycle up and down. To still think about it, and be scared when I do." Which was putting it mildly.

"But why dwell on it?" he asked. "It was terrifying, I know it was, but you're safe now. It's *over*. Seems like you just don't want to let it be over."

"It doesn't feel over, though," she tried to explain for about the tenth time. "I can't just forget it, like it never happened. And what if he does it to somebody else?"

"You reported it. That's all you can do. You're not responsible for everybody else in the world. Move *on*, Ame, or you'll drive yourself crazy."

Well, all right, she was crazy, because she couldn't move on. She didn't feel safe, and she didn't think anybody else was safe, either, not with *him* out there.

She needed help, and Dr. Santangelo had been amazing in the housing office. Amy still couldn't believe that she'd gotten her moved. And today, it wasn't just Dr. Santangelo. She *really* couldn't believe that Cal Jackson was walking into the building with them.

She knew who he was, of course. Everybody knew who he was. But she couldn't believe he was here with her, and willing to help her.

"I really appreciate you doing this," she said as they stood in the unmanned lobby, waiting for somebody to show up. "Both of you."

"No problem," Dr. Santangelo said. "You need to find out what's going on, and this is our best shot. Especially since we've got Cal with us."

"I told you," he said, "I'll do my best, but I can't promise. Cops don't always like me."

"Everybody likes you," Dr. Santangelo said.

"Everybody but cops."

"Huh," Dr. Santangelo said, and she sure seemed to be casual about Cal. Amy didn't know how she could do it.

"*Personal Weapons: Secure Storage*," Dr. Santangelo read aloud from the sign over the door to the right of the reception desk. "Does that mean the officers' personal weapons, or . . . what?" She watched a guy head out of the room, dropping a handgun into his backpack, a uniformed officer locking the door behind him. "Or . . . something else?"

"Oh," Amy explained, "you're supposed to turn in your guns for the day while you're on campus. But I didn't," she whispered.

"What?" Dr. Santangelo stared at her.

"I shouldn't say. Not here. But my dad said to keep it with me all the time." She shifted her backpack on her shoulder, and now Dr. Santangelo was staring at that, as if she'd never heard of anybody carrying a gun before.

"He was right, too," Cal said. "You listen to your dad. Make you feel a whole lot better. If he comes anywhere near you, you pull that thing out first and ask questions later."

"Wait. *What?*" Dr. Santangelo demanded.

"I told my dad I was supposed to lock it up," Amy said, "but he said if I never needed it, nobody would ever know I hadn't. And if I did . . . well, that would be the least of anybody's worries, that I was carrying."

"Carrying," Dr. Santangelo said faintly. "Sounds like some . . . movie."

"Nope," Cal said. "Just sounds like Idaho. Figure everybody's carrying, and you won't be too far off."

"Do you know how to use it, though?" Dr. Santangelo asked Amy. "Otherwise, isn't that really dangerous? I've always heard that a gun is dangerous because your attacker can use it against you."

"Only if he's not dead," Cal said, which was pretty much what Amy's dad would have said.

"Of course I do," Amy said. "You're right. It doesn't do you much good if you don't."

"It's like a whole new world," Dr. Santangelo said.

The officer who'd been locking up the weapons storage room was back behind the desk now, eyeing the three of them without much enthusiasm. "Can I help you?" he asked.

"Yes," Dr. Santangelo said. "We're here to see Officer . . ." She looked at Amy.

"Moore," Amy said. She wanted to talk to him, but she didn't want to talk to him. She was just glad she didn't have to do it alone.

"Wait," Cal said. "Moore? That's who's on the case?"

"Well, yeah," Amy said. "That's the one who did the report and everything. Why?"

Cal groaned a little. "Great. I should probably leave."

"No," Dr. Santangelo said. "No. We need your help."

"I think he's eating lunch," the desk officer was saying.

"Well, since we're here now," Dr. Santangelo said, "maybe you could tell him that a crime victim is here, along with a faculty member, and that we have important information about a case."

"Well . . . I'll tell him," the officer said, picking up the receiver by his side and speaking into it.

"Not that we have new information," Dr. Santangelo whispered. "But whatever works."

"I—" Amy said.

"What?"

"Tell you later."

"I should probably say . . ." Cal told them. "I may not be that helpful, after all."

"Why not?" Dr. Santangelo asked. "So far, you've seemed like the most important citizen of this town. What did you *do*, that cops don't like you?"

"Officer Moore," Cal said. "He's my cousin."

"I thought he was a deputy sheriff," Dr. Santangelo said.

"Different cousin."

Another man in blue appeared through a door behind the desk.

"Oh," Dr. Santangelo said. "That Officer Moore."

NOT GETTING ANSWERS

It was Zoe's dance partner from a couple weeks before. He stopped short, his weight balanced on both muscular legs, his dark eyes slowly surveying the three of them, a little smile curving his lips. Tall, well built, tough, and Zoe could see the resemblance to Cal. And yes, he was good-looking, which was, she remembered to her disgust, why she had danced with him in the first place. She'd had something to say to Cal about men who only cared about women's looks, but really, was she any better?

"Sorry," he said. "Do I know you?"

She knew he did. "Zoe Santangelo," she said. "From the Cowboy Bar," she added. On purpose.

"Oh, that's right. What can I do for you, Ms. . . . Sangelo?"

"Santangelo," she said. "And it's *Dr.* Santangelo, actually. I'm here with Amy Corrigan. I'm sure you remember her."

He looked at Amy. "Sorry. Didn't recognize you. The burglary last week, yes, of course. You'd better come on back."

Burglary. Amy had been right, then. Zoe followed him through the locked door to the back with Amy following her, and Cal, who still hadn't said anything, bringing up the rear. The little procession passed through a hallway into a small . . . squad room, she guessed.

It looked pretty much like on TV. Bare bones. Bulletin boards, file cabinets, metal desks.

Officer Moore waved them to seats on the other side of one of those desks, covered with stacks of paper decorated by brown coffee rings. A tin can held pens and pencils, some adorned with teeth marks. No chair for Cal, but he just walked around to another desk, grabbed a chair, brought it back, and sat himself down on the other side of Amy, so she was flanked by the two of them.

"All right," Moore said. "Officer Sandford said you had some new information?"

"I'm sorry," Zoe said sweetly. "He must have misheard. I said we *wanted* information. Information on the progress of your investigation."

"Ah." He sat back, laced his fingers over his flat abdomen. "Well, I'm afraid we don't have much to go on. If somebody'd gotten a license plate, or seen anything more than the back of a guy running away, we'd be better off."

"I know more than that," Amy said. "He was following me, remember? Pickup truck. Big. Dark. I *told* you."

"Uh-huh." Moore dug in his ear with a little finger. "If it was the same guy. But, yeah. Big dark pickup. Got one of those yourself, don't you?" he asked Cal. "What were you doing on Halloween?"

"Funny," Cal said, barely moving his lips.

The officer shrugged. "So I'm sorry you've taken the time, Miss Corrigan, but I don't have anything new for you, except to say that we're investigating, and we'll keep investigating. I'm not sure why you've brought . . . reinforcements, but I'm afraid it doesn't change the situation. When I have something to tell you, you'll be the first to know."

"After we leave here," Zoe said, "just to keep you in the loop, since I can see how important that is to you, we're on our way to the student newspaper to tell them what happened. So women around here know what's happening and can protect themselves." She caught Cal's look out of the corner of her eye. Well, no, it hadn't been the plan, but it sure sounded like a good one now.

There was real hostility in the dark eyes across from her. "You are, are you? Telling them there's been a burglary. Got news for you. There are burglaries on college campuses. It's not front-page news."

"That's not what this was, though," Zoe said. "This was an attempted rape. And if that isn't front-page news here—well, let's say I'll be surprised."

"Anyway, I do have something new," Amy said, and pulled a baggie out of her coat pocket. "I've got something that tells me what he was there for, no matter what you say. I've got this."

DECIDE AND PLAN

The man read the article again, forced himself to sit back even as the cold rage coursed through his body. His hand closed over the pen in his hand, until he set it back into its holder with deliberate care.

In control. He was in control.

He'd never failed. Never, because nobody was better at pre-engagement reconnaissance than he was. How could he have foreseen the baseball bat? Was he supposed to research their high school sports?

From now on, he decided, he would. If that was what it took, he would. *Suck it up and move on. Decide, plan, and execute.* Nobody was better at that, either.

He'd love to go after Amy again. As scared as she was now, as much as she'd figured out? Hell, yeah. He'd love it. This time, he'd be anticipating the bat, could make a plan to allow for it. The look on her face when he took it away from her . . . that would be so good.

He wouldn't use it on her. He wasn't that kind of guy. But she'd be so terrified he would. He could hold it across her throat, maybe, while he did it. Hold it close, like he was going to crush her windpipe with it, watch her eyes get big, watch her shake, watch her panic. Her arms wrenched behind her back. Helpless. Hurting.

He could do it, too. He knew where she was, he had the skills, and he could get the access. But it was risky. Even if he made sure the roommate was gone—interior hallway in a dorm? Even at three in the morning, you couldn't be sure. With lights on, and not being able to wear the mask . . . no.

He abandoned the night plan, the normal plan, with regret. He either had to get her someplace else, force her off the road, maybe, or find her walking home alone after dark, pull her into the bushes . . . or move on.

He hated the thought of moving on. Once he found his target, he hit it. Always. But he had a feeling she wasn't going to be walking alone after dark for a while, or even driving anywhere alone. She wasn't a soft target anymore, and soft targets were the only ones that made logistical sense.

Maybe later, he promised himself. Much later, when she had relaxed again, when she thought she was safe again. It could be months, but he wasn't going anywhere. And neither was she, it looked like. More fool her. They usually ran away, but she thought she was tough. They'd see who was right about that. But not now.

The smartest choice of all would be to lie low on campus for now, choose a target farther afield. Somebody in town, even. Problem was, he liked the young ones, and high school girls were still living with their families, with their gun-toting, protective Idaho fathers, which made the mission too risky.

Anyway, the college girls were more satisfying. So confident, so arrogant, prancing around like they owned the campus, not nearly careful enough in their newfound freedom. That always made it sweeter.

Another campus again. Or maybe . . . His mind toyed with the possibility. She was a little long in the tooth for him, true. But otherwise . . . yeah. Just his type. And if he was looking for an arrogant bitch who thought she got to call the shots, well, you couldn't do much better, could you?

And he needed somebody. His planning had been so satisfying. He'd enjoyed the preparation, what he always thought of as warming them up for him, more than ever, with the sweet knowledge that it was about to pay off, that he was just about to scratch that itch.

But it hadn't paid off, and he hadn't scratched that itch for much too long. The frustrated urge clawed, and nothing else could satisfy it. No other form of control could possibly match this, because this was the ultimate.

He needed another one, and he needed her now. Time to make a plan.

EXECUTE

Three days after the visit to the police station—and the newspaper office, which had been a little more productive—Zoe nursed her car cautiously around another of the tight curves that snaked their way up the Union City grade.

It had been snowing all day, and more than six inches had accumulated so far. She'd been told that it was only the start of what was to come, but this was already six inches more than she was used to. The highway had been cleared, but she remembered that black ice from the last time, and she wasn't ending up in the ditch tonight. Even though she actually did have Cal's number now, and she had a feeling he'd tow her out again, too. Even in the snow. Even in the dark. Because she'd had lunch with him again after their outing with Amy the other day, and it had been . . . nice. More than nice. And he'd been so . . . so *good,* coming along for that. Even though he'd been right, he hadn't exactly been a big asset with his cousin. But then, Zoe wasn't sure she had been, either.

And if he invited her to go dancing again . . . she didn't think she was going to be able to say no.

She brought her mind back to the tricky S-curve at the top of the grade, breathed a little easier when she reached the top and her little car wasn't laboring so hard anymore. She hoped she could nurse it through the winter. A new car—well, a new used car—was an expense she hadn't counted on and couldn't afford. She'd had no idea, though, how hard cold weather and salted roads could be on a car that was on its last legs anyway.

As long as she could hold out until next fall, she'd be all right. She should be able to get more consulting work, too. She'd just made her very first final presentation, had delivered her report to the city on their aquifer, and they'd seemed pleased. A pleased client meant a referral. And best of all, she'd delivered her invoice, which meant that she'd be paid. Within two weeks, she devoutly hoped. She was so glad now that she hadn't reduced her rate as she'd been halfway tempted to do.

Ask for what you deserve, she'd reminded herself. *Don't put yourself on sale. You'll impress nobody that way. People take you at your own valuation.* All the lessons that Dr. Aaronson, her major professor, had drilled into her when she'd assisted him with his own research. Tough to do when the urge to compromise, to ask for less, to settle, was telling you something entirely different. But for a woman in a man's world, that message was everything.

The bright, high-set lights of a semi loomed in her rearview mirror, and she brought her attention back to the road once more. A rare stretch of straightaway appeared ahead, and the big truck moved out and around her. She hugged the white line and slowed to let it pass, her hands tight on the wheel, then fumbled for her windshield wipers as the truck cut back in front of her, its big tires kicking up slushy spray. She tried not to flinch at the pickup truck that zoomed past in the opposite direction, seemingly only a second after the semi had gotten out of the way. That had been much too close to a head-on collision, with her right in the middle of it.

She forced her mind away from the vivid image and slowed down a little more, focusing on following the big truck's taillights, until even it pulled away.

More lights appeared behind her. Not a semi this time, but somebody else who would probably want to pass, because nobody in Idaho drove more slowly in the snow than she did. She was coming into another curve, though, so he'd just have to wait.

He was clearly impatient, because his lights seemed to be taking up her entire rearview mirror. She tried to ignore him as he dropped back, edged closer, dropped back again, and then, on a straight section, edged up again. Passing, she thought with relief.

He didn't pass, though. He got so close that her attention drifted from the road and turned to the mirror, because she could swear he was going to rear-end her. She sped up again, but he matched her speed, and sweat was prickling under her arms despite the chill.

Five more miles of him speeding up, falling back, speeding up again, and the tension in her arms and legs was making it hard to control the car. She took a curve too fast, felt her back end sliding again despite her new all-weather tires, steered into the skid, and swung back around.

Nobody was coming the other way this time, so her brief foray across the center line didn't matter. Why wouldn't he *pass*? And why couldn't she just ignore him? So he was in a hurry. So what? That wasn't her problem.

A straight stretch, and she slowed deliberately, hugging the narrow strip of shoulder between the white line and the bank of snow pushed aside by the snowplow.

And still he didn't pass. She couldn't see him, could only see his lights in the mirror. It must be his brights, because they were blinding her.

She sped up again, risking the ice. She briefly considered pulling over farther, simply stopping and forcing him to go by, but she'd been seized by a thought that was very nearly paralyzing her.

Somebody was definitely following me, Amy had said. She had been scared, too. Everyone had told her she was imagining it, but Zoe hadn't thought so. Not then, and certainly not later. She'd thought Amy had been stalked. That somebody had either been looking for his moment, or had simply been scaring her because that was part of his plan. Part of his fun.

Just like everything in Zoe's body was telling her that somebody was trying to scare her right now. Or worse, looking for his moment. She had a good fifteen more miles to go to Paradise, and nothing much between here and there. Nothing but farms sitting off the road, a few lonely lights flashing by before she could do more than register them. Farms with unplowed driveways she could get stuck in, and that wasn't happening. She was driving straight into town, straight to the police station. Not the university police. The Paradise police.

What else could she do right now? The semi was far ahead now, no help to her. She needed somebody to notice. Somebody driving in the other direction, as few vehicles as that was. This was Idaho, Cal had told her again and again. People helped here. But how did you get somebody to notice you while you were driving?

You put on your flashers, and you honked, that was what you did. She fumbled for the flashers, punched the button, then laid her hand flat on the center of the steering wheel, pressed hard, and kept pressing.

He was right on her now. So close that she thought he was going to push her off the road. She kept honking. If only somebody would *come*.

Nobody came, though. Nobody at all. The road was curving again, and she had to put her hand back on the wheel.

Too fast. She was going too fast. She had to tap the brake, fishtailed a little. Her breath caught in her throat, her hands tightened desperately on the wheel, but she made it around. Barely. As soon as she was clear, she had her hand on the horn again, was splitting the night with its blare.

He was still back there, still right on her tail, and she'd gone straight into another curve, and her back wheels were sliding out again. She tried to turn into it, but she was going too fast, and the surface was too slippery.

Time slowed as the darkness revolved around her. Like a dream. Like a carnival ride. The other car's lights loomed over her for a flashing moment, and she flinched, anticipating the collision. Then they were gone, and she was still sliding, heading into darkness, her wheels hitting the snowbank with a sickening thud, then climbing over it. The car stopped for a split second, hovering, then the front end tipped downward and rammed into the other side of the concrete ditch with a hard jolt that slammed her into her shoulder belt.

She was in the ditch, and she was stopped, and she was stuck. And he was out there. He was waiting.

IN THE DITCH AGAIN

Cal slowed for the turn. Not that his truck couldn't handle it, but he wasn't taking any chances while he was towing the new Bobcat on the trailer behind him. It was his last time driving this stretch today, and he'd meant it to be in the light, but the day had gotten away from him.

He came around the curve just in time to see the lights hurtling across his path, the car leaping the bank, slamming to a stop.

He had his foot hard on the brake, was slowing fast himself, his big tires biting into the road as the powerful brakes engaged. He threw his flashers on with a flip of a switch, rounded the bend, headed down the straight stretch for a little ways, then pulled as far over as he could get, which wasn't very far at all. Flares and fire extinguisher from under the seat, a flashlight from the glove compartment, and he was out of the truck and running along the shoulder. He stopped halfway along, pulled the cap off a flare, lit it against the asphalt, set it down, and kept running.

He got around the corner, and the blare of a horn he'd been aware of all along got louder. Must have gotten stuck when the car had crashed, because it was steadily, maddeningly loud. He prayed that it didn't mean the driver was draped over the wheel. He'd seen an accident once . . . Let it not be that.

Another truck had pulled over, too. Must have been right behind the car in the ditch. Good. They'd be checking on the car's occupants, and he wasn't smelling smoke or seeing flames, so he didn't stop, just ran on well past the two vehicles, past the horn's continuing blast, lit another flare and set it down, then ran another hundred yards and lit a third before turning around and taking off toward the wreck again.

He nearly had to dive for the ditch himself when the truck roared past, barely missing him, on the wrong side of the road. The truck that had been with the car. What the hell?

He shook it off, ran for the car. Still no smoke, thank God, but no motion, either, and still the horn. But the flashers were on, so the driver must be conscious.

It wasn't until he turned the flashlight on the car that it hit him. The little hatchback. The license plate. It was Zoe.

He wasn't even aware of leaping the snowbank, sliding down the ditch, and clambering up the other side. He had his hand on the door, was trying to get it open, but it was locked. He shone the light inside, dread tightening his chest at what he would see.

Her face. White with shock and fear, her mouth and eyes stretched wide, three black holes, one hand shoving desperately down on the center of the wheel to continue the earsplitting noise, the other raised high, fist clenched. Her hand leaving the horn now, reaching for her shoulder belt, stabbing for the release button, again and again.

She was safe. The knowledge, and the sudden silence after the unbearable noise—it was infinite relief, and it was a hammer blow.

"Zoe!" He shouted it so she could hear through the glass, turned the light on himself. "It's me. Cal. Open the door. Please, baby. Open the door. Let me get you out."

She was trying to punch the lock, but she was missing it.

He crouched beside the car. "It's okay," he shouted. "Just hit the button."

He heard the *click*, was wrenching the door open, reaching for her.

Injuries, he reminded himself at the last moment, and pulled his hands back. "You hurt?" he demanded. "Your neck? Your back?"

"N-n-no," she got out through chattering teeth. "I don't th-th-think so."

He got hold of her, picked her up, pulled her out, set her on her feet, but kept his arm around her. "Up and over," he urged her. "Come on, now. Just a few steps and we're out of here."

She was shaking, holding his arm, and he supported her down the steep culvert, up over the berm, onto the shoulder of the road. "Can you walk?" he asked. "Can you make it to my truck?"

"Of . . . of course," she said, but he could feel her trembling, kept his arm around her, got her to his rig and up inside it.

"My purse," she managed when she was there, and he sighed with relief that her brain had switched on again. "My laptop bag. My phone."

"Going back for them right now," he promised, shoving the extinguisher back under the seat again. "Keys?" He looked at her hand, still grabbing whatever it was.

She looked blank. "They must still be . . . in the car."

"What's that you've got?"

She looked at her hand as if unaware she was holding anything, then opened her fingers. "Limestone."

"Limestone," he repeated blankly.

"To hit him."

"Ah." To hit who? He didn't get it. "Think you could drop it now? You don't need to hit me, I promise. Use your words."

"Oh," she said. "Yeah." She bent over, set it down on the floor.

He wanted to ask, but he couldn't sit here. Too dangerous a spot. "I'm going back for your stuff. Hang on."

"Be careful."

"Aw, sweetheart," he said, "I'm always careful." He grinned at her, because she needed it. "Be right back. You sit tight."

His flares were still burning, and her car was off the road anyway. The only real danger was somebody hitting his truck, but that had him hustling to get her things and get back to her.

He managed it, climbed in beside her again. He switched on the engine, turned the dial to blast the heat, because she was still shaking. Cold, and shock.

"My . . . my car," she said.

"We'll call for a tow," he promised as he pulled out. "Soon as we're out of this. Not while we're on the highway."

"I can't just . . . leave it. What if somebody . . ."

He put the pedal down, got up to speed, because he didn't need to be rear-ended in the storm. "That thing's not going anywhere. Nobody's stealing it, nobody without some serious towing capacity. You're all good."

"No," she said. "I'm not. I'm not all good."

"You hit the ditch again, that's all. That's just Idaho. They practically won't give you your license until you hit the ditch a few times."

"You don't understand," she said. "He was *chasing* me. I know he was."

"*What?* Who?"

"The . . . the car behind me. He was chasing me. Coming so close, dropping back. For miles."

"The truck," he said slowly. "The truck behind you. He left after I stopped."

"Because when I crashed, he was there," she said. "He was waiting."

"Most people would stop if somebody crashed, though."

"No," she said. "I don't think so. He was there after I went off the road. I saw his lights behind me. I was trying to figure out what to do. That's why the rock, because that's what I had. When you came . . ." She stopped a moment, then went on resolutely. "I thought you were him. I thought that was it. And then when you took me out of the car—I realized he'd left, that I'd heard him go, and that must have been why. He left because you came."

He wanted to tell her she'd been imagining the whole thing. Somebody chasing her? It seemed so unlikely. He wanted to think so, but he remembered that truck peeling out. If it was him . . . if it was . . .

He took his foot off the accelerator as he approached the speed limit sign signaling the Fulton city limits—all two blocks of them. He took the turn at the intersection, and she seemed to notice where they were for the first time.

"Wait," she said. "This is the wrong way."

"I thought . . ." he said. "I thought, take you someplace we can call for a tow. Someplace you can warm up, calm down."

"No." She sounded like she was shaking again, and she was punching for her shoulder belt. "*No.*"

"Zoe. Wait," he said urgently. "I don't mean my house. I meant my parents. I meant my mom." He made a quick decision, pulled into the deserted post office parking lot, careful of the trailer behind him, and stopped. "My parents' house, which is just a couple blocks away. I'll call the garage, and you can call the police, tell them what happened. My mom will make you a cup of . . . tea, or something, and you can . . ." He cast around for what a woman would want to do, what would help. "Have a bath. Have dinner with my folks."

She laughed. Barely, but a laugh. "Have a *bath*?"

"Yeah. Well." He looked at her sheepishly. "I don't know why, but when women have a bad day, when something bad happens, they always seem to want to take a bath. Isn't that the deal? I mean, personally, I just want to have a beer, but whatever. A beer's fine by me, too, though. Hell, have two beers. My folks won't mind."

She was laughing a little more, some of the tension easing, and that was so much better. "Yes," she said. "Yes, please, then. I don't think I'll have a bath, but . . . please. It *is* a different house, right?" she asked, a thought clearly striking her. "I mean, you don't . . . live with your parents?"

He laughed himself at that. "Nope. Sure don't. I haven't been living in my parents' basement for, oh, a good year or two now. Not since I went full-time at Pizza Hut."

"Oh. That's right." She looked embarrassed, and he smiled at her and pulled out of the parking lot. "I mean," she said, "NFL quarterback. Duh."

"Farmer," he reminded her. "Living in a farmhouse."

PHASE ONE

The man drove into the storm, his hands clenching and unclenching on the steering wheel. He felt the muscle bunching in his jaw, forced himself to relax it. Not that anybody was here to see, but he couldn't afford to let his face give him away. He never had yet, because he was cool. Because he was good.

That couldn't have gone much worse, not unless he'd been recognized. He hadn't been recognized, though, he was sure of it. Cal had been too busy putting out his flares, being a helpful little citizen, to pay much attention to him. And then he'd been too busy diving out of the way like a scared little bunny.

Zoe had been a scared bunny, too. A *very* scared bunny. He felt better for a minute, remembering, before frustration had him gripping the wheel again. Who'd have expected the stupid bitch to go off the road? It had barely been icy. Who'd given her a driver's license?

He'd wasted a whole late afternoon following her, had risked ducking out of work, making up a story that could be checked, which was always dangerous. For nothing. First she hadn't noticed him at all, not for the entire forty-minute drive to Union City. Too focused on herself to see anything else, even somebody as dangerous as he was. To notice his lights on her pretty little tail the whole way down the grade, through every turn on the city streets, all the way to the courthouse. Who was that oblivious?

He hadn't been able to risk following her in there. No way. He'd figured, when she'd left the university early on Friday afternoon and he'd realized where she was headed, that she was ducking out to go shopping at one of the malls. A normal woman thing, and that would've been perfect. He could have paced her as she walked through the dark lot, as she glanced back at his truck and tried to tell herself it was all right, when her body was telling her it wasn't. Instead, he'd had to sit outside, freezing his ass off, not daring to run the engine, to draw attention to himself, for almost an hour. For *nothing*.

She'd noticed him on the way back. Finally. Only when he'd gotten so close that anybody but a total moron would've had to notice.

It had been fun after that, though. He'd made it extra fun, just to punish her for the time he'd wasted, for her obliviousness. He'd made it a little *too* fun, in the end, had gotten too carried away with his cat-and-mouse game, because he could almost smell the sweet scent of her fear. She'd been scared anyway just from driving in the snow, he could tell. She liked to pretend she was so tough, but scratch that surface and she was weak. Weak all the way through. From now on, she'd be even more scared, and that was good. All part of the plan. And then she'd find out just how weak she really was.

It had all been good, in fact, right up until the stupid bitch had landed in the ditch, and his plan had gone straight to hell.

He'd pulled over. He hadn't been able to resist, not after she'd gotten him off-balance like that. The same way she had this whole time, messing with everything he'd done. So, yeah, he'd pulled over, because if he wanted her scared, there was surely nothing better than wrecking her car, knowing he was there, and that she was helpless. That she was about as stuck as a person could be—until she got even more stuck.

He wondered if she would have run in the end, once she'd figured out that honking the horn wasn't going to work, because there was nobody to hear. Nobody but him.

She probably would have. He'd have smashed the window, reached down for the lock, and she'd have dived out the other side, run straight up the highway. In the snow, in her little heels. Yeah, that would've worked out real well for her. And then . . . he'd have pulled her up into his truck, hit her a couple times, given her a little attitude adjustment to get her in the right frame of mind, gotten her wrists secured, and driven away with her. Piece of cake.

Pull off the road, and that's when the party would start. Do it, let her think it was over, tell her he'd let her go. Then drive her someplace else, someplace more remote, and do it again. Do it worse. Let her hope, then kill her hope, until she'd promise anything, do anything, just to live. Just to hope to survive.

Until he kicked her out of the truck, once he was done with her. Naked, barefoot in the snow, with her wrists still fastened behind her. Man, it made him laugh to think about her trying to flag somebody down like that in the dark. No hands, so she'd have to get right out there in the road. If a guy picked her up in his headlights? Hell, yeah, he'd stop. And then, who knows? That was fun to think about, too.

He wouldn't kill her, because he wasn't a killer. If she froze, though? If somebody ran her over, or if things got even worse for her? He wouldn't be real sad. And there would be nothing to lead anyone back to him. All he'd have to do was dump her clothes and he'd be golden.

It was her own fault anyway. She could have left it alone, and she'd never have occurred to him, because she was too old. Although he was rethinking that, too. The tougher they thought they were, the harder the fall was. That part was good. He couldn't believe he'd never thought of that before.

It had real possibilities. *Real* possibilities. Except that it wasn't time. Not now. Not yet. Too risky. Not in the plan.

Phase One, he repeated to himself, relaxing his grip on the wheel again. All right, she'd screwed it up, had almost pushed him right into Phase Three. Had almost made him abandon his plan, and he *never* abandoned his plan. That's why he was so good at this. Because he was disciplined.

So never mind what she did. It was still Phase One. And everything that had happened so far, everything that would happen next? It would only make Phase Three that much better.

For now, he was headed back to Paradise. He had a house to visit.

THE DECISIVE PEOPLE

It was only a couple blocks, just as Cal had said. But then, the whole town of Fulton didn't seem to be much bigger than that—what Zoe could see of it in the dark, at least.

Cal pulled the truck and trailer into a long driveway. "Hang on," he told her as he hopped down. He was hustling around the front of the truck, pulling her door open. "Careful," he said. "Snow, and you're not dressed for it." He took her hand to help her down, then reached inside for her laptop bag, slung it over his shoulder. "Okay. Watch your step."

He led her across the plowed driveway, up concrete steps that had been shoveled once, were dusted again now by the still-falling snow, to the front door of a neat one-story ranch-style home, illuminated by a porch light that cast a yellow glow over a semicircle of brick siding. He knocked his snowy boots against the wall, gave them a scrape across the mat, then opened the front door and called out, "Hey, Mom!"

Zoe followed him into a tiny entryway. "Here," he said, shutting the door behind them. "Give me your coat."

She was pulling off the puffy jacket and handing it to him when a slim, dark-haired woman came into the hall.

She stopped at the sight of them. "Well, hi," she said with a smile.

"Hey, Mom," Cal said, hanging Zoe's coat on a black iron hook, setting her laptop case and purse on the floor next to it. "I brought you a damsel in distress. This is Zoe Santangelo. Her car's high-centered in the ditch. Zoe, this is my mom, Raylene."

"Oh, no," his mother said. "Poor you. What was it? An accident, or just skidded off in the storm? Is everybody all right?"

"Well," Cal said, looking a little grim, "that's what we need to figure out. Whether it was an accident."

"My goodness," Raylene said. "What does that mean?"

"Tell you later," Cal said. "Zoe's a little shook up. I've got the new Bobcat on the trailer, need to take it on back to my place before the snow gets any deeper. Got to feed Junior, too. I thought you could take care of Zoe for me for a little while, maybe give us dinner."

"I couldn't . . ." Zoe was totally off-balance now. "I don't want to impose. Maybe you could just give me a ride home, Cal. But my car . . ."

"Yeah," Cal said. "Your car, the sheriff, all that. Don't worry, we'll get it done. Give me twenty minutes."

"It's no imposition," Raylene told her. "It's just chicken pot pie. I'll stick a couple more potatoes in the oven and we'll be all set. You can't go home by yourself, not after being in an accident. Come on in. You need a cup of tea, I'm sure, and maybe a hot bath, too. Dinner's not for an hour. Plenty of time."

Zoe caught Cal's expressive glance and almost smiled. "A cup of tea would be great," she said. "Please."

"Twenty minutes," Cal promised. "I'll be back, and we'll get all this figured out."

◆ ◆ ◆

He was out the door again just as a man who looked to be in his sixties came in from the back of the house, saw Zoe, and stopped.

"Well, hi," he said, exactly as his wife had.

"My husband, Stan," Raylene said. "This is Zoe, Stan. Cal brought her home to us."

"Oh?" He lifted gray eyebrows.

Surely this was how Cal would look in thirty-five years or so. Tall and broad-shouldered, which she was beginning to recognize as a family trait. It was more than that, though. It was the way he stood, so upright. The way he took up space. And his face. The face of a man who'd spent his life outdoors, in all the elements. He was a little battered, a little weathered, but still nothing but strong. A little intimidating, and a lot tough. Yep. Exactly what she would have imagined.

"She's been in an accident," Raylene said. "Come on into the kitchen, Zoe. Much nicer than standing around here. Stan, would you go get me four baking potatoes from the root cellar while I make Zoe a cup of tea? You can give them a scrub for me, too, if you don't mind."

"I could do that," Zoe said, trailing after the two of them into a compact kitchen, its yellow walls and cherry-patterned curtains cheerful after the stormy darkness outside. "I don't know where the root cellar is, but I could scrub and . . . whatever."

"No. You sit," Raylene commanded, and Zoe sat.

"And everybody thinks Cal gets that nature of his from me," Stan said. "Shows what they know."

"Yeah, yeah," Raylene said with a laugh. "Potatoes?"

"We live to serve." He gave Zoe a smile, headed through a door at the far end of the room, and came back in a minute with four baking potatoes, dumped them into the sink and began to scrub.

"So," he said again, twisting around to look at Zoe, who was accepting a cup of tea from Raylene. "What's this accident about? Anybody else hurt?"

"No," Zoe said, swishing her tea bag in her mug. "It was just me. My car's in the ditch."

"Ah," Stan said. "Well, it happens. Cal pulled somebody else out just a month or so ago, I heard. Couldn't get you out with that Bobcat on the trailer, I guess."

"Well, actually," Zoe said, concentrating hard on removing her tea bag and placing it carefully in a saucer, "that was me, too. Before."

"Really." Stan leaned against the counter, crossed his arms in his heavy flannel shirt, and looked at her. "Both times?"

"Quite the coincidence, I guess. Or I'm a bad driver," she added with a self-conscious laugh. "I can hear you thinking it. It's a little more complicated than that, though. At least I think it is." She put a hand to her head, which was aching a little.

Raylene saw it. "Don't go quizzing her right now, Stan," she told her husband. "She's not up to it. Time enough when Cal comes back. Not that much of a coincidence, either," she told Zoe. "Cal's driving that stretch a good ten times a day. Lucky for you he was there, that's all."

"He call about her car yet?" Stan asked, keeping to the point. "Or could be he's pulling it out now."

"No," Zoe said. "I mean, he said he'd call once we got here. It's . . . really stuck."

Stan nodded. "I could make that call, anyway. Where did it happen?"

"Um . . ." Zoe shook her head in confusion. "I'm sorry. I don't know. The . . . other way, I guess. I mean, I was coming back from Union City, and Cal was coming the other way, and he didn't turn around, so . . ." She stopped, feeling like an idiot. "I'm sorry. I was a little shaken up."

"North," he decided. "About how many miles from here?"

"I don't know that, either," Zoe admitted. Because she didn't. Had Cal driven for five minutes? Ten? More? She couldn't have said.

"I'm sorry. I don't know. I should have called Triple A right away, but I was . . ." *Terrified.*

Raylene was rubbing olive oil over the potatoes, putting them on a cookie sheet, and sticking them into the oven. "Of course you were," she said. "Never mind. Cal will know. He'll take care of it. You just drink your tea and don't worry about it. And nothing needs to happen now," she told Stan, who had opened his mouth. "Nothing at all. You always want to do something, but you know, sometimes nothing at all has to happen right now."

Which was why she was still sitting there when Cal showed up again. She heard the front door open and close, and a minute later, he'd breezed into the room in his stockinged feet.

"Well, hey, Professor," he said. "You're looking a little more stout."

"Professor?" his mother asked.

"Yeah." He pulled a chair out, sat down next to her, and she felt a little better, a little steadier to have him there. "Dr. Santangelo here is a bona fide professor, up there at the university. And not what you'd think, looking at her pretty face. Not Renaissance poetry or something. Geological sciences. She's an expert in hydrogeology, in fact. She's got plans to tell me all about the water table under the farm. With diagrams. In color, even, with labels and arrows and all that. And a laser pointer."

"Only if the price is right," she said. She was smiling, even though she could tell that this was exactly why he was teasing her. That he was trying to cheer her up, shake her out of it.

"Sounds like you know her from more than pulling her out of the ditch," Stan said.

"Yeah," Cal said with a martyred sigh. "Kinda couldn't help it, once I met her, because she made a play for me right from the start. I had to practically pull her off of me, tell her I wasn't that kind of guy. But I've warmed up to her some since then. She's about sweet-talked me around to her way of thinking. I'll admit, I'm about to go for it, shy as I normally am. She's just too hard to resist."

"Cal," his mother warned, but she was smiling.

Zoe couldn't help it. She was laughing. "I didn't impress him," she told his parents, "when he pulled me out of the ditch the first time."

"Tried to pay me, for one thing," Cal said. "That was pretty flattering."

"It wasn't that I thought you were *poor*," she tried to explain. "It was just that you went to all that trouble. I thought it was the right thing to do."

"Nope," Cal said. "But then, it takes a while to learn the cultural mores of a new society."

"Cal," his mother warned again, "you're *bad*. We're honestly not all that backward," she told Zoe.

"I know that," she hastened to say. "I mean, of course I don't think that."

"We're a little scary, though," Cal said. "Because Zoe thinks that this time around, when she went into the ditch, it wasn't so simple. First time, she just hit black ice, spun out. But this time . . ." He looked at Zoe.

"There was somebody behind me," Zoe said, the playfulness gone. "And he was chasing me. That's why I skidded."

"*Chasing* you?" Raylene looked shocked, and Zoe couldn't blame her. She knew it sounded crazy.

"We should back up," Cal said. "Because it's complicated."

"First, though," Zoe said, "my car? Shouldn't I do something about that? Call Triple A?"

"I already called," Cal said. "Vern over at Vern's Auto will come get it as soon as he can. Probably wait till morning, once the storm blows over and it's light out. He'll give you the special friends-and-family rate on the whole deal, because we had a talk, so don't you worry about that."

"A . . . *talk*? What kind of talk?" she asked in alarm. "I'm grateful that you called," she hurried on at the look on his face. "Don't get me wrong. But I have Triple A. That's what it's for. I can't pay extra for towing."

He sighed. "That's the point. You won't pay extra for towing."

"But . . ." she began, then stopped, put her hand to her aching head again. "Look. You didn't want me to pay you before, and I get that. I do. But I don't want you to pay for me. So we're clear. You didn't do that, did you?"

"I didn't pay the bill, no," he said. "If you don't like what I did, you can go on and rip me a new one tomorrow. I'll put on my flame-retardant suit and everything. Just not tonight, all right? You're not up to your usual standard right now, and it'd wear you right out. Besides, that car's in a little bit of a tough spot. I wanted somebody who knew what he was doing to get it out of there. So I called the best guy I know, and I got you the best deal."

"He is the best," Stan assured her. "Cal's right. Easy to damage a car, towing it wrong. Then you're in a world of hurt, all kinds of expense."

"Yeah, Dad," Cal said, glowering at him. "Thanks. She doesn't need to hear that."

Zoe sighed, rubbed her forehead. "I don't mean to sound ungrateful. That you stopped . . . I'm so grateful. You don't know how much. It's just . . ." She scrubbed at a nonexistent spot on the old-fashioned Formica dinette table with her fist, tried not to let it overwhelm her. The fear, and now the money. More money. And she didn't have a car.

"Yeah," Cal said, his voice gentle now. "I know what it was. That's why the friends-and-family rate. I promise that you don't have to dance with me again, or anything else, either, in exchange. Just a friend helping a friend. All right?"

She felt the tears rising, blinked them back with an effort. "All right," she said. "But please. Ask me first. I mean, explain it to me first. Please." She did her best to ignore the glance Raylene and Stan exchanged.

"Ah," Cal said. "Too bossy again?"

"Well . . ." she admitted.

"What did I say," Stan muttered. "Gets it from his mother."

"Yeah, Dad," Cal said. "I don't think that's the only place. I think there was basically no hope for me."

"So my car," Zoe said. "Do you think it's bad?"

"I'm afraid you could have some damage there, yeah," he said. "Hard to tell in the dark, but the way you hit, how hard you hit? It's possible. Vern said he'll try driving it when he gets it back to the shop, give me a call and let me know what he thinks. I'm guessing you won't know for sure until he can get under it on Monday and take a better look."

"That's what I was afraid of." She tried to shake it off. Worrying wouldn't help. But she knew why she was worrying about money. Because worrying about what had happened was too frightening.

"She hit the ditch mighty hard," Cal told his parents. "I came around the curve near Johnson's and saw it happen. She spun out, did a doughnut, and went right over the snowbank, bottomed out on it, front end slammed into the culvert. Not so good."

His words brought it all back to her. Spinning. Hurtling out of control. And the panic afterward, knowing he was out there, that he was coming, that running wouldn't work, that her only hope was staying in the car, blowing the horn, praying for help. Scrabbling for something, anything, to defend herself. A pen. Anything. Remembering the samples she had on the floor of the passenger seat, and grabbing for one. Knowing she had to move fast, that she had to strike first, and fast, if he broke her window. Hoping she could do it. That it would be enough.

Raylene saw her distress. "Hey, now," she said, coming down to sit beside her, reaching for her hand and squeezing it. "It's okay. Scary, but all over now."

"That's it, though," Zoe said. "I'm not sure it is. It's . . . it's pretty similar to something that happened to a student of mine. A young woman."

After that, of course, she and Cal had to explain, with his mother looking increasingly shocked, his father increasingly grim.

"So Zoe got involved in all that," Cal finished, "and then there was that follow-up piece in the *Idahonian*, too. They just did a story a couple weeks ago about campus sexual assault."

"I saw it," his mother said. "We were just talking about it at our last League of Women Voters meeting, in fact. It's become quite the civil-rights issue, hasn't it? There's been such a sea change, almost overnight, it feels like, in how it's being looked at, in how cases are being investigated, how aggressively they're being pursued, although there's still a long way to go. High time, too."

"Yes," Cal said. "We're aware of the political angle, but thanks for the . . . update." He stopped, mindful of his father's warning glance. "Anyway, that maybe turned the heat up some. I don't think Zoe's made a lot of friends on campus these past weeks, and I've got to wonder if it could have gotten back to the guy. Sounds crazy, but on the other hand . . ."

"Somebody who'd do that," his mother said, "he *is* crazy."

"Or evil," his father said.

"That's all I can think," Zoe said. "I know it sounds so paranoid," she hurried on. "But I swear that I thought he was going to hit me. It felt like he was . . . playing with me. And then when I crashed . . ."

"He pulled in behind her," Cal finished. "And I thought, well, good, somebody else is there. I pulled over, too, and he took off like a rabbit. Now, who would do that?"

"Could have been somebody who saw it happen, saw it wasn't too bad, and took off again," his father said. "Not that most folks around here would do that, not without even checking on the driver. But who knows? Some people."

"I don't think so," Zoe said. "I think he was chasing me, and that Cal scared him off."

His father was looking at Cal again, his gaze serious. "You'd better call the sheriff's office," he said. "Get them out here to talk to her. Just in case."

"Yeah," Cal said. "That's what I'm thinking, too."

"Here's what I think we should do right now," Raylene said. "Cal, you call Jim Lawson, tell him what happened, see if he can come on by later on, if he's on duty. He'd be best."

"Right," Cal said. "You got his number?"

"I should have," she said. "If not, I'll call Vicki and get it. My cousin," she explained to Zoe. "Her son's a deputy."

"Ah," Zoe said. "I think I've met him. If it's him, that's going to make me *less* likely to be believed, though. Since I met him kind of . . . from the ditch. The last time. I mean, the first time."

"Nope," Cal said. "Because I was there, too, this time. He'll believe you."

"Must be nice," Zoe muttered.

"What?" he asked, looking confused.

"To be that confident." She realized what she'd said, where she was, and flushed a little with embarrassment. "Sorry," she told Raylene. "That was kind of rude. I mean, to your son and all, in your house."

Raylene was smiling, though, looking at Stan. "Oh, honey, no. That's music to a mother's ears."

"Hey," Cal said.

"Never mind," his mother said. "You go on and call Jim. I'll get dinner on the table, and Zoe here . . ." She eyed Zoe.

"She'd better stay here tonight," Stan said. "Until we can talk to Jim, get this figured out."

"You're right," his wife said before Zoe could answer. "After dinner, you can have a bath, get changed, get out of that suit. Get yourself relaxed before you have to go through all this again. Because I think you should stay here tonight anyway. Who knows how long it'll take Jim or whoever to show up, and if there really is somebody out there looking for you, we're none of us going to feel good about you going home to an empty apartment."

"I can't do that," Zoe protested.

"And why not?" Raylene demanded.

"Because . . ." Zoe cast about for a reason. "Because I don't have anything to wear," she realized. "And I can't put you out like that."

"Of course you can," Raylene said. "I wouldn't get a lick of sleep tonight otherwise, worrying about you. And I'll get you something to wear, too. You're not so different size-wise from me, just a little shorter."

A *lot* shorter, but not that different otherwise, it was true.

"As long as it's not a turtleneck," Cal said, eyeing his mother.

"Why not?" Zoe asked. "Your mom looks fine. She looks *nice*. And warm, too. What on earth is wrong with a turtleneck? I just can't wait to hear."

"I've looked at you in that suit way too often," he said. "And a turtleneck . . . no. That's just going from bad to worse."

"What a shame, then," his mother said, "that it isn't all about you."

"Nope," Stan said. "It's about me. And I like you in a turtleneck," he told his wife. "So you know."

"You just like me in sweaters," she said.

"Well, yeah," he said with a grin that was surely the original of his son's. "Always have, and I'm happy to admit it. I do love the way you look in a sweater."

"Annnddd . . . an image I did not need," Cal said.

"You're the one who brought it up," his mother pointed out. "Like what I wear is one bit your concern. Here's a real hot news flash for you. And not the menopausal kind, either. Your generation didn't invent sex."

Cal laid his forehead on the table, banged it against the hard surface. "Make the hurting stop," he moaned.

His mother laughed and swatted the back of his head so his forehead hit the table again.

"Ow," he complained, sitting up and rubbing the spot.

"Quit being so silly," she ordered, "and call Jim. Zoe, you come help me set this table. You'll be a whole lot calmer, be able to explain yourself a whole lot better, with a good hot dinner in you."

◆ ◆ ◆

It was like she'd been taken over by the Decisive People, and resistance was clearly futile. Which was why, when the burly, reassuring figure of Jim Lawson was sitting around the kitchen table with all of them a couple of hours later, she was wearing a pair of too-long pants with the legs rolled up and a red sweater.

"V-neck," Raylene had said, pulling it out of a dresser drawer. "Although if you don't want to look pretty for Cal, you just let me know. I've got a real ugly beige turtleneck I bought during some sort of lunatic moment in an after-Christmas sale last year. You say the word and I'll haul that sucker out, because it'll do my heart good to hear him whine about it."

"No, thanks." Zoe hadn't been able to keep from laughing, because she *had* felt a whole lot better after a hot dinner and, yes, a hot bath, too, after being showed into a tidy guest room, knowing she didn't have to go home tonight, that for now, at least, she was safe and warm and being looked after. It wasn't a feeling she was used to, but she'd take it. For tonight.

Now, she sat beside Cal in her borrowed clothes and did her best to explain the circumstances of the night in some kind of lucid fashion.

"So you saw whoever was behind her, too," Jim asked Cal when she'd finished. "Get any impression?"

"Ford F-150," Cal said. "Single-cab. Dark, because I'd have noticed if it had been white."

"How do you know what kind it was?" Zoe asked. "In the dark? In a storm?"

Both men looked at her with surprise. "Headlights," Cal said, like it was obvious.

"Uh . . . don't they all have headlights?"

"Not the same shape," Cal said.

"Well, that's good," Zoe said. "Right?" she asked Jim. "If we know the model?"

"Would be," Jim said, "if that wasn't the best-selling truck in the country, and the rig that about half the male population of this county's driving right now. But it's a start. Occupants?" he asked Cal.

"Couldn't tell you that, either. Too busy diving for the ditch."

"He was that close?"

"Oh, yeah. He was hell-bent on getting out of there before I got close enough to see him, seemed to me. That's the thing that's got me convinced. That and that Dr. Zoe is actually a pretty levelheaded person, at least when her head's actually level. When she's not in a ditch."

"Uh-huh," Jim said. "Not much to go on, somebody following too close."

Zoe had to bite her lip to keep herself from bursting out that he *hadn't* just been following too close. Protesting wouldn't help, though, she knew. Cal put his hand briefly on hers, and she knew he understood, and that helped.

"You said there was something else, though," Jim said.

"Yeah," Cal said. "We can do a little better on this one. Zoe's even got a copy of the police report."

She pulled it out of her laptop case. One of the two copies they'd badgered Greg Moore into giving them during their visit. "This was my student," she said, handing it over. "She had the same experience I did tonight. That's not in there, but she told me about it, and I know she'd be glad to tell you."

"She hit the ditch, too?"

"No," Zoe said, refusing to blush. "Being followed. On foot, she thought, somebody watching her. And by a pickup truck. Before"—she gestured at the report—"this happened."

"She go to the cops about that?"

"No," Zoe said. "Not enough to go on, she thought. Just like me. Just a feeling. Somebody staying behind her. More than once. More than a coincidence. But not doing anything, so there was nothing to report. Would you have taken that seriously?"

"Well . . ." he said.

"No. Of course you wouldn't. Just like you wouldn't be taking me seriously now if it weren't for the pattern." *And Cal.*

"Suppose you let me read this," he said, "get the whole picture, before you go deciding what I think."

Cal's hand was on hers again, and she waited, shifting a little in her chair as Jim read through the report. Slowly. Deliberately. Until she wanted to scream.

He looked up at last. "Based on this and what you've told me, and keeping in mind I'm not a detective, and keeping in mind that this is Greg's case, and Greg's a . . ."

"Yeah," Cal said. "Pretty hard to find the appropriate word in present company."

"All right," Jim said. "Keeping all that in mind, this doesn't sound like burglary to me. Sounds like we could have something more going on here."

"There's another thing," Zoe said. "Not on there, because she didn't know it then. Amy found a zip tie under the bed when she was moving out. A long one. She swears it didn't come from her. She's pretty sure he dropped it."

"Under the bed?" Jim asked. "How would it have gotten under the bed, if he dropped it?"

"She thinks it fell out of his pocket when she hit him, when he spun around," Zoe said. "Maybe he kicked it, or she did. She thinks so."

"Greg know about this?"

"Well, yes," Zoe said. "That is, Amy told him while Cal and I were there at the station with her. He didn't seem too convinced. He said the same thing you did. But she was pretty sure. And it seems like a . . . a clue, doesn't it? I mean, you wouldn't bring zip ties to a burglary. Would you?"

Jim shrugged. "Who knows. But could be." He made a note in his book. "Sliding-glass door, ski mask, zip ties."

"MO," Cal said.

"Could be," Jim said again. "Greg do a search online for patterns, do you know?"

"He didn't share what he did," Cal said. "Not too happy with our being there. Not about to talk to us."

"Want me to try to find out?"

"Why do you think I told Cal to call you?" Raylene spoke for the first time. "That's why you're here, isn't it?"

Cal looked at Jim, Jim looked back at him, and they both smiled a little. "Yes, ma'am," Jim said. "I guess it is."

"Sounds like a good idea to me," Cal said. "I'd sure like to know what's happening myself, and I'm not Amy. Or Zoe."

"Yeah." Jim shoved the notebook back into his pocket and pushed back from the table, the others rising with him. "I sure hope this Amy has something more than a bat next to her bed now. This mutt sounds like real bad news."

"She said that she . . ." Wait. Should she say? It was against the rules, Amy had told her.

"Be surprised if she didn't," Stan put in. "Mr. Smith and Mr. Wesson make a pretty powerful argument. If she were my daughter? You bet she would. No way she'd be back here otherwise."

"You be careful, too," Jim told Zoe. "And remember, somebody comes into your bedroom at night in a ski mask, you've got a right to defend yourself any way you have to. Just in case we do have a pattern here, the best thing would be if you weren't in your bedroom alone for a while."

"That's what I keep telling her," Cal said.

Jim looked at him, smiled a little, shook his head. "Don't shoot Cal," he advised Zoe. "He responds all right to 'no.'"

"I'm not shooting anybody," she said.

"Then," Jim said, "what I told you. Play it safe. Be careful. I'll check this out," he told Cal. "Get back to you."

"And Zoe," Cal said.

"Yep," he said. "Zoe, too."

◆ ◆ ◆

"Feel better?" Cal asked Zoe after Jim had left. "Ready for that beer now?"

She hadn't wanted to drink anything earlier. It had seemed important to keep her wits about her.

"Do," Raylene said. "Time to relax."

"Sure," Zoe decided. "Why not."

Cal got up, grabbed a beer out of the fridge, popped the top, and handed it over. "Dad?"

"No," Raylene answered for her husband. "Dr. Parker told him to keep it at one, except on special occasions."

"Excuse me?" Stan said with some pain. "Is there a reason I can't answer for myself? I'm the one who was there at the appointment."

Cal smiled. "So, beer?"

"No," Stan said. "Because he did say it. To *me*. Nothing wrong with my hearing, or my memory. He didn't tell me I had Alzheimer's."

Raylene looked completely unruffled. "If women didn't look after their men's health, you'd all be eating pork rinds and pizza seven nights a week and dropping dead at forty-five. Consider it my wifely duty to remind you to get your cholesterol and your prostate checked every year. I don't see you doing it otherwise."

"I tend more to consider that you're sitting at home chuckling at the idea of that rubber glove coming at me," her husband growled.

"Could be," she admitted. "I bore you three children. I call that a little well-deserved payback."

"Not so much with the rubber glove," Cal complained. "Could you two give it a rest? I'm trying to make an impression here."

"Seems to me," Raylene said, "that Zoe's had a real tough night, and what we really need is to get you on out of here, Cal, so she can go to bed. You can come over for breakfast tomorrow and see her again."

"I can, huh?" he said. "How about if I get her to sneak out her window and meet me? Roll the truck down the street with the lights off?"

"Did you do that?" Zoe asked.

"What, didn't everybody? Well, I did it until the night Mom showed up at the party and took me on out of there by the ear. I swear, she had radar."

"I always told him I had eyes in the back of my head," Raylene said. "He used to think I was kidding. And you're stalling," she told her son. "Out. Tomorrow."

He sighed pitifully. "All right. I'll come have breakfast with you, Professor. Let you know what I find out about the car, give you a ride back to town, figure out a plan."

"Oh," she realized. "My boots. If I'm staying the night."

"Uh . . ."

"They're in the trunk of my car. Could you . . . would you mind getting them for me? If the car's still there, and it's on your way? Because otherwise, I mean, it's snowing."

"Sure thing." He got up, and she rose with him, walked him to the front door, then stood and waited as he put on his own boots, grabbed his coat off its hook.

"I wanted to say thanks," she told him. "For everything. I don't think I've been grateful enough."

"Oh, I don't know," he said, shrugging into the coat. "I think you've said that word about five times tonight. And tell you the truth, I'm a little tired of it."

"I know," she said, not sure what to do with her hands. "That's just how people are here. But I'm still grateful."

"Well, no," he said. "That's not exactly it. But tell you what. We can talk about that tomorrow, too."

He stood, taller than ever in his boots, and looked down at her, and surely there wasn't enough air in this room. He raised a hand to her cheek, gave her a sweet smile that had none of his usual cockiness.

"Thanks for wearing the red sweater," he told her softly. "You look real pretty. Can I say right here that I'm looking forward to tomorrow?"

"You can say it," she said. Because so was she.

He bent and kissed her cheek. His lips, his hand awakened a response everyplace he touched, and she leaned into him a little.

"Damn, Professor," he said, his thumb stroking over her cheek, his fingers in her hair. "You do bad things to me."

"Oh, yeah?" she managed. "Does that mean tomorrow's off?"

He kissed her lips this time, just a brush of his mouth over hers. "Oh, no," he said, standing back again, dropping his hand at last. "Tomorrow's not off. No way."

A CRYSTALLINE WORLD

Zoe lay in the old-fashioned heavy wooden double bed, covered by a warm down comforter and an embroidered white quilt that she suspected had been fashioned by a long-ago hand in a more patient time, and tried to sleep.

Not a sound, not a single beam of light to disturb her, and she was nothing but safe here. But despite her exhaustion, and no matter how firmly she closed her eyes and concentrated on her breathing, the rest she sought eluded her. Her whirling mind simply wouldn't settle, insisting on ping-ponging back and forth over the day's events.

Two lectures. The presentation that, this morning, had loomed so large, relegated now to a fleeting thought. The terrifying drive through the darkness, the certainty of danger, the crash. The knowledge that he was coming for her, that she had to save herself. The panic, and then the weak-kneed relief at recognizing Cal. His parents. The police. Amy. And Cal again. The pieces swirling like bits of confetti shaken in a jar into ever-changing patterns, refusing to calm.

It felt like hours, but was probably only thirty minutes before the pieces settled, before her mind slowed, before she fell into sleep.

All the same, her dreams were jerky, violent, full of shadows. She woke more than once, her heart racing every time, and lay staring into the dark, her body rigid. Again and again until, finally, from sheer exhaustion, she slept more deeply. And kept sleeping until the smell of frying bacon wafted into the bedroom, until movement in the house, sounds of activity outside, gradually roused her to consciousness.

She threw the covers back and got out of bed, stumbling a little over the overlong legs of her borrowed flannel pajamas, went to the window, and pulled the curtains. And then stood there a minute because it was beautiful.

She was looking out onto a sparkling world. Every tree, every bush and roof wore a thick mantle of white, the bright sun reflecting off each individual crystalline surface. The sky was an innocent baby blue that belied the previous night's storm, but the quiet of the morning was broken by the low growl of a snowplow, someplace not far away. The highway, maybe.

Something closer, too. The scrape of a metal shovel on concrete. She'd never heard that sound before moving to Idaho, but she knew it now. Stan was shoveling the walk.

She poked her head cautiously out of the bedroom into an empty hallway, ducked into the bathroom to clean up. She found herself wishing she had more than a lipstick in her purse, then chided herself for her vanity. Who cared if she was made up?

Well, she did. But she wasn't, so too bad. She got dressed again in her borrowed clothes, made her bed, and ventured into the kitchen to find Stan grinding coffee and Raylene flipping pancakes on an electric griddle.

"Sorry," Zoe said. "I guess I overslept."

"Nothing to be sorry about," Raylene said. "Nothing in the world to rush for."

Well, except a couple of upcoming lectures to review, some labs to plan, grades to enter. But those could wait a couple of hours, surely. Her perspective had shifted quite a bit overnight.

"Go tell Cal that breakfast is ready, will you?" Raylene asked, opening the oven and adding a few more pancakes to a platter.

"Oh." The scraping was continuing, she realized. Cal was shoveling his parents' walk, and she had to smile a little at the thought. It was just so . . . sweet.

She found her boots in the entryway, because he'd stopped and picked them up for her. She got herself outfitted, stepped out the front door into that dazzling light, blinking against the bright white of it. And then couldn't help jumping back as a big brown dog bounded toward her with a woof.

Cal turned at the sound, tossing a shovelful of snow along the way. "Junior!" he called.

The dog stopped in his tracks only feet from Zoe, his long, whiplike tail waving, and turned his heavy head back to Cal.

"He's friendly," Cal told her. "To friendly people. You scared of dogs?"

"No," she said faintly. "No," she added a little more strongly, putting a cautious hand out to the dog. He gave it a sniff, then bounded back across the yard to Cal at a whistle, spurning the shoveled walk.

"He gets all frisky in the snow," Cal said. "Thinks he's a puppy."

"What kind is he?" He wasn't beautiful, that was for sure. Plenty big, mud-brown, short-haired, and ungainly, he didn't look exactly purebred to her inexpert eye.

"US Grade A certified mutt," Cal said, confirming her suspicions. "Junior Jackson." He gave the dog a thump that set his tail whipping furiously. "I'd tell you he was my best friend, but it sounds too pathetic, so I'll just tell you he's my dog. How you doin'? Sleep okay?"

"Not entirely," she admitted, pulling her jacket more tightly around her against the chill. It was colder when the sun shone, she'd already found. The insulating power of cloud cover, of course.

"Bad dreams, huh?"

"Some."

"I guess that's not a surprise. But hey. Everything looks better in the daylight."

"Oh," she remembered, and laughed. "I'm supposed to tell you that breakfast is ready. Since you've obviously been working hard for it."

◆ ◆ ◆

"So what are you two doing this morning?" Raylene asked when they were sitting around the kitchen table again, and Zoe was eating a breakfast that was going to take a whole lot to work off.

Cal took a sip of coffee, his hand looking bigger than ever wrapped around the white ceramic mug.

She was getting gooey looking at his *hand*. She had to stop this.

"Well, eventually," he said, "I'm going to be giving the professor a ride on back to her place. Vern says you've got some damage, like we thought," he told her. "Maybe bent the frame. Sorry."

"Oh." She forgot all about his hand, and the bite of pancake threatened to stick in her throat. "That sounds bad."

"Not great. What's your insurance like?"

She sighed. "Not good enough. Old car."

"You're probably still going to be better off repairing than replacing," he said. "Long as there's nothing else wrong with it."

"No," she said automatically. "No. It's fine. I'll get it fixed."

"Friends-and-family rate," he reminded her. "Won't be that bad, I don't think." She didn't miss the look his parents exchanged. *Had* Cal paid part of it? She should care. She should object. "But meanwhile," he said while she was still trying to work up to it, "it was so pretty driving over here, I thought we should go snowshoeing. Take your mind off the bad stuff."

"Snowshoeing?" she asked blankly, her mind still on her car, and the bill. "I don't know how to snowshoe."

"Do you know how to walk?"

"Of course I do."

"Then you know how to snowshoe. And besides, all those calories in that bacon and pancakes? What were you planning to do about those?"

"Cal!" his mother exploded.

Zoe was laughing a little, though. "And here I was afraid you were going to charm me today."

"What, that wasn't charming?"

"Telling me that I'm eating too much and had better get some exercise? No, oddly enough. Not so much."

"Was that what I was saying? Funny, I was thinking just the opposite. Thinking how good you look, and wondering how I could talk you into spending a little more time with me so I could look at you some more."

In front of his parents. He'd said that in front of his *parents*, was smiling at her like he meant it, and he was melting her as surely as sunlight melted snow.

She did her best all the same. "You know what else I'm wearing? Besides your mom's sweater?"

"Uh . . . no," he said, his eyes sliding toward his mother. He was looking a little rattled now, taking a would-be casual sip of coffee.

"I'm wearing your mom's pants, and your mom's socks," she told him. "And underneath that? I'm wearing your mom's underwear."

He choked on his coffee, grabbed for a napkin, coughed for a full thirty seconds while his father pounded him helpfully on the back, his grin reaching all the way to his blue eyes.

"I've heard," Raylene said once Cal had got his breath back again, "that having two conflicting ideas in your head can paralyze a person."

"You see what I'm up against?" Cal asked, wiping his watering eyes with the napkin.

"Well, yeah," his dad said. "I think we pretty much do."

ONE HELL OF A WOMAN

Cal really did live in a farmhouse. Big and white, its solid lines softened by a wide covered porch that wrapped around two sides, with a porch swing hanging from chains that looked ready for lazy summer evenings. Set on a hill overlooking his fields, above a big metal shed that he called "the shop," and an actual red barn.

"It looks . . . old," she said when they came up the long driveway in his truck.

"You sound surprised." He pulled the truck into the garage, hopped out, and unclipped Junior from his spot in the bed. The dog leaped over the side, headed for the snowy yard, and romped as if he'd been tied up for a week, and Zoe slammed her own door and laughed at his antics.

"I told you," Cal said, leading the way across a shoveled walk and up the porch steps. "A farmer, in a farmhouse."

"I know, but I wasn't expecting it to actually be a . . . *farmhouse.*"

"What? A McMansion, cleverly disguised as a humble farmhouse?"

"Well . . ."

"Nope. Smack-dab in the middle of my fields, the house my great-grandfather built. The house I grew up in. The house I thought . . ." He stopped, shrugged, and held the door for her.

"That your kids would grow up in," she guessed, heading inside.

"Well, yeah. I did. Because I like it. It's a good place."

"But she didn't?" Zoe guessed.

"Nope. She didn't."

Zoe had to wonder at that. Because what she saw inside couldn't have been anything close to the original. The cherry cabinets and high-end German appliances in the kitchen weren't anything his parents had had done, she'd have bet money on it. It wasn't a McMansion, but it was a pretty great house. A comfortable house. She looked out through picture windows over curved lines of white and gray against the horizon of blue, punctuated by the red of the barn, and felt . . . peace. Even after the night before, even facing the week ahead. Peace.

Stomping up the hill in her snowshoes an hour later, she tried to tell him something of that. "This is a good place," she said. "I think anybody would be happy to live here. In all this quiet, all this space. All this peace."

"Ah," he said. "Well. Kind of a matter of opinion, I guess. One man's peace is another woman's . . . boredom."

She hadn't heard that note in his voice before. "Oh. I see."

He laughed, a sharp sound that she hadn't heard, either. "I sound bitter, don't I? Bad idea. Scratch that."

"No," she said. "I asked."

"You did, didn't you?" He stepped over a bank onto an unplowed road that wound up and around the butte, reached back with a gloved hand for one of hers. "Here."

His hand closed over hers, and he helped her onto the bank, set out beside her up the road. They walked for a while in silence, Junior romping ahead, racing back to circle around them before heading off again. Other than that, it was snow, and sky, and silence.

"But it is good here, isn't it?" Cal asked, glancing at her.

"Yes," she said. "It is."

One final turn in the road, and they were cresting the hill. Cal walked to the highest point and stopped, turned in a circle.

"Here you go," he said with satisfaction. "Home."

She turned herself, less gracefully than Cal had in the awkward snowshoes. She nearly overbalanced, and he reached a hand out for hers, then kept hold of it.

It was a sea. That was the only way to describe it. Wave after wave of rolling white, hills and dips delineated by the black stripes of roads, dotted with a farmhouse here, a cluster of outbuildings there, a barn, a stand of trees, all with their coating of white. And the blue of the low mountains to the east providing a backdrop to it all.

"Paradise," Cal said. She thought for a moment he was describing it, then realized he was pointing to the town, the university's water tower and domed stadium clearly visible in the distance. He turned 180 degrees, her hand still in his. "South. That's Fulton, and the grade down there"—he pointed to the canyon—"going on down to Union City."

The road she'd driven the night before. She shivered a little, and he felt it, looked down at her.

"Where did I go off?" she asked.

"Right down there." He pointed to the spot on the highway.

"I was close to your farm, then, because isn't that where we came from?"

"Yep. Lucky thing."

"Yes," she said. "It was."

"Don't worry," he told her. "I know that's easy for me to say, but we'll figure this thing out. Greg's a lousy cop, I'd bet money, but Jim isn't. And you and I are pretty smart."

"So we're going to crack the case? The two of us?"

"We're going to ride Jim's tail until he does. We'll put it like that."

"And meanwhile?"

"Yeah. Meanwhile. What would you think," he said, his casual tone immediately setting off her alarm bells, "about staying with my folks for a while?"

"With your *parents*?"

"Why not? You'd be safe there. They're both around a fair amount."

"Why on earth would they want to do that?"

He looked at her, smiled a little. "You really can't think of an answer to that?"

The warmth she'd felt all morning, in contrast to the chill in the air, increased a little more at the look in his eyes. His hand was still around hers, and she withdrew her own on the pretext of adjusting her hat. *His* hat, a gray wool watch cap he'd loaned her. Nothing fancy, because there wasn't anything fancy about him. Just that strength, and how she wanted to relax into that, to rely on it.

"No," she said. "Thank you," she added hastily. "But I'm not even sure I'm in danger." And it would feel too weird.

"How would you be sure?" he asked. "Wait for him to break in? Not until we know more, and not without a plan for that. Not without a *good* plan."

"You know . . ." she said, and laughed a little. "You take ownership of every single situation you're in. Do you realize that?"

"Ownership, huh?" This time there was heat as well as warmth in his gaze, and she turned away again.

"I didn't mean that," she said, wishing she didn't sound as flustered as a high school girl with her crush. "I meant—"

"Yeah, I get it. I'm bossy. Check."

"I don't mean to sound ungrateful."

He sighed. "Would you stop with that word? I've got to tell you, I'm really hating it. So let's hear *your* plan instead. The one you've worked out for yourself to stay safe."

"All right." She was totally flustered now, but she struggled with herself, focused. "My plan is to call Rochelle and see if I can sleep on her couch for a week or so, until I can beef up the locks on my doors. See what your cousin turns up, if anything. What you said, an MO. See if there really is a predator out there, and make a plan based on that. A plan that's something other than running away."

"Because if he's done it once, he's done it more than that."

"Yes. He will have." She looked away, over those flowing contours, those peaceful rolling hills and valleys. "They always do it again. They do it because they enjoy it. I don't think rape is ever a one-time deal. And you could tell that what he did with Amy was planned. That was a pattern he was working." She rubbed her hands over her arms. "And maybe with me."

"We'll get moving again," he suggested.

She nodded, and he led the way down the hill.

"Sounds like you know," he said after a minute.

"What?"

"That they do it again. And you don't seem as . . . horrified as I'd have imagined about all this."

"*What?*" He didn't think she was *horrified*? "Are you kidding?"

"Whoa." He turned, waited for her to catch up, then started off again, next to her this time. "I mean that you haven't seemed surprised. Made me wonder if all that, the assault on campus thing . . ."

"The rape on campus thing," she said. "Call it what it is. It's always such belittling language, isn't it? 'Date rape.' 'Sexual assault.' Maybe if people said 'rape,' they'd take it seriously." She was getting worked up, and she stopped, took a breath. "Sorry. Not fair to take it out on you."

"So why?" he asked. "What happened to make you care so much? And how you were with me. Why?"

"How I was *what* with you?"

He gestured with his ski pole, and Junior, who always seemed to have one eye on him, bounded back, circled them, and, at some apparent signal Zoe couldn't read, took off again.

"That I was a jock," Cal said. "That you didn't like jocks. Not getting out of your car when you were in the ditch, not riding in my truck. All that. You don't have to tell me why, but I'd sure like a hint."

"That's what women do, though."

"Maybe," he said. "I mean," he went on hastily, "all right. I accept that. But I still think there's more, and I'd like to know what it is."

"You want to know if I was raped. Or if I just know people who were raped."

"Yeah," he said, his gaze steady on her. He had left her the trail groomed by their snowshoes on the way up, was breaking a new one beside her. "I do."

She debated for a minute. "No," she finally said. "It wasn't me. All that happened to me was the usual. I got better-looking, like I told you, in college, but I still thought of myself as a . . . Well, let's say that I was too flattered that anybody would notice me, and I made a few mistakes."

"Ah. Jocks."

"Yep," she said with a sigh. "Especially one jock. And walking by him a week later, hearing him say, 'Yeah, I nailed that bitch' to his buddies, and hearing them laugh? Call it a teaching moment."

"Ouch."

"Anyway, it happened, and I got over it. I got more cautious, and that's nothing but a good thing. But my roommate was raped. My best friend in college."

"By another jock," he guessed.

"Yes." She didn't want to talk about this, or think about it, but it had been coming to the surface more and more these past weeks. Well, of course it had. "We were freshmen," she said. "About Amy's age. Ten years ago. And the thing is—you'd never have known it, to look at him. He hid it, or maybe he didn't feel like he had to hide it, because he didn't think he was doing anything wrong. He had this total confidence. Like a . . . a god. Like you would have been."

"I wasn't a god."

If he didn't know, she couldn't tell him. "You know what I felt really bad about afterwards?" she asked him. "That I'd been jealous. He was in a history class with us, and we both had a crush on him, even though I tried not to. But he was so cool, so far above everybody else. Bigger, and better-looking, and so much hotter than all the other guys. Just like you."

"Except that I'm not that guy," Cal said. "And I never was."

"I know," she sighed. "I know, all right? But you asked."

"Yep. I did. So tell me. You both had a crush on him."

"We sure did. But he paid more attention to Holly. I thought it was because she was prettier. Now, I think it's because I was tougher."

"Bet you're right."

"Yeah. He started out asking to borrow her notes, because he was gone. For games, you know. Before long, she was copying them for him every time. So happy to do it, too. So happy for his attention. Which meant that the day he asked her to a party, she thought that was it, the big step, that she meant something to him, that it was going somewhere. Here he was, a junior, a football player, asking her out. It never occurred to either of us that the guy had never even asked her to have a cup of coffee. Had never done anything but take advantage of her. We should have known that. We should have noticed."

"She blamed herself for that? How was she supposed to know?"

She stabbed her poles into the snow. "I blamed myself. All right, she was dazzled. She was excited. But I should have seen. I wasn't dazzled. But I didn't realize until that year that men would just . . . lie. Flat-out lie, and use, and hurt. I mostly dated my friends, once I dated at all. I didn't know that some men would do . . . what they do."

She stopped, but he didn't say anything, and after a minute, she went on. "It was a frat party. I only found out the rest afterwards. She didn't come home until morning. I'd gone to breakfast, and when I came home, she was in the shower. The worst thing she could have done, not that it would have mattered. Not that anybody cared."

She turned to him, stopped on her snowshoes, and he stopped, too. "You know what he did? He kicked her out. She woke up not knowing where she was. The last she remembered, she'd been dancing with him, and she'd felt so woozy, and he'd put his arm around her, told her she needed to lie down. That was the last she knew until she woke up without her underwear, with him yelling at her to leave. She was crying, finding her way out again from his room in this big building, because she didn't even remember going up there, and some of the other guys were out there, and they were laughing at her. *Laughing.*"

"Because they were assholes," he said.

"All of them? There was nobody who had the guts to stand up and say, *This isn't right. I don't want to live with people like this.* Nobody?"

"I don't know," he said. "I'm not excusing it. But I think when you're young, it does take a lot of guts for a guy to speak up like that."

She started walking again. "Then I think they'd better get some guts," she said. "If they want to call themselves men."

"I think you're right."

She wasn't listening, though. "She didn't even know it had happened," she said, "until she realized she was hurting. She didn't know because she was *unconscious*. What kind of man wants to have sex with somebody who's unconscious?"

"A rapist."

"At least you get it."

"Of course I get it." He was frowning at her now. "That doesn't take a big stretch."

"She didn't even know how many of them it was. She didn't even know if it was just him. Can you imagine that?"

"No. I can't. So what happened? Did she report it?"

"Yes. Because I made her. And what do you think happened next?"

"I think," he said, "that they dropped it."

"You'd be wrong, then. They'd have to have taken it to drop it. They wouldn't even do that. Said there was no evidence. Because she couldn't remember. Because of that shower, although there probably wouldn't have been any evidence anyway."

"He'd have worn a condom," Cal guessed.

"Or they would have. Because she was . . . bruised. Badly. And isn't that evidence? Isn't that enough?"

"You'd think."

"And there she was, because she still had the class. I made her go. *She* was the one who deserved to be there, not him. So we went, and he walked in, and he *smiled* at her. Like it was funny. Like it was a joke."

"So what did you do?"

"How do you know I did something?"

"Oh, Professor, I know you did something. Don't let me down. Tell me what you did."

She laughed a little, shook her head. "You're right. I did. He was sitting there with his legs stretched out, taking up extra room, you know, all cool and casual. I walked over and stood over him. And he looked up at me and smiled some more and said, 'What?'"

"And what did you say?"

"I stopped a minute. I was nineteen, you see," she explained. "I was pretty idealistic. Kind of . . . fierce."

"I'll bet."

"I looked around at his friends, at his little cohorts. All the people who thought he was so cool. I said, 'You guys should feel real good. You should feel real proud. You're hanging out with a rapist. You're hanging out with somebody who raped an unconscious woman.'"

"Whoa. Then what?"

"Nobody said anything. Then somebody laughed, and I was just *burning*. I was *burning*. And he—the guy who did it—he said, 'You wish.'"

"Asshole."

"That's what I thought, later. At the time . . . I didn't think. I got that red mist, you know that thing?"

"Oh, yeah. I know that."

"And I slapped him."

"You didn't."

"Yep. I did. Right when the TA walked in. I belted him across the face. Hard. I mean, I really wound up and let him have it, snapped his head right around. He jumped up, started to go for me, and the TA grabbed him, and a couple other guys did, too, and somebody grabbed me. And I ended up in the dean's office, explaining myself."

"I'll bet you did."

"You bet right. They dropped it. But they dropped Holly, too. They dropped her right out. They wanted a rapist more than they wanted a dean's-list student. Because the rapist could play football."

"She quit?"

"She transferred. She went to a Cal State, and that was just *wrong*. The whole thing was so wrong. I've never forgotten it. And as a professor . . . I know how much it happens, how much it *still* happens, and it makes me sick. I hear about it from my students. And still, girls blame themselves, feel so ashamed that they went to that party, that they drank the punch. They blame themselves, when the guys have *planned* it. When it's some kind of sick game to them." She was shaking a little now, the momentary humor gone. "And what I want to know is," she demanded, "where's the shame for the guys who sit around and watch it happen? Who laugh about it? Who know about it and do nothing? Where's their shame?"

"I don't know," he said. "I don't. And now I see why you care so much about Amy."

"You can't learn when you feel unsafe. And that's not fair."

"Is it your job to keep them safe?"

"Of course it is. At least to help."

"Ah. And see how we came around to it?" he asked. "That must mean it's my job, too. To help Amy, and to help you. And can I say this one thing, Professor?"

"Well." She laughed a little, shook her head, and started walking again. "I guess you can, if you can get a word in edgewise. And you haven't done anything wrong. In fact, you've done everything right. I do get that, by the way. I do. But go ahead. Please. Say your one thing."

"Here it is, then," he said. "I think you've got all the guts those guys didn't. I think you're one hell of a woman. One hell of a teacher. One hell of a friend."

She stopped again, looked at him. "You do?"

"Oh, Dr. Zoe. You bet your ass I do."

SOME OTHER GUY

"Well . . . thanks," she told him, looking surprised. "Thanks."

She didn't even know it. She didn't even know everything she was. He could swear that he'd been through every emotion there was in the past eighteen hours. And still, it was only a shadow of everything she'd felt, and look how she was holding up.

He was impressed by her, yeah. You could put it that way.

They walked the rest of the way in silence, turned in at the mailbox, passed the shop, and started up the track they'd made beside the long drive.

"Got you cold out here," he said, looking down at the pink of her cheeks, the reddened tip of her straight little nose. At his gray watch cap, which shouldn't have looked so cute over the swing of her dark hair. "But it was good. Thanks for going with me."

"No," she said. "Thank *you*. Last night, I mean in the night—I thought I'd never relax again, and you've let me do it. Being out here, being with you, has helped. Even talking about it has helped. So—thank you."

"No problem. How about a cup of coffee before we head back to my folks'?" And maybe, in the warmth of the kitchen, they could have some more emotions. Some quiet time. Some good time.

"Sounds good," she said, stomping up the drive with determination, her arms swinging the poles.

Junior had been trotting a little ahead of them, and now he barked, alerted by something up ahead. Cal looked up, saw the rear end of the car around the edge of the garage. A little black SUV.

Nobody he knew, except it almost had to be. Nobody in it, nobody on the porch, so the person was either walking around, which wasn't likely in the cold, or in the house.

It was a Mercedes, he realized as they got closer. Who did he know with a Mercedes SUV? Nobody around here, that was for sure. Some football buddy, somebody in trouble. Not the time he would have chosen for them to show up.

"Whose car?" Zoe asked, following his gaze.

He shrugged. "Don't know. Guess we'll find out."

"You don't think it's him, do you?" She was half-turned already, looking set to take off down the road, like she was going to snowshoe the whole three miles to Fulton.

"No," he said. "Can't be."

"Why not?" She was still holding back, any ease she'd managed to find gone, and he hated that.

"Not the right rig, for one. And Junior." He pointed a ski pole at him. The dog's tail was wagging, and he had jumped onto the porch, was letting go with another bark or two. "Whoever it is, he's all right."

"How does the dog know?"

"The dog knows. Besides, I'm here. Between me and Junior, you're safe."

He bent to unhook his snowshoes, saw her hesitation before she crouched down to remove her own. He waited for her to finish, took her equipment from her, hung everything up in the garage, then walked with her around the side of the house, scraped the snow off his boots while she did the same.

He opened the door to the mudroom, unlaced the boots and tugged them off, and was shrugging out of his jacket when the door to the kitchen opened, and he saw why he hadn't recognized the car.

"Hi, Cal," she said.

He froze with one arm in and one out of his jacket. Forced himself to move again, to finish taking it off, pulled his hat from his head, and hung them both up on the hook next to Zoe's before he answered.

"Hey," he said, his voice flat as the prairie. "Jolie."

◆ ◆ ◆

She looked perfect, as always. Gray woolen trousers, boots, some kind of sweater that he'd bet was cashmere, and designer, too, the way it wrapped around, buckled at the side to highlight her narrow waist, then spilled over the curve of her hips. In a shade of blue that matched her eyes and made a brilliant foil for the expertly highlighted blonde hair that fell in glossy waves to below her shoulders.

Absolutely perfect, and like absolutely nothing he wanted to see.

"I'd say come inside," he said. "But you're already there."

It truly hadn't occurred to her, he could tell, that she couldn't just walk right into his house and sit on down.

"Zoe," he said, "this is Jolie. My ex-wife."

"Oh," Zoe said, the uncertainty right there to see in her eyes. She smoothed a hand over her hair, rumpled by the hat she'd pulled off, and he wanted to tell her not to worry. When it came to perfect, it seemed he didn't care for it all that much anymore.

"I could . . ." She looked around wildly.

She could what? Nowhere to go.

"Nothing Jolie has to say to me that you can't hear." He headed toward the kitchen door. Jolie stepped back to let them by, and Zoe padded in behind him in her stockinged feet, Junior bringing up the rear.

The dog wagged a time or two, went to his bed in the corner of the dining room, and settled himself. His head was high, everything about him alert, sensing the tension in the room.

"Sit down," Cal said, indicating the round oak dining table that had belonged to his grandma and grandpa. The one he'd grown up with, that had expanded to fit everybody who could cram in around it at every holiday dinner. The one Jolie had wanted to replace with "something from this *century*, at least."

He'd put his foot down at that, one of his few hard lines, and she'd showed him the cold shoulder for a week.

"I'll just . . . go upstairs," Zoe said. She didn't wait for an answer, fled up the narrow staircase without so much as that cup of coffee. Hell of a way to get her up to the bedroom floor.

Cal sat, waited for Jolie to sit, too, sighed, and looked at her. "You in trouble?"

"What? Of course not."

"Then why are you here?"

"Maybe I just wanted to see you." She tried out her sweet, coaxing smile, the one that had used to work so well on him. "Is that such a crime? Maybe I missed you, and I wanted to see how you were doing. We were together a long time, weren't we? You can't just wipe that out like it didn't exist."

"We're divorced," he said, his mouth barely moving. "You're with Ray. You don't get to see me."

She traced the grain of the wood with one perfectly manicured fingernail. "No. I'm not. With Ray."

"And see," he said, "I don't even care."

"Cal." She put her hand on his sleeve, and he stared down at it, then up at her face. The blue eyes were beseeching now, a few tears shining in her eyes, one translucent drop sliding down a sculpted cheekbone. "I made a mistake. Didn't you ever make a mistake?"

He shoved his chair back, stood up, and leaned against the breakfast bar behind him. Got some distance. "Yeah," he said. "I made a mistake."

"You mean marrying me. That wasn't a mistake. We were in love."

"I thought so." All he wanted was for her to leave. "Until the day you took off and went to live with my teammate. What did he do? Cancel your credit cards?"

Her face twisted. "That's cruel."

"Yeah, right." Like she hadn't been. "So what did he do, that I finally look better to you?"

"He . . . he hurt me."

"He *hurt* you? You mean he hit you?" The rage was there, just like that. Ray had stolen his wife, and then he'd hurt her? Cal didn't love her anymore. But he couldn't stand the thought of Ray hitting her. Of anybody hitting her.

A few more tears were trickling down her cheeks. "No. Not that. But everything else he could do, he did. And it made me realize"—she took a deep, shaky breath, wiped away the tears—"that I hurt you, too. But now I know. I know how you felt. I get it now, and I'm so sorry."

She never got splotchy and messed up the way other women did when she cried. He'd always hated to see her cry, had been willing to do anything to make it stop. Now, he wondered if she'd known that.

"He cheated on me on just about every single road trip," she went on, her voice trembling. "He made sure I knew it, too, because I kept finding these receipts that he didn't even bother to throw away. He wouldn't call me, and then I'd find texts on his phone, and he took a *call* once, out in a restaurant. Stepped out and took a call from somebody else, right there. Can you believe that?"

"Well, yeah," Cal said. "He's a cheater. He cheated *with* you. Why was it such a shock that he'd cheat *on* you?"

"He barely even tried to hide it," she went on, hardly listening, because she wouldn't want to hear that. Ray hadn't been the only cheater. "It's like he thought he was *entitled* to it. That it was all right, and I should just put up with it because that was how it was."

"Yeah," Cal said. "I'm sure he did. This something you're just figuring out now? That not all pro athletes are upstanding citizens or great husbands?"

"But you were," she said. "You always were."

"And look how much good that did me."

You're boring, she had flung at him, there near the end. *I thought you were special, but all you want is a boring, ordinary little life. What's the point of getting it all if you're just going to be boring?*

He hadn't known what to say. He'd wanted a bigger life when he'd had it. And then he hadn't had it. He'd hit bottom during the worst year of his life, had come back up again and had figured out that he could be happy with the farm, and his wife, and, someday soon, kids. With working hard and having a family, people to love who'd love him, too.

Maybe it wasn't a big life, but it was a good life. But she hadn't wanted it. She hadn't wanted him.

She was still talking. "He's not . . . he's not a nice person. He's not who I thought he was. He was so cold, and I thought, what have I done? I had something so good. Can't we get that back again? I know I made a mistake. But I hardly even knew what I was doing. It was too hard. The change . . . it was so *much*."

"You might have noticed that it was a bit much for me, too," he said. "Being as how I was the one with the career-ending injury and all. The one who had to give up the dream. You might have noticed that. But you didn't."

She didn't acknowledge that. "But maybe now," she said, "we could do it. It's been such a long year. Such a *hard* year, and I've realized how much I miss you. You can't just wipe out five years together, can you? And I thought . . . we've both changed, now. Maybe we could try again."

"You didn't happen to notice that I walked into the house with somebody else?"

"You mean . . . her?"

"Yeah," he said, not bothering to say that he'd barely kissed Zoe. It didn't matter, because this wasn't about Zoe, not really. "I mean her."

"Even so," she said, because of course she wouldn't think any other woman would stack up. Even now. "You and me? It was so good for those first years, Cal. It could be that good again."

He stood there, ankles and arms crossed, looked down into her beautiful face, and felt . . . nothing.

"You know what's crazy?" he said, almost to himself. "When you left, I would've taken you back. Even knowing what you'd done, I'd have taken you back and tried to work it out. But you know what I found out?"

"What?" she asked, and he could see the confusion. She'd really thought he could just forget everything that had happened? Really?

"I thought I missed you," he told her. "And then I realized all the things I didn't miss at all. I didn't miss you sitting with me at a high school football game, hardly able to even pretend that you cared. I didn't miss you not talking to my parents at Sunday dinner. I didn't miss you looking at my old friends like they were some kind of ignorant hicks with dirt under their fingernails, just because they don't play in the NFL, just because they drive pickups, when any one of them is worth ten of Ray McCarthy. I didn't miss you hating my hometown, and my family, and my friends, and my job, and my whole damn *life*."

He forced himself to stop. There was no point.

"I didn't *marry* a farmer, though," she said urgently. "Can't you see?" She was standing up, coming to him, putting her hands on his folded forearms, and he went poker-straight.

"Can't you see how hard it was?" she begged, leaning into him, trying so hard to work it, to use it. "I married a pro football player. That's the man I fell in love with. I married a *star*. And then you decide—*you* decide—that we're going to live here, and you want me to be some farm wife? Drive a . . . truck or something? Can vegetables and plow the garden? What was I supposed to do?"

He took hold of her upper arms, put her away from him, and took a step toward the door. "I had to have a job," he said, keeping his voice even with an effort. "A man needs a job. And then I remembered I had one, and it was here. You could have gotten a job, too. You could have gone back to school, studied anything you wanted. You could have done just about anything you wanted, anything except what you did. You could even have had a baby. I was all ready to help you have your dream, whatever your dream was. That was all I wanted. But you didn't have a dream. Nothing but . . ." He stopped. What was her dream? He didn't even know. Or maybe he didn't want to know.

"A baby, right," she said, the scorn right there for him to see. "I know that was what you wanted. That was *all* you wanted."

"So what's the real reason you're here?" he asked, feeling so tired. What did it matter? It was dead and gone. Not even worth talking about. "You spend all my money already? Can't find anybody to support you?"

"That's not fair," she whispered, looking so hurt again.

Once, all he'd wanted to do was protect her. Once.

"I think that's just exactly fair," he said. "You need a life? Go get a life. You need money? Go get a job. Maybe if you'd ever gotten up at six to drive a combine during harvest, around those fields until ten at night, day after day after day for weeks on end, you'd have a clue how to do that. It's called hard work, and it's what the rest of the world does."

"You were always so sweet," she said, sounding genuinely sad. "Always. What happened to that? What happened to you?"

"You burned the sweet right out of me," he told her. "That's what. You took my heart, you took my trust, and you ripped them up. I gave them to you, and you smashed them like they were nothing. That's what happened to me."

He walked to the door, pulled it open, let the cold air rush in, then stood back and watched her get the message. Finally.

"And now," he said, "guess what? I'm over you. Got my heart growing back a little. Trying to find some trust again. Maybe even a little bit of faith. Maybe I'll get there, one of these days. But I'll get there without you. You want a better life? Go look somewhere else. Go find some other guy."

COWBOY UP

Zoe had wanted to listen, of course she had. The look on Cal's face when the door had opened . . . she hadn't been able to tell if that was pain, or anger, or just surprise and embarrassment. She could only think of a few reasons for Cal's ex-wife to show up at his house, and none of them seemed like good news.

She hadn't known where to go, just that she didn't belong there in the middle of it, so she'd gone upstairs. Now she stood in the hallway, irresolute. What now?

She could still hear them, barely. "I made a mistake," she heard Jolie say, and that was it. That was enough, and she started opening doors. She couldn't stand here and listen to Cal . . . what? Whatever. Whatever he did. And she didn't want to think about why.

The first door was to a big bedroom at the front of the house, with windows looking out over the shop, the barn, the fields beyond. An old rocking chair in a corner, with another of those old quilts folded over its back. *Double wedding ring*, she thought automatically. A dresser, a king-size bed with heavy corner posts, a door that presumably led to a master bath. The bed was neatly made, but covered with nothing more elegant than a heavy brown bedspread. Cal's bedroom, obviously, and she shut the door again hastily.

The next room was an office. Desk, computer, printer, filing cabinets. Paperwork neatly stacked in a corner of the desk. Also none of her business, and she shut that door, too.

At last, a bathroom. Guest bathroom, she guessed, since it looked unused. More high-end fittings, stonework and tile, the best of everything. Nothing on the countertop, no toothbrush by the sink.

She glanced into the mirror, recoiled in shock, and began a hasty finger-comb of her hair. She'd looked like *that,* was wearing his mother's sweater and stretch pants, and he was down there talking to a woman who looked like she could have gotten a modeling contract just by walking into an office and announcing that she was ready for one?

Of course, there wasn't much point in even trying, because she was never going to compete with that face, that body. She did her best anyway, though.

She finally found a guest bedroom, went in and sat on the bed, looking down at her stockinged feet, wiggling her toes against the oval of braided rug that stuck out from under the bed, and waited, wondering what to do next, and why it mattered so much. How she'd know when it was safe to go downstairs again, what she would say when she did.

The first question was answered by the sound of a car engine starting up outside. She got up, looked out the window, and saw the black SUV reversing, bumping into the snowbank behind it, the tires spinning a little as the driver gunned the engine, then the car shooting forward, barely missing the side of the garage, and heading down the drive a little too fast.

She took a breath, ran her hands over her hair again, and went back downstairs.

He was at the dining room table, sitting there looking down at nothing. Junior was off his bed, lying under the table, his head next to Cal's foot.

Cal turned his head at her entrance, and the bleak expression on his face made her feet stop moving.

"What happened?" she asked, not at all sure he'd want to tell her.

"She wanted to come back." He'd turned away again, was staring out the front window, out into the fields. Out toward the road where she'd driven away.

"But you said no," she said cautiously. "I'm guessing."

He laughed, a sharp sound. "Hell, yeah, I said no."

She stood there a moment more. "Would you like a cup of coffee?" she asked.

He didn't seem to take it in for a moment. "Yeah," he finally said. "Yeah. Sure."

He got up, but she waved him down. She could see the machine sitting on the counter. Nothing fancy. Basic.

"Yeah," he said, following the direction of her gaze. "She took the espresso machine. Surprise. Doesn't matter, because I don't like fancy coffee anyway. Coffee and filters are in the cupboard above the machine. Thanks."

She found them, stuck the paper basket filter into the machine, filled the carafe at the farmhouse sink. She was guessing who had been behind the kitchen remodeling, too. She opened cupboards, found the mugs, milk in the fridge.

"Sugar? Milk?" she asked.

"No, thanks," he said. "Black."

She brought it to him, sat down next to him, but not too close, and took a sip. And waited, because she didn't know what else to do.

"You know what?" he asked her after a minute. "I got to say all the things I wanted to for so long. All the things I'd rehearsed. All the things I wished I could say, all those nights when I was lying there on my back in the dark. I got exactly what I wanted back then. Her coming back to me, asking me to give her another chance. I got to tell her no, and I got to tell her why. I thought, if I could just make the speech, I'd feel better. I'd win again."

"And it was . . ." she said cautiously. It didn't look like it had been anything great.

That laugh again. "And it stunk. It hurt."

"It still hurts, then. That she left."

He looked at her this time. "No. It hurts that I don't care. That I looked at her and I didn't feel anything. Anything except wanting her gone. When she walked down the aisle to me, looking so beautiful, I felt like I'd won the lottery. And all of that . . ." He made a sweeping motion with his arm, dropped it into his lap again. Helpless. Final. "It's just . . . gone. And the worst part is, I don't even know if it was ever real. It's like everything she said, everything I felt, everything I thought she felt—it's gone. Everything I thought was true was a lie."

He stopped, ran his hand through his hair. "And, so what? It's all over now. I'm guessing you know why we split."

"Well, yes," she admitted. "Rochelle told me."

"Turns out she didn't want a farmer, and I'm not even sure she ever wanted me. Not the man I am. That's what hurts, being so wrong, being so blind, being . . . fooled. It wasn't the money. I didn't care. I told my lawyer not to fight that hard. Just get it done. Just get her gone. Just let it be over. She got half of everything I'd made, everything I'd worked for, and I didn't even care. But you know what she kept saying today?"

"No, what?" She was trembling. It hurt, watching him, hearing him. It hurt her own heart.

"That she'd made a mistake. A *mistake.* Like she'd bought size four pants instead of size two or something. She didn't make a mistake. She made a choice. I should have said that, I guess. But . . ." He sighed, took a final swallow of coffee. "What did I just say? That it didn't matter what I said, because it's over, and there's no point in any of this. Cowboy up and move on."

He stood up, took his cup and hers to the sink, rinsed them out, and stuck them into the dishwasher. "I'd better give you a ride back to town so you can grade those papers or whatever," he said, coming back to lean against the breakfast bar. "Vern said he'd get to your car first thing. You should have it Monday, Wednesday at the latest. You okay driving back and forth with Rochelle until then? Because otherwise, I could come get you."

She could feel him closing off, and she didn't stand up to leave. "Of course I am. But that's it? We're all done here? You get to be upset for ten minutes, and then it's 'cowboy up and move on'?"

"What's the alternative? Wallow in it a little more? Sit around and drink beer and talk to the dog? I tried that. No, thanks. I'll do what I've always done. Get back to work and get over it."

She did stand up, then. "You could ask a friend for a hug."

"A *hug*?"

"Yeah," she said, her throat dry. "Don't cowboys hug?" She stepped closer, put her arms around him, and held him. Felt him standing rigid for a moment, then his arms coming around her, pulling her tight. She felt how much he needed somebody to touch, and was glad she could be the one to do it. That she could be here for him.

Her head was against his chest, under his chin, and he felt so good. Warm, and strong, and so solid.

"Jolie was a fool," she said quietly. "It doesn't matter what you are. It matters *who* you are. If she couldn't see that, if she couldn't see you, she was a fool."

A REAL GOOD HUG

She could feel the tension in him softening, the deep breath he took, the slow, controlled way he let it out. She stood quietly and held him, and waited.

She waited, and after a while, she realized that he wasn't soft at all, and her heart stopped beating for a moment, and everything else started up, despite everything that had happened, all the emotion. Or maybe because of it.

The thrum. The sizzle. The heat.

He eased back from her, his hand coming up to frame her face, to tip her head back.

"This probably isn't the right time," he sighed. "But what the hell."

Another thud of her heart, and her lips had parted, because all she could see was his mouth, and her body wanted that mouth. She wanted it right now.

She got it. His lips descended on hers, softly at first. It was all soft, and slow, and patient, until her mouth opened and his hand was clenched in her hair.

He deepened the kiss then, his lips and tongue still in no hurry, still exploring, starting a slow rhythm that told her what else he could do. Everything he could do, everything he wanted to do. The fire was licking down into her breasts, her belly, into every warm, sweet spot that needed his touch, and she pushed up against him, trying to get closer. Trying to get more.

She was trying to move forward, but he was moving her backward. His other hand, the one that wasn't still fisted in her hair, had been on her lower back, holding her tight. Now he sent it lower, stroking her curves, and she gasped into his mouth at the sensation.

An upward jerk, and he was lifting her, setting her on the edge of the table. Her legs parted with a will of their own, because they wanted him between them.

"You're too small for me," he said. "I need you up here where I can reach you." He had a hand in her hair again, his thumb stroking over her cheek, and she was leaning into it. He still wasn't rushing her, and she found herself wishing he would. That he would hurry.

"Or maybe," she said, doing her best to curb her body's headlong plummet, "you're too big for me."

A husky laugh at that. "Aw, sweetheart. No such thing as too big. And I take it back. No such thing as too small, either. Just sweet and fine and so damn hot. We'll fit just right. You'll see."

He was finally moving closer, putting a hand on each thigh, gently moving them farther apart so he could get there, right where she needed him to be. She could feel the size and the heat of him even through the layers of fabric separating them, and her own hands had gone to his hips, then had grown bold and were holding him to her, pulling him closer, because she needed him to be closer. She needed him to be *there*.

He closed his eyes and groaned a little. "You're killing me here, darlin'."

"Then kiss me some more," she said, loving that she could do that to him. "Because you're killing me, too."

She found out why he'd put her on the table. So he could give her more of those long, slow kisses. So he could nibble, and lick, and tease her mouth. So he could slide a hand up, when she thought that he never would, that she would explode if he didn't do it, and close it over her breast.

And that was when the teasing began in earnest. His hand stroked, still so slowly. Fingers, and palm, and best of all, his talented thumb. Every touch was a lick straight to her core, like she was connected that way, like there was a wire going right to that one sweetest spot. She was hanging on to his broad shoulders for dear life, moaning a little, and when his mouth trailed across her cheek, found the side of her neck, all gentle lips and barest graze of teeth, she was squirming. A strangled moan escaped her, and his mouth wasn't quite so gentle anymore. He was biting a little, moving down her throat, teasing out a response in every place he touched.

She was gasping, and when he got a hand under her sweater, touched bare skin at her waist, she jumped.

"I need to touch you," he told her. "So if you don't want it . . . tell me."

She wasn't going to tell him that. But he was asking. He was *asking*.

"I want it," she managed to tell him, and she felt him sigh. With relief, she thought, and pleasure, the same pleasure he was giving her.

She should be touching him, too, she realized fuzzily. Not just sitting here letting him do whatever he wanted, and not giving him anything in return. And then she forgot all about it, because his hand was leaving a trail of heat all the way up her side, all the way to the lace of her bra, sliding over the pebbled nipple and drawing another jump and gasp out of her.

"So sweet," he murmured, and he was kissing her again, his hand still touching her through the lace, the extra friction of the material only adding to the pleasure. His other hand was holding her lower body tight against his, his hips beginning a slow grind, and she was whimpering into his mouth, spiraling up farther with every stroke.

"I need more," he told her. "I need it now." He traced the lace edge of her bra over and over again with his fingertips, the light contact over the swell of her breast at once frustrating and so incredibly stimulating. And then, when she thought she couldn't stand it another minute, he slipped his hand inside and touched her.

Hard hand on soft, warm flesh. Stroking, circling, pinching. Teasing and playing until she was writhing, until she was calling out.

"Please," she begged. "Please. I need . . ."

"I know you do," he said. "That's why we're going to let you do it."

He stood back a pace, and she reached to pull him close again, because she had to feel that slow, grinding pressure. She *had* to.

He smiled a little painfully. "I know you need it, sweetheart. But I've got something even better for you." He put a hand out, traced the center seam of her pants, up and down, over and over. His fingers moving slowly at first, still not rushing it. And then, finally, when she thought she'd die if he didn't, he slipped that hand inside, found the spot, began a slow, steady circling, even as his other hand stayed on her breast, still moving inside her bra.

She was caught in it, right there against his hand. This was all there was, and it was everything.

"Feels so good, baby," he told her. "Feels so good."

She was bucking, higher and higher, his hand was moving harder and faster, and the pressure was building. She was so close. So close.

"We're going to do it just like this," he told her. "Just this hard. So come on. Show me how much you want that. Let me feel it."

She was there, shaking, crying out, jerking into his hand, and his other hand slid around to her back, held her there for him during the endless seconds it lasted. Until the spasms slowed, until she slumped, panting and spent.

He stepped close again and kissed her, long, drugging, and deep, while her chest heaved and her breath came hard.

"Damn," he said when he came up for air, his hand smoothing down her back, soothing her. "You're the best thing I've ever had on this table. You're so sweet. That's so good."

"I just meant to . . ." she managed to say, "give you a hug."

"And you did." His smile did something to her. Everything about him did way too much to her. "You gave me a real good hug. Made me feel a whole lot better."

"We need to . . ." she said, feeling shy, which was ridiculous.

"Yeah," he said. "We sure do. Need a bed for that, I think, don't you? This first time?" His hand was back on her face now, and she rubbed her cheek against it, loving it.

Then it was dropping from her, and he was stepping back, pulling her off the table by the hips and setting her on her feet. "Damn it to *hell.*"

"What?" She didn't have to wonder for long, though, because Junior had got up from his bed with a *woof* and a wag of his tail, and a white pickup was pulling into the space beside the garage, the space where Jolie's SUV had sat.

Her hands went to her hair, smoothing it even as he tugged her sweater down a little more securely, then reached down into his jeans, gave himself a quick adjustment, and grimaced.

"My mom will tell you," he said, "that when Luke was born, I asked her to take him back, because I didn't want a brother. And I don't want one now."

The door to the truck opened, and sure enough, Luke was heading around the rear of it, jumping up the steps onto the porch, giving his boots a scrape on the mat, and coming right on inside.

"Hey, Cal," he began, then stopped at the sight of Zoe. "Well, hi there," he said slowly, a grin starting on the handsome face. "Didn't realize you had company, Cal."

"Yeah," he growled. "Obviously."

"Um . . ." Zoe said. "We were just snowshoeing. I mean, not now," she hurried on. "I mean we were. Before. And Cal was about to give me a ride home. Because my car's in the shop."

"Uh-huh," Luke said. "And see, I'm not actually illuminated by all that. But never mind. I just came by to borrow your chainsaw, Cal. Dorothy Taylor next door had a tree down in that storm."

"Yeah," he said.

"Okay if I take a can of gas, too?"

"Okay if you take the whole damn shop," Cal said. "Just go."

Luke scratched his cheek, tried without much success to hide a grin. "All righty, then. I'll just let you two finish your . . . committee work, and head on out. See you at the meeting next week, Zoe."

"See you," she said weakly.

ALL GOD'S CHILDREN

"So," he said when Luke had finally gotten out of there, about one second before Cal would have given in to the urge to help him along his way, "where were we? I think I was kissing you. And I think we were about to go upstairs." He sure hoped they were, anyway.

"Uh . . ." She looked uncomfortable, and his heart sank. "I'm not sure it's a good idea. I mean," she hurried on, seeing the look on his face, "it *feels* like a good idea. But I wasn't going to do this. I wasn't going to do it at all. And then I did, we did, but I still . . ."

He perched himself on the edge of a barstool and folded his arms. "I knew it," he said with resignation. "Go on, tell me."

"I'm just so . . ." She was looking anxious, and here was one more emotion for today, because now he was the one wanting to give her a hug.

He sighed. "Zoe. Just tell me. It's all right. I'm a big boy. I can be disappointed, and I can get over it. And besides," he said, trying to make her smile a little again, "it's that ulterior motive. So tell me, baby. Tell me what's holding you back, and if I can make it better, I will. If you need more time, we'll take it. I'm not going anywhere."

She was leaning back against the table, struggling against the tears and not quite making it, and he *was* giving her a hug, and keeping it at that, too. Which deserved at least a medal.

"I'm not usually nearly so high-maintenance," she said, pulling away, trying to laugh, wiping at her cheeks with the heels of her hands. "It's been too much emotion today, I guess. And last night. Being so scared, and glad to have you with me, and then so sad for you, and now this. Too much. Too many feelings."

"Funny," he said, going into the living room and coming back with the tissue box, pulling one out and handing it to her. "I was just thinking the same thing."

She blew her nose, wiped her eyes. "Really?" She sniffed again. "You?"

"Yeah. Me." She did get messy when she cried. Her nose was red, her eyes were puffy, and that was all right, too. She was real, had her heart right out there on her sleeve for him to see, and he loved knowing that he was seeing it. "Come on," he coaxed. "Just tell me."

"It's that . . ." she began. "It's that I don't know where we are, and this isn't what I planned, and you're . . . not the kind of guy I'm used to. And now, bam, it happened, and then Jolie . . . I like you so much, though, even so, even knowing all that, and that's making me stupid. I can *feel* it making me stupid right now, just looking at you. How I'm not making any sense, and you're looking at me like I'm . . . nuts."

"No," he said. "I'm not. Go on."

"If I go upstairs with you now, what am I doing?" she asked him, her face urgent, because she wasn't casual. She was never casual. "What are we doing here? I don't know, and it's all so fast, and I didn't even mean to do that, and I'm not sure you did, either. And everything that's happened. I'm not sure I'm making good decisions right now."

He leaned back again, frowned down at his feet. "Wow. That was a whole lot."

"Yeah." She laughed, although it didn't sound too convincing to him. "Sorry."

"If I said it was more than that," he said slowly, "if I said, yeah, I want it to be real. Would that be enough?"

"I don't know," she said. "I hope so. But maybe not today. And I'm sorry."

He sighed. "In other words, no. It wouldn't be enough." He shoved off his stool. "Come on, then. I'll give you a ride home. And," he said, trying another smile on her, "I'll ask you out again, too. You can bet on it. Even though you've messed me up bad already, every single time I've been with you. Even though I don't have a clue what's going on here, either."

She was smiling back. A little shaky, but a smile all the same. "I guess if I let you give me the orgasm of my life on your dining room table, I could go out with you. You think?"

"I guess you could," he said, the grin starting slow, then growing. "I won't make you a bunch of promises we're not ready for, and that you won't believe anyway. But I'll promise you this. If you think that was the orgasm of your life . . . I'm just getting warmed up here. You haven't even seen my good stuff."

"Oh, yeah?" she asked, the teasing light back in her eyes. "You got good stuff?"

"Darlin'," he said, "I've got stuff that'll rock your world. That's a promise. And I can't wait to show it to you."

◆ ◆ ◆

"Thanks," she said quietly when they'd gone back to his parents' place, collected her things, and were in his truck again for the twenty-minute drive into town, Junior right there between them, hogging the middle. "For everything. I guess it hasn't been an easy day for either of us."

"Nope," he said. "I guess not. Although some parts were better than others." He grinned at her. "Way better."

She smiled back, gave Junior's head a rub. "Well, for me. Not so much for you."

"Oh, I don't know. I may have gotten a little charge out of it, too. But I'll just put it out here—on the table, as it were—that you've got pretty much free rein to consider my body yours to use. Because it's been a while, and tell you what, I'm ready to break that drought any old time."

"Really? You haven't been . . ."

"Not so much. Just like you haven't been. I know that's hard to believe, but divorce can be tough on a person. Found that one out the hard way."

"How long has it been since you split up?"

"Since the divorce was final? Four big months. Since she left? A little over a year." He laughed, although it didn't come out quite right. "But who's counting."

"Makes dating again tricky, huh? We've got a few strikes against us, seems to me."

"Or we're two people who understand each other. You could think of it that way. And anyway, I'm past the rebound stage. Unfortunately."

She'd been looking out the window, but now she turned to look at him again. "Unfortunately?"

"Well, yeah. Because when you're on the rebound, you get to think you're right and that she was wrong. Nice and simple. Of course, you're also walking around like a great big gaping wound. That part wasn't too good."

"No," she said. "I'm sure it wasn't."

"And unfortunately, like I said, I'm all the way to the point where I can see her side of the story now. Pretty damn uncomfortable. I'd sure rather go back to where I was right."

"What could her side of the story possibly be?" Zoe demanded. "I'm just fascinated."

"You really want to know?"

"Hey. I shared all my naked truths with you. It's the least you can do."

"Well not *all* your naked truths," he reminded her. "Still got a few of those I'd like to see."

"Come on. Tell me. Please," she added hastily. "If you want to. If it would help."

He slowed to twenty-five for the city limits, got stopped at a red light, but he didn't mind this drive taking a while. She was so sweet, and she didn't even know it.

"I changed the rules," he said. "She married one guy, and I turned into another guy."

"You mean, not a football player."

"I mean more than that. When I found out I couldn't play anymore, when I finally faced the fact that I couldn't rehab my way out of this one . . . Let's say it was a dark time. I thought football was all I could do. Hell, I thought it was all I could *be*. It was who I was, and it always had been, at least that's how it felt."

"But you must've known you could get injured. You must've *gotten* injured. Doesn't that happen all the time?"

"Sure. And you recover, and you come back. I didn't prepare for that not working out. I thought of retirement as something that would happen later. You know, when I was thirty-three, thirty-four. Three or four big long years away. Nothing I had to plan for now. And then—" He hit the steering wheel with the flat of his palm. "Bam. It happened, just like that. My right shoulder, my throwing arm. Dislocated one too many times, and they couldn't keep it from happening anymore. Couldn't fix it enough. My career, who I was—it was all over. And I didn't handle it well. But she stuck around anyway. Give her credit."

"What did you do? That wasn't handling it well?"

He was turning into her street now, pulling up outside her house. He shifted into neutral, but didn't turn the car off. He let the motor and the heater run, sat there and thought a minute, and she waited.

"Got mad," he finally said. "Got quiet and angry and . . . sullen, I guess you'd call it. Or you could come right out and call it pouting. Drank too many beers. Stopped working out much. Stopped talking to Jolie. I sure wasn't thinking about what she might be feeling, how it was for her."

"But that changed? Or did it?"

"Yeah, it changed, but not in the way she wanted. That went on for a couple months, and then my dad came over for the weekend by himself for once, not with my mom. Told me flat-out that I needed to come on home and help him on the farm while I decided what to do. Quit sitting around on my butt feeling sorry for myself. I wasn't too happy to hear that, I'll tell you. He had a few words to say about that, too."

"Like what?"

He turned and looked at her. "Well, as I recall, it was along the lines of, 'Oh, you've got a football injury. You've hurt your passing arm, can't keep making millions of dollars a year and being on TV. Well, suck it up, buttercup. I want you to sit here a second and think about some kid who joined up with the Marines because he didn't see any other options. Who got blown up by an IED and came home, not with a bum shoulder. With no arm at all, or no legs. Those boys are out there learning to live again. They don't have millions of dollars. They don't have *legs*. And they're out there learning to walk on those artificial limbs. They're sucking it up and getting on with it. Go on the Internet sometime for something other than looking at what you don't have. Go on there and think about what you've got. And then sit still for a minute and thank God. And then come home and get to work.'"

"Wow," she said blankly.

"Yeah." He laughed. "Did the trick, tell you that. My dad's not one to dance around it. Tell you straight out. He sure told me. So I did what he said, came home, and Jolie came along for that, too."

"But it wasn't just for a while," she guessed. "Because you stayed."

"Yep. I stayed. My dad yanked my butt out of bed every morning at six no matter what I'd been doing the night before, or how late I'd been up doing it. Took me along to work like he always had, since I was about four. Spring work. Harvest," he explained. "All those hours on the tractor, in the combine, you've got nothing to do but think. And I remembered that this was who I was before I was anything else. That I was the son of a farmer, and the grandson of one, and for all I know, the great-great-great-grandson of one, too. That this was in my blood before football ever got there." He shook his head. "That's the only reason anybody would farm in the first place. Hell of a way to make a living. You could always do something easier, because just about anything *is* easier."

"You could have been a mechanical engineer, seems to me," she said.

"Well, and in a way," he said, "I am. I'm that, and a businessman, and a laborer, and a mechanic, and a whole lot of other things, too. I remembered all that. And all that anger, all that bitterness . . ." He spread out a palm, pushed it sideways. "I guess I drove it away, somewhere around the thousandth time up and down a hillside in that combine. And then, you know, my dad told me he wanted to retire. I realized I had something that was mine, after all. Something to believe in again. Luke didn't want to farm, so I did what every single generation before me has done. Started paying off my brother and sister out of the proceeds—which takes about twenty years, by the way—so it would belong to me someday. So it would be mine."

"And Jolie?"

"Yeah." He sighed. "Jolie. I kind of left her out of that equation, didn't I? That's where she had a point. That's where she was right. That's her side of the story."

"Because she didn't want that."

"She sure didn't. She wasn't a country girl, and she'd never pretended to be. She stuck around at first, thinking I was getting back on track. My old track. Her track. Begging me to move to California and take the color commentator job the network had offered me. It was a good job, too. A whole lot easier. And as you've pointed out, I can talk."

"But you didn't want it."

"Nope. Didn't want the job, and sure didn't want to move to California. I lived in California. Stuck on the freeway every time you wanted to go anyplace, living in some gated-community ghetto with a bunch of other rich people? No, thanks. I told her that, and for a while, she didn't believe me. And then she started getting mad. Started heading off to Seattle to be with her friends, because it was too boring here." He gave a sharp laugh at that, because the pain and anger were still there after all when he thought about it. "Yeah. Her friends."

"And she had an affair."

"Yeah. That's the part I could never get past, that I had such a hard time forgiving. I mean, if she'd had the guts just to say it. Just to leave me. It would still have been tough, but this was . . ."

"Betrayal."

"Betrayal," he agreed. "But after a long time and a whole lot of denial, I realized that she thought I'd betrayed her, too. I hadn't kept up my end of the deal."

"That was the deal?" she said, sounding outraged for him. "I didn't think that was the way the deal worked. I thought that was what the whole 'for richer, for poorer, for better, for worse' thing meant. And you weren't even poorer, right? You weren't even worse."

"Call it not richer. Not that I have anything to complain about. I invested, and anyway, I've got the farm. I could live just fine on the proceeds of that. It doesn't do bad at all. That ground rent I told you about, that I pay Luke and Theresa? That's a hundred grand apiece. Just the rent on a thousand acres."

"A hundred . . . thousand . . . *dollars*? You mean . . . *extra*? A year? Apiece?"

"Yep," he said. "It's hard work, but it's a good farm. A good living. But not private-jet money. Not vacation-house money."

"Not a house in Puerto Vallarta."

"Pretty good memory you've got there, Professor. Of course, she could buy it herself. She got half of everything I'd made since we got married, and we were married for three very good-earning years. But she doesn't tend to look at it that way."

"I think you're being way too charitable," she said. "Way too understanding. I think you should be *mad*."

"Well," he pointed out, "I tried that. It's been more than a year now, remember? I tried the mad thing. I tried it *hard*. It didn't exactly make me feel better. So after a while, I decided to try something else. Been doing all right with it, up until today. And I'll do all right again. Just might take me a little while to remember that."

They'd been sitting in front of her house for more than fifteen minutes, and she seemed to realize it at last.

"All right," she said, sounding a little shaken. "All right. You're not on the rebound."

"Nope. But ready to start up with somebody new, maybe? Yep. I'm that."

"Even if she's got demons of her own?"

"Hell, darlin'," he said with a sigh, "we've all got demons. You've got demons. I've got demons. All God's children got demons. I guess the only difference is, who's running the show. You, or the demons."

FOOTPRINTS

"Well," she said, because she was too rattled by everything he'd shared to say much else. This wasn't who she'd thought Cal was. For somebody who was supposed to be so smart, she wasn't feeling very smart at all. There was so much more to him than she'd ever guessed, and it made her want him more than ever. "I guess I'd . . . better go in. Since Rochelle won't be home until later on this afternoon, and I can't go over there now."

She was babbling, because he already knew that. She'd already told him that she'd called Rochelle and made the plan.

"I'll come in with you," he said. "Check it out."

He got out of the truck with her, and she was glad of it, and they walked around the side of the house together.

"Nobody's shoveled yet," he said, his boots sinking into the drifted snow of the walk.

"I think my landlords are out of town."

The significance of that hit her at the same time it did Cal. "So who," she asked slowly, "made these?"

Tracks through the snow. Barely indentations, because they were partially filled in. Because it had snowed through most of the night.

"Junior!" Cal called sharply. "Come back." The dog circled around, sat in the snow beside them, and Cal crouched to examine the faint marks. "Somebody walked this last night," he said. "Come on. Let's take a look."

They walked the rest of the way to her door, and the faint tracks continued on and around the walkway to the . . . Her heart gave a sickening thud. To the sliding-glass door at the back.

"He thought it would be shoveled," Cal said. "Or he didn't think it mattered."

"Because even if I saw it, even if I figured it out," Zoe said, "nobody would believe me." She was shivering from more than the cold. He'd been here. He'd looked into her windows, checked for . . . checked for access. He'd been planning. She could swear she felt his presence, and the hair on the back of her neck was rising.

It wasn't just fear, though. It was anger. That he could wipe out all the closeness of the day, all the good things, just like that. Just by leaving his tracks in the snow.

"I'm not going to let him do this," she said, her voice low. "I'm not going to let him take away my life like this, or anybody else's life. It's not fair. It's not right."

"No," Cal said, and there was nothing easygoing about his face now. "You're cold. Let's go in. He's not inside," he added, seeing the moment when the thought struck her. "Those tracks are from last night, and they go both ways. He came, he looked around, and he left."

She tried to laugh. "Sorry. I'm not much of an outdoorsman."

"Luckily," he said, "I am."

Inside, he prowled around, Junior at his heels, testing locks, rattling windows. "We'll go to the hardware store," he told her. "Get a dowel to put in the runner of that sliding door, get some alarms for that and the front door. And I've got a couple other ideas, too. But I don't think you should be here alone today."

"No." She didn't even want to sit down. "I'll go work at my office," she decided. "Can you give me a minute to change?"

"I can do better than that. I'll wait for you, and we'll go out to lunch. Then the hardware store, get this place fixed up so at least you can come back and forth. Then Junior and I will take you on up to the university, walk you up to your office. As long as you get Rochelle to pick you up from there tonight, get a ride with her on Monday if your car's not done, you'll be all set. Well, mostly set," he amended, "because I'm going to be giving you girls some self-defense instructions, too. And some home protection. I don't really like the two of you being alone at her place. That's not very secure, either. I'll come by tomorrow and get you started with that."

"Whoa," she said. "I mean, sounds good, but . . ."

"Yeah," he said. "Bossy. Can't help it. My mom says I came out like that. All right, let's try this a new way. That's my idea. How does it sound to you?"

"Good," she decided. "Great. How do you know what Rochelle's place is like?" she asked distractedly. She could stay with Rochelle for a week or so max, because her friend's apartment was just too small. What about after that? Maybe Rochelle wanted a roommate, a bigger place? Zoe would feel so much better if she weren't alone. If there *were* a bigger place to rent, which wasn't likely, not in the middle of the semester, and anyway, she had a lease, and she couldn't afford double rent, that was for sure. So she was going to be coming back here alone. No choice. She hoped that Cal did have some ideas. She was going to need some ideas.

"Well, not because I slept with her," he said, and she tried to remember what they'd been talking about. "I walked her home, remember? After I danced with you, walked you home, and you shot me down."

"Oh, yeah." She was smiling again, because Cal had that effect on her. "I do remember that. Did you mind?"

"Hell, yeah, I minded. But I got my kiss in the end, didn't I? Goal-oriented, that's what we call that. But then, you know all about that, too, don't you? Just a different goal, maybe."

"Or a one-track mind."

"Can't help it," he sighed. "My mind just keeps going right on down that track. Even if you're wearing my mother's underwear, and princess, anytime you want to go on and change out of those, it won't be soon enough for me."

She laughed. She might have a crazy stalker after her, she was being forced to escape her apartment until she and Cal could fortify it—and still, she laughed.

"I didn't notice it stopping you," she said. "But you wait here, and when I come out again, I'll be wearing my own underwear. I'm not saying you're going to be seeing it right away, but I can put your mind at ease, in case you're imagining it."

"Oh, darlin'," he said, "I'll be imagining it."

◆ ◆ ◆

Cal did everything he'd promised. And the next day, he came over to Rochelle's, too, gave them both some pretty good self-defense instruction, and then took them out to dinner. If there was one thing Cal was, it was thorough.

"The only thing I miss about California and Seattle," he said, taking a dubious bite of Senor Fred's special enchilada, "is the ethnic food. A beef enchilada isn't supposed to have hamburger in it. Or canned sauce on top of it. But there are still some things we do better around here. Music and beer, for two. And that was a segue," he informed Zoe. "Since I know how you love a man who uses those two-bit words."

"Mmm," she said, reflecting that fish probably wasn't the wisest choice of dinner entrée in the Inland Northwest. "A segue to what?"

"I'm about to smoothly invite the two of you to go dancing on Friday. They'll have a band again, and I think you both need a distraction from recent unfortunate events. And as for you, princess—I think you need another lesson from somebody who knows how."

She paused with the bite halfway to her mouth, then went on and ate it, taking her time. "Uh-*huh*," she said, doing her best not to read the light in his blue eyes. "That was really smooth right there, too, by the way."

"Well, I thought so. So, dancing?"

"Both of us?" Rochelle asked from beside Zoe. "You going harem-style these days? Because, bud, think again."

He laughed. "Nope. I'm going to get Luke to come along and be your date. If you say yes, of course," he amended quickly.

"And does he know this?" Rochelle asked. "Because I'm not exactly getting the warm fuzzies here."

"He will when I tell him," Cal said cheerfully. "So, what do you say?" he asked, looking between the two of them. "Two good-looking Jackson brothers? Pretty hard offer to refuse?"

"I told you," Zoe said, trying hard to look lofty and not to laugh, "you're not that good-looking."

Rochelle stared at her, a startled laugh escaping, and Cal grinned.

"My body's all right," he informed Rochelle. "But I'm afraid that's where it stops. That's all right, princess. I'll let you be the good-looking one. Plus, if we dance real close, you won't have to look at my face."

"Just feel your body, huh?" She couldn't believe what was coming out of her mouth, but here it came anyway.

"Well," he said, "that works for me, yeah."

◆ ◆ ◆

She didn't have to wait, it turned out. He walked them home, looked at Zoe when they were standing outside Rochelle's door, and said, "Want to climb up in the truck with me a minute, say good night?"

"Well, yeah," she said. "I do." Because she did. She wanted to kiss him, to snuggle up close and run her hands over his shoulders and arms, to feel him holding her. So big, and so secure.

They couldn't do more than that, not parked on Main Street with the truck running, but it seemed she wanted whatever she could get. And Cal was generous. He gave it to her. For a good long time. He held her against him while his mouth nibbled and played, and when his lips slid around to the side of her neck and he bit down, she gasped.

"Cal," she said.

"Hmm?" he asked against her skin.

She shifted on the seat, got a hand in his hair and drew him to her. "Oh," she said. "Don't stop."

That got a laugh, and he obliged. He stayed there and teased her, found all her most sensitive spots until he had her leaning back against the door and writhing a little. Just from his mouth on her neck.

"I need . . ." she breathed.

"I know." He brushed his mouth over hers again. Her lips were so sensitized they were tingling, and so was every other part of her. "I know what you need. But maybe not on Main Street."

Now it was her turn to laugh. Not too steadily, because she was off-balance and no mistake.

He sat back, pulling her with him, and rested his forehead against hers. "Feels pretty good, huh?"

"Mmm," she agreed, running a hand over his cheek, around to the short hair at the back of his neck. "Making out in a truck. Another new Idaho experience for me."

"Well, I'd tell you it was new for me, but you've just described my entire teenage courtship ritual. But I never did it with you before, and that's fairly special. Kinda looking forward to Friday. I hope you are, too."

"I don't really . . ." She backed off a little. "I don't really have time for a relationship, though. I mean, I work a lot. A *lot*. Especially this year. And I don't want you to be disappointed."

"I noticed that," he said. "Just wait until spring work starts. You'll see that I don't have time, either. But I'll make some time for you all the same. It's all about priorities."

"You going to make me a priority?"

"Seems I just can't help it." He stroked her hair, smiled into her eyes. "It doesn't seem to be the mind that's calling the shots around here."

"I guess the question is," she said, "what is? The heart or the body?"

"Couldn't it be both?"

"I guess." She relaxed into his hand. "It feels like both," she confessed. "But I'm glad you know about working a lot, too. I've always drawn these . . . boundaries, you know?"

"Yep," he said. "I know all about boundaries."

"But I wasn't counting on this place. I wasn't counting on you. Who knew I'd be such a sucker for a take-charge guy with a kind heart?"

"I've moved from bossy to take-charge, huh? I kinda like that. And I like the kind heart, for sure. You've got a pretty good heart of your own, Professor. Seems like you've got just the kind of heart I like."

◆ ◆ ◆

"I've got to say, you give it right on back to Cal," Rochelle said.

Zoe had said a reluctant good-bye to Cal and gone back inside, and she and Rochelle were in their pajamas now—well, Zoe's pajamas and Rochelle's much more elegant version of nightwear. Drinking wine and half-watching a movie on the couch, with Zoe doing her best not to think about the work she wasn't doing.

"Mmm. Because it's so much fun," Zoe agreed, smiling a little at the memory.

"And he's loving it," Rochelle said. "If you're trying to whet his appetite, I'd say you're doing a good job of it. I don't know how the heck you're holding out, but it's working. I know I'd hit that. Of course," she acknowledged, "I'm getting a little desperate here."

"Oh, yeah?" Zoe turned down the volume on the TV. "I thought maybe you and Deke would go out."

"Well, not *that* desperate. He's all right, but I just can't bring myself to break my long drought with somebody who mostly stands out for wetting his pants in the second grade."

Zoe laughed. "I guess that's the downside of small towns. Knowing all their history."

Rochelle sighed. "All I want is tall, dark, and handsome. Plus strong and sweet, of course. And somebody who wants to settle down and have lots of sex and babies with me. That too much to ask?"

"And a good job," Zoe suggested.

"Well, yeah. A job, too. Not working on his carburetor on the coffee table would be a plus, and not living in a shack. I'm prepared to be flexible on the handsome. I can even be flexible on the tall and dark. But I'm not going to compromise on the strong and sweet."

"Or the sex and babies," Zoe said.

"Well, that goes without saying. How about you? What do you want?"

"Well . . . nothing. I mean, I've never wanted anything."

"You telling me you don't have standards? Girl, I don't believe that for a minute. You've got standards out the wazoo. Either that or you're nuts. You're holding out on *Cal*."

"I mean," Zoe tried to explain, "I can't do the settling down and babies, not now. And the problem is, I've always been attracted to the wrong guys. What you said. The strong, take-charge guys like Cal."

"And that guy's the wrong guy," Rochelle said dubiously.

"For me. Because is that kind of guy attracted to a woman like me, long-term? No. He isn't. He wants somebody younger, and less educated, and less career-oriented. Somebody to put her career second and his first. Somebody to put *herself* second and him first."

She had Rochelle's full attention now. "And you know this how?" the other woman demanded.

Zoe gestured impatiently with the remote. "Everywhere. Anywhere. Some Hollywood actor makes it, what does he do? Dumps his wife, the one who's his equal, maybe the one who supported him when he was starting out, and marries somebody younger who'll worship him. Doctors marrying their receptionists. *Everyone* marrying their receptionists, or their assistants, or their . . . whoever. Because that's what that kind of guy wants."

"Uh-huh." Rochelle still didn't look convinced. "Never seemed that way to me. Always seemed like a good, strong man would want a good, strong woman."

"All right," Zoe said. "My parents. My dad's a research fellow at USC, right?"

"I don't know," Rochelle said. "Is he?"

"Yes. He is. And my mom's main job—until they were divorced, that is, because he found somebody younger—was to take care of my dad. She was happy to do it, too. She was crazy about him, and she still is, and even that wasn't good enough for him. He wanted somebody to take care of him *and* be young and hot. And he got it, too. Anyway, I work in a male-dominated field. They might talk about work/life balance, but nobody's *living* work/life balance. You get ahead because you put in the hours. You *focus.* I have all these strikes against me anyway as a woman, not being part of the group. I can't afford any more."

"And that's all right with you," Rochelle said.

"It has to be, doesn't it? Because A, the guys I want have never been the guys I get."

"Except Cal."

"Well, yeah. I mean, maybe. But that's . . . that's an anomaly."

"Uh-*huh,*" Rochelle said. "An anomaly."

"And B," Zoe went on, "the guy I would want, even if by some miracle he wanted me? I probably couldn't have him anyway. Not and do what I've spent the last ten years of my life preparing to do. So it has to be all right with me."

"And does Cal know this?"

Zoe shifted her gaze to her wineglass. "I was just talking to him about it tonight. Telling him how hard I have to work right now."

"Well," Rochelle said, "he works pretty hard, too. So this is just for . . . what? Fun?"

"No. Yes. I don't know. I'm not good at relationships. They're like clothes. They confuse me. But I just can't help it, you know?"

"Yep," Rochelle said. "The heart wants what it wants."

"*Le coeur a ses raisons,*" Zoe said.

"What?"

"*Le coeur a ses raisons, que la raison ne connaît point.* The heart has its reasons, that reason knows not of."

"Hmm. Yeah," Rochelle decided. "I suppose that just about covers it. Do you know any more about it than how to say it?"

"No," Zoe said. "I sure don't."

"But then," Rochelle said, "who does?"

CLOTHING CHALLENGES

Zoe had showered, was in her underwear when the knock came at the front door on Friday night.

She jumped and stared at Rochelle, who stared back at her.

"The guy wouldn't knock," Rochelle said. "He doesn't strike me as the knocking type."

"No," Zoe said with relief, feeling foolish. "Of course not." She pulled on her robe and followed Rochelle out through the minuscule kitchen into the living room all the same, and stood with her beside the door. Safety in numbers, and if she and Rochelle didn't like the answer they got, well, they had a response for that.

"Who is it?" Rochelle called.

"Cal," they heard. "And Luke."

Rochelle's hand dropped from her chest, and she flipped the deadbolt and swung the door open. "Well, damn, boys. That's what the phone's for, you know?"

"What?" Cal asked, stepping inside with Luke right beside him. He shrugged off his jacket, hung it on the brass tree beside the door while Luke did the same, and Rochelle watched them do it and raised her eyebrows comically at Zoe.

"We supposed to call you instead of knocking on your door when we're standing outside it?" Cal continued. "This some New Age social media rule I haven't heard yet?"

"Well, yeah," Rochelle said. "If one of us might have a crazy stalker after her, and you're here this early, I'd say you *are* supposed to do that."

He looked taken aback, shot a look at Zoe. "Oh. Sorry."

"Why are you here?" Zoe asked, pulling the belt of her robe a little tighter around herself. "You said eight. It's not even seven thirty."

"Aw, honey," Cal complained. "What a welcome."

Rochelle had her hands on her hips. "It's true that you're not supposed to mind waiting on a woman," she said, "but this is ridiculous. Zoe's in her *robe*."

Cal cast a glance over the white fleece robe patterned with blue snowflakes. "Yeah," he drawled, "and that's pretty much setting me on fire."

"Hey," Zoe objected. "It's *cold*. It's *winter*. Excuse me for not being in some . . . satin negligee with marabou slippers. Sorry to burst your bubble. I didn't know you'd be showing up to criticize my lingerie."

"Honey, that's not lingerie," Cal said. "I'm pretty sure my mom has a robe just like that."

"So why are you here?" Rochelle asked, her toe tapping dangerously in its red cowboy boot. "Our hair isn't done. Our makeup isn't done. Unless you're going for candid before-and-after shots, which wouldn't win you one single point with me, what's the deal? I thought you were trying to get somewhere. This is you trying?" She looked at Luke. "Do you have absolutely no influence? I mean, all right, Cal hasn't gotten out much lately. But seems to me you could've set him straight, a tomcat like you."

Luke's mouth opened in shock. "I am not a tomcat. *When* am I a tomcat?"

"Right," Rochelle scoffed. "You think you can just cross the state line and that's going to keep the gossip from getting back here? I've got news for you, big boy. The gossip gets back. We all know."

Luke was spluttering a little, and Cal was laughing. "Man," he said. "I love it when the heat's falling on somebody else. But to answer your question, we're here to make sure the professor gets dressed right. I had a dream last night that she showed up in that black suit and I had to blow my brains out from sheer despair."

"You came over to help me get dressed," Zoe said slowly. "Both of you. Now I have heard everything."

"Yep," he said. "We sure did. Closet back here?" he asked Rochelle, already heading farther into the apartment.

She raised both arms from her sides, dropped them in surrender. "Well, go right ahead," she told his back. "Be my guest."

"Thanks." Cal led the way into her bedroom, lit by the two lamps draped with pink silk scarves, one on either side of the canopied brass bed.

"Nice place," Luke said, looking around.

"It isn't," Rochelle said, "but I do my best. I always wanted a bed like this. Of course, I used to want Cal in it, too, but I've changed my mind on that one."

"Good," Cal said absently. He had her closet door open, was sorting through it. "You've got your clothes color-coded."

"No shit, Sherlock," she said. "Because I get to be organized, now that I'm not married to the biggest slob in the Western Hemisphere."

"This it?" Cal asked Luke, pulling out a dress. A red dress. A *dark* red dress.

"Yep," Luke said. "That's the one."

Cal took it off the hanger, tossed it to Zoe, and she reached out reflexively to catch it. Some kind of soft material that draped easily over her arm. She was sure it had a name. All she knew was, it felt nice.

"There you go, darlin'," he said. "That's your color. And that's your dress."

She held it in front of her, looked down at it, then back at Cal.

"Come out here with me," she told him. "I want to talk to you."

"Uh-oh," Luke muttered.

Zoe barely heard him. She was stalking into the living room, as much as a short woman in a snowflake-patterned bathrobe and slippers could be said to stalk. He'd better be following her. He'd *better* be.

She turned around when she got there to find he had been, because there he was. Levi's, black T-shirt, cowboy boots and all. Hard muscle, hard man. And she wasn't one bit intimidated.

"What school of charm did you go to," she asked him, "that you think you can come over here, barge into my closet—well, Rochelle's closet—and tell me what to wear? I thought we were all clear on this, that my body belongs to me. I'd think that would mean that what I put on it is my choice, too, but apparently not."

He had his hands out in front of him. "Whoa. Hang on. Okay, I'm going to apologize. You ready?"

"Yeah." She crossed her arms, still holding the dress, and scowled at him. "Waiting."

"All right. I'm sorry. I just started thinking about it, and I . . . I wanted to see it, all right? I wanted to be sure you wore it."

"Wore what?" She looked down at the dress, then back at Cal. Her eyes narrowed. "You are kidding me."

"What?"

"Don't give me that innocent face. You bought me a *dress*? And then you came over to make sure I *wore* it?" She held it up in front of herself, confirmed her suspicions. "You did. You totally did. This is way too short for Rochelle. It would be up to her butt. For that matter, it's kind of short for me. You *bought* this?"

"Well, me and Luke," he said. "Online. And it's not too short. You've got real pretty legs. Can I help it if I wanted to see them?"

"You and Luke went online and picked out a dress for me?" The image was too funny, and despite her earlier annoyance, she was having a hard time not laughing.

"Luke said red, and I got to thinking about it, and it sounded so good, I wanted to see you in it," he said, looking a little sheepish. "I was thinking about going dancing with you, and it just . . . one thing led to another, all right?"

She had to laugh then. She couldn't help it. "You and Luke," she managed, "sitting in front of the computer, clothes shopping. For *me*. The planet's most clothing-challenged woman."

"Well, yeah." He was grinning now, then laughing himself. "I wanted you to like it. I wanted to buy the right thing. And he's better at it than me. I'm a little clothing-challenged myself."

"But I would have liked it anyway. Couldn't you have trusted that Rochelle would have told me to wear it, and I'd have done it? She's obviously in on this, because somebody told you guys my size, although I wouldn't put it past Luke to be able to guess it. And then she hung that dress up in its color-coded spot so she could, what? Pull it out and say, 'Hmm. How about this?'"

"Well . . ." he admitted.

"Uh-huh. And I would have said, 'Fine,' and worn it. I'm not the most confident person in my fashion choices. And then you could have just . . . acted all surprised at how beautiful I looked when you came to pick me up. At *eight.* A way better strategy. Just for your information."

"Right," he said, still grinning. "In future, I'll be much sneakier with my clothing purchases for you. And are we good? Am I forgiven? Because, baby, I want to see you in that red dress. I hope I didn't blow it so bad that you won't wear it for me."

She was still shaking her head. "Stay here," she commanded. She headed for the kitchen again, then turned around as a thought struck her. "You may be thinking you get to pick out my underwear, too," she informed him. "But you're just going to have to be surprised on that one."

She went back into the bedroom, where Luke was leaning against the door leading to the courtyard, watching Rochelle put on her makeup at the dressing table.

"Looks like I'm changing," Zoe told him. "Go talk to your brother. Contemplate your sins."

"Yes, ma'am," he said. "Cal talked his way out of it, huh? I should never have doubted it."

"You've both got way more charm than is good for you." She put a hand on the doorknob, jerked her head at him. "Out."

When he was gone, she shut the door again, looked at Rochelle. "You could have *told* me."

Rochelle was looking a little guilty. "I thought it was kind of romantic, and sweet. I thought I'd let Cal tell you, and it could be a moment."

"It was a moment, all right." Zoe was shrugging off her robe, tossing it on the bed, and pulling the sleeveless dress over her head. She settled the mock-wrap waist around her, adjusted the V neckline, looked in the mirror, and sighed.

"It would be a whole lot easier to be mad at him," she told Rochelle, "if it didn't look good."

"Try it with your boots," Rochelle suggested.

Zoe pulled on her socks, then the cowboy boots, stood up, and posed again. The skirt fell just below midthigh, and the deep red brought out the brown tones of her skin and hair. She looked . . . well, no doubt about it. She looked sexy, even without makeup.

"Purple and red," she said dubiously.

"Yep," Rochelle said happily. "Dynamite."

ONE FOR THE SINNERS

"I told you so," Luke said. "Bad idea."

They were sitting on the couch, and Cal was flipping through a magazine from Rochelle's coffee table.

"Huh?" Cal asked absently, because he was somewhere else.

You may be thinking you get to pick out my underwear, too, she'd said. *But you're just going to have to be surprised on that one.* He hoped that meant what he thought it meant. Man, he hoped so.

He lifted the magazine he'd been leafing through, turned it around so Luke could see it. "Nine Ways to Drive Him Wild Tonight," he informed his brother.

Luke grinned back at him. "Yeah. What I said. Show up and get naked. Two ways. Or even better, show up and let me know she'd like *me* to get her naked. Now we're down to one. Guess that wouldn't make for much of an article, though."

By the time the door opened and the girls came out, Cal had gotten himself informed about all nine ways, and was about ten ways turned on himself, because those had been some pretty specific instructions. He'd had no idea that women were getting all that . . . information.

And then he was about eleven ways turned on, because here came Zoe. Her round brown eyes, which could look so sweet and innocent, were smoky with shadow and liner again, snapping at him like she was daring him to think she didn't look good enough. As if that were going to be a possibility. With a spot of color on each cheek that he didn't think was makeup, and her full lips, parted a little now, painted a deep red. Rochelle's doing, obviously, because they matched the dress.

And *damn*. That dress.

That red dress. The style making the most of her curvy shape, all that leg showing between its hem and the tops of her cute little boots. And that wonderful deep V between her full breasts, that shadow that he knew he'd be sneaking a look down while he danced with her. Oh, yeah.

"Luke," he told his brother without taking his eyes off her.

"Yeah?"

"You're a real good shopper."

"That's all you've got to say?" she asked. She was still trying to be sassy, and he still loved sass, so that was fine by him.

She pirouetted in her boots, swung back around to face him, her perfectly mussed fall of dark hair going right along with her. "Am I acceptable?" she asked. "Or do you have any further instructions?"

"You're acceptable," he said, smiling at her. "And, yeah, darlin'. I might have some further instructions."

Luke coughed a little. "Pushing," he muttered.

Cal didn't think it mattered. He thought it had worked, because her color was even higher, and she dropped her chin, looked sideways at him with a flirtatious challenge he'd never seen from her before. Because she was feeling sexy, and pretty, and a little bit wild.

Nothing like a red dress to set a woman free. Nothing at all.

◆ ◆ ◆

And when he was dancing with her in that dress, he was sure of it.

It was a different band tonight, featuring a girl singer with a sexy, smoky voice, taking turns on lead with the guitarist. There was a fiddle, too, and it sounded great. Cal was twirling Zoe, watching her dress swirl around her thighs, then catching her again, feeling her come into his arms, his palm firm against the warm, damp skin of her back.

The band was rocking, and she was, too. Dancing like she loved it, laughing up at him. He was forgiven, because she looked beautiful, and she knew it.

They danced fast, and they danced slow, and she still had her thumb on his collarbone, but there was a lot less tension in that arm, and the longer it went on, the less there was.

Another fast one, whirling her, doing some fancy double twirls, a few tricky moves, and then the band paused, and the girl singer was stepping up to the microphone.

"We're going to slow it right on down," she drawled, punctuating it with a toss of her blonde hair over one bare shoulder. "This one's for the sinners out there. And yeah," she added with a wicked smile, "I know you're out there."

No instruments to start it out, just a slow snap of fingers, and she had a hand on the microphone stand, was leaning in, cradling it, making love to it. Singing about how strong and wild that sin felt, creeping up on her, pulling her down. About fighting the temptation, and losing the fight. About wanting, and longing, and falling. About the hot, sweet release of giving in.

The guitar wailed, the drums offered up every hard beat, the male singer had joined in, and Cal had Zoe in his arms, was swaying with her. And the thumb was gone. Her hand was on his shoulder, all the way over on the other side where it belonged, her rounded arm resting right there against his.

One last moment when she looked up into his eyes, and he looked down, and his heart pounded with a slow, steady beat that matched the irresistible pull of the drums.

"The thumb's optional," she told him softly. "And I'm opting right now. I'm opting to give it up."

She stepped right up into him, and he had every bit of her pressed up against him at last, strong and soft and . . . wonderful. Her feet moving, her body swaying softly like she was meant to do this, like she was meant to fit with him. Her cheek turning, pressing into his shoulder.

It was dancing, and it was making love standing up, a slow, sweet, delicious rock. And it was so good.

◆ ◆ ◆

She'd known she was his from the moment she'd seen him look at her in the dress he'd bought for her, just because he wanted to see her in it. And every single song they'd danced to since, every single step she'd taken in his arms, had walked her a little farther down that path.

He hadn't even pretended to want to dance with anybody else, and she was so very far past pretending herself. And now, she was all the way there. She was pressed into him, feeling him telling her how much he wanted her. His hand on her back, guiding her so surely. His other hand around hers, warm and strong. And the rest of him. That, most of all. Warm, and hard, and ready to give her everything she wanted. Everything she needed.

The song went on and on. She had a feeling he'd had something to do with that, could have sworn she'd seen money change hands. But she didn't care. She just held on to him, danced to the music, with the smooth texture of his T-shirt under her fingers, covering all that hard muscle. With the roughness of denim against her thighs, his belt buckle against her lower ribs—and everything else, too. Feeling him wanting her as much as she wanted him.

Every song had to end, though, and this one did, too. The singer gave her hair one final toss, the drums offered a last emphatic beat, the guitar let out a last languid lick, and the room erupted in applause and whistles.

Cal wasn't clapping. He couldn't, because he still had hold of her hand, had barely stepped back from her. He was taking her back to the table, grabbing her coat and his own, holding hers for her, helping her on with it.

"Going so soon?" Luke asked, sitting back with a beer in his hand. Rochelle must be dancing with somebody else, Zoe realized hazily, although she didn't much care.

Cal didn't even answer. He had hold of Zoe's hand again, was leading her between crowded tables, the cluster of patrons by the bar, barely acknowledging the greetings he gathered along the way.

The cold hit, as always, when they got through the outer door, but for once, Zoe barely noticed it.

It seemed to sober Cal up, though. He stopped, looked down at her. "I've got this right, haven't I?" he demanded. "If not, tell me now."

"You've got it right," she managed. "Please."

He let out a breath. "Then let's go."

"Rochelle," she began.

"Luke," he answered, and that was that. He had his hand around hers still, was hustling around the corner toward the spot where his truck was parked on a side street. He was taking her home.

INSPIRATIONAL

They reached the truck, and Cal was there at her side, his keys in his hand. He looked down at her, his breath puffing out in a cloud of white that matched her own.

"Got to kiss you first," he said. "Cold and all." He reached for her, pulled her against him, and his mouth was on hers.

Not sweet this time. Hot, hard, and demanding. She uttered a little sound of surprise into his mouth, and his tongue was there, plunging, retreating, his hips rocking into her in the same urgent rhythm, and her hands were on his broad shoulders, grabbing him, pulling him down to her, trying to get him closer.

"Too small," he said on a gasp, and he was reaching under her, picking her up, turning her so her back was against the door of the truck. Her legs wrapped around him like they needed to be there, and she was grabbing either side of his head, her fingers curling into the short, dark hair. She was kissing him right back, giving him everything she had, tasting beer and salt and man, drowning in him.

One of his hands stayed underneath her, holding her up, and the other one was on her bare thigh, the short dress and coat falling away. His hand was on her, broad and hard, stroking up, and up some more, and she was gasping into his mouth.

Male laughter from the sidewalk beyond brought her back to herself with a start. "Man, get a room," she heard somebody call.

Cal must have heard it, too, because he pulled back, set her on her feet, and finally got her door open. "Yeah," he said, sounding shaken. "Good idea. Up in that truck, sweetheart. Slide right on over there next to me, because I'm going to need to hold on to you."

She should care that he was ordering her around again, but she didn't. She got up there and slid, catching her breath as her bare legs hit frigid leather.

He was around, up in his own seat, turning the key. "What?" he asked as she shoved her hands under her thighs.

"C-c-cold," she managed.

He turned the dial for the heat, and the fan blasted. More cold air, and she was shivering. "We'll get you warm," he said. "That's a promise."

"It's my th-th-thighs," she said. "F-f-freezing."

"Them, especially." His forearm was on the back of the seat behind her again, his head turning to back up into the street. He got the truck pointed toward Main, then stopped. "But where are we going?" he asked. He shook his head, laughed a little. "I just wanted to get you out of there, get you someplace where I could take off your clothes. Please don't tell me we have to go all the way back to my place. I don't think I'll make it. We need a bed, not my truck pulled over to the side of the road."

"My apartment," she said, pulling the keys out of her little purse.

"You feel safe enough there?"

"With you? Oh, yeah. But could you quit talking and *drive*? Please, Cal. Take me home."

He breathed out a laugh. "Hell, yeah. I could do that." He put his foot down, and they were turning onto Main.

She put her hand on his hard thigh, exactly the way she'd wanted to do on that high school stage, and she could swear he jumped a little, so she did it some more. She curled a little bit closer, got her right arm around his chest so she could stroke the side of his face, then leaned over and kissed his neck, thrilling at the rasp of whiskers under her lips.

"Zoe," he ground out. He was stopped at the light. Almost on Maple. Five blocks from home.

"What?" She kept her hand stroking over his jaw, twined it around to the back of his head where the hair was cut short, and rubbed her fingers over his nape, while she licked her way to where the pulse beat steady and strong under his ear, and kissed him there.

The light had turned green, the driver of the car behind him blasted out his impatience at the delay, and Cal started up again with a jerk, took off up the Maple Street hill.

"One minute," he told her. "Sixty seconds. And you aren't going to believe how fast you lose that pretty little dress."

"Promises, promises." Her fingers were still playing, her hand moving a little farther up his thigh. "You sure you've got something good enough for me?"

"Oh, darlin'," he said, pulling onto Jackson at last and turning into her driveway. "I've got so much for you. And I can't wait to give it to you."

He cut the lights and the engine, leaped out of the truck, and was around to her side before she'd had time to do more than slide over and get a hand on the door handle. Then he was lifting her down. He kept his arm around her, was taking her keys from her, hustling her along the sidewalk to the basement door, fitting the key into the lock, shoving the door open and hitting the light switch, all in about fifteen seconds.

It was freezing in here, too, musty with a week's worth of disuse, and she was shivering again.

"Thermostat," he muttered.

She went across to it, shoved the lever to the right. "We'll have to keep our coats on," she teased, coming back to him where he still stood by the door. "Have a hot drink."

"Hell we will." He was pulling her up on her toes, kissing her some more, his lips trailing over her cheek, around to her neck. "Little girls who tease men when they're trying to drive," he murmured into her ear, his lips sending shivers down her spine, "get in trouble."

"Oh, yeah?" she managed to say. "What happens to them?"

"They get their clothes taken off." He was unzipping his coat, tossing it onto the easy chair, and then getting to work on hers, adding it to his own, looking at her where she stood in the red dress he'd bought her.

"This," he told her. "Got to touch this." He slid a slow hand right inside the neckline of her dress, held her there. "Oh, yeah," he sighed, "that's good."

It was. His hand was moving, his thumb was tracing, and she had her hands on him, too, was tugging his shirt up. She stepped a little closer, kissed him right under his collarbone, spread her palms flat on his broad chest, and nudged the shirt over his shoulders. Then pulled it over his head, and was finally able to toss it.

He stood in front of her, bare-chested and powerful, and she drank in the sight of him. Shoulders, chest, arms, all of it narrowing so perfectly down to his waist and hips. She traced her fingernails over his pectorals, down the ridged lines of his abdomen, bent and licked a flat brown nipple. The air hissed between his teeth, and he jumped.

"Here I thought I was going to be in trouble," she told him as she straightened, "and the only one getting naked is you."

"You want a take-charge guy, do you?" His hands were stroking from her shoulders down her bare arms, every nerve ending they encountered on their journey sending a message straight to the part of her that was waiting for him, that was so ready for him.

She lifted her shoulders, let them fall. "Maybe not." She did her best to make it sound sassy, even though all she wanted to do was lie down for him. "Not if that's too much of a challenge for you."

He laughed, low and soft. "Here I thought this was going to be my lucky night," he said. "Turns out I didn't have a clue."

He got the hem of the dress in both hands, pulled it up over her head, dropped it to the floor. "Now, that's what I call pretty," he said with satisfaction.

"I told you I could pick out my own underwear," she managed to say. She'd worn the blue lace ones again. Her favorites.

"Oh, yeah." His hand traced the edge of the bralette. No wires, nothing but lace. "You did a real good job. Not much at all between you and me right here. I like that. Let's see what we can do with this."

He had a hand under her thighs, the other one around her shoulders, and before she knew what was happening, he was striding across the living room with her in his arms, kicking open the bedroom door with a booted foot, dropping her onto the bed, and coming down over her.

"Heater," she said.

He looked around for it, got up again and switched it on, then came back and stood over the bed, looking down at her. "Still giving me instructions, huh?" he asked her. "Thought I was taking charge here."

"Well," she said, trying to shrug again, "only if it's necessary."

"I don't think it's going to be necessary anymore." His eyes were on her body. "Blue lace and cowboy boots," he said. "One hell of a combination. I'd call that downright inspirational."

He sat on the edge of the bed, pulled off his boots and socks, and she sat up to reach for her own.

His hand was on her shoulder, giving her a gentle shove that put her on her back again. "Oh, no," he told her. "No undressing. That's my job."

"My *boots*?" she asked, trying to laugh, but it wasn't easy, not when he stood up and began to unbuckle his belt. Her eyes were glued there as he pulled the tongue of leather free, began to work on his button fly.

"Seems to me," she told him, "that a take-charge guy would want a woman doing that."

"Well, you know," he said, a slow smile growing, "I think you're right. I think you'd better get on over here and do it."

She sat up, walked across the bed to him on her knees, got a hand under his waistband, and looked into his eyes. And then she started to unbutton. Her mouth was dry, her breath was coming hard, and she could see his chest rising and falling, because his was, too.

She finished, carefully not touching what lay beneath, because she could tease, too, and shoved the jeans over his hips, down his thighs.

"Hang on," he said. "Condom." He grabbed a couple out of his pocket, tossed them onto the bed, dropped the jeans down the rest of the way and kicked them off, stood there before her in navy-blue briefs.

"Got another job to do, haven't you, darlin'?" he asked. "Better get to work on that."

She didn't need telling. She was pulling them down, and then the briefs were gone, too, and he was standing there, all six foot three of hard-muscled man. Every single part of him looking more than ready to take her on, and win.

She swallowed. "Is that all for me?"

"Oh, yeah," he told her. "You did real good, sweetheart. Now lie on down there, because we're going to see just how much I can do to you before we even get that pretty underwear off."

She did what he said, because she needed to.

He got her boots and socks off first, dumped them on the floor. "Not that I don't love the idea of doing you with just these boots on," he told her. "It's just that I'm saving that one up for when I've got you over the tailgate of my truck."

The jolt of arousal went straight through her, and he saw it and smiled. "Yeah," he said. "That works real good, doesn't it? It'll work even better when you've had a while to think about it first."

"I . . ."

He wasn't listening to whatever she would have said. He was sliding over her, covering her with his big body, kissing her again at last, and she was hanging on to him, kissing him back, stroking her way over his back, his shoulders, his arms. Smooth skin over hard, bunched muscle, and she couldn't get enough.

He didn't stay there very long. He was pulling her hair back to get to her, biting his way down her throat, around to the side of her neck. His mouth closed on the sensitive spot under her ear, and she moaned.

"So good," he said. "Let's do some more." His hand drifted down her throat, over her shoulder, and headed for her breasts at last, because they needed him, and he knew it.

She expected him to take the bra off. But he didn't. His fingers trailed over the edge of the lace, and his thumb flicked lazily over the hardening nipple, over and over, teasing mercilessly until her hips were moving in invitation and she had her hands on his shoulders, trying to pull him closer, making urgent little noises.

He still didn't take it off. Instead, he lowered his mouth to her, bit her, sucked at her through the lace. And when the friction was almost unbearable, he transferred his attention to the other breast, until, when she was actually squirming underneath him, he finally pulled the bra up, freeing her.

"Goes over your head, huh?" he said. "I love this." He hauled it up over her arms, then stopped.

"Now, that's a real nice look," he said. He'd only gotten it halfway, and her arms were stretched overhead. "How about we pause this a minute and you stay exactly like that? Seems to me I could spend some more time here. Because this is real, real good."

Another thrill, sharp and electric, as his mouth closed on her breast. She began to pull her arms down to hold him, and his hand shot up, grabbed her wrists, and held her there.

He looked up. "Okay?"

"Uh . . ." It felt so good. So good. "Okay," she gasped, "but thanks for . . . asking."

He smiled, but didn't answer. Just got busy again, his other hand working on one breast while his mouth made love to the other one, and she was moving hard against him, because he was going so slowly. Taking so long, and her legs were parting as if they had a mind of their own.

"Cal," she managed to get out, "touch me."

He looked up at that, his hand still imprisoning both of hers, and smiled, slow and lazy. "You need me?"

"Yes. Yes."

"Then I'd better give you some more, hadn't I?" He was finally pulling the bra the rest of the way off her, releasing her hands, sliding down her body some more, yanking the blue bikini panties down her legs and dropping them to the floor to join the bra. And then his hands were on her thighs, spreading them wide as her hips rose beneath him, trying to make it happen faster.

"Oh, honey," he said with a sigh, "on second thought, let's take our time."

"No," she insisted. "No. Now."

All he did was slow down. He nibbled his way down, licked into her belly button, then, finally, when she thought he never would, moved a tantalizing little bit lower. His hand took a maddening detour over her hip, the top of her inner thigh, and it felt good, but it didn't feel good enough.

"Cal," she moaned. "Please."

"What?" he asked against her skin. His hand was stroking up her thigh, and when he finally took it higher, one finger flicking delicately over her, a feather touch against the sensitized nub, she jumped.

"Now," he said.

When his mouth finally found its target, she actually screamed a little. He gave her a long, slow lick, and she nearly climbed off the bed. He laughed against her, his hands gripped her inner thighs more tightly, and he got serious. And if it had felt good before . . . now, there was nothing but this. Nothing but those strong hands, that talented, willing mouth.

It didn't take long at all, because he had wound her up so tightly already, and he was so good. So hard, and so sure. He knew how, he knew where, and he hit it, and she was there, singing out with the dark, hot pleasure of it, her upper body jerking off the bed, the waves slamming through her, wild and relentless.

He worked her through the whole delicious process until she was limp and shuddering, then lifted himself off her, got the condom on, grabbed a pillow from the head of the bed and slid it under her hips. And then another one. Finally, he pulled out the pillow from behind her head so she was upended.

"Ah," he breathed, sinking into her, and she was opening, stretching to receive him. "What did I say? So sweet. So tight. Damn, baby. This is my place."

Not that he went fast even now. Slow and smooth, long and sweet, until slow and smooth weren't enough and he was rocking her harder, her arms twining around him, the position he'd put her into pulling him so deeply into her, and she couldn't do anything but hang on and feel it, until that wasn't enough, either.

"I need . . ." she begged. "I need . . ."

He groaned, pulled back a little, got a hand between their bodies. The strain of holding back bunched the muscles of his shoulders and arms, the sweat stood out on his forehead, the dark shadow of his upper lip, but he did it anyway.

"Come on, darlin'," he urged her, stroking fast. "Come on and let me have it." He was driving her, her body arching beneath him, because he was thrusting again in time with his hand.

"Come on," he said again. "Give it to me. I'm dying here. I need you so bad."

His panting breath was loud in her ears, and he was inside her, on her, over her. She was there, and she was his.

And this time, when she was flying again, so long and so hard, he went right along with her.

It took a few minutes to come back to earth. For both of them, because he wasn't talking now. He was just holding her like that was exactly what he wanted to do. One big hand stroked down her back, leaving a warm trail of pleasure in its wake.

"Wow," she sighed, rolling to lie on top of him. "Way to break a drought."

She felt the rumble of his laughter, propped her chin on his chest to smile up at him.

"So that take-charge thing worked out for you, huh?" he asked.

"Yeah," she said, still smiling. "I might ask you to do some more of that. What do you think?"

"Oh, princess," he told her, "we live to serve."

FLOWERS

Two nights later, she wasn't enjoying herself nearly so much.

She and Cal were sitting around the kitchen table after dinner at his parents' house, and once again, Jim Lawson was sitting with them. Only this time, he was the one handing out the police reports.

"Two cases," Jim said. "Two different towns, two different states. Spokane and Coeur d'Alene, Washington and Idaho. And now here in Paradise. So, three. Which isn't many at all, not for this kind of guy, and the different jurisdictions—that's why it hasn't been picked up on. And by the way, this visit is unofficial," he warned as they started reading. "I'm showing you this so you both know what you're up against, and if Cal weren't my cousin, I wouldn't even be doing that."

Zoe had one of the reports, and Cal was scanning the other. She didn't linger over hers, because the details made the elk steak she'd just eaten threaten to rise in her throat. Cal flipped through his just as fast, then traded with her.

"The same," she said when she'd finished.

"Yep," Jim said. "Amy was right. Stalking them first. Zip ties, ski mask, and he likes to come in through the sliding-glass door. Organized, got a pattern. Power-control rapist."

"I'd think that would be all of them," Zoe said with as much composure as she could manage, her mind doing its best despite all her efforts to take the bald facts she'd just read and turn them into a horror movie. Doing its best to send her back to that ditch, with him out there waiting. Wanting to do all the things she'd just read about. To her. And how close Amy had come . . . The girl was doing better these days, seemed so much steadier. Surely it would only be good for her to know that the police were on her attacker's track at last, and that she still needed to take care, but Zoe wouldn't be sharing everything. She wouldn't be sharing all this. Because that wouldn't do Amy any good at all.

"It's all relative," Jim said. "You don't want to know. The sadistic ones . . . no. But this guy . . ." He flicked the reports Zoe had handed back, because she couldn't stand to touch them. "He uses force to subdue them, binds them, does it multiple ways, multiple times. Maximum humiliation, that's the point."

He saw Zoe shudder, and stopped. "Sorry," he said. "We don't have to do this. You wanted to know."

"Yes," she said, "we do. I have a right to know what I'm up against. Go ahead."

Cal took her hand, laced his fingers through hers, set it on his thigh, and she felt stronger for the support. "Go on," she said again.

"Like I said," Jim said. "Control. He doesn't get pleasure from the hurting so much. It's about the power. And then there's his organization. He's got a pattern. He's got a victim type." He looked at Zoe again. "Short. Dark. Good figure. Except . . ."

"Young," Cal said. "They were both students. Well, all students. Amy, too."

"At college campuses, yeah," Jim said. "He could be affiliated with a college, but probably not, not with it happening at three different schools. Probably just got a thing for college girls."

"But then why me?" Zoe asked.

Jim rubbed a broad thumb over the bridge of his nose. "Yeah. Well. Remember that power-control thing? I'd say you were a threat, and a challenge to his power. A danger both ways. To his safety, and to his sense of himself. You got involved. You got Amy moved, you got the campus force moving, you told the paper about it. He lost Amy, and I don't think he's lost before, because we didn't find any attempteds that matched these."

"And now he's lost again," Cal said. "Ran Zoe off the road, wasn't able to . . . follow through, and hasn't gotten to her since."

"Can't get at Amy, can't get at Zoe," Jim agreed. "Because you've got her with you, right?"

"Yeah," Cal said, a muscle working in his cheek, his hand tightening around hers.

"Well, take my advice," Jim said. "Keep her with you until we figure this thing out. We're getting there, even though it's likely to take a while. And here's another thing I didn't tell you. When I was checking around, talking to a buddy of mine, deputy up in Kootenai County? He was over in Iraq, and he said it reminded him of a perp they knew about over there, back when he was an MP. There were at least a couple victims that they knew about, but probably a lot more, he said, because they didn't talk. It's major shame over there for women, being raped. They won't report it, don't want their families to know. But the MPs heard anyway. Word got back."

"Wait. What?" Cal asked. "The same guy?"

"Could be. Serial rapist," Jim said. "The investigation never got far, because like I said, the victims wouldn't talk. But what they heard, the word on the street, they thought he was American, even though he was masked. Just like our mutt. Zip ties. Gloves. And he dropped a flower by them when he was done. Like a date, my buddy said. Some kind of sick insult. Like a thank-you. Salt in the wound. And that's another part of the pattern we found. Flowers."

"Flowers?" Zoe asked.

"Yeah. These two . . ." He indicated the reports. "It was part of that organization, his rituals. We checked with Amy, and she got flowers, too. They all thought they were from somebody else—boyfriend, admirer—didn't connect it until later. But they all got them beforehand, which shows you he chose them, planned it."

"Then," Zoe said, taking her hand out of Cal's, wrapping her hands together on the table, "can't you trace that, through florists?"

"Not that kind of flowers, unfortunately," Jim said. "Grocery-store flowers. Cheap-ass flowers."

"Still," Zoe insisted.

"Not a cash sale three weeks ago," Jim said. "We'll check it out, but he wouldn't have used his loyalty card. It's another piece, though. We get enough pieces, we've got the whole puzzle."

"He didn't send me flowers," Zoe said.

"No. He doesn't do that until later," Jim told her. "He stalks them first. Then he does the flowers so they'll be there in the house, like he brought them. Like a date. He probably didn't mean to attack you that night in the car, because that's not how he does it, and it's all about how he does it. It's all about the pattern. He was doing his thing, but you ran off the road. And then he went to your house to check it out, right? That looks like the MO. Exactly."

"Air Force," Cal said slowly, clearly having been thinking about something else. "Iraq. North Idaho, Spokane. Fairchild."

"Fairchild?" Zoe asked.

"Fairchild Air Force Base," Cal explained. "It's in Spokane. Somebody who was in the Air Force until . . . when?"

"Two years ago," Jim said. "For the first one in Spokane. And that's when the Iraq ones stopped, which is pretty indicative."

"So now we're looking for, what?" Cal said. "Somebody who was in the Air Force in Iraq up until two years ago. Who was stationed at Fairchild after that."

"*You're* not looking for anything," Jim said. "*We're* looking."

"Would he have to have been stationed at Fairchild?" Zoe asked, ignoring that. "Couldn't he just be from around here? Because isn't Coeur d'Alene in Idaho? And obviously, we're in Idaho now."

The guys looked at each other. "Well, yeah," Jim said. "Obviously."

"Nobody has a description?" Cal asked.

"Not much of one," Jim said. "Only the relevant piece. He stayed dressed, and he kept it in the dark. Used a flashlight, shone it in their eyes, blinded them. But they all said he was strong. They all said he flipped them hard and fast."

Zoe shuddered again.

"Sorry," Jim said.

"No," she said. "I need to know. But how would he be on campus here? I mean, over and over? First Amy, and now me, and it's been weeks since it started? Doesn't he have to be here now? At least able to come here? Can you spend a lot of time someplace else if you're in the military?"

"No," Jim answered. "But if you're ex-military, you can."

"Something," Cal said slowly. "Something I noticed. This six-foot guy, Air Force, Spokane or Fairchild connection, with the black Ford F-150, who'd have been beat some with a baseball bat on Halloween. That would still have hurt a few days later, even if Amy didn't crack any ribs. That kind of bruising doesn't fade very fast. I ought to know. Left arm, back, right?"

"Right," Jim said. "What are you thinking?"

"About a week after Amy was attacked," Cal said, "I was in the high school gym, and Greg came in. Did some lifting. And he was uncomfortable. I thought at the time he was just putting too much on the bar to impress me, dickhead move, you know. But what if . . ."

"Ford F-150," Jim agreed. "That's his rig. Physical description matches."

"Air Force," Cal said.

"Wait, what?" Zoe demanded. "You mean the *cop*? Your cousin?"

"Yeah," Cal said. "He was an MP."

"Security Forces, technically," Jim put in. "He wasn't ever at Fairchild, though. He was working up at Washington U outside of Spokane for a year before he came on back down here, because it's where he's from. He got hired by the university police about a year ago."

"But the other thing, the thing last year," Zoe objected, "wasn't here. It was north of here."

"Makes sense to me," Jim said. "You move someplace, got an MO going, and immediately start some action in your own backyard? Way to point the arrow right at you. Nope. You'd decoy away. You're in Spokane, you do it in North Idaho, at the college there. You move down here, you do it up in Spokane. But my guess is, eventually, it's just too tempting. And you start needing it more. I'll have to check, but I think that's how it works." He caught himself. "But this is all speculation. He's our cousin, and he's a cop, and this is nothing but coincidence."

"Whole hell of a lot of coincidence," Cal said. "He's got an anger problem, we both know it, and according to my mom, they're not too sure about what's happening at home. Looking way too coincidental to me."

"All right," Jim said, shoving back from the table. "I'm way out of my league here, criminally speaking. This is one for the sheriff. And we're in multiple jurisdictions, fellow officer . . . and I shouldn't be talking to you at all. This has to head right on up to the sheriff."

"Today?" Zoe insisted.

"Today," he promised. "Nobody's taking this lightly, believe me."

"You need me to call," Cal said, "I'll call."

"I don't need you to call. I need you to stay right on out of it. We're talking about *one* possible suspect, based on pure coincidence, out of hundreds of possibilities. And don't get thinking you're going to investigate by yourselves, go confronting anybody. This guy's real dangerous. You poke him, you're going to get bit. Or Zoe's going to get bit. You just focus on looking out for her. And you," he told Zoe, "you focus on being careful, and letting Cal look out for you. Nobody's going to give you police protection, not for somebody following too close on the highway, whatever kind of pattern you might or might not fall into. Your best bet is being careful, and Cal."

He stood up, grabbed his hat from the table, and put it on. "You got a plan?" he asked Cal.

"Oh, yeah," he said. "I've got a plan. Same one I've had all along. Basically, stick with her. Me and Junior."

"Not a bad plan," Jim said. "Guys like this? They don't want to take on other guys." He gathered his reports, tapped them together, and turned to go, then turned back. "I mean it," he warned. "Look out for her, and that's exactly where it stops. We'll do the rest."

VOLCANIC ACTIVITY

Two weeks later, Cal was watching for the moment when Zoe recognized him.

She'd walked briskly into her rock lab a few minutes before two, had begun setting up for her lecture before she registered his presence at the back of the class, together with the buzz of excitement, the turned heads, the whispering. He raised his eyebrows at her, saw her intake of breath, then her shoulders straightening before she moved smoothly on with her preparations.

He smiled a little. That was how it was going to be, was it? She was taking his visit as a challenge? That was interesting.

He'd just wanted to see her teach. Or, let's face it, he'd just wanted to see her. It seemed that being at her house, or having her at his, every night for the past couple of weeks wasn't quite enough.

For protection, of course. That was why he had to be there.

The clock ticked over to two, and she clicked the mouse on her laptop. An image of a steaming mountain filled the screen behind her, and the class quieted.

"Happy Monday," she said. "You may have noticed that we have a special guest today. Hello, Cal. Glad you could join us."

"Glad to be here," he said.

"And for any of you who have found Geology 101 extra fascinating thus far," she said, "and are thinking about your major, this would be a good opportunity to point out that Cal's done a few things to make sure that our science and engineering classes are even better in the future. I could give you some more incentive, starting with the fact that physical science and engineering degrees are some of the most sought-after by employers, and among the most lucrative career paths you can take."

"Except for football," a short kid near Cal threw out. Clearly the joker in the pack.

"Cal could probably give you a breakdown on the probability of success in that career, too," Zoe said. "If you want to have that chat. He's an engineer himself, which means he knows a bit about probability."

She raised her eyebrows right back at Cal, and he grinned at her, leaned back in his chair, stretched his long legs out in front of him, and prepared to be the badass in the back row.

"All right," she said crisply, "let's get to it. As I'm sure you all know from doing the reading"—she looked around, caught a few eyes—"we're continuing our exploration of seismicity today with a look at volcanoes." She clicked on her laptop, and a video began. The familiar dramatic eruption, lava and smoke shooting high in the air.

"Explosions are always fun to watch," she said. "Hollywood knows that, and so do the rest of us. But what's actually going on here?"

For the next thirty minutes, Cal watched as she held them. Walking, talking, clicking, moving smoothly from one subject to the next. Turning it into a story.

"Let's look now," she said at last, "at a stratovolcano, the kind you'd see around here. We watched Mount St. Helens erupting at the beginning of class. What caused that to happen?" She moved to the white board, picked up a marker. "I could show you a nice slide of this," she told them. "And you could look at the diagram again in your textbook and call it good. Because, yes, this will be on the test." She paused for the laugh, her timing as good as any comedian's. "But I'm not going to do that, because here's another study tip from me, absolutely free of charge. Some of you may have heard this already, the ones who've been to all my scintillating lectures. But for those of you who may be hearing it for the first time . . ." Another pause, another laugh. "I'll tell you again. You retain a whole lot more when you write it down."

Her glance swept the room, catching the unlucky souls who weren't taking notes, and there was some scrambling.

"So," she said, "assuming that you'd like to be able to reproduce this next artistic effort on demand in, oh, about three weeks, you may want to follow along here."

She began to sketch the familiar cone shape. And all right, maybe he wasn't watching as carefully as he could have been. Maybe he was distracted, as he had been the whole time, by her white blouse and knit skirt, which she was wearing with sassy black tights and little boots. Fortunately, not her cowboy boots, because then he'd have been in real trouble.

"Here's your stratovolcano," she was saying as she drew. She labeled it at the top of the sketch. "I'll draw in some features, and you all just shout it out. Go ahead and feel free." She drew a long conduit down below the cone, a broad pool far beneath the surface. "So what do I label this?"

"Magma chamber." That was Amy, sitting in the second row, sounding proud.

"Good." Zoe wrote it in, drew a horizontal line above it. "And in what region of the earth is that magma chamber sitting? Come on now, sing out. I know you all know it."

"Deep crust," Cal heard from more than one mouth.

She went on, bringing them right along with her until she had a fully detailed sketch up there and, Cal was pretty sure, etched in everybody's notebook and brain as well.

"And there, boys and girls," she said, stepping back with a satisfied smile, "is your annotated diagram of a stratovolcano. I'm erasing it," she added, suiting the action to the words, "because I know you've all got it, and because we're moving on to Hawaii now, and our shield volcanoes. So flip a page, and away we go."

When she finished, Cal sat and waited until the last student had left the room, then untwisted himself—damn, these desks were cramped—and sauntered up to where Zoe was packing up, still not acknowledging him.

"So," he said, "that a pretty good example?"

"Of what?" she asked, looking up at last and giving him a cool smile.

"Of your teaching technique. I might actually have retained something if anybody had lectured at me like that. And here I thought," he sighed, "that I was doing you some big favor getting you on that committee. Joke's on me."

"Oh," she said, zipping up her laptop case again, "I suspect you retained a little bit. And I figured you might be here checking me out for the committee, making sure you hadn't embarrassed yourself."

"Checking you out, maybe," he said, "but not for the committee. Though I do have to say—color me impressed, Professor. Good to see you in your natural habitat. You got another class right now?"

"No, I'm done for the day. With classes, that is. Got some more work to do, of course."

"Uh-huh." He scratched his cheek. "In your office?"

"Well, yes. Of course."

"Going to show me that?"

"You've seen it." She looked a little rattled, and he smiled again, slow and lazy, because he knew that worked on her.

"You know," he told her, "I kinda want to see it again. I was thinking, watching you up there, about these real bad thoughts I used to have about my French teacher in high school." He sighed. "Flirty little skirt, flirty little voice, pretty little mouth? Oh, man. I didn't learn too much French."

"And you want me to go back to my office with you and pretend to be your *French* teacher? Somebody you had a crush on? Somebody *else*?" Her innocent round eyes had narrowed at him, but her dimples were peeping out all the same, because she was fighting a smile. "My, how flattering. Why does this not sound like it's going to be my most cherished moment?"

"Oh, sweetheart," he said, "I plan to do some real good cherishing. And I'm not going to be asking you to pretend to be anybody. I'm going to have my eyes wide open the whole time. I'm going to know that every inch of you is . . . you. And I'm hoping to get you familiar with every inch of me."

FANTASYLAND

He was kidding. He had to be kidding. Having sex in her office was some dirty-movie cliché, not something real people actually did. Wasn't it?

"Then," she said, keeping it cool, "if you've got all that planned, I guess we'd better go someplace where I can lock the door."

The smile was all the way there in his blue eyes, although his mouth stayed serious. "Now, see, Professor," he said, "this is why I'm so crazy about you. It's that logical brain of yours."

"Oh, is that it?"

"Well," he said, "it's one of the factors."

He walked sedately down two flights of stairs with her, then along the hallway, and she did her level best to calm the excitement heating her blood, the spark that had started low in her belly and moved even lower, buzzing her so hard it was almost unbearable.

She shifted her bag, opened the office door, and he stepped through behind her, slammed the door, and punched the lock. She swallowed, but walked on over to her desk, set her bag on the floor beside it, then stood back and looked at him.

"So," she said, "where does this deal start?"

He dropped into her guest chair, and she relaxed a little. Or felt disappointed a little. One or the other.

"You know," he said, "for somebody who says she wants a take-charge guy, you sure do like to set the tone. Is this my fantasy or yours?"

"Hey. I just *asked*."

"Yep. You sure did. How about this? How about if you just relax? Figure you don't have to ask, because I'm going to tell you. If you want to let go of the reins for a little while here, I'm pretty sure I can do the driving."

"I could do that," she said, trying to look unconcerned and, she was pretty sure, failing miserably. "Since it's your fantasy and all."

"Now, that's real good news." He looked her over. "Fantasies always have these technical difficulties, though. I think you'd better take off those cute little boots. The tights, too. They're going to be in my way."

"I've got underwear on, too," she said.

He sighed. "Here you go, driving again. Don't you worry about that. I can take care of your underwear. You just do what I said."

That tingle had set up full residence now, even as she wanted to laugh. She stared right back at him, tossed her hair a little, and pulled the boots off, then shimmied the tights down her legs and threw everything into the corner with her bag, like that had been her plan all along.

"Now, that's what I call fantasy material," he said, standing up and coming around the desk.

"What, me in a white blouse and a skirt?"

"Yep," he said, putting his hands on her shoulders . . . and *not* kissing her. Turning her so her back was to him, then setting those hard hands on her hips, pulling her back into him, doing a little grinding. And it felt so good.

"Standing up at that board," he said, shoving her hair back with one hand to kiss her neck, making her shiver and shift, drawing a gasp and a moan from her. "That fine little ass of yours talking to me."

His other hand had a button undone on her blouse, because he was coordinated. Another one, and his hand was inside, stroking over her, his lips still moving on the side of her neck, biting her nape, moving around to catch an earlobe between his teeth. "Thought I saw some lace in here," he murmured in her ear. "When I was trying to see through your blouse, thinking about what a bad boy like me would do to a sexy little professor once he got up behind her and felt that lace for himself."

His hand was inside her bra, had slipped right in there as he talked, and she was arching her back, because his fingers had captured the nipple between them, his thumb was brushing over it, and his lips were still there, tormenting her.

"And this bra's pink," he said, looking down her shirt. "You're killing me here."

His other hand had her hips tight against him again, and she could feel every inch of hard urgency. But he didn't rush, because he was still teasing.

"Of course," he said, "there's a whole lot more to this fantasy. Put your hands on that white board right there."

"What?'

"You heard me."

She swallowed. And did it.

He had her skirt pulled up with one hand, had settled his other hand over her cheek where he could hold her, stroke her, and his touch was igniting her.

"Aw, sweetheart," he sighed, "you shouldn't have worn the pink lacy underwear, too. That's just cruel and unusual."

"You don't . . . like them?" she managed to ask.

"I like them so much, I'm having some blood pressure issues here." One hand was on a breast now, he had her skirt pulled all the way up, and he was still pressed into her from behind, but his other hand was wandering up the inside of her bare thigh.

She wriggled back, needing to get closer, needing to feel him.

"What do you want?" His breath was warm in her ear, his big hand hard on her thigh.

"I want . . . you," she said. "To touch me. Please."

"And, see," he said, his hand still on its lazy journey, not in one bit of a hurry, "that's the kind of request a take-charge guy likes to hear."

She was sighing, her hands pressed against the board, her legs shifting farther apart, because his hand was stroking over the lace trim now, sliding inside the silky material. When he got all the way there at last, she jumped, then pressed back into him even more tightly.

He chuckled, low and soft. "Oh, that's real good, sweetheart. You're doing so good. You just stay right there and hold still." He yanked the skirt down over her hips, the stretchy knit material making his job easy. "Don't you move, now," he cautioned. "Step out, but leave your hands right there."

His fingers were probing, and she shifted her legs a little more to give him access, breathing hard. When his hand began to move at last, she moaned.

"Yes," she said, leaning her forehead against the cool white surface of the board, between her hands. "Please."

"Need to get fucked hard on your desk?" he asked her, his hand working.

The jolt went straight through her, and she was spiraling up. "Yes." It was almost a sob.

"That's what you're going to get. You're going to get it so hard. So, come on now. Show me how you want it."

She was over the edge, crying out, her hands fisting on the board, jerking back against him, and he took her all the way, let her ride out every last delicious spasm. It didn't matter that she was in her office. It didn't matter that they needed to be quiet. She couldn't be quiet, because it felt too good.

He didn't let her rest. As soon as she finished, he was pulling the underwear down her legs, unfastening the remaining buttons on the blouse, reaching around between her breasts to unhook her bra, dropping everything on the floor. And then he had her around the waist, was shoving everything on her desk aside, laying her down along it lengthwise, and pulling her hips to the edge.

She lay there, looked up at the high ceiling, and trembled. A few seconds, and he had his hands under her, raising her to him, his thumbs digging into her hips, and was inside her.

Fast and urgent, hard and strong, again and again, until she was moaning, trying to squirm toward him, because she needed more, and he had his hand there, helping her out. It was all she needed.

"Now," she managed to say. "Now. I'm . . . Cal. Come on. Now. Harder. Please."

He groaned, paused for just a moment, on the brink, his hand finishing the job, and she was calling out, over the top, and he plunged, dove, and they went under the wave together, again and again.

◆ ◆ ◆

She lay there afterward and tried to get her breath back, then finally struggled to her feet with the help of a strong hand around her own. He grinned at her, collected her clothes and dumped them on her desk, then went around the desk and sat in her guest chair again. He was looking nothing but cool, while her knees were still wobbling.

"You know, Professor," he told her as she wriggled into the pink panties and pulled on the black tights, "I've got to say, that was some pretty fair fantasy fulfillment. Especially having you buck-naked on your desk. Although I do love watching you get dressed, too. Almost as much as I love undressing you."

"Huh," she said. "I still think it was a little cheesy of you to make me act out a fantasy you had about somebody else."

"Well . . ." He rubbed his nose, grimaced. "I may have been, ah . . . embellishing a little."

She stopped in the act of picking up her bra. "What?"

"Yeah," he said, sounding a little abstracted, looking at her dressed only in her black tights. "Wait, what?"

She shrugged into the pink lace, arched her back a little more than was strictly necessary, then pulled it closed around her and snapped the clasp, and he sighed.

"Your fantasy," she reminded him.

"Like I said. Embellished. I didn't actually take French. Too hard."

"Too . . . hard." She put her hands on her hips, ignored the fact that she was wearing her underwear, and gave him her best basilisk stare. "So you never had this fantasy."

"I didn't say I didn't have it. I just may have had it a bit more recently than I gave you reason to believe."

"You had it about . . ."

"Well, yeah. If you're going to get all technical about it, I may have had it today. Not that your talk about volcanoes wasn't real riveting and all. I can't help it if you're distracting."

"You made up the whole *thing*?" she demanded. "I should be so mad at you right now. You dirty liar."

"Seems I'll do just about anything to get you where I want you. And, man . . ." He sighed. "I really, really wanted you right there."

"You got me, too," she said, pulling on her skirt. "Guess it worked. You are one sneaky . . ."

"Bastard," he finished. "I sure did. I got you real good. We're going to do it again, too. Because I've got a couple more teacher fantasies you could help me out with."

"As long as they don't involve rulers," she said, trying for severity.

"Well . . . not *rulers*."

She was staring at him again, and that flame had come right back to life. "Do not tell me," she said slowly, "that you've got a fantasy about spanking me in my office."

"Okay," he said, "I won't. I won't tell you that I've got this real dirty little fantasy about sitting right here in this chair, putting you over my knee, flipping up that pretty blue sweater dress of yours, and giving you the spanking of your life while you wriggle under my hand. I'll just keep that one right off the table. So to speak. Because the desk might figure into it again, too. I'd have to look at what I did, wouldn't I? While I did . . . everything else."

The flame licked harder, and he saw her shudder, because he never missed a thing, and he gave her that slow, lazy grin that weakened her knees every time and was weakening her now.

"Oh, Professor," he said, his voice liquid sin that made all the blood rush right back where he had meant to send it, "if you tell me that I'm going to be able to count on that one, too, I might just have a heart attack."

"Well . . ." She swallowed. "You know how I like a take-charge guy."

"Yeah," he said, blue eyes alight with mischief and lust and everything that made him Cal. "I do, don't I? Darlin', you just made my day. Twice. But for right now, why don't you come on over here, sit in my lap, and let me button up that proper little blouse of yours for you, kiss you a little bit, and feel you up while I'm doing it? Because I just realized that I never did kiss you, and that'd be real good, too. For now."

THE MINOR LEAGUES

They left her office fifteen minutes later. She'd decided she could finish her work at his house, with a little extra persuasion that he'd been more than happy to provide. She pulled the door closed and gave it a quick test before heading down the corridor, and he had to smile, because she might not be walking quite as steadily as she had been going in there.

"Feeling a little shaky?" he murmured in her ear. "I get you a little bit weak in the knees there? Never mind. We've got a treatment for that."

"I don't think I can take any more of your treatments," she said, keeping her voice down, out of the hearing of two of her colleagues standing outside an office at the far end of the hallway.

"Oh, sweetheart, I think you can take it. You're made of some pretty tough stuff. I think we can test you a whole lot more before you break." He saw the shiver and smiled again. Look what kind of woman had been hiding under that black suit. Exactly the woman for him.

She slowed, and he thought it was reluctantly, as they approached the two men still standing near the stairway. "See you guys tomorrow," she said.

They looked up, and Cal saw the recognition on both faces, resigned himself.

"Well, hello, hotshot," one of them said. Not to him. To her. A lean man in his early forties with a sardonic mouth, he was wearing baggy khakis and a button-down shirt. All he needed was a tweed jacket with leather patches to shout "professor" a little more loudly. "Who do you have there? It wouldn't be the university's favorite son, would it?"

She stopped. "If you mean this is Cal Jackson, then yes, your eyes don't deceive you. You know I'm on his committee. Cal, the rude guy here is Roy Blake, and this is Aaron Mortenson, my department chair."

"Pleasure," the older man said, shaking hands. "Well, I'm out of here. My daughter's got a volleyball game this evening, and I promised I'd go. See you all tomorrow."

Roy was still looking from Zoe to Cal. "You know," he said, "the last time I was forced to attend a university function—kicking and screaming, I might add—all I got were a couple of stale crackers, some discount American cheese, and not enough glasses of very cheap wine. You go to one—*one*—so-called cocktail party, and here you are, on about the highest-profile committee you could possibly swing, and . . . everything. You could fall into a septic tank and come out smelling like roses. This girl's going no place but straight to the top," he told Cal. "And I called it. How I love being right."

Zoe was flushing a little, standing up straighter, the way she did when she was under the gun. Hardening under pressure, just like one of her rocks. "Thanks so much for offering us your astute observations, Roy. Remind me tomorrow to let you know how much I appreciated them."

He laughed. "Oh, I don't think Cal minds," he said, and Cal wondered just how soundproof those walls actually were. "All good things," he told Cal. "Nothing to say but good things. Stars have to rise. That's how it works."

"Actually," Cal said, "I thought stars mostly tended to fall."

"Oh, that's right," Roy said. "What can I say, astronomy's not my subject. I don't think there's going to be a whole lot of falling here. For the hotshots like our Dr. Santangelo, it's a couple years in the trenches, and hello Stanford. Got your cushy graduate seminars, got all those doctoral students doing your scut work for you, and bye-bye, gatekeeper classes. So long, hormonal eighteen-year-olds who haven't figured out that you actually have to study in college. They'll be some other unlucky slob's problem. Some doctoral student's problem."

The skin on Cal's arms was prickling. He looked at Zoe, could see that she was uncomfortable, and this wasn't looking good at all. "Is that the plan?" he asked her. "I didn't realize that."

"Well," she said, and laughed, although he couldn't see what was funny. "This is a teaching university."

"I thought they were all teaching universities," he said. "I thought that was kind of the point."

"This is the minor leagues," Roy said. "Our Zoe here is headed for the majors. There's a sports metaphor for you."

"Thanks," Cal said. "I sure appreciate you putting it in terms I can understand."

"A research institution," Zoe hurried to explain, her color even higher, "is a university that's focused on—well, research. Which means professors do more research and less teaching, especially undergraduate teaching."

"And let me guess," Cal said. "Being at a teaching university is low-rent. Means you'll never make the big time."

"That's right," Roy said cheerfully. "Which for some of us is just fine. But for somebody like Zoe, we're nothing but a way station on that bright road."

"Uh-huh," Cal said. "And this way station is, what? A couple years? Three?"

"Unless she gets stuck here," Roy said. "Gets lazy like me, decides it's all too hard and she might as well settle for second-rate. If you want to hit the big time, you've got to go where it's happening."

"And that's not here," Cal said.

"Nope," Roy said. "That's a couple of mountain states and about a thousand miles away from here."

"Uh-huh," Cal said again. He looked down at Zoe, tried not to let his feelings show. Tried not to let the anger take over, and failed completely. "Ready to go? Because I am."

"Uh . . ." She glanced between him and Roy. "Sure. See you, Roy."

"Sure thing. Nice to meet you, Cal."

"Yeah."

He knew Zoe was looking at him, but too bad. His boots rang in the hallway, as out of place as a sheep at the symphony, and they were both silent until they'd made it to the stairway and were headed down. And then she finally talked. And said nothing he wanted to hear.

THE MOMENT OF TRUTH

Zoe felt sick. The look on Cal's face . . .

Maybe it was just Roy. Or maybe she'd screwed up. Maybe, and this was the bad thing, the worst thing—maybe she'd hurt Cal.

"I'm sorry," she ventured. "He's . . . not bitter, exactly. He thinks he's funny."

He turned halfway down the steps and looked at her. "You think I'm upset about that? Garden-variety envy? Think I've never seen that?"

"But you seem so annoyed," she said cautiously. "Is it that I'm friends with Roy? Please tell me that's not it, that you're not jealous."

"Oh, because it's all about what *you* want?" He was walking again.

"What?"

They'd reached the bottom of the stairs, and he stopped and turned to face her, his face harder than she'd ever seen it. The sickness was worse now, was actually making her feel a little faint.

"It wouldn't occur to you," he said, "that I might be upset to find out that I'm, what was it? A way station?"

"Um . . ." She didn't know what to do with her hands. "Well, eventually, yes, that'll probably happen. This is a step, just like . . ."

She cast around for an example. "College football for you," she said with relief. "A starting place. And then you guys move around, try to find the place where you fit, where you can star. It's like that."

"You know," he said, "I can understand regular grown-up topics without people putting them into sports terms. I've worked real hard to raise my IQ past double digits."

"I was just trying to find an applicable example," she said. "That's all."

"Yeah, thanks. I got it. And that's what you want. To be a star."

"Well, isn't it what you wanted, too?" He knew how much her work mattered to her. At least she'd thought he did. "I want to do research. I want to *be* somebody."

"I thought people here did research. I kind of thought that was the idea of the money I gave. To make us more competitive."

"But it's still not—"

"Not the big time," he finished for her. "Not the biggest time, anyway, and it never will be, and that's all you care about. So where does the rest of your life come into this?"

"What rest of my life?"

He gestured impatiently. "You know, that thing most women start thinking about at some point here. Marriage. Family. The rest of your life."

She tried to laugh, but it didn't come out right. "Are you asking me to declare my intentions?"

He went rigid. "Don't be trying to make this funny," he warned her. "Don't you dare try to make me look stupid for caring about you."

"I'm not," she said. "I'm not." She was trembling a little now. She needed to sit down, and she couldn't, so she straightened up instead. She had to face this. She had to face him. "I'm sorry. It's just . . . not what I'd have expected you to say. I didn't think you were really . . . serious. That you really cared." *Not as much as I did.*

"Why not?" he asked. "For a person who's supposed to be a scientist, you make a lot of assumptions, don't you? And they don't even seem to me to fit the evidence."

"What . . ." She swallowed. "What do you mean?"

"Why would you assume I'm just messing around here? What evidence do you have?"

"I don't know," she said. He didn't get it? Really? "Maybe that you're Cal Jackson, and I'm . . . me? So I thought I should guard my heart? That doesn't make any sense to you?"

"When did I make you feel that way?" he demanded. "When? All right, I wanted to sleep with you. Of course I did. I'm a guy. It's how we're made. That doesn't mean I wanted to sleep with you and dump you, or that I was going to dump you if I couldn't sleep with you fast enough. I didn't do either thing. Even though I'm a guy, and a jock, too. I didn't, and I would've thought that was obvious."

"But . . ." She tried to focus, and failed, so she just stood there.

He sighed, some of the anger seeming to drain away, but what was left behind looked like . . . resignation. And pain. Half an hour earlier, he'd been inside her body, and now, everything they'd shared was gone. Just like that.

Loss. That was what she saw on his face. And that was what was making her own heart thump in dull agitation, making her own breath come choppy and short. Loss.

"Look," he told her at last, "I'm thirty-two years old. I've been divorced once already from somebody who didn't want the things I wanted, who didn't want to live in the place I live. My career isn't what you'd call portable. I'm here to stay, and I don't have a couple more years to mess around with somebody getting my kicks, or giving her hers."

"I'm not saying mess around, though," she protested. "When did I say mess around?"

"What do you want to call it? You think of the name, and we'll call it that. If it's not going anywhere and doesn't have a chance to go anywhere, to me, that's messing around."

"But wait. Wait," she insisted, because this wasn't fair. Was it? "Is it my fault that I didn't say, before I slept with you, that I didn't want to settle down and marry you? Was I supposed to say that? You would have thought I was delusional."

"Go on," he said. "Make me ridiculous. You can even win. I'll give you the trophy and tell you that you won. But I've been straight-up here. You're the one with a hidden agenda, and you can't even see it. You've been so busy assuming that you can't trust men, that you can't trust me, you've gone and done the exact same thing to me you're always worrying about. You telling me you don't see that?"

"But I . . . I didn't know you'd want all that," she tried to explain again. "Not with me."

"How would you think I didn't? You sat in my dining room and listened to me tell you about Jolie. You saw how busted up I was about that. You knew I wanted a family, because I told you. What did you think I was doing hanging around with you? Amusing myself until something better came along?"

"I—" She'd gotten herself stuck again. She hadn't looked past the present, because she hadn't dared to believe it was more than casual. That was the answer. And she hadn't wanted to think about why that was.

"The truth is," he told her, "the one who's been doing that? It's you. If somebody's using somebody here, if somebody's stringing somebody else along, it sure as hell ain't me."

She couldn't be mad. She only wanted to cry, because this hurt. It hurt so much. But she couldn't cry, because that would hurt him more.

"I'm sorry," she said, knowing that wasn't good enough. "I should have told you, and I didn't. I just wanted to . . . be with you. I didn't think it through. And I'm . . . I'm sorry."

"Yeah, well," he said. "So am I. And what the hell." He sighed, leaned back against the wall, ran a hand through his hair, and she hated the fatigue she heard in his voice. "I screwed up, too. Picked the wrong woman. Again."

It was a punch to the gut. Because it was true. And she had nothing to say.

"If you're not in," he said after a moment, "you're not. And I don't have time in my life to hang around waiting for another California girl to decide whether this Podunk town is someplace she can stand to be. I tried that already. It didn't work out then, and I've got no reason in the world to think it'd work any better now."

"I can't say anything else, though." She tried to stop the tremble in her voice, and failed. "And I'm not sure it's fair to ask me to."

"Maybe not," he said. "But I can't help it. I guess we just want different things, and that's the way it is. I'm a simple guy. I'm in or I'm out. I play hard or I go home. And I want a woman who's the same way. I want a woman who's in."

"Well," she said, and swallowed against the pain, "I can't say that. I'm sorry. I can't. I can't promise to stay here, because it'd be a lie."

"Yeah," he said. "I got it." He shoved off the wall. "Come on. I'll give you a ride home."

"And that's it?" she asked. "That's all?"

"Yeah," he said. "That's it. Play hard or go home. You don't want to play hard, so I guess we'd both better go home."

LISTENING

The man swung by the house, the same way he had every night for the past two weeks. Casually, not slowing. Checking, just in case. He didn't want to change his methods now, as frustrating as it had been to wait.

The first couple of his American girls had been so easy. Not much harder than in Iraq. Sitting ducks. Since he'd come to Paradise, though, everything had gone straight to hell. He'd had nothing but aggravation, and it was all her fault. Everything that had gone wrong had started with her. Which meant it had to finish with her, too.

He'd never hurt them. Much. But maybe it was time to change that. Let her know who she was messing with. Let them both know, because Cal was every bit a part of this, too. He thought he could protect her? That he could win this game, like he'd won all those others? He was going to find out that this wasn't a football game. This was a whole different game, and there was no rulebook except the law of the jungle. Winner take all, and there was only going to be one winner here.

Nine o'clock. The light shone through the window beside her front door, and her car was there, and his truck wasn't, for once.

Was she there, though—that was the question. But every question had an answer.

He swung into a driveway up the street without slowing, with purpose, in front of a darkened house whose unplowed walk showed as clearly as a "Vacancy" sign that its owners were gone. Invitation to burglary right there. There was a sucker born every minute.

He pulled his duffel out from under the seat, pulled out a penlight to select a few things, not risking the cab's overhead light, zipped the bag up, and stowed it again. No sense leaving evidence for anyone to see, unlikely as that was. You could never be too careful.

Across the street, down the sidewalk, walking like a guy with a plan and not any kind of loiterer. He cast a casual glance behind him. Nobody, so he cut fast through her neighbors' side yard, past another big dark house with nobody home. Around the back, over a short hedge that he jumped with ease.

He spared a thought for footprints, then shrugged. The snow would have filled them by morning, and he was wearing boots, size ten and a half. What were they going to know from that? Not a damn thing. That he was a guy with regular-size feet, wearing boots in the snow.

His movements were stealthier now, because there *were* lights on here at the back of the house, on the second floor as well as in her apartment. He skirted the pools of yellow light beside her door and the back door of the main house and made his way quickly around to the back, where her bedroom was. The pleasurable excitement wound higher at the thought.

Not yet, he reminded himself. *Recon.*

He crouched low, invisible in the dark. Dark clothes, dark hat, dark gloves. He pulled the little box from his pocket, put in the earbuds, and switched the machine on. Directed it toward her wall, sat still and listened.

Music. Classical. He made a face. Of course. She *really* wasn't his type, other than physically. No kind of party girl. But he'd have a party with her all the same.

He hunkered down for ten long, cold minutes, waiting. Listening. And heard nothing but the music. No conversation. Then a scrape that was a chair being pushed back, footsteps coming closer, and another light switched on, farther down the wall. Bathroom. Toilet flush, sink. The light went out, and he heard the footsteps again, the chair.

Working in the kitchen, he decided. A lonely night grading papers.

You're lonely now, Zoe, he promised her. *But you won't be lonely long.*

He didn't know why, but she was alone for once. She thought she was safe, or Cal did. Or maybe she hadn't been good enough, and Cal had gotten bored.

That was the beauty of this line of entertainment. It didn't matter if they were good in bed or not. It was always good for him. And it was never boring.

He couldn't follow all his usual steps, but it would be good enough. He'd make sure of that. He'd add some . . . enhancements. Take his time and do it right, give her some memorable moments. When he got done with her, she'd have some souvenirs to mark the occasion.

He put the device away, stood up, and retraced his steps, checking before he left the shelter of the neighbors' house for passersby. Nobody, not in the dark, not in the snow, not in this peaceful, quiet neighborhood. This safe neighborhood.

Back across the street, into his truck, and home. He had an invasion to plan.

WIND CHIMES

Zoe woke again. Woke scared, just like every other time, her muscles tense, her ears straining to hear something that wasn't there.

She couldn't sleep without Cal. She couldn't think without Cal.

The misery engulfed her again. She'd worked late, trying to distract herself, to get tired enough for sleep. Until eventually, she'd been unable to focus on the screen and had climbed gratefully into bed. And had lain awake all the same, thinking about what had happened.

Everything she'd been so wary of, everything she'd suspected Cal of doing—she'd done it all to him, and she hadn't even realized it. The look in his eyes, the expression on his face, the knowledge that it was over, that he didn't want her, because she wasn't enough, because she couldn't be enough—it had all hurt her heart with an actual physical pain that still ached in her chest.

She didn't understand her foolish heart. Or rather, she did. Her heart wanted him. It was her head that kept insisting on the plan. And all she felt was confused. Confused, and miserable, so sorry for how she'd hurt him, and so lonely for him.

The tears trickled down her cheeks despite her efforts to suppress them, and she wiped them impatiently away with the sheet, then abandoned the effort and let them come, let the waves of sorrow and guilt overtake her until she had cried herself to sleep.

◆ ◆ ◆

She wasn't sure how long it had been before she woke again. The same fear, the same straining ears, the same eyes, open and staring into the darkness. The same terror. Again.

She should have gone to Rochelle's. Cal had wanted her to. After all that he'd said, all she'd said, he'd suggested that she pack a bag and call her friend, had told her she shouldn't be alone. She'd promised him she'd go later, but she hadn't. She hadn't been able to face the thought of being with somebody else, not tonight. Having to tell Rochelle what had happened, that she'd lost him. That would have made it true, and she couldn't stand that it was true. She'd told herself that she'd been safe so far, that tomorrow was soon enough to make another plan.

Now, she wished she'd gone to cry and drink too much with a girlfriend like a normal person, because she was scared. She told her racing heart to settle down, tried to close her eyes, but they stayed open, and she was sitting up now without even realizing it, sitting up and listening.

Nothing. Or something? She held her breath, strained toward it, tried to hear.

Clink. She knew that sound, and she was moving.

Clink-clink-clink-clink. The bamboo wind chimes Cal had hung in her bedroom doorframe resonated with their cheerful music, a low voice uttered a curse, and there was movement in the dark, then a penlight shining on the bed. On where she'd been a moment earlier.

It all happened in a second. The next second, she had the gun in her hands, had racked the slide.

Ka-chunk. The unmistakable sound of the shell sliding into the chamber of a pump-action shotgun, and the light was swinging around, blinding her where she stood tucked into the wall in the shelter of the bedside table.

"I've got my finger on the trigger," she said, her voice shaking only a little. "Aimed right at that light. Got four more in the magazine in case I miss."

"You *bitch.*" It was a hiss.

"I'd love to splatter your brains on my bedroom wall. Just give me an excuse." Her voice was stronger, because Cal had been right. There was nothing like a 20-gauge to give you confidence. She held the gun in one hand, and her other hand found the light switch, exactly like she'd practiced. She got her hand back onto the grip fast, steadied the gun, and looked at him.

Amy had been right, too. Big and strong, wearing a ski mask, the white circles around eyes and mouth making him a monster. A nightmare. His hands outstretched, glistening in surgical gloves.

Monkey paws, Amy had said. Still holding his light, because he was frozen. Because he was the one who was scared now.

"Put the light down," she told him. "Hands on your head."

"You won't," he said, and there was a sneer in his voice despite everything. "You don't have the guts."

She braced herself, jerked the gun to the side, and fired into the closet wall a bare two feet to his right, a galvanizing explosion of noise in the night, and saw him leap. She didn't hesitate, racked the slide again instantly, exactly like she'd practiced, like Cal had taught her. *Four more. One to put him down, one to make sure he stays down, and two more for insurance.* "Just give me one reason," she told him. "Toss the light on the bed. Do it now."

He didn't. She saw the hesitation, and her finger tightened on the trigger. She was going to shoot him. She knew it. She was going to shoot him the second he moved toward her. And then she was going to shoot him again.

He didn't move toward her, though. He turned and ran, crashing through the wind chimes again, leaving them swinging wildly, tinkling merrily in his wake. She followed, but she had to scramble around the end of the bed, focus on keeping the gun level.

By the time she got into the living room, he was climbing out of the window, the beam from his flashlight making him easy to spot, then dropping down onto the ground below and running across the yard.

She wanted to shoot him in the back. But she didn't. She couldn't.

CALL IN THE NIGHT

Cal woke to the sound of his phone.

Zoe. Calling to . . . what? Apologize? Talk? He'd take the call, he knew he would. Call him a fool.

But when he rolled over and picked it up, it wasn't her name he saw.

"Jim?" His voice, his brain were still fuzzy with sleep. He sat up, switched on the lamp, blinked against the glare. "What? What time is it?"

His cousin didn't answer that. "Do you know that the city cops are headed over to Zoe's house?"

"*What?*" He was already climbing out of bed, grabbing his Levi's out of the closet.

"Isn't she 247 Jackson?"

"Yes. What?" he demanded. "*What?*"

"Our mutt, I'm assuming," his cousin said, his voice so maddeningly calm. "Broke in. Just heard it on the scanner."

Cal's hand was frozen on his jeans. "Zoe," he said, his throat so dry he could barely get the word out.

"Don't know," Jim said, understanding him perfectly. "Ten-seventy-one. Shots fired. That's all I've got."

"I'm headed over there now." He had his jeans buttoned, had grabbed his wallet and his keys, was out the door and down the stairs. Junior was off his bed already, standing by the door waiting for him. "Call me."

"Will do," Jim said. "But you'll know before I will. Probably."

◆ ◆ ◆

Probably. Probably, if there weren't more news on the scanner first. More bad news.

The drive into town took forever, and it was agony. Junior sat beside him in the cab, perched high, looking out the window, and Cal drove just as fast as he dared, took the curves at the screaming limit of the truck's capability.

Shots fired. The guy had never used a gun before, but nobody'd been on his track before, and what if that had gotten back to him?

Was it actually Greg? Cal hadn't believed it, not really. It had been a way-out idea. Could his own cousin really do something like this, be this kind of monster?

However quiet the investigation had been, Greg could have caught on, sniffed it out. Or somebody could have told him. Somebody who thought that the brotherhood of law enforcement came before everything, even before this. *The thin blue line.*

And Cal had left her alone, where the bastard could get at her. He'd done that. Him.

Why hadn't he checked with Rochelle? Why hadn't he made sure she was safe?

Because he'd been mad, that was why. He'd been picturing her over at Rochelle's drinking wine, talking about him. He'd assumed she was sitting on the couch telling Rochelle that it wasn't her fault, when it was actually *all* her fault. Both of them talking about what jerks guys were. He'd thought about it all night, had run through it again and again in his mind until he'd made it true.

Because his pride had been hurt. That was the real reason. His heart had been aching, but his heart would have made sure she was safe, if not for his stubborn pride. His pride had been stronger than his heart. And now . . . *shots fired.*

"Come on, baby," he found himself muttering. "Please. Please have shot him. Please."

He saw the pulsing reflections of red and blue flashing against the snow even before he turned into the street. Three cars, the lights in their bars revolving, parked on the street outside the house. Neighbors on front porches despite the hour, despite the storm. But no ambulance. No ambulance.

He pulled up next to one of the cop cars. "Stay," he told Junior, and slammed the door.

He was up the walk, around the side, but a figure was blocking his way. "Stop right there," the voice said.

"It's Cal Jackson," Cal said, his voice coming out too tight. "That's my girlfriend. Zoe Santangelo. That's her place. Is she all right?"

A flashlight scanned him, then lowered, a hand coming off the barrel of a gun. "Hey, Cal. Jesse Hartung."

"Zoe," he said again.

"She's okay," Jesse said, and Cal's knees buckled a little.

"Okay how?" he insisted.

"All the way okay. Well, shook up," Jesse amended. "She chased him off. Let off a shotgun doing it."

"What about the guy?"

"We're checking with the neighbors, doing a search, but he'll be long gone."

"She in there?"

"Yeah. Hang on a minute." Jesse was raising his radio to his lips, but Cal was already moving around him.

The door was unlocked, and the two men standing in front of Zoe's couch turned at his entrance, opened their mouths to say something. What, he never found out, because he was already past them.

She was wrapped in a blanket, sitting dry-eyed and straight, but shaking. She started to stand up at the sight of him, but he grabbed her, pulled her back down onto the couch, and held her, fighting the emotions back.

She hung on. He could feel her trembling, and he was smoothing her hair, kissing her forehead. "It's okay, baby," he told her, even though it wasn't. "It's okay. You're all right."

She nodded jerkily against him, and he could feel the struggle for control as if he were inside her body, maybe because he was fighting the same fight. She took a few deep breaths, and he did the same, and then she pulled away and sat back.

He kept his arm around her, because he couldn't let her go. "What happened?" he asked.

"We're just getting her statement now," the guy in charge said, somebody Cal didn't know. He said it pretty pointedly.

"And you can wait about two minutes until she tells me what happened," Cal said, because his rage had to go somewhere. "She might have told you that I was around the last time this scumbag went after her."

"And when was that?"

"Check with the sheriff's office," Cal said. "Jim Lawson. It's all on report. For that matter, check with the university cops, too. Maybe if you guys worked together, you could actually catch the guy."

"Sir," the cop said with a sigh, "that's what we're trying to do. If you'll calm down, maybe we can get the lady's statement and make some progress."

"Two minutes. What happened?" he asked Zoe again.

"He cut the window glass," she said, jerking her head toward the corner of the room, and Cal realized for the first time that it was freezing in here and the cops still had their jackets on.

"Pretty professional job," the cop said, apparently deciding to forgive him. "Didn't break it. Cut out a semicircle with a glass-cutting tool, probably used some putty to remove it, took it away with him. Quiet. Neat. He's practiced that."

"I didn't hear it," Zoe told Cal. "I heard the wind chimes. He wasn't expecting the wind chimes. Thanks."

"That your idea?" the cop asked.

"Yeah," Cal said. "I figured it might give her a couple seconds, just in case. Jim said shots fired, though," he told Zoe. "Who fired? Him?" He tensed even more at the thought. If the guy was willing to shoot her, that cast a whole new light on things.

"No," she said, and actually looked a little proud. "Me."

"But you missed? Damn, baby, that's real disappointing."

The cop looked startled, but she smiled, because yeah, she was just that tough. "On purpose," she assured him. "He said I wouldn't do it. I was just trying to be convincing. I think I was pretty convincing."

"Buckshot has that effect," the cop said. "Pretty dangerous letting that off in an inhabited area."

"Pretty dangerous for me if I hadn't," she snapped back before Cal could answer.

"Just keep in mind," the cop said, "you start carrying concealed or anything, you need a license."

"She was in danger," Cal said. "I gave her a pump-action and taught her how to use it, and you can assume we've applied for that concealed-carry permit, too. Not her fault that the system takes forever. You didn't see him applying for a license to rape her. So if arming her was a crime, I guess I'm going to jail."

The cop chose to ignore that. Probably wise. He could probably tell how close to the edge Cal was.

"I wanted to keep him on the ground," Zoe said. "I was planning to call 911 so they could catch him. But he ran."

"Could have shot him then," Cal said.

"Hey," the cop protested, and now Cal was the one ignoring *him.*

"I could have," Zoe admitted. "But first, it was shooting him in the back. I don't think I could have. And second, he was on his way out the window. The Dolans' house is right there. I couldn't risk that, could I? They have *kids*. I don't even know which thing was working harder in my brain, but I couldn't shoot him. Even though," she confessed, "I so wish now that I had. I so wish he'd made a move. Another step and I was going to shoot. I wish he'd taken that step."

"Not more than I do," Cal said.

"And if you're all done here with your own investigation," the cop said, "maybe it would be all right with you if we kept going here so the lady can get this over with, get some sleep tonight."

Yeah, like that was happening, but Cal made a gesture of acceptance, sat back with Zoe, and waited while she answered. Over and over. Not telling him anything they didn't already know. Tall, because the guy had hit the wind chimes good and hard, but shorter than Cal, she thought. Big, but not huge. Dark clothes, ski mask, gloves. No zip ties, but that was because he hadn't *gotten* to the zip ties. Thank God.

"Did he do the flowers?" Cal interjected as the thought struck him.

"Flowers?" the cop asked.

"That's his calling card," Cal said. "Ask Jim Lawson. He sends flowers ahead of time. Like it's a date."

"No," Zoe said. "No flowers."

"Not enough time," Cal guessed. "He didn't know you'd be alone until the last minute. Which means he was watching."

"We've checked with the neighbors," the cop said. "Nobody's noticed anybody suspicious. Dark Ford F-150, she says? Not that anybody particularly saw, or remembers."

"How suspicious is a guy driving by in a pickup?" Cal agreed with frustration. "I'm sure he wasn't circling the block or anything. He's careful."

"So he didn't know she'd be alone," the cop said. "Why was that? She normally not alone? Why are you so sure he was watching?"

"Zoe and I had a fight today," Cal said. No point not saying it. "I wasn't here. I've been here until now, or she's been at my place. She was alone, and he saw it, and he jumped."

"Uh-huh," the cop said, making a note. "Targeted, you're thinking."

"Absolutely. That's his pattern. It's all there in the other reports."

More questions, more answers, over and over and over the same ground, and Zoe was clearly flagging, the terror headed straight into exhaustion now.

"We about done here?" Cal asked after she'd described what the guy had said, what he'd done, for what seemed like the fourth time. "Because I think you've got it."

"*You* don't decide if I've got it," the cop said. "*I* decide if I've got it." He closed his notebook, though. "But I've pretty much got it. I'll be coordinating with the other agencies, and we'll have a report for you to sign tomorrow, ma'am. I can find you at the university? Or here?"

"Not here," Cal said immediately, before Zoe could answer. "At my parents' place." He gave the address.

"I could—I can't—" Zoe began.

"What?" Cal demanded. "You can't stay here. Tell me you aren't thinking that."

"No," she said, and she was trembling a little again. "But—"

"But what? Rochelle? You going to put her in the guy's sights, too?"

"No," she said, her face stricken. "No. I can't do that. Not even with the shotgun. Who knows if he'd go after her. I can't do that."

"So it's my parents'," he said. "Only place where I know you'll be all right, and where you'll feel all right."

"Bossy," she said, with the hint of a smile.

"Yeah," he told her, and his heart twisted, because he still wanted her, and what was he going to do about that? Nothing but suffer, because nothing had changed, except that it was even harder now. "Bossy."

◆ ◆ ◆

Zoe hesitated a little upon entering her bedroom, and Cal stepped through first, ducking under the wind chimes that had saved her. That, and her own quick action.

"Suitcase," he said, trying to stay businesslike at the sight of the bed with its covers twisted to the side, the shotgun against the wall. "And did you unload it?"

"Oh." She looked blank. "No."

"Never mind." He picked it up, racked the slide, gathered the shells, opened her bedside table, and put them into the ammo box he'd installed there, then lifted the whole thing out. "Take this with you," he advised. "Keep it in your car."

"In my *car*?"

"Hell, yeah, in your car. You want to land in the ditch with him behind you without it?"

She flinched, straightened again, and said, "No. I don't."

He said, "Good," and that was that.

He studied the neat pattern of holes drilled into her closet door as she opened it, hauled out a big suitcase, and tossed it onto the bed. "Good job," he said. "Center mass. Just wish it had been *his* center mass."

"I know," she said, with another of the flashes of spirit she'd showed that night. "But would you quit *saying* that? I should have just shot him. I've wished and wished I had. Your saying it doesn't help."

"Sorry," he said with surprise.

She sat on the bed with a thump. "I just . . . couldn't. If he'd been coming at me, I could have. But I couldn't stand there and shoot him."

"Fairly hard, I imagine, to shoot somebody in cold blood," Cal said. "Unless your brain tells you it's him or you. We're pretty wired not to kill, I'd say. Most of us." He smiled a little, sat beside her, took her hand. "Hey. Here I am comforting you because you didn't kill somebody. Not what anybody would have thought a few weeks ago, huh?"

She laughed, sounding better. "I guess I've changed."

"I'd say you have."

"Have . . . you, though?" she asked cautiously. "I mean . . . what you said before. Is that still . . . the same?"

He stood up again. "Yeah. It is. I'll keep you safe. And I can't promise not to care about you. But I can't just put my heart right out there to get broken. Not again."

"Okay. I understand." She looked rattled, but she stood up again, went to her closet, and started to pull clothes out, because nobody had more guts than Zoe.

She carried an armful to the bed, tossed it down, began to strip items from their hangers, and stopped. "Oh, no. Oh, *no.*"

"What?" he asked in alarm, because she sounded truly distressed.

"I . . ." She picked it up. Her black jacket, punched neatly through in two places. Two round places. "I shot my suit." And then she started to laugh.

He went for the skirt that lay under it. Another couple of holes. The blue blouse beneath. Also wrecked.

"Five yards away," she said, her shoulders beginning to shake with it. "That means a pattern five inches across. I shot up my entire professional wardrobe. All five inches of it."

She was flipping through one ugly item after another. Those black pants. Another blouse, a pair of khaki pants that had fully deserved to die. All of them ventilated now, and he was laughing with her, both of them overcome, sinking down onto the bed again, and she scooped everything up and flung it into the air, watched it land on the floor.

"Sayonara," she said, gasping a little, wiping her eyes on the sheet. "You said you hated them over and over. And now I've shot them all, and the only thing they're good for is a bonfire."

"I can't think of any clothes that deserve it more," he said. "Death by firing squad. I told you that you were a natural shooter. Right through the closet door and everything."

"I'm going to be wearing jeans to work," she said.

"Oh, I don't know." He went to her closet again and pulled out the blue sweater dress, a short knit skirt, a white blouse with a V-neck. "I'd say some of your better investments survived."

"Those are too feminine for work," she said. "It's better to look more . . ."

"No," he said, pulling them off their hangers and beginning to fold as she stared at him and shook her head. Probably thinking he was bossy again, and too bad. "It's not. You don't look masculine, and you're never going to, so you can just give it right up. You're not a man, and nobody's ever going to mistake you for one. So, look like a woman, get them off guard, because nothing messes a man up more than a good-looking woman. And then hit 'em with your smarts. One-two punch. My advice, and you don't even have to pay for it. Ten Tips for Showing Them Who's Boss."

"Did you read that?" she asked suspiciously, getting up and gathering more hangers full of clothes from the closet.

"Nope," he said. "I made that up all by myself. Might even sell it to a magazine."

SAFE HARBOR

Zoe couldn't get into her car alone, when it came down to it. Everything that had happened tonight, everything she'd done, and she couldn't do this. She couldn't stand the thought of taking that snowy, lonely road by herself, even with Cal following behind. It was irrational, and it was stupid, and she still couldn't do it.

He saw her hesitation. "Come on," he said, throwing her suitcase into the bed of the pickup and opening the passenger door to an enthusiastically tail-wagging canine welcome from Junior. She rubbed the big dog's ugly head while he grunted his satisfaction and politely refrained from licking her, and she felt better for it.

"Hop on up," Cal said, "and Junior and I will take you home. Bring you out here again in the morning, follow you to the university in the daylight. With the shotgun right there in your car. As long as you've got the doors locked, you've got the time to load. If you need to practice that, my dad will help you out."

"I don't need help," she said when he'd started the truck and was pulling out. "At least, I'll be practicing some more, yes. But I practiced before. I practiced with Rochelle, with the dummy shells you gave me. I can load fast. And now I'll be practicing taking it out of the backseat, grabbing the shells. Like you said. Training so

I don't have to think, because you were right. There's no time to think. No space to think."

"You did good," he said. "In case I didn't say."

She steeled herself for it. "And because I didn't say, either," she said, "I need to say it now. I appreciate what you did, and what you're doing. Tonight. I guess it doesn't change anything between us, and I know you'd rather not have anything to do with me right now. And you're still doing this."

"Yep," he said, and she could see the hard line of his jaw, his mouth. "I am. But no, it doesn't change anything. So I won't stick around, if you don't mind. My folks can handle it. I can't."

"I used to wonder," she plowed on, something inside her dying a little at how she had hurt him, at how much she was still hurting him, "if there was any man I could trust. If there was any man I believed was decent, all the way down. I want you to know, no matter how you feel about me, that you're that guy. I know you are. I . . . I like you. And I admire you. So much." *And I want you, and I need you, and I think I love you*, she didn't say, because if she said it, if she even allowed herself to think it, those last fragile pieces of her will and her strength might just crumble away. And she had to hold on to those. They were all she had.

He'd picked up speed, was on the highway, and he didn't answer for a minute, and she sat there, her heart beating hard, and waited.

"Doesn't do me a whole lot of good," he finally said. "But all right."

"I want you so much." There she was, letting herself say it, and it was just as bad as she'd feared. "But I want this, too," she tried to explain, wishing he could understand, "and I can't just suddenly . . . not want it. This is my dream, and it always has been. You had a dream, too. You must know."

"I did," he said. "And I found out there was more than one dream that worked. I found out that happiness wasn't in just one thing."

"Well, I guess I haven't found that out yet. If I'm ever going to. I've worked for this all my life. I've planned for it. I want to be with you. I don't want to break up." If that was begging, too bad. She was begging. "But I can't just give up my dream, can't you see that?"

"So it's all or nothing, is it? I don't want to ask," he said. "I don't want to talk about it. But here I am asking anyway. It's the whole enchilada, or that's it, you're a failure? Because if there's one thing I've figured out during all that time down there at the bottom of the bottle, the bottom of my life, it's that it isn't the life you have. It's what you do with the life you have."

"That sounds good," she said. "That sounds right, but it doesn't *feel* right. It wasn't for you before, and it isn't for me. To get to the top in the hard sciences or engineering, whether it's in research or academia? Yes, it's all or nothing, because it's almost all men. It's all about your career, or it's not. You don't make it all about that, you're second best. You're not at the top, and you'll never be at the top."

"Ah," he said. "None of those men have families?"

"Sure they do. And they all have wives. Wives who take care of absolutely everything else, so they can be a hundred and ten percent."

"I'd point out that women can have husbands, too," he said. "Grandparents to help with the kids. Nannies. Whatever. But no matter what, that sounds like too high a price to pay. For a man *or* a woman."

"It might be," she said, "but it's the price. It feels too high." She drew a ragged breath. "Right now, it feels way too high. But it's the price."

"Then," he said, "I guess it depends whether you're willing to pay it. I guess it depends what you want on your tombstone."

"On my—no. I can't think about dying. Not tonight. Please."

"Maybe tonight's the right time," he said, taking the curves in the dark without slowing, like he knew them by heart, because he did. "Sometimes you don't know what matters most until you're staring down the barrel of a gun. Or until you're on the wrong side of one too many shoulder surgeries, wondering if that's all your life was. If you're anybody at all now that you're not somebody. And I never heard of anyone whose tombstone said, 'NFL quarterback.' Mostly they tend to say, 'Beloved husband.' 'Beloved father.' 'Beloved wife and mother.' Maybe there's a reason for that."

"Women shouldn't have to choose. But they do." She dropped her eyes to Junior, lying between them, because looking at Cal's profile was too hard. Because she wanted to scoot over and sit close, to feel the strength of his body, and she couldn't. She wanted him to hold her and tell her it would be all right, and he couldn't, because it wasn't all right. Because nothing was all right.

"And there's no other choice," he said.

"It's my dream," she said again. There was nothing else to say. "It's always been my dream."

"Then," he said, "I guess you have to go after your dream. But you'll pardon me if I step out of the way while you do it. I'll drive you in tomorrow. I'll keep on pushing to find out who's doing this. I'll do everything I can to keep you safe. But I'll do it from a distance. I won't come around while you're at my folks' place. Don't ask me to. It's too much to ask."

"I know. And I appreciate that." Her voice came out small. She was so tired, so beaten, and all she wanted to do was cry. "I'm grateful."

"Yeah," he said. "I've heard that one, too."

◆ ◆ ◆

He pulled off the highway, through Fulton, and up into the driveway of the tidy brick ranch house. This would make the second time he'd dumped her on his parents without warning, and she wondered what kind of welcome she'd get this time. Now that she'd hurt their son.

He grabbed her bag of files from the floor, hopped out and pulled her suitcase out of the truck bed, and left her to come along after him across the snowy drive, Junior trotting along behind. Cal opened the door, flipped the light switch.

"What time is it?" Zoe asked quietly.

"Five. Somewhere around there." He set her things down, started peeling out of his outdoor clothes while she did the same, her arms leaden, because it all just seemed way too hard.

The male voice made her jump, booming out from the back of the house. "Who's there?"

"Cal," he yelled back. "And Zoe."

A pause, and Stan came around the corner, still shrugging into a flannel button-down, his gray hair sticking up from his head, and a bristle of whiskers covering the hard planes of his jaw. He looked them over. "I'm sure there's a reason," he said.

"There is," Cal said, and now Raylene was hustling out, still tying the sash of a fleece robe. A robe that actually was almost a twin of her own, just as Cal had said. Zoe had an absurd urge to giggle, born of exhaustion and nerves.

"What?" Raylene asked in alarm. "What's happened? Cal?"

"Zoe's coming to live with you for a while," he said. "Sheets on the bed?"

"Of course," his mother said automatically. "And of course Zoe's welcome. But . . ."

"I should have called," Cal said. He laughed a little, and Zoe realized that he was almost as shaken up as she was. "Sorry. The . . . the guy. He broke into Zoe's apartment tonight and went for her. She let off that shotgun I loaned her."

"Oh, my," Raylene said faintly. "Did you hit him?" she asked Zoe.

"No," she said. "I was just trying to stop him."

"Should've hit him," Stan said.

"Yes," she sighed. "So I hear."

"And he got away," Cal plowed on. "So she needs a safe place. And we broke up," he added baldly. "So I thought here."

Stan was looking at Raylene, who didn't miss a beat. "Of course," she said. "Don't just stand there, Cal. Put Zoe's things in the bedroom."

"I'm going to leave Junior here, too," Cal said, and the dog, sitting at Cal's side as always, pricked his ears at the mention of his name. "At night, anyway. Dad, you got that shotgun handy?"

"In the bedroom closet," he said. "It can be by the bed instead. Can be there right now."

"I'd say that's the place for it," Cal said. "Come on, Zoe. Let's get you squared away."

No "princess." No "professor." And definitely no "darlin'." She was just "Zoe," and it hurt. And all the same, here she was with his parents and his dog and his dad's shotgun, all to keep her safe. Because that was Cal.

She followed him into the guest bedroom. "You aren't going in to work today, I figure," he said as he heaved her laden suitcase up onto the top of the low dresser.

"I have to. I have classes."

"Can't you cancel?"

Her chin went up at that. "No. Then he wins."

He looked at her, frowning, measuring, then nodded. "Okay. When do you have to get there?"

"Uh . . ." She ran her hand through her hair. "What day is it?"

His face softened. "Tuesday. You sure this is a good idea?"

"It feels like I have to." She didn't know why. She was too tired to tell. "I have to keep going. And I'm prepared. It's just . . ." She tried to think. Tuesday. "My advanced-topics seminar and a lab. And I'm not in class until ten. So . . . nine thirty."

"Pick you up at nine, then," he suggested. "To get your car."

"Okay." She sat on the bed, because she needed to. Because standing up was way too hard.

"Why don't you get some sleep?" he asked. "My mom will feed you when you wake up, and you'll feel a whole lot better."

"I'm not sure I could. Sleep."

"How about with Junior right by your bed?" he suggested. "After this, he'll stay out in the living room. One eye on the back door, one eye on the front door, and his ears all over the place. But for right now, this rug right here looks like a real good spot. Nobody's getting at you, not with my dad in the house and Junior in your bedroom." His hand went out to smooth her hair back from her face, and his touch was pure comfort. "You're nothing but safe, baby," he said gently. "I promise."

She nodded jerkily, tried not to cry. Tried hard, because that wasn't fair to him. "Okay." She got up so he couldn't look at her, unzipped her suitcase, and pulled out her pajamas. "I will. Good idea."

"Right here. Down. Stay," Cal told Junior, who'd been sitting near the door. The dog walked over and lay down exactly where Cal had pointed, sat poised like a sphinx and looked up at him, ears cocked. Down, but every inch alert.

"Guard Zoe," Cal said, and the dog's tail thumped once and was still.

"Get some sleep," Cal told Zoe again, and then he was leaving the room, closing the door behind him, and her hands were still holding her pajamas. And shaking.

Junior helped. So did exhaustion, a late night, a few hours of broken sleep, and the most frightening experience of her life. But what made the treacherous tears leak from her eyes, lying in the sanctuary of the dark before she finally, gratefully, escaped into sleep . . .

It was Cal. Not having Cal's big arm over her chest, Cal's solid body enfolding her so she could relax. Knowing it was her own fault that she didn't. And knowing that there was nothing she could do about it. It was done. It was over.

A SOFT PLACE

Cal closed her door, went into the kitchen. His parents were both there, his mom still in her robe, starting coffee.

"Sit," she told him. "I'll fix you some breakfast, and you can tell us."

She wasn't asking, and anyway, he needed them to know what they were dealing with. So he sat across from his dad, accepted the mug of coffee his mom handed him, and took a grateful sip.

They listened without commenting until he'd finished telling them, and by the time he was done, his mom had served up the eggs and toast, and he started to eat and tried not to think about what he'd just said.

"Shotgun by the bed," his dad said after a minute. "You got it."

"Sorry," Cal said. "You and Mom . . . I don't think he'd try it. But I didn't even think about that, that it's risky for you, and I'm sorry. I'd have her with me, but I . . . couldn't." He reached for the jam, spooned it onto his plate, started spreading it on his toast. Keeping busy.

"That's a shame," his mom said. "I like Zoe."

He laughed, quick and short. "Yeah. Me, too." He took a bite of toast, a sip of coffee, and didn't look at her. "But she's not sticking around," he found himself going on, "and I can't do that again."

"Huh. I thought she liked it here," his mom said.

"So did I. But it seems the big guns in her line of work don't hang out in the sticks. Bright lights, big city. Same old story, same old song."

His mother shot another look at him, but didn't say anything more. And neither did his dad, of course. But then, his dad usually didn't need you to draw him a map.

Cal finished up, stood, and put his dishes into the dishwasher. "Thanks for breakfast. I'll be back in a few hours to take Zoe into town again. She has to teach today. Would you make her something to eat, Mom? She's pretty tired."

"Of course," his mother said automatically, then shut her mouth on whatever else she would have said.

"I'm not sure when she'll be back," Cal said. "You all will have to work that out, I guess."

"Don't worry," his mom said. "We will."

His dad got up with him, put on his own outdoor gear along with him without saying anything, even though it was still dark out there and would be until nearly eight, and followed him out to his rig.

Cal stood and waited, and his dad sighed, looked at the ground, then looked at him. "Don't beat yourself up for loving her," he said.

Which wasn't what he'd expected at all. "Yeah," Cal said. "Well."

His dad smiled, a little twist to it. "Hell, boy. We can't help it. Every man needs a soft place to put his heart."

He was going to cry in front of his dad, and that wasn't happening. He nodded once, opened the door, and swung on up into the cab. Then he hesitated, his hand ready on the door handle, and looked at his father. Standing planted there, steady and strong, the rock he'd always been. Immovable.

"Take care of her," Cal said over the lump in his throat.

"Don't you worry," his dad said. "We've got her."

◆ ◆ ◆

He went on home, got his morning chores done, took a shower, and went back out to get her.

She was waiting as promised. Of course she was. Wearing the blue sweater dress, because as he knew, she didn't have much else. Looking pale and tired, but ready to take on the day anyway.

"You might be able to get Rochelle to help you go shopping," he said on the quiet drive back to town.

She turned her head from where she'd been watching the snow-covered fields go by. She still had her hand on Junior's head, though. The dog was showing Cal his butt, Cal having clearly been relegated to an also-ran. "What? Sorry," she said.

He took a hand off the wheel, gestured at her dress. "You know. Since you shot up your clothes."

"Oh." She rubbed a hand over her forehead. "I guess. She's too tall for me to borrow pants. Maybe a couple of skirts. She's too tall for those, too, but she wears them shorter than I do. Or I could borrow from your mom."

"Please. No. Anything but that."

She smiled a little, the first time she had all morning. "You don't get to say, I guess. I can wear all the turtlenecks I want. Your mom and I think they look nice. Your dad does, too."

"Still got that sass, haven't you?" he said. "I'm glad he didn't take your sass."

"Oh, I don't know," she said. "He made a pretty good dent. Him and . . ."

"And me," he said.

"No." She sighed. "And us. And me."

He was in town now, stopped at a light behind four cars on Main. Idaho traffic jam. He couldn't think of much to say to that, so he didn't say anything, and there was silence in the truck until he was pulling up outside her place, helping her transfer her things to her car.

He opened the back door, flipped up the blanket on the floor of the backseat to show her what he'd done the night before. "Shotgun right here," he told her. "Keep it there. Shells in the glove compartment. You see something, you get a bad feeling, you get a tickle? Load first, think second. Long as you don't rack the slide, you're all good. And keep the doors locked."

She was inside, her hand on the door. "Doing it now."

"I'll follow you on up there," he said. "Walk you to the door."

"All right," she said. "I have to go now," she added patiently, because he was still standing there holding that rear door open like he wanted to get in.

He slammed it, followed her as promised into the lot of her building. Only thirty yards from the front door. Not too bad.

"Get somebody to walk you all the same," he said when she was out of the car again.

"I will," she said. "Don't worry."

"The cops are coming by with that report today, I guess," he said. "Make me a copy, and you can give it to me tonight when I drop off Junior, and I'll share it with Jim, too. I'll let you know if I hear anything, and you do the same."

"Thanks," she said soberly. "For everything. I appreciate it. Really."

She headed inside, and his arms hung there by his sides with nothing to hold. He got back in his truck instead, and Junior wagged that whip of a tail, looked up at him inquiringly.

"You and me again," he told the dog. "Just you and me, but at night, you hear? You take care of her."

The dog cocked his blocky head, his eyes intent on Cal's, and Cal reached a hand out to fondle the soft ears.

"You keep her safe," Cal told him. "That's your job. And meanwhile, I ride Jim's ass hard to find out what's going on, make sure they're on it. He's got a new best friend, and it's me."

MUDDYING THE WATERS

The man sat at his desk two weeks later, his hand still on the receiver, and stared out at the mounds of mid-December snow that made up his crappy view. He wasn't sweating, because he didn't sweat.

"Just rumors," he'd just heard from his buddy up at Fairchild. Well, not a buddy. More of a stooge, but then, stooges were useful, too. "But I heard they were asking about you."

"They?" he'd snapped.

"That's the thing," the other man had said, almost whispering. "Not SF. OSI."

Not the Security Forces. The Office of Special Investigation. The big guns, asking about him. "Huh." He laughed, made it a joke. "Sure it was me? What the hell would there be for OSI to investigate me about? I'm out, remember?"

"I know," the other man said. "Total clusterfuck, as usual. It wasn't just you. They're asking about a bunch of guys, I heard."

"Asking about what? Not like you or I had any military secrets to sell."

"They aren't asking about me," the other man said in alarm.

"Sure?" He leaned back a little, making it casual. "If they're asking about me . . ."

"Shit," the other man breathed. "I'd better get on that."

"You got some boxes gone AWOL?" he needled. "Bet you do. You always did. Could be they want to talk to me to find out what I know. But don't worry," he went on smoothly, "I've got your back."

"Thanks, man."

He could hear the relief, almost smell the sweat, and he smiled. It was so easy. All you had to do was shift it to a personal threat, and everybody refocused. So very few people could actually think, there was almost no challenge in it. Which was why he'd taken to getting his kicks in more entertaining ways.

"I've got to go," he said now. "Keep your nose clean, or . . ." He laughed again. "Fake it good."

Now, he sat and thought. This wasn't good, but it wasn't bad, not really. His tracks were covered. If they hadn't been, something would have happened long before this. Five long years doing this, and not a single suggestion of anything leading back to him. Not a whisper of suspicion.

On the other hand, he was going to have to lie low for a good long time, and that wasn't optimal at all. He never failed, and this was more than annoying. This was personal.

How about if he redirected the suspicion so it fell on somebody else? He could think of a couple ways right off the top of his head. Time to get on that.

How had they connected the dots, though? Why now, after all this time? The answer to that was staring him in the face.

Zoe. It had all started with that bitch Zoe. He'd tried to finish it with her once, and he'd had to put it off. Anyway, he needed to muddy the waters. A suspect would be good, but a suspect and the loss of a witness would be even better, especially if it seemed unrelated. Two birds with one stone.

He had a pattern. That was his strength, and his weakness. He was organized, but that made it easier to spot his pattern, even though he'd spread the love around, thrown everybody off. Once you crossed a state line, you were halfway home. And now there were four cases out there. Four witnesses. A whole lot more if you counted Iraq, and they were obviously counting Iraq.

But if there wasn't a pattern, it wasn't the same guy. He knew how profilers worked. If it wasn't the same MO, and it wasn't even the same crime . . . it *really* wasn't the same guy.

Zoe and Cal had broken up. He was sure of it. He'd followed her leaving work a couple of times, staying well back, and she'd been alone when she'd left. He knew where she was living, and it wasn't with Cal. Which meant that no matter what else had happened in her life, the cops would be thinking Cal first, because they always thought of the woman's partner first. Especially her *estranged* partner. For good reason, because there wasn't a man in the world who hadn't wanted to kill the woman who'd left him, especially if she was screwing somebody else, and every cop knew it. Dress it up all you wanted, it was evolution. It was biology. All he had to do was let that work for him.

He needed her gone, and he needed Cal under suspicion. And dead was about as gone as you could get.

If he made it look like a lovers' quarrel, or even a random attack. Coincidence? Yeah, but coincidences happened, too. It meant he wouldn't be having much fun at all, and that was a real loss, but sacrifices had to be made. Dump the pattern completely. Different place, different MO, no rituals, no calling cards. Just the heat of the moment, and she was gone, and whodunit? Nobody more likely than Cal. Nobody at all.

Or better yet, suicide. What could be more likely than that? She'd been attacked, wasn't in her right mind. She was falling apart. Her boyfriend had dumped her, because they always dumped them afterward. Nobody wanted damaged goods, and he always made sure they were damaged. Zoe might not have gotten all the attention she deserved, but she was damaged just the same. He could see it in the jerky way she walked. All he had to do was leave the possibility open, and he knew exactly how.

If he was going to do it, he should do it now, and there would be nothing easier. All he had to do was plan some surprise inspections. A five-minute detour beforehand, and if he were seen on the street—nothing more natural, because he would belong on the street.

People in the building, though. But that was easy, too, he realized when he thought about it. He'd do it in the late afternoon, because all these assholes went home at five like they were punching a time clock. All of them but Zoe. Miss Conscientious. It would be dark, and he could come up the far staircase, and then out the same way.

It wasn't without risk, but then, nothing worth doing ever was. Doing nothing was even riskier, and anyway, doing nothing wasn't his style. What was life without risk? Boring, that was what.

Time to make his move. He'd waited long enough.

A PIECE OF PIE

"You know I'm not allowed to talk to you about this," were Jim's first words as he slid into the booth at the Garden Café.

It was mid-December, more than a month had passed since the investigation had begun, and from everything Cal could tell, the cops were not one bit closer.

"I'm not wearing a wire," he told his cousin, "and I'm buying the pie. If something slips out by accident while you're eating, I'll never tell."

"This is my job," Jim reminded him. "Those are the rules, and they're there for a reason."

"Come on, man. You're my cousin. And we're talking about Zoe's safety here."

"Thought she was staying with your folks. And your dog."

The waitress hustled up to take their order, and conversation ended for a couple minutes.

"She *is* staying with them," Cal said after she'd left, "and you heard right, I've got Junior over there every night. Nobody's getting into that house that he doesn't want to let in. But what about when she's not at home?"

"You know," Jim said, "somehow I have a feeling you've taken care of that, too. And I don't want to know, because she can't have gotten that concealed-weapons permit yet."

"She's at the university all day long," Cal pointed out. "Without Junior. Without any protection."

"And you care about this so much, why?" Jim asked, taking a sip of coffee. "For a smart guy, you aren't always too smart, are you?"

"Nope," Cal said, "I'm not. Thanks for pointing that out. I should just wash my hands of her, then? We're not together anymore, so it's okay for somebody to rape her? You read those reports. You know what he does. So come on. Tell me what you've got. Tell me what I can do."

"What you can do," Jim said, "is just exactly nothing. What we've got . . ." He stopped again, took a bite of the apple pie the waitress set in front of him, and sighed. "All right. Here you go. The Air Force is cooperating. They've wanted this mutt, too, thought he was one of theirs, like I said at the time, and they were real glad to know about the pattern we're seeing stateside. They've got OSI on it, because they think—"

"OSI," Cal said.

"Office of Special Investigation. Taking it out of the Security Forces' hands—the MPs."

"In case he was one."

"Jumping right to that conclusion again, aren't you? Which would be why you aren't a cop. Maybe just because it's better to have the investigation happen from outside for something this big. They're pulling the service records of every guy who was in Iraq at the right times and who was stationed at Fairchild afterwards for the past couple years. Which is a whole hell of a lot of guys. Checking into who fits, doing some discreet questioning, when they can find anybody still around to question, and they've promised to pass along anything interesting to us if the guys aren't at Fairchild anymore, if they got out and ended up around here. But it's all a slog, and it's going to take time."

"If the guy wasn't at Fairchild at all, though," Cal said.

"They're looking at that, too," Jim said. "But that's even slower. And they're thinking . . ." He looked at Cal. "I didn't say this."

"Nope," Cal said, sitting up straighter. "Say what?"

"Information. That's the key. The women, at least the ones here—they thought they'd been followed after classes. Afterwards, they all said what Amy said. That they'd felt like somebody was following them, had been uneasy. Which means he was able to get class schedules, probably living situations, too. You can't follow somebody day after day to find that out, not on this size of campus, let alone up there at College of Northern Idaho. Not if he isn't a student, isn't the right age, because he'd stand out, hanging around after class to follow her, trailing her back to her dorm. They're looking at somebody with a specialty that would allow for that, some computing background, maybe. Which is why they're looking at a security specialist, or just a tech weenie. Fits the profile better, actually. This guy isn't just a basher. He's a planner."

"MP," Cal said slowly.

"Which is why Greg's off the case," Jim said. "Even though their profiler says no. He says, wrong kind of guy. Our mutt's a planner. Organized creep. Greg would be disorganized all the way. You know him as well as I do."

"He wasn't told that was why, was he?" Cal asked with alarm.

"No. Far as I know, he got reamed out for how he handled it, which was true, too. Didn't push it up the chain fast enough, didn't investigate hard enough. Don't think he's long for the job there, no matter what, and you didn't hear that here, either. He's had some issues with excessive force."

"And Kathy's left him, my mom says," Cal pointed out. "Gone home to her mom, finally. With the kids. All kinds of anger there, and it'll only be worse now. Which could make him our guy, no matter what some profiler says."

"Which could," Jim said. "And they're looking at that, which I didn't say. That'd be hell to pay for Kathy and the kids, whether they're with him or not. I hope for their sakes it isn't him."

"They got any other suspects?"

Jim hesitated. "Yeah," he said. "And I'm not going to tell you who they are," he added before Cal could say anything. "Because I know you. You'd go after them. Screw up the whole investigation, for one thing. And for another thing, you're a civilian. This isn't a football field, you don't know what you're doing, and you're not in charge. You're not on the team. You're not even the water boy. So stay out of it. I know Hollywood would like you to think that law enforcement are all idiots, but we're going to get there. This has priority, and it's going to happen. But it all takes time," he repeated. "You don't go arresting somebody because he's an asshole who was an MP in Iraq, and now he lives here. We actually need evidence. That's the way the system works."

"The way the system works is too damn slow."

"Yep," Jim said. "And that's the system we've got." He finished wolfing his pie, declined another cup of coffee, and stood to go. "So, you just let us handle it," he warned again. "Protect her all you want, and man—" He shook his head. "You're a bigger man than I am, I'll tell you that right now, because I couldn't do it. But let us handle this."

Cal didn't go with him. Instead, he lingered over another cup of coffee.

Somebody who could track them. Somebody who knew where they lived, what their schedule was. A cop could find that out. Couldn't he?

He thought about staying out of it. He really did. For about thirty seconds. And then he thought of a way.

◆ ◆ ◆

"Well, hey," he said when he walked into the housing office, offering the woman at the front desk his best lazy cowboy grin. "How you doin'? Cal Jackson, here to talk to the big guy. He in?"

Her hand had gone to the hair, which told him he'd got it right. "Mr. Winston? No, sorry, Mr. Jackson, I'm not sure where he is. He must have just stepped out."

"Mr. Jackson's my dad. It's just Cal. Mind if I wait a sec?"

"Of course." She indicated the chair on the other side of her desk, trying to keep it cool. "Did you have an appointment with him? I can't believe he'd be late."

Another woman walked through carrying a sheaf of papers, saw the two of them, faltered, and Cal gave her a smile for good measure. "How you doin'?" he said again. "You know, you two ladies could probably help me some, too, if you've got a minute." Sometimes, the women who did the actual work knew the most. They'd probably been here the longest, too. And women usually talked to him.

"Sure, if we can," the woman opposite him said.

Cal read the nameplate in front of him. "Vanessa. That's a real pretty name. I had a girlfriend named Vanessa once. I have to say—" He sighed. "I'm guessing you're a whole lot brighter."

She laughed. Defenses down. Check. "Well, I hope so."

Cal stood up, addressed the other woman. "I'm sure hoping you'll sit down, too, because my mama always told me not to sit when a lady was standing, and I'm real tired."

She looked around a little nervously. Young, pretty, and what did she have to be nervous about? "Mr. Winston doesn't like us to waste time," she said.

"Mr. Winston isn't here," Vanessa said with a snap to her tone. "And Cal's not asking us to waste time. He has a housing question. Sit down, Isabel."

"Isabel." Cal smiled. "Another good name. Please. Sit down."

"At least," Vanessa told Cal when the young woman had perched on the edge of the chair as if she were about to take flight, "I assume it's a housing question. What can we do for you?"

"Well, you know," Cal said, scratching the back of his head and leaning back, "I gave this little gift to the university recently. The idea of it is to attract the best students, you know, especially women, make sure there are opportunities for them in-state so they don't have to leave to get good jobs."

Except some of them, of course. Some of them left anyway.

"We heard about that," Vanessa said, glancing at the other woman.

"And a friend of mine was saying," Cal said, "a female friend, that I'd overlooked something. That I hadn't thought enough about women being safe on campus. And after I looked into that a little, I thought, well, duh. I guess men don't always know what women go through."

"No," Vanessa said, "they sure don't. Are you asking about safe housing?"

"Exactly." Cal beamed at her. "And it just occurred to me that your boss might not be as concerned about that, or as tuned into that, either, as you ladies probably are. I mean things like, how hard does the university make it to know who's living where? Suppose some guy has a class with a girl, and he's a little off. Suppose he's, oh, some technical whiz. Or not even a student at all, somebody working in an office like this. If he's even a cop, say. In law enforcement somewhere. Just to get all wild, take it to the max," he apologized as the women exchanged glances. "Could he get her address? Her phone number? Because all those things are on file, right?"

"Well, of course," Isabel said. "But the records are encrypted. They're secure, unless there's a reason for somebody to get into the database. I mean, I guess the police, but other than that . . . no. We've never had a data breach that I know of. That's my job," she said a little proudly, a little self-consciously, too. "To keep the information safe. So, no. Unless somebody actually worked here or I suppose in IT, or in the registrar's office, or for the police, like you say. They'd be able to get in, because those guys can get into anything."

"And just about everyone working in this office or over at the registrar's is a woman," Vanessa said. "Anybody doing anything with computers, anyway."

"Really." Cal raised his eyebrows. Unfortunately, this was about as far as he could push it with these two, because they wouldn't know exactly what the police had access to. Winston would, though. And if Cal was right, he was done waiting for any process. It was going to be time to pay Greg a visit. Better safe than sorry. If he was wrong, well, he might have punched out his cousin, who'd earned it over and over.

But he was here and Winston wasn't, so he sat back and relaxed. Might as well keep them chatting, see if he got anything else. "And yet the director's a man. Huh. See? What I'm talking about. But he's probably been here forever."

"No," Vanessa said, and she looked like she wasn't happy about it. "Barely a year."

"Hmm," Cal said. "A long year, I take it."

"Huh." She snorted. "You could say that."

"Came in from outside and took the job over somebody who should have had it?" Cal guessed. "And that somebody was a woman?"

"You've got it," Vanessa said. "The good-ol'-boys' network."

"It was the military thing, I think," Isabella put in.

"What military thing?" Cal asked.

"Mr. Winston worked in housing for the military," Isabel said. "And the vice president of operations is an ex-military guy, too."

"The vice president of operations is an ex-military guy," Cal said slowly. Who would have access to absolutely everything, in that job.

"About a hundred years ago," Isabel said, loosening up a little. "I think he was all impressed with Mr. Winston because he acts like he was in the danger zone, like he was all secret Special Forces or something, when he was in *housing*. Just like us. Same exact thing."

"Where did Winston come from, then?" Cal asked, the hair on his back of his neck standing up straight. He kept it casual with a major effort.

"Francis Xavier," Vanessa said. "You know, the Catholic school up in Spokane. He was their housing director, for just a year or so, I think, and then he came down here, I guess because we're bigger."

"We thought, good news," Isabel put in. "Well, me and the other girls. Because our last director was really grouchy, couldn't wait to be retired, made it really tense in here. He'd yell at you when you made a mistake. And Mr. Winston was young and good-looking. But he's . . . he's even worse."

"Oh?" Cal tried to look encouraging.

"Not outright," Isabel said, "but underneath. Cold."

"You think that, too?" Cal asked Vanessa.

"You bet I think it. You can't exactly miss it. Gone half the time, too," she said, on a roll now. "Lazy. Comes in whenever he likes, leaves for 'meetings.' Not fooling any of us. He shoves everything off on the staff, and what are we supposed to do about it? Who would we complain to? It's not fair, not when he's making twice what anybody else here does. He says it's because of the carpal tunnel, that he can't type for more than a few minutes. But I've known a lot of people with carpal tunnel, and I don't believe it. I think it's an excuse."

"Wait," Cal said. "Carpal tunnel? Isn't that your hands?"

"Yeah," Vanessa said. "It gets really painful, and you really *can't* type, not if you actually have it, that is. He's got all the equipment, all right. Got the splints on both wrists, the arm supports fixed to his desk. He's got the works, and complains about it plenty, too. But I never knew anybody with carpal tunnel who didn't start out small. Who didn't start with numbness, tingling, because that's what it is, your nerves. They don't even know what it is at the beginning. Then it aches, and *then* you go in and find out that's what it is, get the splints. Not all at once. Not without complaining. He would have complained. He would have bitched."

"When," Cal said, his tongue sticking to the roof of his mouth. "When did it . . . come on?"

Vanessa looked at Isabel. "When? A couple months ago, that was all. That's why I think he's faking. Too sudden."

"I remember," Isabel said, "because it was right when the November reports were due. Right after Halloween."

ZOE SANTANGELO, PERSON

Describe the characteristics that typify/differentiate continental and oceanic volcanoes, including lithology and behavior, and give examples of each.

Zoe erased "differentiate," began to type a sentence about sketches. They'd better be able to do those sketches.

Just a couple more questions to go, and she'd finish up and go home—well, she'd go back to Cal's parents' place. She'd been delaying going out there every night, even as she welcomed the safety she felt as soon as she walked in the door. But it was so awkward. And it made her miss Cal so much.

Not being there, though, felt even worse. She'd gone to her mother's for Thanksgiving, and it had felt . . . alien. LA had seemed so noisy, so manmade, so full of strangers and cars, and strangers *in* cars. And so hot, too. It had been eighty degrees on Thanksgiving Day. How could she have changed so much in such a short time, that all those things felt wrong? It was as if the peace of North Idaho had settled into her bones, even when she had no peace at all.

Telling her mother what had happened had been terrible, and not telling her about Cal had been worse. Her mother wouldn't have understood her conflict, though, even now. Cal would have seemed like manna from heaven to her mom.

Talking it over with her father, of course, had been out of the question. He'd always been her advisor, her confidant. She'd always made him proud. But he wouldn't have come close to understanding this. So she'd ended up not telling either of them about Cal, and that had felt lonely, too, and so sad.

Especially since she understood her mother a little better now, and felt sorrier for her than she ever had. All her mother had ever wanted to do was love her dad. The one thing, the only thing, and he hadn't wanted it.

Her mom's life had been a lie, and if she'd coped by trying to deny it, by still insisting on loving her husband even when he wasn't her husband anymore, when he loved somebody else—well, sometimes your heart didn't get to choose. It wasn't easy to stop loving somebody. In fact, sometimes it was just about impossible.

The truth was, Zoe seemed to understand herself and her heart less every day, and she was so tired of trying to figure it out that, instead, she just worked until she was too tired to work anymore, slept, and tried not to feel scared and lonely. And in another week it was going to be winter break, and she was going to be finding a new apartment with Rochelle, and then the connection would be gone entirely. Then, as hard as it would be to stay with Cal's parents, she'd find out how much harder it was not to. How much harder it would be to have him completely out of her life.

"Dr. Santangelo? Can I talk to you a minute?"

She shut her laptop on the final exam even before she turned, the action automatic. It was Amy.

"Sure," she told the girl. She wasn't getting her work done anyway. She might as well pack it up.

Neil, the grad student who'd been working in the corner of the room, looked up as well. "I'm going to take a break for dinner," he said. "You okay if I leave for a while?"

"Of course. You go on." She had to smile a little. Ever since they'd heard about the attack, her students had gotten so protective of her. She suspected them of working out a rotation, because it seemed that she was never alone. Which was one of the reasons she'd taken to working in the rock lab instead of her office, because she wasn't comfortable being alone, not someplace where she could be trapped so easily. She felt safer up here, especially with a male student parked in residence, clearly ready and willing to repel invaders.

"What can I do for you?" she asked Amy. She indicated the chair beside her desk, swiveled to face the girl.

"I just wanted to come up before the semester ended and say thanks," Amy said. "For all your help. Even though you ended up in trouble, too. I'm so sorry about that."

"No," Zoe said automatically. "We already discussed this. It isn't your fault. I got involved because I needed to get involved. It was my choice. And you don't have to apologize for being a victim any more than I do. That's not how this deal works." She began to gather her papers, stack them on the desk. She wasn't in any position to give Amy advice. Not when she was still so fragile herself. Better that she get it at the counseling center. "So . . . you're welcome. And it's almost time for me to get out of here, and you, too. Somebody walking you home? It's dark out there."

"I'm meeting a friend," Amy said. "It's been harder since Bill and I broke up. To get somebody to go everywhere with me, I mean."

Zoe knew she shouldn't ask, but she did anyway. "Oh?"

"Yeah," Amy said. "He was getting antsy. Impatient. He thought I should get over it. I guess I'm not as much fun as I was. And I always wanted to be walked places. He said I was needy. I don't think I'm needy. I think I'm scared, and that I have a right to be. But he didn't want somebody who was scared."

"Huh," Zoe said. She knew she shouldn't say it, but she did. "I guess that means he's the wrong guy. A guy who can't understand how hard this is, who doesn't want to listen, to hear how you feel, who doesn't want to keep you safe—that's not the right guy."

"You're right," Amy said. "I know you're right. That's why I broke up with him."

Zoe brought her mind back with an effort. From Cal, who understood how hard it was, who wanted to hear how she felt. Who cared more about her being safe than about her being with him. That guy. The right guy.

"I had something else I had to tell you, too," Amy said. "I wasn't sure if I should. That's why I waited so long. I thought . . ." She gave a quick shrug. "It was like sucking up, you know? Coming and talking to you before the final. But I have to leave right afterwards. My dad said I shouldn't hang around, but I don't want to anyway. I want to get out of here."

"I know," Zoe said. "It can be awfully hard to stay."

"It can. I just can't help it, you know? I just can't . . . sleep. But I'm trying."

"You are trying," Zoe said. "He hasn't driven you away. He hasn't beaten you. You should feel really proud of yourself for that."

"See," Amy said, "that's why I had to come talk to you, because you say those things. And anyway, you wouldn't grade somebody higher just because they sucked up."

"Well, no," Zoe said, startled into a laugh. "I wouldn't. You'll get the grade you earn."

"I know," Amy said. "I know I will. And that's what I wanted to say. I wanted to tell you . . . I feel stupid saying it, but you're kind of my role model, you know? You're kind of my idol."

She was blushing, and Zoe reached a hand out and set it briefly on hers, gave it a squeeze.

Never touch a student. Sometimes, though, rules were meant to be broken. "Well, thank you," she said quietly, releasing the girl's hand. "That means a lot to me. You still have to study, though," she added with a smile. "Because you're right. That's not going to help you on the test."

Amy laughed, but her face was still working with emotion. "I mean," she said, "you're a great teacher. I wanted to tell you, I want to do something that well someday. I don't know what, but I want to be respected like that, the way you are."

"Does this mean you're going to major in geology?" Zoe asked, teasing a little.

A stronger laugh this time. "Um . . . no. I can pass the class. I hope. But still. I wanted to come in and tell you thanks. For everything."

"Well," Zoe said, the glow warming her, "you're welcome. For everything. And now get out of here, please, so I can finish writing a test that will kick your butt and remind you how hard you're supposed to be studying to earn this good degree you're going to be getting."

"Okay." Amy laughed again and stood to go, slinging her backpack over her shoulder. "I'll do well," she promised. "You'll see."

"I know you will. Take care."

Zoe sat back, tapping a pencil on her desk, and watched her leave. Well, wasn't that something? Sometimes, this job was worth every late night, every Saturday spent grading papers. Sometimes.

A couple more years in the trenches, and hello Stanford. Got your cushy graduate seminars, got all those doctoral students doing your scut work for you, and bye-bye, gatekeeper classes. So long, hormonal eighteen-year-olds who haven't figured out that you actually have to study in college. They'll be somebody else's problem.

Except that she didn't want them to be somebody else's problem. Except that she didn't want to teach less, because she loved teaching.

A top-tier research institution. That had always been the goal. Always, ever since she'd set any goals at all. She'd aimed for the top, and she'd never understood why anybody would aim lower. There had never seemed like any real alternative.

But a teacher was what she was. It was *who* she was. And what if . . .

She sat, pencil still tapping, and stared into space. Brought the thought into focus, examined it from all sides as if it were a scientific problem to be solved.

Assumptions. She'd been operating all along on assumptions. But what if the assumptions were flawed?

What happens in science is what's supposed to happen. One of the fundamental principles, drilled into her so many years ago that she couldn't even remember where she'd first heard it. If the results of the experiment weren't what you'd predicted, that didn't make the results wrong. It made something else wrong. And that something was probably your hypothesis.

How many of the goals she'd set for herself had been about achievement for achievement's sake—or for her father's sake—and how many had been about true satisfaction? How many had been about achieving the life she really wanted?

It isn't the life you have. It's what you do with the life you have.

Cal. It was Cal, but it wasn't just Cal. It was her. It was what mattered at the end of the day.

What do you want on your tombstone?

What she wanted was for her former students to remember her, for them to think, *There's somebody who made a difference.* Maybe even, *There's somebody who changed my life.*

What she wanted most of all, though, was for somebody to care enough to pick out her tombstone. For somebody to care that she was alive, to feel sorry when she had to leave him, because his life had been better with her in it. She wanted to matter more than anything else to him, and for him to matter like that to her. Not to Zoe Santangelo, PhD, hydrogeologist. To Zoe Santangelo, person.

What she wanted was good work to do, work that mattered, and somebody to love her that she could love back. What she wanted was a real life, a full life. A life that didn't just have work in it.

She'd always thought that she couldn't settle. But what if "settling" was the opposite of what she'd assumed? What if "settling," for her, was settling for a career over everything else? Over a life that had love, and family, and a real home? That had real friends, not just colleagues? What if "settling" meant settling for a life without somebody like Cal?

Somebody like Cal? her brain mocked. Because she was still trying to hedge her bets. Time to face it. *What happens in science is what's supposed to happen.* She wanted Cal.

How could she say that, though? She'd known him all of a couple months.

But he wasn't asking her to marry him. He was just asking her not to have one foot out the door of this place. This good place, this real place. He was asking her to want to stay here. To want a whole life. And she did.

She needed to talk to him. She needed to tell him. She needed to get out of here.

◆ ◆ ◆

Except that she couldn't. Because Greg Moore was walking into the room, an extra swagger in his step.

"Officer Moore," she said before he even made it across the room. She stood up herself, grabbed her laptop case, and began to stuff papers into it. "I was just going."

"Really," he said, sitting down opposite her in the chair Amy had just vacated, his eyes sweeping her figure again the way they always did, making her wish she hadn't worn the sweater dress, no matter what Cal had said. "So you aren't interested in the investigation into Amy's case? Or yours? Since you think they're the same?"

She sat down again with reluctance. "Of course I'm interested, if you have something to tell me, or ask me. And of course they're the same."

"Which would explain," he said, his gaze scanning the room now, "why you aren't in law enforcement. Ever heard of a copycat?"

"Oh, really?" She crossed her arms, aware of her body language and not caring a bit. "You've got two serial rapists in town?"

"Hmm," he said. "Maybe one serial guy. Maybe. And maybe one guy with a grudge."

"What do you mean?"

"What happened that day," he asked, "when that guy showed up in your bedroom? Some other . . . major life event?"

"Oh, no," she said. "You're not going to make this about Cal."

"It's not me," he said. "I'm off the case, thanks to you. But as a cop . . . Know who it usually is, when bad things happen to women? The boyfriend. The husband. That's who does it, every time. When did he show up that night?"

"No," she said, and she was trembling. "No. Nobody's thinking that."

"You don't think so?" He smiled, and it was an ugly thing. "Sweetheart. Everybody's thinking that. Your boyfriend's about to be in a world of hurt. Why do you think his wife left him?"

She didn't want to answer, but the urge to defend Cal was too strong. "Because she cheated on him."

"You think? Maybe so and maybe not. Just because a divorce is no-fault . . ." He sighed. "Some guys have a way of making themselves look good, but when you scratch the surface, what's underneath can be some nasty stuff. Money's a pretty good deodorant. He didn't contest the settlement, gave her everything she asked for. What kind of man does that? I'll tell you. A man who doesn't want the publicity. A man who wants to make it all go away, because having it come out would ruin him. A guilty man."

She did stand up then. "If that's all you've got to tell me," she said, her voice shaking despite her efforts to control it, "I think you'd better leave. Because I don't believe it, and I won't. You can say anything you want, and I still won't believe it. So if that's it . . . please go away."

He didn't move. "Oh, honey," he said. "That's not all I've got to tell you."

TO THE TOWER

Cal got back in his truck. Junior sat up and looked at him, but Cal didn't say anything. He was pressing the button to dial even as he was driving. Against the rules? Too bad. It was only five blocks across campus to Zoe's building. He needed to tell her about this right away, to warn her. But first, Jim.

"What?" he heard at the other end. "It's been two hours. Even Miss Marple doesn't solve the crime in two hours."

Cal ignored that. "Richard Winston," he said. "Director of housing. He's the guy. I'm sure. Tell me he's on your list."

"I'm not going to tell you that," Jim said, his alarm coming through loud and clear. "One way or the other. Tell me you haven't been investigating. Please."

"Shut up," Cal said, then filled Jim in as quickly as he could.

"You went to the office," Jim said, sounding stunned. "You talked to his staff. Oh, my God. You've screwed with the investigation, not to mention you've screwed with my job. I've broken so many regs here it's not even funny, and that's not even the problem. The problem is, even if he *is* the guy, now you've alerted him. Brilliant. Just brilliant."

"No, I haven't," Cal said. "His staff hates him. They're not going to be talking to him. Did you even hear what I said? About his hands?"

"I heard it," Jim said. "And if he's on our list—*if*—maybe I just made a note. But I'm not sharing another damn thing with you. And I'll remind you, a couple hours ago you were just as sure it was Greg. It can't be both, Sherlock. So stay the hell out of my case. I'm telling you this once, and the next time, the sheriff's going to tell you. Stay out."

"I don't care who you tell," Cal said, pulling into Zoe's lot. "In fact, tell everybody. Tell the whole damn world. But check out his hands. I'm begging you, man. Check out his hands."

◆ ◆ ◆

He hung up, climbed out of the truck, and Junior looked at him inquiringly. "Let's go," Cal told him, and the dog jumped out. It was after five. Nobody around to object to Junior.

He was through the doors, up the first flight of stairs, around the corner, Junior right beside him. The nearly deserted building was heavy with winter silence, broken only by the sound of boot heels and dog claws on limestone.

And then another sound. A warning growl from Junior, low and menacing. Cal looked down, saw the short hair standing up all the way down the ridge of the dog's broad back. And that rumble again, coming from deep inside his heavy chest.

Cal's own adrenaline had kicked in even before the legs came into view on the stairs above. The blue-uniformed legs, and then the muscular body. And then the face. Greg.

Greg stopped on the landing, looked warily at Junior. The dog was poised on the steps beneath him, body stiff with tension, that hair still up, that low growl still sounding.

Cal walked on up, and Junior walked with him, every muscular bit of him alerted on Greg.

"Get that dog out of here," Greg said, "or I'm writing you a ticket right here. Hell with the ticket, I'm calling the pound. He's not allowed in the building, he's not even on a leash, and he's a menace."

"He's not a menace," Cal said. "He just doesn't like you. You want to write me a ticket, go right ahead, but I'm not sticking around for you to do it. You know where I live."

Greg's hand was on the butt of his gun, and Cal stared at him with astonishment. "What? You going to shoot me?"

"I might shoot your dog," Greg said. "Call him off."

"Junior. Sit," Cal said, and Junior sat.

Cal went to move past Greg, but Greg shot an arm out to block him, and Cal couldn't hit a cop.

"What?" he asked. "I need to go."

"You go when I say you can go," Greg said.

"No," Cal said. "I'm going now. I'm going up to see Zoe. Write me up. Write Junior up."

"Zoe, huh?" Greg started to laugh, but it wasn't funny. It was ugly. "I don't think she's going to be receiving."

"What?" The word barely came out, and Junior was up again.

"I had a chat with Zoe," Greg said. "Shared a few unsavory items from your past, that minor in consumption, the drunk and disorderly. And that wasn't all. There may have been some . . . other things. She might be a little under the weather right now."

Cal's blood froze. Could he have been wrong after all? *Oh, shit.* Zoe. He started to move past Greg, but his cousin shoved that arm out again, blocked him.

Cal didn't think. He hauled back and connected with his cousin's jaw, and when Greg staggered, he elbowed him hard in the kidneys, watched him go down, gave him a push with his boot for good measure, then left him there and took off running up the stairs.

He'd just hit a cop. Or he'd just beaten up a rapist. Or he'd just thrown a punch at his asshole cousin. He needed to find out how many of those it was, and he needed to find it out now.

He took the steps two at a time to the third floor, Junior keeping up, until they pushed through the double doors that led into the foyer, the final short flight to the tower. Zoe's tower.

Junior stopped and raised his ugly head, and the rumble began again, deep and menacing as thunder. He wasn't looking behind them where they'd left Greg. He was looking ahead.

Zoe.

Now the dog was running again, sprinting, taking the stairs so fast that Cal couldn't keep up. He saw Junior's muscular hindquarters disappearing around the corner, his back feet sliding out from under him with the force of his turn, and the dog was gone.

By the time Cal made it around the corner, Junior was out of sight. He could hear him barking as he went, though, and it was a sound that struck terror all the way to his bones.

Fear. Aggression. Rage.

THREE TO TANGO

Zoe needed to find Cal and tell him what had happened. Most of all, she needed to tell him how she felt, everything she felt. She needed to tell him all of it, and the phone wasn't going to work, not for this. She gathered her papers for the third time that evening, knocked them against the desk a couple times to straighten them, and turned to grab her laptop case from where it sat on the floor next to the wall.

"Going so soon?"

Her hand stopped in midair, but the rest of her didn't freeze. She was up, whirling, the second she heard him.

No ski mask. An ordinary face, an ordinary man. Except he wasn't. His posture. The way he moved. It all fell into place.

"You," she breathed. "It's you."

Something changed in his eyes, and the next moment, he was coming for her. From arrogant poise to full-out aggression, like somebody had thrown a switch.

Richard Winston. The director of housing. Who didn't have any braces on his wrists. Whose hands were glistening in the fluorescent light. Surgical gloves. *Monkey paws.*

She was up, and she was diving, shoving the chair out hard against him as she went, putting the chair and table between them. Obstacles. She needed obstacles.

She thought of the fire escape, rejected the idea instantly, because she'd have to open the door. Instead, while he was following her around the table, she'd have gained a precious half second, and the door to the corridor was open. She was fast, she could scream, and there were people out there. People who would come.

It was a good plan, except that he'd anticipated her and was already pivoting, headed around the table to cut her off, and she wasn't going to make it to the corridor. So she turned again, dodged, kept the table between them. It was going to be the fire escape, and she was dancing, feinting, trying to get him off guard.

She didn't make it. He reached out, grabbed her left arm, and began yanking her straight across the table toward him.

She fought him, her right arm flailing, connecting with his face, his arm as her feet scrabbled for purchase.

He hissed as her fingernails raked his cheek, but she was too short to mount an effective resistance, and he had hold of both arms now, was dragging her bodily across the wooden surface, her laptop and papers sliding along with her, crashing to the hard linoleum.

He backed up as he continued to pull her, and she tried to hook her foot under the table, but he was too strong, and she lost her purchase. It wasn't going to work.

Curl up. The long-ago self-defense class came back to her. *He won't expect you to drop.* She drew her knees in close as he dragged her, then launched both legs out with all her might to kick him, to throw him off balance.

He anticipated, twisted, and she missed, but he was forced to shift his grip as he pulled her the final inches. She sagged at the knees when she came off the table, and he had to adjust again to combat the force of gravity carrying her toward the floor.

She kicked from her low position, tried to punch at him, but he was lifting her despite her efforts, turning her, pulling her back against his chest, his arms wrapping around her torso, going for a bear hug that would leave her helpless. She lunged forward with her upper body before he could do it, reared back with all her might, felt the back of her head hit soft flesh, heard his gasp of pain. She thought she'd gotten his nose, and it had worked, so she did it again. Hard.

His grip loosened, the air leaving his lungs in a hiss, and she was twisting out of his arms, running blindly, but he grabbed her arm again, yanked, was running with her.

"Bitch," he panted. "You *bitch*."

He pulled her hard to the left as she aimed to the right, swinging her around, and her hip slammed into the side table with its long row of rock samples. A juddering impact, the rattle of stone on melamine, and he was on top of her, pressing her down onto the table, into the jagged edges of rock, and she was gasping with the pain even as he used all his weight to subdue her. She kicked out blindly, her boot raking down the inside of his shin, then reared back and kicked again, as hard as she could, in the center of his shin.

"*Fuck*," he gasped. "Fucking *bitch*." His lower body twisted away from her, and finally, she had a hand free. She reached out blindly for something, anything, and her hand hit a sharp edge.

Obsidian, her mind automatically recognized even as her hand closed around it. She barely registered the pain of the knifelike edge scoring the tender undersides of her fingers and palm as she brought the chunk of rock around with a scything blow, slammed it with all her strength into the knuckles of the hand that grasped her other arm. He let out a yelp and jumped away, shaking his hand.

A second later, he was lunging for her again, and she was swiping with the rock, bashing at his arm, his shoulder, his head. She hit him as hard as she could in the side of the head and, when he staggered, levered herself off the table and ran for it. Ran for the fire escape, because it was the closest, got her hand on the door.

He was there again, twisting her around by the arm, making her lose her grip on the door, and she swung her rock, connected with his side, forced him back.

"You've got nowhere to run this time," he taunted, even as he dodged. "Nowhere to hide. No shotgun, and nobody to hear you scream. You are going to *die*."

Her groping left hand found the door again, and she swung her rock as she shoved down on the handle, yanked the heavy door toward her, and was through it even as she pulled it closed behind her.

It wouldn't close, though, and she yanked hard at it again, irrationally, because how could she hold him back? How?

She heard the scream, looked down and saw the fingers protruding, and then he was pulling the door from his side, snatching his hand out of the opening. She let go fast so he would fall back, and turned to run.

She barely made it two steps. He pulled the door with such force that it slammed against the opposite wall and stayed open. Which gave her two ways to escape him.

The thought formed even as he came at her, backed her against the metal rail, and left her with nowhere to go but fifty feet down. And she had dropped her rock in the struggle for the door.

He wasn't talking. He was snarling, his face twisted with rage, and he was trying to lift her, to push her over the edge. She grabbed the railing in desperation with her left hand, twisted her right leg around the metal post beside her, and hung on. She was going to fight, and if he threw her over, she was going to do her best to take him with her.

His left hand, the one she hadn't crushed, went back, and she raised her own bloodied right hand reflexively, caught his fist. Her own knuckles slammed into her forehead, his fist following right behind, and she fell back a little more, but didn't let go. She couldn't let go.

He was punching her in the shoulders, the chest, as she protected her face, speaking in time with the blows, and she was gasping, shuddering, trying to protect her head, trying to keep him from knocking her out, because she would have no chance then. No chance.

"You're going to *hurt.*" He came for her again and again as she twisted and ducked and threw her elbow across her face. "I'm going to fuck you *up.*"

He reared back for the blow that would surely knock her out, and she held her arm up and waited for it.

He connected even as she shifted, his fist landing square against the delicate bones of her wrist, her hand and his crashing into her eyes, and she felt something snap. Her arm fell to her side, and the pain bloomed, a red mist in wrist and head. He was wrenching at her other arm, prying it loose, was pushing her higher as her leg clung desperately around her post.

Don't let go. Don't let go don't let go don't let go.

And still, she began to slip. She was going to go, and she reached for him, trying to pull him with her.

Then he was falling back, because there was a snarling fury launching itself at him, a blur of brown muscle and teeth. Vicious growls, a shout of pain, and Winston had let go of her, because Junior's teeth were latched into the back of his thigh.

Zoe dropped to the metal grating, her left hand going out to break her fall, and her wrist buckled, wresting a cry of pain from her as she rolled out of the way of Winston's kicking, stomping boots. He was kicking at Junior, dropping to a knee, twisting the dog's head, forcing a yelp of pain from him. Then his fist, landing again and again on Junior's blocky head, his body, a gleam of black showing in his hand. Beating him with her obsidian, and Junior was falling. Twitching, and finally lying still.

Winston turned in a flash, was back on Zoe even as she struggled to stand. Only for an instant, because Cal was there, grabbing his upraised arm, spinning him around.

Winston lashed out with his left fist as he turned, connected, and Cal's head rocked back. A wild blow to Cal's left arm with the rock, and Cal was twisting to the left, punching with his right even as Winston sidestepped, grabbed Cal's right arm, and swung him around. Trying to throw him down the stairs, Zoe realized.

Cal was too coordinated for that. His feet were dancing, pirouetting, but a harsh cry came from him that didn't sound like Cal at all. Nothing like Cal, and his arm had dropped from Winston's grasp, was hanging weirdly by his side.

Dislocated. His shoulder was dislocated, and he was staggering, bouncing off the railing opposite Zoe.

She was already moving as it happened. Moving like a crab on her bloodied right palm, her feet, kicking out at Winston's legs, then shoving herself up to stand, raking at his face with her nails, shoving vicious fingers into his eyes, and Cal was pulling himself up with his left arm on the railing, was grabbing Winston by the arm, swinging him around, putting all his muscle behind it. Slamming into his chest with his left shoulder, sending him backward.

Winston flailed for a moment at the top of the iron stairway, his arms windmilling for balance, then righted himself, lunged forward again, and Cal reached a boot high, kicked him straight in the gut, and Winston was falling back, sailing through the air, coming down on the metal stairway with a sickening thud, thumping down a few more stairs. And lying still.

◆ ◆ ◆

"Inside," Cal said, his breath hissing out through gritted teeth. He had his good arm around her, was pulling her through the door and slamming it shut. She wanted to lock it, to shut the monster out, but there was no way, because it was a fire escape.

"Junior," she said, the word coming on a gasping sob of pain and fear. Somehow, it mattered so much that Junior was out there. Out there with Winston.

Cal wasn't listening, was fumbling for his phone in his right hip pocket, but he was shaking, his face bloodless, and he couldn't reach it.

She didn't think. She couldn't think. Her head was swimming, her arm was useless. She reached for the red fire alarm beside the door with her left hand and pulled it.

The clanging filled the room, echoed from the hallways, filled her throbbing head. Cal had dropped to his knees, was rocking back and forth, and she lunged for her desk, opened the bottom drawer with fumbling fingers, pulled out her purse, and grabbed her phone, all with her clumsy, bloodied hand.

She hurt, but she didn't hurt as badly as Cal. Not as badly as Junior. She pressed the "1" button with her thumb, held it down despite the blood, despite the pain, because she had to.

Hang on, she told herself. *Hang on*. And she did.

GOING HOME

"Damn, bro." Luke came into the surgery waiting room on a swirl of energy and dropped down to sit in the upholstered chair next to Cal. "You look like shit."

Cal stopped staring at the soothing landscape picture, the blue walls that were supposed to be calming. He tried to pretend he was fine, that he wasn't half out of his mind. "Hi."

"What happened?" Luke asked. "I came as soon as Jim called me. Mom and Dad will be headed out, too."

"Then I'll save the story and tell all of you at once," Cal said, doing his best to maintain.

"How's Zoe?"

"Banged up all to hell. But alive."

"I guess you found out who did it," Luke said cautiously.

"We did. The hard way. And he's *not* alive."

"He isn't?" Luke looked startled.

"Jim didn't share that? Yeah. He's dead. The cops told us. Broke his neck, I guess. I wasn't listening too close. I was a little preoccupied at the time."

In forcing the paramedics to put his shoulder back in, actually. He'd still been on his knees when the cops had come, with the paramedics right behind them. He'd wanted to tell them to check Zoe out first, but he hadn't been able to. Because he'd barely been able to talk.

"We'll get you to the hospital, get that fixed that for you," one of them had said, after he'd touched Cal and Cal had nearly screamed.

"Hell you will," Cal gasped. "The muscles will go into spasm. Once they do that, they won't get it back in there without surgery, and I'm not doing that again. You'll do it now, or I'll kill you." And he wasn't at all sure he'd been exaggerating.

"Come on, Frank," the other guy said. "I know how. And it's killing him. Let's do it."

"But what about *her*?" Frank asked.

"Never mind me," Zoe said, and Cal wanted to say that that wasn't right, but he couldn't. "Take care of Cal first. Please. Please take care of him."

"Let's do this thing," Frank said. "I think there's been enough killing for one night."

Zoe had watched, had flinched, had shuddered for him despite her own pain, and Cal hadn't screamed. Some . . . sounds might have come out, but he hadn't screamed.

"Is he dead? Winston?" Zoe asked once Cal was able to focus again, once he was sitting in a shuddering heap on a classroom chair, because he'd refused the gurney. Once they'd gotten to work on her, were putting her onto the gurney, which there'd been no way in hell he was letting her refuse. "Is that what you meant about killing?"

The paramedic hesitated, looked to the cops, who included Greg, a bruise on his jaw and a scowl on his face.

One of them—not Greg, because Greg hadn't been talking to Cal, or to anybody else, either—answered.

"Dead as a doornail," the cop said. "We'll go on to the hospital with you, because we'll need to ask you some questions about that."

"What?" Cal managed to say, wiping the sweat and blood from his face with his good arm. "Zoe got him up here so she could throw him down the fire escape? Even you guys couldn't be that stupid."

"Watch it," one of them warned, and he didn't, because he was cold, hard mad. Mad that they'd been too slow, that they hadn't protected her. Mad that he hadn't. Mad that she'd almost died. So mad, looking at her battered face, her bloody hands, the pain she was trying not to show, that if Winston hadn't already been dead, he'd have killed him right then and there.

Once they'd gotten him to the hospital, they'd taken him through it again and again while he'd gotten himself cleaned up and waited for Zoe. He'd never been good at waiting, but this was the worst. The cops had been there at first, and then they'd left him alone and Luke had come. And Cal was still waiting.

Finally, though, a guy came into the room. Green scrubs, stethoscope. "Cal Jackson?" he asked, and Cal stood up, his heart knocking against his ribs, and Luke stood up with him.

"That's me," Cal managed to say.

"Dr. Marshall," the guy said. "We're all done with Ms. Santangelo. We got that arm set, did some tests and some X-rays, a little suturing, and she can go on home."

The relief about knocked Cal over, but he forced himself to stay upright. He didn't dare look at Luke.

"I told the police they'd have to wait for the rest of her statement until tomorrow," the doctor went on, "because she's concussed. I wouldn't say she's a flight risk. She's not getting far tonight. In fact," he said, eyeing Cal, "you don't look like you are, either. You need some pain pills yourself? They hook you up already?"

Cal brushed it off. "She's okay, though?" he demanded. "She's going to be all right?"

"As okay as somebody who's been beaten that badly is going to be," the doctor said. "In other words, about like you after a hard game. I guess you know how that feels. A week or two, six weeks for the wrist, and she's good. But I should see the other guy, huh?"

"The other guy," Cal said, "is wearing a toe tag."

"Well," the doctor said, "Hippocratic oath and all . . ." He smiled. "From what I heard in there . . . good job."

◆ ◆ ◆

When Cal walked into the tiny curtained cubicle with Luke right behind him, it didn't matter that he and Zoe weren't together anymore. She was lying there all battered, all broken. She was the strongest thing he'd ever seen, and seeing her open her eyes, try to smile at him . . . it was going to destroy him. He was going to bawl, right here and now, right in front of his brother.

"Hey, princess," he said, sitting beside her, wanting to take her hand in his, but one of them had a cast on it, and the other one was covered with a bandage, and every bit of her hurt, he could tell. "Remind me never to make you mad."

She smiled again, even though he could tell it hurt her face. His heart twisted up tighter, and the tears tried a little harder to get out.

"We did good," she said, the words not coming out very strong.

"Yep," he said. "We did. You're one hell of a fighter. One hell of a woman."

A couple of tears escaped, rolled down her cheeks. "I'm just so glad . . . you came. Because I was losing. And Junior," she said urgently. "Please. Tell me. Nobody will tell me. Please tell me Junior didn't die. He saved my life. And then you did. Is he . . ." She swallowed. "Is he okay?"

"No," Cal said, "he's not okay, but he's alive. He's at the vet's, and they're working on him." He looked across the bed at Luke.

"Hard to say," Luke said. "But Junior's hard to kill." He smiled at Zoe. "Kind of like you."

She closed her eyes, and there were some more tears now. "I'm going to hope," she said. "I'm going to believe. I didn't think I'd get out of there, but I believed. I kept fighting. And so did you, and so did Junior. We made it, and I'm going to believe he will."

He loved this woman. It didn't matter what happened. He loved her.

"Why did you come, though?" she asked. "How did you know?"

"It was the braces," Cal said. "I went to the housing office, thinking I'd find out what kind of student data Greg could have had access to. And I found out that Winston's so-called carpal tunnel came on right after Halloween. The way I figure it, Amy beat him with a baseball bat, and he had to explain why he was sore and couldn't move one arm. If he pretended it was his hands instead, and that it was both of them, he could explain the soreness without drawing attention to his real injuries, and he'd rule himself out for anything that happened in the future."

"Like attacking me," Zoe said.

"Yep."

"But people with carpal tunnel . . . you can't just say you have it. You get diagnosed. There are tests."

"If it's real. I'll bet he stuck some braces on there and told the staff he had it. How would they know? I was coming over to tell you that. Then I met Greg on the stairs, and he'd been up there with you, said some things about it, and I thought it could be him, after all. But Junior knew it wasn't him. He knew you were still in danger. That's why he got there first."

"I thought it was Greg, too," she said. "At least, I thought it could be, especially when he was in my office. When he started getting . . . nasty. But it wasn't. He just wanted to talk trash about you." She smiled at him, so painful, so sweet. "But I wouldn't listen."

That got him again, and he was choking up. "Yeah," he managed to say, "he told me what he said, because he's an asshole. But that's all he is. Whereas Winston . . . he was something else. At least those two women in the States, and Amy, too, can know that it was Winston who attacked them, and that he's dead. Too bad the Air Force can't tell all his victims over in Iraq, but they'll never even know how many there were. He did this for five years, and he got away with it. But it's all over now."

Her eyes were closing again, and what was he doing, wearing her out? "But this is all for tomorrow," he told her. "We'll have all kinds of time to talk about it then. Right now, I need to take you to my folks', if you're really supposed to go home, because I'm having a hard time believing it."

"No," she said, opening her eyes, although he could tell it was an effort. "I needed to know. I'm so glad he can't hurt anyone again. I need to rest, that's all. Just like you, because you're hurt, too."

"Oh, darlin'," he said, and grinned at her. "It's just a flesh wound."

"Yeah, well," she said with another of those flashes of spirit and heart and pure guts that she'd showed him since the moment he'd met her, "me, too. And I don't want to stay here anyway. I'm all right."

"No," he said, "you're not. But you will be. Want me to get a nurse to help you get dressed?"

She hesitated, her eyes searching his face. "No," she said. "I want *you* to help me."

"Uh . . ." He glanced at Luke, and his brother looked back at him, brows lifted. "You sure?"

"That's what I wanted to tell you tonight," she said. "I wanted to tell you how I felt. What I figured out. I'm so . . . so tired. I can't say it all. But I have to say something."

His heart was hammering out a dance beat. He was working on his next broken heart for sure, except maybe he wasn't. Maybe his heart wasn't going to be broken, not this time. Maybe his heart had come home at last.

"What you said," she told him. "Before. I'm ready. I'm ready to play hard. And I don't want to go home. Please don't make me go home. I mean, I . . . I mean . . ."

His heart was pounding, his blood was singing in his veins, and he could barely say it. Could barely ask it. "You mean that you're already home," he said slowly. "That we're home. Both of us."

"Yes," she said. "I do. I do. I want this, and I want you. So if that offer's still open . . ." She stopped, breathed, and said it. "You've got a taker."

She was crying. His tough, feisty little professor was crying, full-tilt and no joke. The tears running down her cheeks, her nose getting even redder, one eye swollen almost shut, her cheekbone bruised and swollen, her arm in a sling, and every inch of her aching.

She looked like hell, and she looked like the most beautiful thing in the world.

"Oh, sweetheart," he told her, his heart doing its best to swell up until it left his chest entirely, "the offer's still open. The offer couldn't be closed if I wanted it to."

"Then . . ." she said. "Could you . . . could you come down here and give me a kiss?"

He bent over the bed, and it felt bad, but it felt so good. He put that bad arm of his around her and held her. Gently, because she hurt so much. His lips brushed over hers, and his arm told him it had had more than enough that day, that he wasn't supposed to be moving it, but who listened to arms? He had a woman to hold.

So he laid his cheek against hers and held her. And then he kept on holding her, because he hadn't been able to do it for so long, and he'd been sure that he'd never be able to do it again. It was necessary, that was all.

"If I've got a taker . . ." he told her, the tenderness trying to make him cry. Trying its best, and he wouldn't say it wasn't winning. "That's good. Because you've got a giver."

She cried some more, and they lay there like that for long seconds, until the voice floated in from beyond him. Of course it did, because his brother had never, ever been known to shut up.

"Is there love in here?" Luke asked the room. "Or is it just not me?"

EPILOGUE

It was Saturday, the first of July, and Zoe was going to be spending it on the river with Cal.

She met him at her front door with a kiss, and he stood back afterward and looked her over, and she didn't mind a bit. He took in the sleeveless blouse, buttoned up to the top, the flirty skirt, the strappy sandals, and she preened a little, because she could tell by the gleam in his eyes that he liked what he saw.

"All ready to spend your day with me?" he asked. "Inner tubes in the back of the truck, beer in the cooler. Redneck cruise."

"Just let me get my stuff." She smiled up at him, and he smiled back and followed her inside.

"Where's Junior?" she asked.

"Ah. Junior had to stay home. He's kind of a menace on the river. Gets way too excited. My folks have him over there, watching their granddog. Or having him watch them."

It had become almost impossible to dislodge Junior from Cal's side since the dog had made his slow recovery. Junior seemed almost disappointed when another day went by when he didn't have to rush in and defend his master. Or Zoe, because he'd offered his ferocious loyalty to her as well, which sometimes almost made her cry, it was so sweet. The Junior Jackson Insurance Policy.

And his parents . . . that was pretty funny. His dad had never been all that fond of indoor dogs, Cal had told her, had tolerated them in the past for his wife and sons' sakes. But Junior had earned a big, ugly, permanent spot in both of his parents' affections with his heroics. And a spot on the couch, too, when Cal's dad wasn't looking.

Now, Cal picked up her bag from the couch. "All set?"

"In a sec," she said, the happy smile still on her face. "Because I got paid for the summer, you know. And I got you a present."

"Is it that your lease is up? Because that's the present I want, and you know it."

"No," she said, but she was still smiling, because she couldn't help it. "Stop."

"Thought you said you were playing hard."

"I am. I'm playing hard. I'm playing just as hard as you like."

She was, too, because it was so good. Spending her Saturdays working at the desk he'd set up for her in the guest room, with Junior curled up on the braided rug next to her. Cooking a meal together that she didn't have to eat alone, or going over to his parents' place for Sunday dinner, their warm acceptance enfolding her. Walking over to a high school basketball game with Cal and cheering for the team. Going dancing with him on a Friday night, and going home with him afterward to his house or hers, depending on whether they could wait, and knowing that when they got there, it would be special.

Even her mother loved him. Of course she did. Cal had gone home with her over Memorial Day, had teased and charmed her mother mercilessly, and then had sealed the deal by offering to fly her up to visit over Labor Day weekend.

"To celebrate harvest being done," he'd said. "I'll have a little breathing room then, be able to pay proper attention to my ladies. Zoe will be starting her semester, but I think between the two of us, we could talk her into taking a couple days off. You could meet my folks, too. I think you might like them. And you know what would really help me out? If I could persuade you to borrow my credit card and take Zoe up to Spokane for a day and help her get outfitted for school. She shot up her work wardrobe, you know. She's pretty impulsive that way. They've got a Nordstrom there. Don't you think Zoe should go to Nordstrom?"

"Oh," April Santangelo assured him, "I do. You don't know how long I've been waiting to hear those words."

"Dirty play," Zoe told him, although she couldn't help laughing.

"Whatever it takes, baby," he told her with a completely unabashed grin. "Whatever it takes."

"You hang on to this one, honey," April told her daughter. "This is a once-in-a-lifetime man."

"Hear that?" Cal said. "That's me. Mother knows best."

Zoe couldn't argue. For the first time in her life, she and her mother were in complete agreement.

Her dad had been another story. He was still too upset with her for changing her career goals, and with Cal for being the cause of it, to be more than civil to Cal. He wasn't going to be visiting anytime soon.

It hurt, but it wasn't his life, and they weren't his choices to make. They were hers, and they were right. She'd gotten another consulting job in the spring, and she had an idea for a research project for the coming year. She could have her career—maybe not the career she'd originally planned, but the one she wanted—and she could have Cal. She needed both. They were like . . . air. And she needed to breathe.

But her dad . . .

"You're his only child," Cal had told her after an awkward lunch with her father that had left her shaken. "And he's crazy about you.

Give him a year, keep on calling him, leave that door open, and he'll walk on through, because dads love their daughters. You'll see."

It had made her cry, which had made him hold her and kiss her and tell her again, and that had helped. She still called her dad every week, and he still talked to her. He didn't ask about Cal, but that didn't seem to bother Cal one bit.

"He's jealous," he told her matter-of-factly when she raised it with him. "Because he's always come first with you. But he'll come around. He may never love me, but that's okay. He doesn't have to. He just has to love you."

She couldn't imagine, now, how she'd ever resisted Cal. How she'd ever resisted all this, because this was *life*. This was *living*. And today, she was going tubing on the river with the man she loved, and she couldn't wait.

"I got you a present," she reminded him now. "Don't you want to know what it is?"

"Sure," he said. "You didn't have to do that, though. I'm not all that crazy about . . . stuff. Unless it's a new tractor, of course. Nothing runs like a Deere. They're having a sale, too."

"I don't get paid that much," she said, but she was laughing. "I would have gotten you something. I wanted to, but I couldn't think of what you wanted. Until I did. Maybe you don't want it, though."

She was unbuttoning her blouse, and that got his attention.

"Oh, yeah," he said, setting her bag down and reaching for her. "I want it."

She slapped his hand, smiled some more.

"Damn," he groaned. "Those dimples . . . I need to kiss you. Now."

She kept unbuttoning, showing him what was underneath her prim and proper little white sleeveless blouse. Because what was underneath was red. And low. And exactly what he liked.

She shrugged the blouse off, unbuttoned her skirt, and started unzipping. "What do you think?" she asked as the skirt hit the floor and she stepped out of it, wearing her brand-new deep-red bikini. His favorite color on her. "Good present? Do you want me to take it back? Or do you want to . . ." Her hand trailed over the side of his neck, down his chest. "Take it off?'

"You bought a . . ."

"I bought you a present," she repeated. "I thought about what you'd want. And I decided you might just want me to float down the river next to you in an inner tube. I decided you might want to watch me lying back in a little red bikini, drinking a beer and smiling at you. So that's what I did. That's what I've got to offer. You want it?"

"Oh, darlin'," he said. "I want it."

◆ ◆ ◆

She looked good dressed, she looked better undressed, and she looked damn good in a red bikini. He could have looked at her all day, so he did.

And five or six hours later, she was looking sleepy, and happy, and pretty well satisfied. Off the river again, cooled off and relaxed and messy, eating a hamburger in a booth in a little diner in a tiny Idaho town. Dusty pickup trucks in the parking lot, heavy fans turning lazily overhead, fake flowers hanging in baskets from the ceiling, an old-fashioned jukebox playing country music, low and soft and sweet. Summer in the country.

He took a sip of chocolate milkshake and looked her over. "You know," he told her, "you're a pretty quick study. I've got to say, I'm approving of your wardrobe more and more these days."

"Well, thanks," she said, looking a little startled, but pleased.

"Except I think you could still improve."

She set her paper-wrapped burger down and stared at him. "Excuse me?" The fire was lighting up those innocent round eyes of hers, and it made him smile inside.

"I had plenty of time to read those magazines at Rochelle's," he said conversationally, ignoring her expression, "back when you were staying with her. They had a bunch of stuff about accessorizing. It made me realize that you never accessorize, and I think that would look a whole lot better."

"You do, do you," she said, her tone level and dangerous, and she was sitting back, folding her arms. "And that's required? I'm not up to standard yet?"

"Mmm . . . close," he said, looking her over critically. "Just need a few more . . . touches."

"You are the most—" she started. She stopped, took a deep breath, and visibly calmed herself. "I'm reminding myself really hard right now," she told him, "that you don't call the person you love names. Because I've got so many words I want to use on you. Keep talking, though, and I might not be able to hold back."

"Let's see," he said. "I'm thinking obnoxious. Arrogant. Presumptuous. How'm I doing?"

"Keep going," she said, but she was starting to smile. "You're getting warm."

"All right, then," he said. "Let's narrow it down. How about if you just wore some jewelry? Kind of . . . brightened up a little?"

"I don't like lots of jewelry, though," she said. "It gets in my way. Earrings, that's about it. You like jewelry so much, *you* wear it."

"Hmm. I might just be doing that," he said, and she looked even more startled. "One piece, then. How about that? I'm negotiating here, princess. I'm compromising. Isn't that what you're supposed to want in a life partner? Isn't that one of the rules?"

"In a . . ." She was sitting up straighter, and her arms had fallen to her sides.

"Yeah." He knew he was stalling, and he knew why. Because now that it was time, he was nervous. Hell, he was more than nervous. He was terrified.

Cowboy up.

He reached in his pocket, pulled out the box. "One piece," he told her, opening it, turning it around so she could see it. "Please. If you'd wear this for me . . ." He swallowed. "It would mean a lot. It would mean just about everything."

"Cal." She was staring at it, then up at his face. "That's . . ."

"Yep," he said. "That is. I'm asking you to marry me in a diner. I'd have done it more fancy, but you know the Breakfast Spot's the best restaurant in Paradise, and even I couldn't really do it over bacon and eggs."

He was rambling. Time to cut to the chase. "So, Zoe Santangelo," he said, "I'm asking you to change that pretty name of yours. I'm telling you that I love you so much. I wish I could tell you how much, but I can't figure out any good enough words to explain it. So I'm just asking you to marry me and live with me and love me back. I'm asking you to have my babies and help me raise them out there on the farm. I'm asking you to make some kids with me who'll slide down the banisters and swing on a rope in the hayloft and be farm kids and hicks and jocks. The girls, too, because I hate to tell you this, but girls can be jocks. And, because they're your kids," he said, looking into her eyes, trying to tell her everything, to show her everything that his stupid tongue couldn't say, "they'll probably be brains as well. They could even be geeks. But that's okay, because I love geeks."

"How many kids are in this plan of yours?" she asked, and she was trembling a little, but still trying so hard to be businesslike. "Sounds like six. I'm twenty-nine."

"I told you," he said, "I'm good with compromising. I'm ready to negotiate here. I'm all right with two. But I'm holding out for two. You've got to give her an annoying brother to tease her and provoke her and stand up for her if anybody tries to mess with her. Our daughter's going to need a brother."

"Then," she said, and those were definitely tears shining in her eyes now, "I guess we'd better give her one. But I'm not changing my name. At least professionally," she amended. "Research, you know. Consulting."

"Done," he said promptly.

"What is this?" she asked with a shaky little laugh. "A business deal?"

"Nope," he told her, and, finally, he reached for her hand, pulled the ring from the box. He lifted his eyebrows at her, got a smile, and slid that ring right onto her finger. The diamond winked in the shaft of summer sunlight that fell across the red-checked vinyl tablecloth, George Strait sang about loving somebody forever, and Cal knew that as always, old George had gotten it just exactly right.

"This isn't a business deal," he told her, his ring safely on her finger, right where it belonged. Right where it was going to stay. "This is the real deal."

ACKNOWLEDGMENTS

As always, many people aided in the research for this book. Any errors or omissions, however, are my own. My sincere thanks go out to, in alphabetical order: Lisa Avila, Barbara Buchanan, Rick Dalessio, Bernie Druffel, Jake Druffel, Mary Guidry, Erika Iiams, James Nolting, Sam Nolting, and Wayne Stinnett, for their help with trucks, guns, farm life, campus life, military life, bad guys, good guys, fighting, driving in the Idaho winter, and hitting the ditch.

Thanks to my awesome critique group: Lisa Avila, Barbara Buchanan, Carol Chappell, Mary Guidry, Kathy Harward, and Bob Pryor, for telling me what I needed to hear even when I didn't want to hear it.

Thanks, also, to my editors at Montlake Romance. To Maria Gomez for reaching out and taking a chance on me, and to Charlotte Herscher for guiding me toward the best book I could write.

And as ever, thanks to my husband, Rick Nolting, for keeping me fed, keeping me sane, reading the book first, and telling me to stop working and get some sleep.

ABOUT THE AUTHOR

Rosalind James, a publishing industry veteran and former marketing executive, is the author of more than a dozen contemporary romance and romantic suspense novels, set both in the United States and New Zealand. Originally from North Idaho, she now lives in Berkeley, California, with a husband, a Labrador retriever named Charlie (yes, she named a character after her dog, but she swears she didn't realize it until later), and three extremely spoiled, non-egg-laying bantam chickens.

Made in United States
North Haven, CT
10 June 2023

37597032R00232